THE FINAL STEEP

A. K. HAYAT

Steep House Press

Copyright © 2026 by A.K. Hayat

This is a work of fiction. Names, characters, places, and incidents either are the product of the author's imagination or are used fictitiously. Any resemblance to actual persons, living or dead, events, or locales is entirely coincidental.

Book Cover and illustrations by Sarah A. Hayat

Steep House Press, an imprint of Al3abna LLC

First edition 2026

ISBN-13: 978-9948-6269-4-7

UAE Regulatory Compliance

Printing Permit Approval No.: MC-02-01-3441171

Age Classification: 17+

Printer (UAE edition only): Lightning Source Sharjah FZC LLC

Printer Address: Sharjah Publishing City Free Zone, Sharjah, United Arab Emirates

This permit and printer information apply only to copies printed and distributed within the United Arab Emirates; copies printed in other countries may use different printers.

تم تصنيف وتحديد الفئة العمرية التي تلائم محتوى الكتب وفقا لنظام التصنيف العمري الصادر عن المجلس الإمارات للإعلام

For my daughter — who is still finishing her novel.
I won the race. You started the journey

Athergard
District of Ink
Greythorn Estate
The Royal Palace
The Records Hall
Hollow Stair
The Final Steep
Tamber Canal
Merchant Square
Meat District
Night Market
Tanners' Quarter Safe House
Greythorn Bone Chamber

When a Thornwick sits upon the Athergard throne,
the city shall burn
and the kingdom shall fall.
The crowned head shall become
the destroying hand.
So it is written.
So it shall be.
— The Sealed Prophecy of the Cathedral Vaults,
confirmed by twelve seers, 1697
blood-warded vault

Chapter One

THE STRANGER IN THE STEAM

DAY ONE: SEVEN DAYS REMAIN

THE RAIN WAS TRYING to get inside.

It had turned vicious three hours ago, throwing itself against the windows of The Final Steep with the mindless persistence of a drunk who'd forgotten why he started swinging. The shop anchored the corner of Weaver Street, deep within Athergard's Hollow Stair neighborhood, and tonight the city felt like it was trying to wash them all away. Each gust of wind sent water streaming down the warped glass, turning the gas lamps outside into orange smears that wobbled and ran like wet paint.

The rain left a film on everything it touched, a faint grey residue that clung to the windowsills and collected in the cracks between cobblestones. Teyra had scrubbed it off the shop's front glass that morning, as she did every morning. By nightfall it was back. It was always back. In the Ashmore District, across the river, the rain fell clean. But Hollow Stair rain carried passengers, a gritty, ashen quality that her grandmother had called "the Unsettled." The residue of spirits who couldn't afford a proper passage, dissolving into the water table drop by drop, year after year, until the whole neighborhood tasted of unfinished goodbyes. On bad nights, the neighbors still left cups of cold tea on their windowsills, an old Hollow Stair custom, giving the Unsettled something warm to pass through so they'd move on quieter. She'd always called it runoff.

Teyra had begun to wonder if it was leaking up.

Teyra Tepes squeezed out her cleaning rag over the copper sink and watched a glob of grey slime spiral down the drain. It smelled like ozone and old pennies. Mrs. Pemberton's dead husband, as it turned out, had not forgiven her for the affair with the butcher. Forty minutes of spectral ranting about "that ham-fisted adulterer" had left the shop smelling like a lightning strike and Teyra's head feeling like someone had shoved ice picks behind her eyes.

And a residue the Academy textbooks never mentioned. A residue beyond the physical. A splinter of Mr. Pemberton's bitterness still lodged behind her sternum, hot and acrid, borrowed bile that burned like her own. It would fade by morning. They always did, mostly. But for now his betrayal sat in her chest like a coal, and she had the irrational urge to march to the butcher's shop on Gallows Lane and give someone a piece of her mind.

She turned off the tap and stood there with her hands braced against the edge of the sink. The metal left white dents in her palms. The Grave-Chill had settled into her bones as it always did after a session. It was a deep, interior frost that came from channeling death magic, leaving her fingers stiff and clumsy, the joints aching like she'd been making snowballs without gloves.

But lately the cold had changed. It had grown teeth, pushing past numbness into erasure. Like standing at the edge of a well that had no bottom, and the well was breathing.

She'd mentioned it to Dr. Voss at the Guild last week. He'd laughed it off. "You're overworking yourself, Tepes. The Chill plays tricks when you're tired."

Maybe he was right. But the cold didn't feel tired. It felt hungry.

Most professional necromancers had heated stones for this. Thermal baths infused with salamander scales, assistants to brew warming tonics. They also had the clinical detachment the Academy drilled into every graduate, the ability to channel a spirit's energy without absorbing its feeling. The Grave-Chill was clean, professional cold. Teyra's cold was messier. It came tangled with the dead's emotions, their unfinished sentences, the weight of what they'd left unsaid. The Academy called this "Resonance bleed" and treated it as a deficiency. Teyra's grandmother had called it a gift. Either way, it meant every ghost who sat in her shop left a residue, and the residue wasn't always ectoplasm.

Teyra had a hot water bottle with a slow leak, a vocabulary of profanity she'd learned from a dead sailor, and on bad nights, his lingering ache for open water and salt air that surfaced whenever she stood too long at the sink, watching things circle and disappear.

She dried her hands on her apron and didn't look at the rent notice sitting on the counter behind her. The notice radiated judgment anyway, cream-colored paper that meant "official" and "consequences." Forty-two gold sovereigns. She had eleven.

"Boring," a voice croaked from the shadows.

Teyra didn't look up. She started wiping down the counter, scrubbing at a ring of ectoplasm that clung to the wood like old honey. "It's peaceful, Lenore. There's a difference."

"Peaceful is for corpses." The raven hopped from the bookshelf onto the marble bust of some dead poet, a minor Romantic whose name Teyra could never remember, her talons clicking sharply against the stone. She was a big bird, glossy black, with a beak that could crack walnuts and a personality that could crack patience. "I need scandal. I need betrayal. Something with teeth. The last ghost who came through here just wanted to complain about his grandson's choice of curtains. Curtains, Teyra. My brain is rotting. I'm going to start pulling out my own feathers for entertainment."

"Please don't. I can't afford a vet."

"You can't afford anything."

"Thank you, Lenore. Very helpful."

Teyra turned to the kettle. It was a heavy iron-belly model, forged in the Dwarf Districts where they still used coal fires hot enough to melt stone. The thing cost more than two months' rent and weighed as much as a small child, but it was worth it. She held her hands over the rounded sides, feeling the heat work its way into her frozen fingers, a stinging thaw as blood crept back to the tips.

The tin she reached for was marked Velvet Dusk in her grandmother's careful script. Real silver, tarnished now but still beautiful, with tiny moons and stars etched into the lid. When she popped it open, the smell hit her, dried lavender and smoked vanilla and the charged stillness before a thunderstorm.

The shop fell away. She was sitting on a kitchen floor in a house she'd never visited, watching flour dust settle in a bar of morning light while someone hummed a song she didn't know the words to. The image was warm and aching and entirely wrong, because it belonged to the old widow from last Tuesday, the one who'd died in her sleep and couldn't understand why her cat kept walking through her. Teyra had helped her say goodbye. The widow had left behind a yearning for ordinary mornings that had been surfacing in Teyra's chest ever since, triggered by small domestic comforts. Like tea.

She blinked it away and focused on the tin in her hands.

It was a comfort blend. The kind of tea you brewed when the world felt too loud and your rent was too late and you were twenty-six years old with four useless years of Applied Necromancy and a shop that specialized in helping dead people with their problems because you weren't cut out for the living ones.

She was going to sit in the velvet wingback by the window, the one good piece of furniture she owned, salvaged from an estate sale, and drink this tea, and forget for ten minutes that she was a failure.

The kettle whispered, the preliminary hiss before the boil.

That's when the bell above the door rang.

It shivered with a high, thin sound that seemed to come from somewhere other than the metal. The temperature in the shop dropped so fast that Teyra's breath misted in front of her face. Her ears popped. Frost webbed across the inside of the windows in delicate crystalline patterns, spreading outward from the center like cracks in ice.

The door swung open, bringing with it the smell of wet cobblestones and rain, undercut by something older, something that lifted the hair on the back of her neck. Old water and rotting lilies, the shut-in mustiness of crypts that have been sealed too long.

A man stepped out of the rain.

He stood on the floor, which was the first odd thing, because most spirits floated. His boots hit the floorboards with a solid thump she felt through the soles of her shoes, but the air around him was wrong. It shimmered and warped like heat rising off summer pavement, and when he moved, his edges stuttered, there and gone and there again, like a candle flame in a draft.

Water dripped from his coat in a steady rhythm, pooling on the worn wood in a puddle that didn't look right. Darker than water ought to be, and unnervingly still.

"You're dripping," Teyra said.

The words bore no resemblance to the opening line she'd rehearsed during her Academy training for dangerous supernatural encounters. Professor Grimwald had been precise about maintaining authority and establishing boundaries. But her brain was stuck on the incongruous detail of muddy water on her clean floor, and the words came out before she could stop them.

The man stopped moving. He looked down at his coat as sleepwalkers do—fumbling, half-absent. It was a long trench coat, navy blue, the kind with wide lapels that looked like it had been tailored in another century. Soaked through. Heavy with water and dark stains that might have been mud, or might have been something else.

He blinked, slow and dazed, water clumping his eyelashes.

"I..." His voice came out rough, gravel grinding together in a riverbed, as though he hadn't used it in a long time. He looked up, and his eyes found hers.

Teyra's breath caught somewhere between her ribs and her throat.

Grey eyes—sharp, though, with none of the washed-out pallor of a long-dead spirit. The grey of storm clouds when the lightning's about to strike, of steel just before it cuts. His face was angular, the bones prominent under skin that was too pale, too smooth. Several days' worth of stubble shadowed his jaw. His dark hair was plastered to his forehead, dripping onto his collar.

He was staring at her, straight at her, with the desperate focus of a drowning man who'd found a rope. She almost stepped back. Almost.

"Is this The Final Steep?" he asked.

"That depends," Lenore squawked, leaning forward on her perch with predatory interest. "Are you dead, or just rude?"

The man didn't look at the bird. His eyes stayed fixed on Teyra with an intensity that prickled along her skin. He walked to the nearest table, moving with a strange, liquid grace that didn't match the heaviness of his steps, and dropped into her velvet wingback chair. The wood frame groaned under him. So much for her ten minutes of peace.

As he gripped the armrests, his hands wavered. They turned transparent for a heartbeat, bones visible through spectral flesh, the wood showing through his palms, then snapped back to solid. The snap back was brutal.

Teyra came out from behind the counter, wiping kettle-steam from her hands on her apron. The cold in her blood was reacting to him, recognizing the proximity of death magic. Her teeth chattered, her fingers twitching with the old Academy reflex to start weaving containment sigils.

She kept her voice steady. "Sir. You're fading. You need to tell me what happened."

"I don't remember dying." The man was staring at his hands, turning them over like he was seeing them for the first time. The light from the gas lamps shone through his palms when they went transparent. "I remember cold, and water. And a name."

Teyra's pulse kicked up. "Whose?"

"Yours."

The word landed between them like grave-soil hitting a coffin lid.

She'd never seen this man before. That face wasn't the kind you forgot—those cheekbones, that jaw. How did he know her name? Why did he—Then his eyes flashed white.

The grey in them burned away, replaced by a white-hot, like lightning trapped behind glass. The temperature dropped again, so fast that frost raced across the windows with an audible crack. The teacups on the shelf rattled. One of them, the blue willow pattern her grandmother had loved, split down the middle with a sharp snap.

She knew the sensation at once, dread turning sharp and heavy in her gut. She knew what this was. She'd seen it before, in her third year at the Academy, when a student's summoning went wrong and they had to evacuate the building.

Poltergeist transformation. The violent shift from coherent spirit to mindless, destructive force.

She gave him minutes, if that.

"Do it, Teyra," Lenore hissed, abandoning her perch in a rustle of black feathers. She launched herself toward the top of the highest cabinet. "If he pops in here, he'll blow the roof off. I just organized my nest. My acorns are arranged by size."

The air pressure dropped. The ghost let out a sound that didn't belong in a human throat, half-groan and half-growl, as his form was shredding at the edges. The solid mass of him was unraveling, replaced by grey energy that lashed at the air.

Another teacup exploded. Shards of porcelain rained onto the floor.

Teyra cursed, a string of words she'd learned from that dead sailor, foul enough to make Lenore proud, and ran for the back room. Her hip clipped the counter. The impact shot up her side, but she didn't slow down.

She fell to her knees before the hidden floorboard under the threadbare rug, prying at it with shaking fingers. The wood was swollen from years of moisture, resistant, and her nails scraped against the grain. The cold from the ghost in the other room was seeping through the walls, into the wood, into her bones.

Finally, the board gave with a groan.

Inside was a lead-lined box wrapped in oilcloth and warded with sigils she'd drawn in her own blood two years ago. The metal was freezing, burning her fingers, but she didn't let go. She fumbled with the latch.

Inside sat the forbidden ingredients, nestled in beds of salt and ash. Graveyard Moss, harvested at midnight from a murderer's plot in the Old City Cemetery. Dried Moonflower petals that had never seen the sun. And tucked in the corner, a small glass vial of bonemeal, a necromancer's last-resort weapon, the kind of thing the Academy pretended didn't exist.

"This is treason," she muttered, her heart hammering so hard she tasted copper in the back of her throat. "I am brewing treason for a stranger."

Illegal, a binding offense. The Inquisitors hanged necromancers for less. *Meridia Ashworth heard this argument too*, whispered a voice in the back of her mind that sounded like Professor Grimwald. She ignored it.

But what choice did she have? Let him tear himself apart? Let him destroy her shop and half the street?

She grabbed a pinch of the moss, cold and spongy under her fingers, and a single petal. The vial of bonemeal she shoved into her apron pocket without thinking, a reflex drilled into her by four years of Academy training. Always carry your last resort. Then she ran back to the front.

The shop was shaking now. Books rattled on their shelves. The ghost had almost disappeared, just a violent swirl of grey energy thrashing in the chair.

The kettle was screaming, steam pouring from the spout. Teyra threw open the lid and dumped the ingredients inside.

The water turned black. Absolute black, like a hole had opened in the bottom of the kettle. The smell that rose was foul, wet earth and decay, and underneath it a sweetness gone wrong.

She grabbed the bone stirrer from its hook and plunged it into the liquid. The tea hissed and spat like a living thing. Droplets spattered onto her wrist, burning through her sleeve.

She stirred. Three circles clockwise, one counter, three clockwise. Then hissed the incantation through gritted teeth.

"Anchor the drift. Bind the blood. Root the spirit. Still the flood."

The magic hit her.

It felt like someone had shoved an icicle through her skull and was twisting it against the bone. Her vision whited out. Warmth dripped from her nose. She touched it with shaking fingers. Blood, bright red against her skin.

This was worse than the usual occupational frost. This was the price of forbidden magic, and her channels dilated, the Resonance pathway widening as it always did when she used magic the old way, her grandmother's way, the way that listened instead of commanded. For a terrible moment she felt the stranger's confusion as if it were her own, the drowning thrash of a man who didn't know who he was, where he was, why the world kept sliding through his fingers. And beneath the confusion, so faint she almost missed it, the smell of flour and morning cold. Then the tea took hold and the connection snapped shut, and she was just Teyra again—though for one fading instant, she could have sworn the connection had pulled both ways—shaking and bleeding and adding another man's memory to the collection she carried behind her ribs.

She swallowed it down.

She poured the sludge-thick liquid into a chipped mug, the one with the faded blue flowers that had belonged to her mother, and rushed to the chair. He was thrashing now, his head thrown back, his features gone, replaced by a blur of white noise and static.

She shoved the mug against his intangible lips. The magic in the steam forced contact, solidifying him just enough. A mouth, a throat, enough for him to swallow.

"Drink it!" she yelled over the sound of rattling windows. "Drink it or we both die!"

He gasped, a drowning sound, and downed the brew in one desperate gulp.

He arched his back with a strangled cry, and the air around him cracked. The shockwave blasted outward, slamming into Teyra's chest and sending her flying backward. The mug spun from her grip and shattered against the floorboards, blue flowers and old porcelain scattering like teeth. Her spine hit the counter. The windows rattled so hard the glass spider-webbed. The lights guttered and died.

Then silence pressed against her eardrums, thick as fresh-turned grave soil.

Teyra's ears were ringing. Her heart was going too fast. She couldn't see anything. The darkness was absolute.

Slowly, the warded emergency lamps sputtered back to life. Pale yellow light spread across the wreckage of her shop.

He was still in the chair.

The flickering had stopped. He was solid, pale as marble, but solid. His breathing had steadied, his edges sharp and defined. Seven days. That was the limit her grandmother's notes had warned about, and after that the anchor would dissolve and whatever was left of him would come apart for good.

Lenore swooped down, landing on the back of his chair. She tilted her head, examining him with one bead-black eye. Her gaze fixed on his left hand, on the heavy signet ring that clung to his fourth finger, gold darkened almost to black, its crest worn to the bone but still legible if you knew what you were looking for.

"Which one?" Lenore's voice was delighted. "A Thornwick crest! The dead dad? The dead uncle? Or the baby who got turned to ash in his crib?"

The man flinched. The air around him shimmered, a quick, violent blur, before snapping back to focus. His jaw clenched, his knuckles going white on the armrests.

Teyra shot Lenore a glare sharp enough to draw blood. Thornwick. A dead king's crest on a dead man's hand. The implications stacked up faster than she could count them.

"Ignore her," Teyra said, gentler now. "She's soulless in the most technical sense."

She walked toward him, unhurried. When the cold pouring off him reached her—the chill of the space between heartbeats—she stopped.

"I need to check your anchor," she said softly. "Make sure the magic took properly. Make sure you're not going to destabilize."

She reached out, her fingers hovering above his forehead.

This close, details she'd missed sharpened into focus. The silver threading through his dark hair. A small scar above his left eyebrow, pale and raised, shaped like a crescent moon. How his pupils dilated when he looked at her.

He went very still. His eyes locked onto hers.

The air crackled between them, charged with nothing magical. He looked at her the way you look at a candle in a storm.

Her fingertips brushed his skin.

For one heartbeat, he was solid and warm under her fingertips—the texture of his skin, the faint ridge of that scar beneath her thumb. Heat, startling heat, like touching sun-warmed stone.

A flush swept through her, sudden and unwelcome.

Then his eyes widened, and the warmth vanished.

Her hand plunged through his forehead like she'd stuck it into a frozen lake.

The cold was vicious. It bit into her bones, racing up her arm in a wave of frost. For one raw second she felt the emptiness inside his skull, the hollow space where thoughts should be, where warmth and breath should pulse. Nothing. Just void. Just the endless, aching cold of the space between worlds.

And beneath the void, faint as a voice under ice, came another impression. A flash of red, silk, wet-looking, the color of arterial blood. The smell of roses. A woman's mouth forming words Teyra couldn't hear. And beneath all of it a weight vast and annihilating, the weight of a man who had lost everything and didn't even know what everything was. It crashed through her Resonance channel like a wave through a drainage pipe, too fast to process, too big to hold.

She yanked her hand back with a strangled cry, cradling it against her chest. Her fingers were white, bloodless, numb to the elbow. Her eyes stung with tears that weren't hers.

The stranger solidified instantly, jerking backward so hard the chair groaned. He looked stricken, his face pale as ash.

"I'm sorry," he breathed. "I didn't... I don't know why that happened."

Teyra couldn't answer. She was rubbing feeling back into her arm, her fingers clumsy as she massaged her wrist, trying to coax warmth back into the frozen flesh. It was like the professional cold, only it went deeper. Like she'd plunged her hand past the skin of the world and found nothing on the other side.

"Emotion," she finally managed, her voice shaking. Her teeth were chattering. It was textbook, Professor Grimwald's first lecture on spectral mechanics. The stronger a ghost felt, the more real it became, but push too far and the whole thing fell apart. "The tea anchors your soul to the memory of your body, and strong emotions disrupt it. If you're frightened, if you're angry..." She couldn't bring herself to say *attraction*. "You come apart."

"So I can't..." He looked at his hands, flexing his fingers. "I can't touch anything? Anyone?"

The way he said *anyone* hit harder than it should have.

"You can," she said carefully. "As long as you stay calm. Detached." She swallowed. "No strong emotions."

He held her gaze. A wry smile touched his lips, smaller, sadder, edged with resignation. "So I stay numb. I stay still." He paused.

"I stay... nothing." The unspoken words hung between them.

His hand rose, slow, unconscious, the way a hand moves in a dream. His fingers drifted toward her cheek, close enough for the cold to prickle her skin. Then he caught himself. Stopped, an inch away. Held there, trembling, in the space between wanting and being allowed. He lowered his hand. Said nothing. Neither did she.

"It feels heavy," he said. "Being solid. Like wearing armor made of lead."

"That's the tea. It's giving you substance. Weight." Teyra pressed a rag to her nose. The cloth came away spotted with blood. Her head still throbbed, a steady pulse of ice-cold behind her eyes. "Gravity is part of the package."

She studied him, a question nagging at the back of her mind. "How long have you been... wandering? Before you found my shop?"

He shook his head. "I don't know. There was darkness. Something between death and whatever comes after. Like being unwoven. Like something was trying to erase me thread by thread." His voice went distant. "And then I heard rain, and smelled tea, and something else—a word, maybe, I don't know—and I followed it here."

Teyra's chest tightened. The storm. Her shop. Her magic. She'd had the Velvet Dusk open when he appeared, her grandmother's blend, heavy with necromantic resonance. The scent alone could have been enough.

Had she called him back? Without meaning to, without trying, had she reached into whatever void had been holding him and pulled?

The question was what else she might have let through.

Teyra cleared her throat and turned away, needing distance. "We need to call you something. I can't keep calling you 'Hey You' or 'The Dead Guy.'"

He looked at the ring. "Thornwick seems dangerous."

"Agreed." Teyra scanned the room. Her eyes landed on the bookshelf, where a tattered copy of *Tales of the High Guard* sat on the middle shelf, its spine cracked from a hundred readings. Her grandmother's collection of old legends, the ones she used to read aloud on storm nights. The knight on the cover had a jawline that looked familiar now.

"Ash," she said. The name came out before she'd thought it through.

He blinked. "Ash?"

"It's a good name. Strong. Simple." Defensive, suddenly. "And it sounds like it ought to mean something in the Old Tongue."

She didn't tell him it was actually the name of the knight in the book. Let him think it was more than a spine she'd read a hundred times.

He tested it. "Ash." He nodded. "It fits better than nothing."

Teyra looked at him, at Ash, sitting in her shop with a dead king's ring on his finger and seven days before he turned into a monster. Seven days to untangle a dead man's past and a ring that shouldn't exist on a hand that shouldn't be solid.

She should turn him away. Call the Inquisitors. This wasn't her problem.

But she'd already broken the law for him. Already bled for him.

Besides, Lenore was right. She'd been bored.

"Alright then, Ash." Teyra grabbed her coat from the hook, heavy wool that smelled of sage and rain. "Get up. We have work to do."

"Work?"

"We have seven days before you turn into a monster." She saw his face and added, quieter, "The anchor holds your soul together. When it burns out, you either dissolve into nothing or you become a poltergeist—mindless, violent, and impossible to stop. Seven days."

He was quiet. The kind of quiet that has weight.

She opened the door to the rainy street. The smell of wet stone and coal smoke rushed in. "And you have a ring that belongs to a dead royal family. We're going to the Records Hall."

"Tonight?" He looked at the driving rain with undisguised dismay. "In this?"

"The dead don't sleep, Ash," Teyra said, stepping out into the storm. The rain hit her face like cold needles. "And neither do I."

But as she stepped over the threshold, a memory brushed against her, cold and foreign. Someone else's memory—foreign, unbidden, older than the rain or the Grave-Chill.

Thomas. The soldier.

The scar on her palm, star-shaped, white against her skin, twinged, and for a half-second she was him. Seventeen, the taste of iron in her mouth, an arrow lodged between ribs she didn't have. The bone-deep pull of a boy dying six hundred miles from his mother's kitchen. She'd carried that pull out of the Academy examination hall four years ago, and it had never left. It lived in her now, a splinter of borrowed loss lodged so deep she'd stopped noticing it most days, surfacing only at odd moments. The smell of baking bread. The sound of rain on a tin roof. Any small, domestic thing that Thomas would never experience again.

The professors had seen it happen in real time. Had watched her crumble to her knees inside the summoning circle, sobbing a dead stranger's tears. They'd failed her before she hit the floor.

"A necromancer commands the dead, Miss Tepes. She does not weep for them."

What they didn't say, what she'd only learned later, buried in the footnotes of a textbook they'd since removed from the library, was why. Meridia Ashworth had wept for every spirit she touched, just as Teyra had. She'd healed hauntings that the clinical practitioners couldn't reach. She'd been celebrated. And then the accumulated weight of a thousand borrowed losses had cracked her open, and the dead had spoken through her mouth for six years while her body wandered the Lower Wards, feeding on scraps and rainwater.

The Academy banned Resonance precisely because it was powerful—a river, and the last person who'd opened the floodgates had drowned in other people's sorrow.

Maybe they'd been right to fail her. Maybe compassion was a professional hazard in a trade that dealt in death.

But Thomas had been so scared. And nobody else in that room had cared.

"Are you alright?" Ash's voice, from behind her. Concerned. As if a dead man had any business worrying about the living.

"Fine," Teyra said. She rubbed the scar; the grey film of the Unsettled was already settling on her coat, fine as ash. "Just cold."

She walked into the rain, and the ghost of a dead man with a king's ring followed her into the dark. Behind them, a streak of black shot from the shop's eaves and disappeared into the storm overhead.

Chapter Two

SEVEN DAYS TO REMEMBER

Day One, continued: Seven Days Remain

The walk to the District of Ink was miserable.

They'd barely made it out the door. Mrs. Pemberton from the herbalist's guild had stopped Teyra on the step, squinting past her into the shop with an expression that was two-thirds nosiness and one-third suspicion. "Your windows are frosted on the inside, dear. In September." Teyra had mumbled an excuse about a preservation charm gone wrong and pulled the door shut before the woman could see the chair that was rimed with ice where no living person had been sitting.

Athergard's rain soaked into you, grey and heavy and faintly wrong, settling somewhere behind the skin where no towel could reach. As they left the shelter of Hollow Stair's eaves, it fell in thick sheets that turned the cobblestones slick as old ectoplasm and filled the gutters with rushing water carrying debris from the upper districts, rotting vegetables and coal runoff and the usual urban filth. But there was more in the water tonight. The grey film she'd noticed on her windows was thicker here, where the gutters funneled it downhill. It pooled in the cracks between cobblestones and left a dull tarnish on the iron railings, as though the rain itself were corroding the city one storm at a time.

The farther downhill they walked, the worse it got. In the Ashmore District, the gutters ran clear because the Guild maintained spiritual drainage there, wards sunk into the sewer grates that filtered spectral residue the way coal screens filtered soot. Hollow Stair had no such luxury. Whatever dissolved into the rain here, old hauntings left unfinished, the residue of spirits too poor to afford a proper passage, ran downhill and collected at the bottom.

They walked east, toward the old part of the city. The buildings changed as they went, newer brick giving way to older stone, the neat grid of the Merchant Quarter crumbling into the crooked lanes that had been here before the fire codes, before the zoning laws. These buildings leaned into each other like drunk men holding one another up, their upper stories jutting so far over the street that the eaves nearly touched. Gas lamps flickered in recessed alcoves, their light failing against the perpetual twilight. Some lamps stood dark on purpose-looking corners, as though the shadows had claimed them for good. The shadows they left behind were thicker than they should have been, nearly solid. Teyra walked faster through those patches without thinking about why.

Ash walked beside her, his long coat swinging with a heavy, sodden weight too real for a ghost. He moved with a strange alertness, upright and watchful, his eyes cataloguing the shadows the way trained men do, marking exits and blind spots before his conscious mind caught up. Halfway across the bridge over the Tamber Canal, he stopped.

His form stuttered—a sharp, involuntary jerk, different from the emotional destabilization she'd seen at the shop, as if a hand had yanked him downward. His knees buckled. One hand shot out and caught the railing, passing through the iron twice before his grip held.

"What is it?" Teyra asked, reaching for him.

"Nothing." He straightened, but his eyes stayed distant, fixed through the canal, past the water and the stone and whatever lay beneath. "For a moment I felt... pulled. Like something beneath the city is starving." The word choice prickled against her skin.

Teyra looked over the railing. The Tamber Canal was black and sluggish, choked with runoff. But there was a presence down there, faint as a toothache, pressing against her raw Resonance channels. Older than any spirit or haunting, less defined, like the memory of a wound that had never been treated. And beneath the old ghosts, beneath the burial-channel residue, a deeper presence. A hunger with no mouth, pressing upward against the bedrock with the patience of a predator that had never needed to hurry. She pulled back from the railing. Below, a shape moved in the water—a fish, pale and belly-up, drifting past with the current. Then another. Then a third. Whatever was down there, the canal's last living things could feel it too. Somewhere above the rooftops, the Merchant District clock tower struck the quarter-hour, and the chime hung in the air a beat too long, as if the sound itself had forgotten how to end. The canal had been a burial channel centuries ago, before the city paved over its dead. Now the water remembered, even if the city didn't.

He shook his head and started walking again. "It's gone now."

But his hand stayed on the railing longer than it needed to, the grip of someone who'd learned that shadows sometimes had teeth. She didn't look back. If she had, she might have noticed how still the water had gone.

A carriage rattled past, its wheels sending up a spray of muddy water. The driver hunched under a tarp, the horses' hooves clattering on wet stone.

Ash's arm shot out instinctively to shield her from the splash.

But he stopped inches from her shoulder. His hand hovered there, trembling slightly, the cold from his skin sharp enough to prickle hers. Then he jerked it back as though the air between them had bitten him.

"I forgot," he muttered, shoving his hands deep into his pockets. A muscle jumped in his jaw. "I can't even offer you a coat. I'm useless."

Teyra wiped a spot of mud from her cheek. "You're not useless. You're just... intangibly challenged."

The ghost of a smile touched his lips, already fading. "That's a terrible joke."

"I know," Teyra said. "But you almost smiled."

He said nothing, but she saw his hands clench inside his pockets. The impulse ran deeper than touch. Some older instinct in him, one that predated the death and the forgetting, wanted to shield her from mud and rain and carriages and the world's general indifference.

And the magic wouldn't let him.

They turned a corner, and the District of Ink opened up before them.

The noise dropped as they entered. Rain fell more softly here, muffled by overhanging eaves and thick stone walls. The buildings were different, pale limestone instead of dark brick, their facades covered in elaborate carvings. Symbols of knowledge. Open books. Quills crossed like swords. Eyes that followed you as you passed.

Or they had, once. Teyra noticed it as they walked deeper into the district. Some of the carved symbols had gone dark. They'd been snuffed, quick and clean, as though someone had pinched them out. Preservation runes that had glowed for centuries were now grooves in limestone, their light faded to nothing. The oldest ones predated the Thornwick dynasty by ages, carved in a script no living scholar could read. She counted and the number sat wrong in her stomach. One in three. One in three runes dead, their knowledge-keeping magic gone, as though the stones had forgotten what they were for.

Now it was mostly empty. The scholars had fled a generation ago, when the runes began failing. The buildings remained as gravestones remain, marking a place where something had once been alive. The air smelled of parchment and old ink, steeped in the particular staleness of knowledge no one consults anymore.

"Here," Teyra said, stopping before massive iron gates. The metalwork was intricate, wrought into patterns of interlocking letters that shifted and rearranged as you looked at them, spelling out different words in different languages. "We're here. And Lenore, you stay outside."

The raven, who had been circling overhead like a bad omen, landed on a stone gargoyle above the gate. She shook her wings, sending droplets scattering. "Fine. Smells like dust and bureaucrats in there anyway. Gives me a headache. I'll keep watch."

"Please don't scream at anyone."

"No promises."

Then, quieter, from the gargoyle, "And Teyra? Royal archives are curated, not written. Remember that."

Teyra pushed open the heavy doors. They swung inward with a groan of old hinges that echoed in the vast space beyond.

The smell hit them instantly—dry and suffocating. Parchment and binding glue and a wrongness underneath that made the hair stand up on her arms. Centuries compressed into dust.

The Records Hall was a cathedral of information.

The ceiling vanished into darkness somewhere far overhead, lost in shadows that the gas lamps couldn't penetrate. The walls were lined with shelves that stretched up for stories, rising so high that the topmost levels were barely visible, accessible only by floating ladders that drifted through the air like sleeping birds. The shelves themselves were dark wood gone black with age, their surfaces carved with preservation runes that glowed in the gloom.

Books—tens of thousands of them, leather-bound tomes beside cloth-wrapped scrolls, with loose manuscripts tied in ribbon. They filled every shelf, packed so tightly that Teyra couldn't see how anyone could remove one without the rest collapsing.

"Silence," a voice hissed from the darkness.

Teyra jumped. Ash tensed beside her, his form flickering, the edges going blurry before solidifying again, then forcing himself still.

A wizened old man sat behind a high desk near the entrance, blending into the surroundings so thoroughly he might have been made of the same parchment as the books. His skin was thin and papery, stretched tight over prominent bones, his fingers long and skeletal, stained black with decades of ink. He looked at them with eyes that were cloudy and colorless.

"We need the Lineage Records for the Royal Houses," Teyra said. She pulled her Necromancer's License from her pocket, bent at one corner with the seal slightly smudged, and placed it on the desk. "Official business."

The archivist picked up the license with painful slowness. He held it close to his face, squinting, lips moving silently. Then he looked at Ash.

"Who is this?"

She should have prepared for this. She opened her mouth to fumble an excuse.

"Consulting specialist," Ash said. His voice had changed, gone precise and clipped, the vowels flattened into something formal that Teyra had never heard from him before. "Retained under Provision Twelve of the Lineage Access Charter. The necromancer's license entitles her to one specialist of her choosing for cross-referencing purposes. You'll find the clause on the back of the seal."

Teyra stared at him. The archivist turned the license over, squinted, and grunted.

There was nothing on the back of the seal. Teyra knew this because she'd had the license for four years and had read every word of it. But Ash had said it with such smooth, bored authority that the archivist didn't check twice. The truth wards in this place should have flared at a lie, but they stayed dark, humming quietly, as if whatever Ash was had satisfied them. That should have been impossible. She filed it under the growing list of things about this man that didn't add up. The old man grunted again and waved them through.

"How did you know that?" Teyra whispered as they moved deeper into the stacks.

"I guessed." Ash looked faintly surprised at himself. "It just came out. Like my mouth knew the words before I did." He flexed his fingers, frowning. "Court protocol. I think I was trained in it. Whoever raised me made sure I could talk my way past a bureaucrat."

Teyra tucked that away and said nothing. Whoever he'd been, the man had known his way around authority.

The archives were old magic, built on layers of preservation spells and truth wards. If anyone could sense a ghost walking around in borrowed flesh...

"Section 4," the archivist repeated, already looking back at his manuscript. "The Crimson Aisle. Don't touch the Cursed Tomes, or you will be eaten."

He said it so matter-of-factly that it took Teyra a moment to process. "Eaten?"

"Digested, technically. But the end result is the same." He was already looking down at whatever manuscript he'd been reading. "Section 4. Second floor."

They walked deeper into the stacks. The silence was absolute, broken only by the soft sound of Ash's boots on the wooden floor and the occasional whisper of pages turning themselves somewhere in the darkness.

The stairs were narrow and steep, winding up into the gloom. Teyra counted steps automatically, forty-three of them, each one worn smooth in the center from centuries of feet.

The second floor was darker, the gas lamps sparser, the shadows thicker. The shelves here were different, the wood almost black, and the books looked wrong. Their bindings were strange colors. Wine-dark and violet and sickly green, and some of them pulsed.

"Section 4," Teyra whispered, scanning the brass plates mounted at the end of each row. "Thornwick... Thornwick..."

She found it. The Crimson Aisle.

The archivist had been right, you couldn't miss it. The entire section glowed with a faint red light, as if the books themselves were on fire. Heat radiated from the shelves.

She pulled a massive, leather-bound volume from the shelf, heavy enough that the weight of it made her arms shake, and carried it to the nearest reading table.

"Here." She traced the family tree with her finger. "House Thornwick."

The page was illuminated, hand-painted in the old style. The Thornwick crest, a rose wreathed in flame, was stamped at the top in faded gold, and beneath it a motto in the old language that someone had translated in pencil: The crown serves the root. The family tree spread across two pages, three hundred years of names branching outward, dozens of them, kings, their queens, and the consorts folded into the line beside them, the lineage of a dynasty that had governed the city since its founding. She noticed the Thornwick names repeated across generations—Alaric, Isobel, Evelyn, Ashen—the same names cycling back, parents naming children after grandparents, an unbroken chain of inherited identity. At the bottom of the tree, the last two entries.

The page was already marked.

Someone had been here before them. A thin strip of silk, black, almost invisible against the dark leather, had been slipped between the pages, marking this exact entry. And in the margin, in handwriting so precise it looked printed, someone had written a single word in silver ink.

Patience.

She pulled the bookmark free. The silk was embroidered with a tiny moth.

"What is it?" Ash asked.

"Nothing." She pocketed the silk strip, her pulse ticking faster against the side of her throat. "Just a placeholder. Someone was here before us, that's all."

She kept the rest to herself—the trail of breadcrumbs leading to exactly the information they needed, and what the moth embroidered on the silk meant. Every debtor in Hollow Stair knew that sigil, because it belonged to the man who ran the city's invisible economy. And if he had planted this bookmark here, in a restricted archive, then a man who collected rare things had apparently been collecting their story for a very long time.

Ash leaned over her shoulder. The dead had no need for breath, but the cold radiating from him raised goosebumps along her arms.

"There," he said, pointing. His finger hovered just above the faded ink.

Teyra read the entry aloud.

"Lord Alaric Thornwick. Lady Isobel Thornwick. Deceased, The Year of Ash."

She moved her finger down, following the line to the next generation.

"Ashen Thornwick. Heir Apparent. Deceased, The Year of Ash. Age seven."

She stopped. She looked at Ash.

Ashen. Ash. The name she'd pulled from her grandmother's book of legends, the throwaway nickname she'd invented on the spot, two letters away from his real name. Her skin prickled. Coincidence, she told herself. But necromancers didn't believe in coincidence. They believed in resonance.

"The Year of Ash was twenty-five years ago," she said. "The records say you died in the fire with your parents. You were seven years old."

Ash stared at the words. The air around him vibrated, a low hum that made the gas flames flicker.

"I died as a grown man," he whispered. His voice was rough, scraping. "I remember a sword. I remember a woman in a red dress. I was a man. Fully grown."

"Then you survived the fire." Teyra's mind raced. "You grew up somewhere. In hiding. And you were killed later, as an adult."

"But where? By whom?" He pressed his palms against his temples. "Why can't I remember?"

She looked at him. The ghost in front of her was a grown man, late twenties, maybe thirty. And the way he moved, how he spoke—these were the mannerisms of someone who had lived a full and guarded life.

She looked back at the record. Deceased, Age 7.

Then at Ash, a grown man, fully solid, and recently dead.

"This doesn't add up," she said. "If you died in the fire twenty-five years ago, your ghost would be a child. Ghosts don't age. They're frozen at the moment of death." She met his eyes. "But you're a grown man, Ash. Which means either you didn't die in that fire..."

"Or someone lied about my death," Ash finished.

Teyra braced herself and reached for her Resonance, brushing the edges of his death-imprint. The contact sent a lance of cold through her temples, briefer than the shop but sharp enough to make her wince. The fire was twenty-five years ago. But the residue clinging to him was recent, years old and fresh-stinking with violence. Whatever had killed him, it hadn't happened in a nursery.

"Then someone else died in your place," Teyra said, piecing it together. "Or there was no body at all. Just a story. The Crown declared you dead, but you were smuggled out. Hidden somewhere. Raised in secret."

"By who? For what purpose?"

"To reclaim the throne someday." Teyra's voice was quiet. "You were the heir. If loyalists saved you from the fire, they would have trained you. Prepared you. Waited until you were old enough to come back and challenge whoever took power."

Ash's edges blurred. "And then someone killed me before I could."

"Someone who knew you were alive. Someone close enough to get past your defenses." Teyra's gaze dropped to the signet ring on his finger. "The woman in the red dress."

"I don't know!" Ash shouted, his voice cracking.

The book slammed shut with a force that shook the table. The floating ladders stopped drifting and shook. The temperature in the aisle plummeted. Frost spread across the table, creeping up the legs of the chairs.

Ash was losing coherence. His solid form was tearing apart at the edges. The handsome man was disappearing, replaced by a presence with more teeth than a man.

He gripped the edge of the table, and his fingers sank into the wood, phasing through it.

"Ash, stop!" Teyra grabbed his wrist without thinking.

Her hand passed straight through him. The cold burned, but she didn't pull back. She stepped into his space, right into the freezing aura pouring off him in waves.

"Look at me," she commanded. "You are here. You are solid. You are Ash."

His eyes locked onto hers, white and empty and enormous. She held his gaze, forced herself to look into that storm.

Slowly, agonizingly, it receded. He held. The shaking stopped. The cold eased.

He stood there, his form flickering at the edges, his jaw clenched so tight she could see the muscle jump.

"I remember something else," he rasped. "Look at the margin."

Teyra opened the book again. There, scribbled in faint, faded ink next to the entry for the "dead" child, was a note.

Elias T.—Ward of the Crown. Adopted by House Greythorn.

Teyra scanned the rest of the record. Another entry, smaller, almost hidden.

Elias Thornwick. Second son. Age 4. Survived. Ward of the Crown.

"Elias." The name tore out of him like a wound reopening. "I had a brother."

His hand moved to his chest, fingers splaying over the place where his heart would have been. "I had a brother, and I don't remember his face."

Teyra watched something move across his features that she couldn't name, only feel at the edges where her Resonance bled through. She reached for him. The cold stopped her.

"You'll remember," she said. "We'll drag it back."

Heat moved through her chest. She checked, the way she always checked. This anger was hers, clean and unfamiliar, with nothing borrowed in it. Anger at a world that could murder a man and bury the evidence in a filing cabinet. She looked at the note again.

"He didn't die in the fire," she said. "He was adopted by the rival house. By House Greythorn. The house that rules the city now."

Ash straightened. The confusion drained from his face, replaced by iron. And cold.

"We need to find him," he said. "Because if I had a brother, he knows why I'm dead."

They didn't go home.

Teyra knew they should. She was exhausted, bone-deep tired, the forbidden-magic-and-too-much-adrenaline kind. But the discovery had lit a fire behind Ash's eyes, and the look on his face made it clear that sleep was off the table.

Instead, they found an all-night café in the District of Ink, a cramped, smoky place called The Broken Quill that catered to scholars and insomniacs. The coffee was terrible and the pastries stale, but the place was warm, dry, and otherwise empty except for an elderly historian snoring in the corner.

Ash paused in the doorway. His eyes moved across the room—back exit behind the counter, windows facing the alley, narrow corridor to the kitchen—before he chose the chair facing the door and sat with his back to the wall.

He'd done the same thing at the shop. Teyra filed it away. Wherever he'd been before the darkness, he'd learned to sit where no one could come up behind him.

Teyra wrapped her hands around a chipped cup, willing her thoughts into some kind of order.

"House Greythorn," she said. "The most powerful family in Athergard. They've been advisors to the Crown for three generations, but that undersells it. They own half the shipping routes into the harbour, they control the Hessian foundries, and every judge on the High Court was appointed by a Greythorn. Lord Greythorn sits on the City Council. His wife died three years ago, no children of their own, but the family has cousins in every major house and nephews in every regiment. When a Greythorn sneezes, the whole city reaches for a handkerchief."

"If Elias was adopted by them,,," Ash sat across from her, his coffee untouched. Could ghosts even drink coffee? She made a mental note to ask. "He's not just alive. He's powerful. Connected."

"Untouchable," Teyra agreed. "At least by normal means."

The café was quiet except for the tick of a clock on the wall and the soft patter of rain against the windows. The gas lamps were turned low, casting long shadows across the scarred wooden table. Ash's fingers moved on the wood—lighter than the tapping pattern she'd catalogued, tracing a different pattern entirely. The ghost of a melody his hands remembered but his mind had lost.

"Tell me something," Ash said suddenly.

Teyra looked up from her cup.

"Tell me about yourself," he said. "You know everything about me now, or at least you know I'm a dead prince with a lost brother and seven days to live. But I don't know anything about you."

"There's not much to tell."

"I doubt that."

Teyra took a sip of the terrible coffee, buying time. "What do you want to know?"

"Why do you help ghosts? You're clearly good at it, the tea, the readings, talking me down from becoming a poltergeist. But you run a shop with a leaking roof and one good chair. You could be doing something bigger."

The question landed closer than she'd braced for. She set down her cup.

"I was supposed to do something bigger," she said, her voice dropping. "I was a top student at the Academy. Highest scores in Necrotic Theory. Professor Grimwald said I had 'natural talent.' My thesis on spectral anchoring was published in the *Journal of Mortuary Sciences.*"

"What happened?"

The words came out before she could stop them. "I felt too much."

Ash waited.

"The Practical Exam," Teyra said. "The final test before they let you attempt a Command Word, the high necromancy, the kind that can bind a spirit or break a ward or drag someone back from oblivion. Dangerous magic. It burns your channels if you do it wrong."

She stared at the table. "The theory is straightforward. Command Words channel power through the Grave-Chill, clinical and tightly controlled, flowing in one direction. The necromancer commands, the spirit obeys. Clean lines. No bleed-through." She traced a circle on the table with her fingertip.

"But there's an older theory, pre-Academy, before the Grave-Chill was standardized, that the strongest Commands don't run through the Chill at all. They run through connection. Emotional bond. The deeper the bond between necromancer and spirit, the more powerful the Word." She dropped her hand. "It used to be the standard practice, actually. Before the Academy existed.

Necromancers worked through empathy, through shared feeling. They called it Resonance. And for a long time, it worked."

She paused. The coffee was cold. She drank it anyway. "Then it stopped working. A necromancer named Meridia Ashworth, she's the cautionary tale in every first-year textbook. Built her entire practice on Resonance, bonded with every spirit she touched, and the accumulated weight collapsed on her all at once." Teyra turned the coffee cup in her hands. "But the textbooks only tell you half the story."

"What they leave out is what happened six months before that." She met Ash's eyes.

"Meridia performed a mass Resonance event. Nobody has a name for what it was. The Academy scrubbed the records after the incident, called it an 'uncontrolled escalation,' buried it in a footnote. But from the witness accounts that survived, she connected simultaneously to dozens of spirits across the city. Held all of them at once. Channeled their accumulated weight as a unified force to close a Spectral Breach in the harbour district that had been killing people for three years. It worked." Teyra's voice was flat. "It worked. Forty-seven hauntings resolved in a single night. The harbour district was clean. The breach was sealed. Meridia was celebrated. For six months, she was the greatest necromancer the city had ever seen."

The clock on the wall ticked.

Ash said nothing.

"And then the bonds didn't release. The spirits she'd held during the mass event, they hadn't left. They'd gone quiet, the way a crowd goes quiet when the music stops. And when they woke up, she wasn't a necromancer to them anymore. She was a door, and they walked through her. All of them at once."

"The Academy was founded in the aftermath. The Grave-Chill method, clinical and controlled, no emotional contact, was their answer. Their way of making sure it never happened again. And it worked. It made necromancy safe and predictable." She shrugged, aiming for casual and landing nowhere near it. "It also made it cold. Mechanical, even. The spirits aren't people to the Academy. They're cases to be processed."

"And you couldn't do that."

"I couldn't do that."

"So. Step one, prove you can command a spirit through the Chill. Clinically, without emotional contamination."

She stared at the table, at the ring left by her coffee cup.

"They summoned a soldier. Seventeen years old. Died with an arrow in his chest six hundred miles from home." Her voice went flat. "The other students just commanded. Clean, clinical. One girl, she was good, the best of us besides me, she finished her summoning in forty seconds and didn't spill a drop of her tea. She watched me break the circle, and I saw her face. Relief, plain on her face, not disgust. Relieved it was me and not her, because she'd felt it too and she'd learned to pretend she hadn't."

"But when I reached out, I didn't just get his voice. I got everything." She didn't elaborate. The memory was a splinter she'd carried for four years, and she wasn't going to pull it out in a café at two in the morning. "I broke the circle. The professors failed me on the spot."

Silence.

She looked up. Ash was watching her with an expression she couldn't read—tender, unguarded—and it made arguing feel pointless.

"They were wrong," he said.

"Were they?" She hadn't meant to say it. But the question had been sitting in her chest for four years, and the late hour and the terrible coffee had loosened her guard.

"Meridia Ashworth felt everything too. She wept for every spirit she touched. She was celebrated for it. And it destroyed her. It destroyed an entire neighborhood." She turned the coffee cup in her hands. "Maybe the Academy wasn't wrong. Maybe they were just answering a question I didn't want to hear. How much feeling is too much? Where's the line between compassion and self-destruction?"

"You're not Meridia Ashworth."

"How do you know? You've known me for six hours."

"Because Meridia Ashworth didn't have a talking raven to keep her humble."

The laugh surprised her, a short, startled sound that broke the tension like a cracked window letting in air. "That might actually be the worst joke I've ever heard."

"Worse than 'intangibly challenged'?"

"Significantly worse."

But she was smiling. And the question, the real question, the one about where compassion ended and destruction began, settled back into her chest unsolved, the way it always did. She suspected it would stay unsolved until she was forced to answer it. She hoped the day was far away.

He went still. His head tilted slightly, his nostrils flaring. "Do you smell that?"

Teyra sniffed. Stale coffee and coal smoke from the fireplace, layered under the faint must of old books that permeated every building in the District of Ink. "Smell what?"

"Roses." His voice had changed, gone distant, uncertain. "Red roses. And something else. Wet earth. Morning dew." He pressed his fingers against his temple. "It slipped."

"A memory?"

"I don't know. It felt like… like standing in a garden I can't see. Like being very young and very safe." He shook his head. "It doesn't make sense."

And it was there, just at the edge, leaning against her Resonance channels. His childhood certainty that the world was good and the garden would always be there. It ached with the sweetness of a life ripped away, and her eyes stung with the same tears that weren't hers, the ones she'd felt when her hand had plunged through his skull in the shop. His loss, leaking through the cracks in whatever wall she was supposed to maintain between herself and the dead.

She blinked it away. Filed the roses beside the exit-counting and the back-to-the-wall habit. Whoever Ash had been, he'd known gardens. He'd known safety. And he'd known roses.

She was going to find out why someone had taken all of it away from him. And she was going to make sure it cost them.

He reached out. His hand hovered over hers on the table, the cold of him pressing against her skin without weight. He didn't touch her. He remembered the shop, her hand plunging through him, the cold that had burned her white to the elbow.

But the space between their hands felt charged. Electric.

"I'm glad you were the one who found me," he said.

She pulled her hand back, too fast, pulse kicking against her throat, and wrapped both hands around her cup. The coffee was cold. She didn't drink it.

"Kindness doesn't solve murders," she said. "Evidence does."

She set the cup down too hard.

"You said you remember a woman in a red dress. A sword. We need to know more. If we're going to figure out who killed you, and why, we need to see what you saw."

"How?" Ash asked, voice tight.

"A reading. Something stronger than tea leaves. I can read the residue of your last strong memory. The moment of death." She met his eyes. "It leaves a mark."

"You want me to relive it."

"I want you to show me."

Ash was quiet. Then he nodded.

Somewhere in the building, a clock struck two. The sound was thin, distant, absorbed by all that paper and dust.

"Tomorrow," he said. "When we're back at the shop. When you've rested."

"I don't need to rest."

"You're bleeding again."

Teyra touched her nose. Her fingers came away red.

"Fine," she said. "Tomorrow."

She stood up, leaving coins on the table for the coffee. Her legs were unsteady beneath her, the exhaustion arriving all at once like a debt called in.

Ash stood with her, moving like a man trying not to spill himself. "Teyra. Thank you."

"Don't thank me yet. We still have seven days left."

"No." He stopped her with a single word, his hands never moving. "Thank you for not looking at me like I'm a monster. For telling me about the soldier. For…" He searched for the words. "For being kind. Even when you didn't have to be."

The knot between her ribs gave, just a little.

"You're welcome," she said softly. "Now let's get out of here before I fall asleep standing up."

They walked out into the rain together, a necromancer and a ghost prince, with seven days between them and the end of the world.

Behind them, in the Records Hall, the preservation runes on the Crimson Aisle flickered once, and another one went dark.

Chapter Three

THE TEA LEAVES DON'T LIE

Day Two: Six Days Remain

D AWN WAS TRYING TO break over Athergard, but the storm was putting up a fight.

The sky was bruised purple and swollen, streaked with darker veins where the clouds were thickest. The rain had turned from a downpour into a cold, persistent mist that clung to everything, clothes, skin, the warped glass of the shop windows. The grey film was worse this morning. It coated the outside of the glass in a dull sheen that turned the gaslight murky, and where it had pooled on the windowsill overnight, it left a residue like dried tears. Teyra had stopped scrubbing it off months ago. It always came back.

Teyra woke in the velvet wingback, her neck stiff and her mouth tasting like a crypt.

She couldn't remember sitting down. Last thing she recalled was locking the door behind them, engaging the wards, turning to say something to Ash. Then nothing. The exhaustion had come down on her like a collapsed ward.

Someone had slipped a notice under the door while she slept. Guild letterhead, official seal. The Ward Inspectorate would be conducting routine spectral emissions checks in the Hollow Stair district this week. Random selection, the notice said. Purely standard. Teyra read it twice, then folded it into a tight square and put it in the stove.

Ash was sitting on the counter. More than watching. His hands were moving, she caught it as she blinked awake, fingers tracing a pattern on the counter's surface, tapping in a sequence she didn't recognize. Index finger, middle, ring, thumb. Index, middle, ring, thumb. Over and over, unconscious, as though tapping out a melody he couldn't quite hear.

When he noticed her looking, he stopped. Stared at his own hands like they'd betrayed him.

"What was that?" she asked.

"I don't know." He flexed his fingers, frowning. "I wasn't thinking about it. My hands just... did it."

Another fragment: the exit-counting, the roses, the habits his body kept shelving where his mind couldn't reach them.

She filed the sequence: index, middle, ring, thumb. Four beats, repeating—muscle memory worn so deep the hands kept going long after the mind stopped paying attention. And beneath the rhythm, so faint she almost missed it, a murmur at the edge of his presence. The ghost of a voice, gruff and patient, the cadence of someone who had drilled a boy through this pattern until the boy's hands knew it better than his name. It was gone before she could catch the words. But her Resonance channels had brushed it, and the impression stayed: hay and sword oil and a man who had cared enough to make him practice.

He looked better than he had last night, more present, less like smoke fighting to hold shape, and the Moonflower tea was doing its work. But there was a quiet intensity in his expression, that made her wonder how long he'd been watching her sleep.

"Morning," she croaked.

"You snore," he said.

"I do not."

"Like a congested badger."

Despite everything, the absurdity of their situation and the looming deadline and the ache in every part of her body, Teyra felt a smile tug at her mouth. "Nobody asked you."

She stood, her joints protesting, and made her way to the brewing station. Her hands moved automatically, filling the kettle and lighting the burner, measuring tea leaves into the pot without thinking. Silver-Needle for restoration. A pinch of Iron-root for stability, the standard anchoring blend she used for nervous ghosts.

The shop was quiet, almost peaceful. Morning light filtered through the rain-streaked windows, turning the shop the color of old pewter. She could almost forget what they were about to do.

"The reading," Ash said, as if he'd read her thoughts. "Are you ready?"

Teyra's hands stilled on the teapot. "Are you?"

"No." He was honest about it, at least. "But we have six days. I don't think we can afford to wait until I'm ready."

He was right. She hated that he was right.

She poured him a cup of the restoration blend and set it before him. He picked it up with both hands, and she watched carefully, saw the slight hesitation, how his fingers passed through the ceramic before thickening enough to grip it.

"Drink," she said. "It'll help stabilize you for what comes next."

He drank, grimacing at the taste. "This is not Velvet Dusk."

"Nothing is Velvet Dusk." She watched him swallow, watched the color return to his face, watched him become more real by the minute. "Ash. About the reading. It's going to be intense."

"I assumed."

"I mean for both of us." She turned away, reaching for a white porcelain bowl, one of her grandmother's pieces, fine china with pale painted roses around the rim. "The tea shows the moment of greatest extremity. The moment when the soul screamed loudest. I'll see what you see. Feel what you feel. If it's too much..."

"It won't be."

"You don't know that." She set the bowl on the table harder than she meant to. "Last night, when I brewed the anchoring tea, when the magic hit, I felt your confusion. Just a flash. Your disorientation, your not-knowing. It was in me for less than a second, and it nearly knocked me down." She met his eyes. "This reading will be worse. The death-moment is the strongest imprint a spirit carries. When I open the channel, I see what happened to you. All of it. I feel the blade go in. The betrayal. All of it. And it won't just pass through me, Ash. Some of it will stay."

He watched her face. "Stay how?"

"The way Thomas stayed." She said it before she could stop herself. "Four years later, and I still get homesick for a village I've never been to, because he was homesick when the arrow hit. I smell bread baking and I'm in his mother's kitchen. Rain on a tin roof and I'm six hundred miles from home." She looked at the bowl, at the pale roses painted by her grandmother's steady hand. "Some of what I take in doesn't leave. That's what I'm asking you to understand before we start."

She almost told him about Meridia Ashworth again. About how a thousand borrowed deaths had cracked open the most gifted Resonance practitioner Athergard had ever produced. About how the Academy had been founded in the aftermath, specifically to prevent it from ever happening again. But she'd already told him that story in the café, and repeating it now would sound like she was trying to talk herself out of helping him.

She was trying to make sure he understood what he was asking her to carry.

"I need answers," he said. "And you're the only one who can help me find them." He paused. "But if the cost is too high…"

"It's always too high. When has that ever stopped me?"

Her hands were steady. Her heart was hammering so hard she could feel it in her wrists.

She pulled a canister from the top shelf, small, marked with an open eye painted in silver ink. Inside were the Dream-Shade petals, purple and bruised-looking, their edges curled and black. They smelled wrong, sweet and rotten at the same time.

"Put your hand over the bowl," she instructed. "Don't touch the water. Just… remember. Focus on the last thing you felt before you died."

Ash hesitated, his hand hovering uncertainly. Then he nodded, sharp and decisive.

Teyra poured hot water over the petals. Instead of floating, they swirled and danced, sinking and rising in a hypnotic pattern. The water rippled outward in perfect concentric circles. A pale, sickly green vapor rose in tendrils, curling and writhing.

"Focus," Teyra whispered. "The red dress. The sword. Show me."

The steam shimmered. Coalesced into shapes.

Flash.

A ballroom, grand and high-ceilinged. The ceiling soared overhead, painted with frescoes of angels, gilt trim catching the light from crystal chandeliers. The chandeliers were swaying on their chains. A waltz played somewhere, violins and cellos, the melody distorted and slow.

People danced in elegant circles, their faces blurred. Women in ball gowns beside men in tailcoats, the smell of perfume and candle wax thick in the air.

Flash.

The edges of the ballroom were wrong. Where the far wall should have been, where the orchestra should have sat, there was nothing. An absence so complete it made Teyra's eyes ache, like staring at a hole cut in a painting. The nothing pulsed, once, as if it were breathing.

Then the vision lurched sideways and the wall was back, solid and gilded and draped in silk, as if it had never been gone.

Damage to the memory, Teyra told herself. Spectral degradation. Even so, the distortion felt profoundly wrong.

The steam thickened.

A woman.

Dark hair piled high, held in place with pins that sparkled like stars. Skin pale as porcelain. Lips painted the same deep red as her dress, dark red silk that clung to her figure, shimmering like wet silk. Like liquid.

She was smiling, though her eyes stayed flat and empty.

The floor rushed up.

Her hand raising a crystal glass. On her wrist, a heavy gold bracelet, thick, carved with a serpent eating its own tail. Ruby eyes glinting in the candlelight.

The Ouroboros.

Teyra felt Ash tense beside her. Heard his sharp intake of breath.

Flash.

The perspective shifted sickeningly. The floor rushing up. A bright, blinding lance through his ribs. Cold steel sliding between bone, scraping. The sensation of drowning on dry land.

The woman in red standing over him, looking down. Her face calm. Her lips moving, whispering something, but the words were lost in the static of death.

Darkness creeping in at the edges, and cold. God, the cold.

Flash.

The bracelet again. The serpent. The rubies glowing.

Then silence.

Teyra blew on the steam, scattering the images. Her hands were shaking, her face drained of color.

The blade-sensation still lived in her, steel parting flesh between her third and fourth rib, the scrape of metal against bone, the horrible wet wrongness of something being inside her that shouldn't be. Her body knew it hadn't happened to her. Her Resonance channels didn't care. They had absorbed the death-moment the way a sponge absorbs water, and now the phantom wound sat in her chest like a coal, pulsing with someone else's final seconds.

She pressed her hand against her ribs. No blood, no wound. Only the echo, and the knowledge that this one would stay. Thomas's homesickness. The widow's yearning for mornings. The sailor's ache for open water. Mr. Pemberton's bitterness. The little girl's winter cold, the oldest of them, the one she'd been carrying since she was twelve. And now this, the horror of being murdered by someone you trusted.

She added it to the collection. Seven, now—though the flour-and-morning-cold wisp from the anchoring was already fading, thin as smoke compared to the others.

Ash gasped, stumbling back from the table. His hand flew to his ribs, the place where the blade had entered, and she swore she saw blood seeping through his shirt. Just a shadow, though. A phantom pain.

They were both holding the same wound, she realized. His body remembered it. Hers had just inherited it.

"Seraphine," he choked out. The name came out like a curse.

"That bracelet. The Ouroboros, the serpent eating its tail. It's the mark of the Queen's Personal Guard. Only members of the Guard are allowed to wear it."

Ash was shaking. Actually shaking, his whole frame vibrating like a bell struck too hard, and when he looked at Teyra the rawness in his eyes was so total it made her chest ache. She couldn't tell anymore whether the ache was hers or his. The line between them was thinning.

"She smiled at me." His voice went flat. "While she was doing it. As if we were dancing."

She knew the name, felt it land in her throat. Everyone in Athergard with a Guild license knew the name. "Lady Seraphine. Commander of the Queen's Personal Guard. The title dates from the Thornwick era, and Greythorn kept the institution, kept the name. The Queen's right hand."

Ash's eyes widened. "The Queen's Guard killed me?"

"And if she killed you," Teyra said, "the order came from the Throne."

Three heavy knocks hit the shop door.

Teyra froze. Lenore puffed up on her perch, silent. Ash turned toward the door, and his form dimmed, once, twice. He let go, she realized. Released his grip on the physical the way you'd open a fist that had been clenched too long. He vanished into invisibility.

But she could still feel him there. A cold spot in the air. A presence.

"Open up," a deep voice boomed from outside. "In the name of the Crown."

The knocking stopped.

"Open the door, Miss Tepes." The voice was patient but implacable. "Or I will be forced to dismantle it."

Teyra looked toward where she knew Ash was standing, a shimmer in the air, heat haze in reverse. The temperature in the shop had dropped another five degrees. Frost was beginning to web across the windows.

She pointed a finger at the empty air. *Stay.*

Then she smoothed her apron, straightened her shoulders, and unlocked the deadbolt.

She pulled the door open.

It was a Gilded Hessian, a clockwork soldier used by the Palace for high-priority errands. Seven feet tall, maybe more, its body constructed from brass and polished oak. The brass was worked to a mirror shine. The face was a smooth, blank mask of gold with no features and no expression.

Rain hissed and steamed as it hit the Hessian's heated chassis. The thing radiated dry, metallic heat.

Inside its chest, gears turned. A steady tick-tick-tick.

"Miss Teyra Tepes," the Hessian droned. "Necromancer, Second Class. License Number 409-B. Certified for Standard Passage, Spirit-Ease administration, and basic anchoring. Restricted from Resonance work, advanced summoning, and unsupervised high-risk operations."

"That's me." Teyra gripped the doorframe. "Is there a problem? My license is paid up."

The Hessian raised one heavy brass hand. It held an envelope of thick, cream-colored parchment.

"Correspondence from the Commander of the Queen's Guard. Delivery priority, Immediate."

It thrust the letter at her.

Teyra took it. Her fingers brushed the Hessian's brass hand, and the metal was hot enough to sting. The wax seal on the back was blood red, stamped with a familiar symbol.

A serpent eating its own tail.

The air in the shop dropped ten degrees. The windows rattled.

"Thank you," Teyra said quickly. "I'll…"

The Hessian didn't move. Its blank golden face tilted down. "Scanning perimeter. Large magical signature detected. Unregistered. Ectoplasmic origin."

Her mouth went dry, heart slamming against her ribs.

"I'm brewing," she lied. "A very large batch of Spirit-Ease. For the Widow Gable's cat. It died yesterday. Tragic."

The Hessian paused. Gears clicked inside its chest.

"Acknowledged," the Hessian finally said. "Widow Gable, residence 47 Weaver Street, filed a death certificate for one feline familiar yesterday at 14:32. Spirit-Ease is an approved restorative. Have a pleasant day, citizen."

It turned and marched away, its heavy footsteps ringing against the cobblestones.

Teyra watched until it disappeared around the corner. Then she slammed the door and threw the deadbolt.

"Okay," she breathed. "That was close."

Ash materialized in the center of the room. He was staring at the letter as though it might bite.

"Open it."

Teyra broke the seal, her fingers trembling. The handwriting inside was elegant, sharp, the kind taught to noble children by expensive tutors.

"Miss Tepes,

It has come to my attention that you have acquired a new… acquisition. A lost antique, one might say.

I have a fondness for antiques. Especially those I thought were lost in the fire.

Join me for tea. Tomorrow. 3:00 PM. My conservatory. Come alone. Or don't come at all, and I will send the Hessians back to dismantle more than just your door.

—S"

"She knows," Teyra said. "She knows you're here."

Lenore hopped onto the counter. "Tea with a murderer. Delightful. Should I send flowers or a funeral wreath?"

"Good," Ash said. The word was sharp, edged with violence. "Let her know. I want to look her in the eye when I ask her why she murdered me."

"It's a trap, Ash!" Teyra whirled to face him. "She's the Commander of the Guard! She has an army of those clockwork nightmares. You walk in there, and she'll exorcise you before you can say hello."

"I don't care," Ash shouted.

The display case of porcelain figurines exploded. Glass shards flew outward. The lights died.

"Stop it!" Teyra stepped toward him. "Look at me! You're here. You're solid. Stay with me."

He was breathing hard, his chest heaving even though he didn't need to breathe. He looked at the broken glass, then at Teyra. The tension drained from his shoulders, and he sagged.

"I'm sorry." He wouldn't look at her. "I can't control it when I think of her."

"I know." Teyra stepped over the broken glass. "But you have to try. If you flicker in front of her, she wins. If you lose control, she wins."

She took a breath.

"We go tomorrow. But we do it my way. I go in the front door. You go in invisible. You listen. You gather evidence. You do not manifest unless I give the signal."

"No."

The word came out flat and controlled, from a man who was used to refusing things.

"Excuse me?"

"I go alone." Ash's jaw was set. "Invisible, like you said. I find her. I watch her. I learn her patterns, her guards, her weaknesses. And then we decide what to do. But you stay here."

"That's not..."

"She killed a prince, Teyra. She drove a blade through someone's heart and walked away. You're a bleeding necromancer with a familiar whose flight is questionable at best. If she decides you're a threat..."

"Then I handle it. That's my job. That's what I do."

"Your job is brewing tea for grieving widows. This is different."

The silence that followed had an edge to it, the kind that dares someone to break it. Teyra stared at him. He stared back. Neither of them blinked.

She'd been wrong about him. Underneath the gratitude and the grief, there was iron, a stubbornness that didn't need memories to function. The same reflex that made him count exits and put his back to the wall. Whatever crown he'd once worn, he'd earned it.

"Ash," she said. "You're a ghost. You can't open doors. You can't carry evidence. You can't read documents because your hands pass through the pages half the time. You need me."

His jaw worked. She watched the argument die behind his eyes, killed by logic rather than agreement.

"If anything goes wrong," he said, "we leave. Immediately. No heroics."

"No heroics," she agreed.

They both knew it was a lie. But it was the kind of lie that let people move forward, and right now, forward was the only direction they had.

"And if she tries to kill you?"

"Then you can break everything in the room."

He almost smiled. Almost.

"She said come alone," he pointed out.

"She also murdered you. I think we can bend her rules."

He held her gaze for three seconds, then turned toward the brewing station without another word.

They spent the rest of the day preparing.

Teyra brewed a fresh batch of anchoring tea using the last pinch of Moonflower from the lead-lined box. Her wrist still ached from the spatter burns of the first batch. She scraped the bottom of the tin with her fingernail, gathering every precious grain.

"That's it," she said, showing him the empty container. "After this dose, you have maybe two days before you start fading again. Three if you're lucky."

"Then we'd better make this count."

He drank. The transformation was becoming familiar: transparency sharpening to presence, color bleeding back into him like ink through wet paper. She looked away before he caught her staring.

Night fell, the grey day fading into darker grey. The rain finally thinned to a whisper, leaving the city quiet and dripping. Teyra lit the gas lamps, turning the shop into a haven of shadows and warm light.

"Tell me something," Ash said.

He was sitting on the counter again, watching her sweep up the broken glass from the display case.

"That scar on your hand. The burn. Is that from the exam?"

Teyra looked at the star-shaped scar on her palm. "No. That was my first ghost. Before the Academy. I was twelve. A little girl, she was lost in a blizzard. Didn't know she was dead. She kept asking for her mother."

Her voice thinned to almost nothing.

"She was so cold. I tried to warm her up. Held her hand too long without knowing what I was doing. The cold burned me. The star shape is from her fingers."

She rubbed the scar absently, the habitual gesture whenever it ached, which was whenever the temperature dropped or the rain came or she thought too hard about children who died alone. "She was the first one who left something behind. The scar healed. But on winter nights, when the wind sounds a certain way, I still feel her. A cold spot. A smallness shaped like a six-year-old girl. My grandmother said that was the gift. That the dead trust us with their feelings because we're strong enough to carry them."

She paused.

"The Academy said it was a disorder."

Ash looked at her.

"You really are too kind for this job," he said softly.

He hopped off the counter, landing lightly on the floor. He stood close to her, too close. The air between them hummed with that electric tension.

He reached out, his hand hovering over hers. The temperature dropped between them.

"Tomorrow," he said. "We get answers. I promise."

Teyra nodded, unable to speak.

She turned to lock up for the night. One last glance out the front window.

She froze.

Across the street, standing in the darkness between two gas lamps, was a figure. Tall and hooded, perfectly still, not even pretending to have a reason to be there.

Just watching.

On the lapel of his coat, even at this distance, she caught the glint of silver. A pin shaped like a moth with spread wings.

The same symbol as the bookmark in the Archives.

She thought of the silk strip in her pocket, the silver ink in the margin, the word *Patience* written by someone who had been waiting for exactly this. And now a figure standing across the street, unhidden, making sure she knew she was being watched.

Someone had been circling her, first with the bookmark in the archives, then the watcher across the street, and now by closing in.

"Ash." A sharp, heavy dread pooled in her stomach. "We're being hunted. That watcher was there to control the distance, not keep it."

The figure in the street didn't move.

But as she watched, a second shadow detached from the darkness behind him. Then a third.

"Teyra." Ash's voice was tight. "Get away from the window."

She stepped back just as the first stone came crashing through the glass.

The stone hit the floor with a heavy thunk, followed by a rain of broken glass.

Teyra threw herself backward, shielding her face. Shards caught the gaslight as they fell, tiny knives glittering in the dark.

"Down!" Ash grabbed her, his hands solid enough in that moment of pure protective instinct, and pulled her behind the counter.

His fingers phased through her arm halfway through the motion, the Touch Barrier kicking in the moment his concern outran his control, but by then she was already moving, dropping to her knees on the hardwood floor.

"What's happening?" she gasped.

"They're coming in."

Through the broken window she could see three figures, moving with coordinated precision. Professionals, all of them. The kind who got paid to make problems disappear.

"The back door," Teyra hissed. "Go. Now."

"I'm not leaving you."

"You can't fight them like this. One strong feeling and you'll flicker into nothing. Go. Get out. I'll meet you at the Records Hall."

"Teyra…"

"That's not a request, Ash."

She grabbed the iron poker from the fireplace, the closest thing to a weapon she had, and stood up.

The first figure was already climbing through the broken window. In the dim light, a moth pin gleamed on his lapel, identical to the watcher across the street, his face hidden behind a mask of plain black cloth.

"Miss Tepes," he said. His voice was pleasant, conversational. "We don't want trouble. We just want to talk."

"People who want to talk don't throw rocks through windows."

"A necessary attention-getter. Please put down the poker. My employer has questions."

"Your employer can make an appointment."

The second figure was through the window now, flanking her left. The third was circling toward the back. They were boxing her in.

"I'm going to count to three," the first man said. "Then my colleagues will subdue you. It will be unpleasant for everyone involved."

"Teyra." Ash's voice was in her ear, invisible again, standing right beside her. "I have an idea. But you need to trust me."

"One," the man counted.

"What idea?"

"Two."

"Do you trust me?"

"Thr..."

Ash's hand closed around hers. She felt the cold, biting and vicious, as he channeled everything he had into that grip. For one impossible second, he forced himself solid, using the sheer drilled instinct of a soldier, completely devoid of feeling. And then he threw her.

His hand dissolved into mist the moment it left hers, and she saw it dissolve, watched the ectoplasm scatter like ash. When he reformed, the fingers were translucent, barely there.

She flew through the air and slammed her shoulder against the back door. The old wood splintered around the latch, and the door burst open. She tumbled out into the alley behind the shop, landing hard on wet cobblestones.

Behind her, she heard chaos erupting. Glass breaking. Men shouting. A sound like thunder, Ash's spectral energy turning the temperature in the shop to freezing.

"Poltergeist!" one of the men screamed. "It's a goddamn poltergeist! Fall back!"

Teyra didn't wait to hear more. She scrambled to her feet and ran.

The alley was narrow and dark, slick with rain and worse. The grey film was thick here, pooled in the gaps between cobblestones and coating the walls at ankle height in a grim tide-line. Her boots splashed through it, and it clung to the leather, gritty and faintly warm in a way that rain shouldn't be.

She took the first turn, then the second, putting as much distance between herself and the shop as possible, lungs burning. The scar on her palm throbbed in time with her heartbeat, and Ash's phantom blade pulsed between her ribs with every step, a stitch that belonged to a dead man

She ran until she couldn't run anymore, until she was doubled over in a doorway somewhere in the District of Ink, gasping for air.

Ash materialized beside her, barely there, edges fraying, the blue light of his spectral energy guttering low. The throw had cost him.

"Are you hurt?" he managed.

"No. You?"

"Fading." He leaned against the wall; transparent patches showing through his coat. "The cold... I used too much."

"You saved me."

"I threw you through a door."

"You counted," she said, still breathless.

"Waited for the weak point. Used the burst to cover our retreat."

She looked at him.

"That wasn't panic."

Ash blinked. "I don't remember knowing how."

"Your body does."

"Now come on. We need to find somewhere safe. Somewhere they won't look."

She took his hand, or tried to. Her fingers passed through his palm, cold burning against her skin.

"Can't hold on," Ash managed. "Too weak."

"Then stay close. And try not to flicker."

They moved through the empty streets together, a necromancer and a fading ghost, with six days left before the end of the world and the Moth's agents hunting them through the dark.

"Ash," Teyra said as they ducked into another alley. "That man. The one who was watching. He wasn't just watching for someone else. He was watching for himself."

"What do you mean?"

"I mean the Moth doesn't send lackeys for reconnaissance. He does it himself." Her skin prickled. "That was him, Ash."

Ash processed this. "He wanted us to know."

"Yes."

"Why?"

Teyra didn't answer. But she was starting to piece together a picture, a conspiracy that was bigger than a murdered prince, bigger than a centuries-old lie.

The Queen's Guard had killed Ash. The Moth was watching them. And someone, somewhere, was pulling strings that stretched from the Palace to the underground.

"Tomorrow," she said, "we're walking into a trap. You know that, right?"

"Yes."

"Seraphine will have Hessians. Wards. Probably holy water, given what we're dealing with."

"Yes."

"And you want to go anyway."

Ash looked at her. In the dim light of a distant gas lamp, his eyes were more solid than the rest of him, grey as storm clouds, burning steady.

"I spent five years dead," he said. Grief had scraped his voice thin. "Five years lost in the dark. I don't remember my parents, or my brother. I can't picture my mother's eyes. I can't hear my father's voice. All I have is this, this borrowed time, this fading existence, and you."

He went quieter.

"I won't spend what's left of it running or hiding. If I'm going to die again, really die, this time, I want to know why. I want to look the woman who killed me in the eye and ask her why I wasn't worth saving."

Teyra said nothing for a while.

Then she said, "Six days."

"What?"

"You said we have seven days. We've already used one. That means we have six days left to solve a five-year-old murder, unravel a conspiracy two generations deep that reaches the throne, and figure out what the Moth wants with us." She smiled, a small, tired, slightly unhinged smile. "Better get started."

Ash stared at her. And then, against all odds, he smiled back.

"You're insane," he said.

"Probably." She started walking. "Come on. We need to find somewhere to sleep that isn't being watched by a crime lord. And tomorrow, we're having tea with a murderer."

They disappeared into the fog together.

Behind them, in the shadows, a figure watched them go.

The silver moth pin glinted on his lapel.

And beneath his mask, the Moth smiled.

Chapter Four

THE CONSERVATORY

Day Three: Five Days Remain

T HEY'D SPENT THE NIGHT in a storage cellar behind the Widow Harkness's apothecary, a woman who owed Teyra two favors and asked no questions. Neither of them had slept. Teyra had brewed four cups of tea by candlelight while Ash sat against the wall, flickering whenever a rat scratched too close. By dawn, the Moth's watchers had moved on. Teyra had crept back to the shop long enough to grab her grandmother's formal robes from the upstairs wardrobe and her portable brewing kit, and to check that nothing else had been taken. The watchers had moved on—or at least become harder to see.

The Garden District began where the cobblestones stopped being cracked.

The change was abrupt—one block, broken stone and overflowing gutters; the next, smooth granite slabs swept clean by servants who rose before dawn. The air was different here. It smelled of roses and cut grass instead of coal smoke and horse dung. Even the rain was more polite, falling in a gentle mist rather than the aggressive downpour that battered the lower city.

And the grey film was gone. Teyra noticed it as you notice silence after leaving a noisy room—by its absence. The granite was clean, the iron railings untarnished, the cracks free of pooling Unsettled. The drainage wards were set into the gutter grates every thirty feet, small bronze discs inscribed with Guild-standard purification sigils, each one maintained, each one glowing with active magic. The spiritual infrastructure here was immaculate. Whatever the wealthy dead of the Garden District carried, it was filtered and dispersed before it could stain a single cobblestone.

The dead here were managed. The dead in Hollow Stair dissolved in the rain.

Teyra's boots, resoled twice, the leather cracking at the toes, announced her poverty with every step. The sound they made on the pristine walkway was too loud, too flat. Wrong.

She'd worn her grandmother's formal robes. Black wool, severe cut, silver embroidery at the cuffs and collar. The kind of thing a respectable necromancer might wear to a guild function or a formal summoning. But the hem had been let down twice, the faint lines where the stitching had been still showed, and the silver thread was tarnishing despite the hour she'd spent polishing it that morning. Next to the gleaming brass of the Hessian guards at the gate, next to the manicured hedges shaped into perfect spirals, she looked like a crow that had wandered into a peacock garden.

"Remember," she murmured to the empty air beside her, keeping her lips still. "You're invisible. You stay invisible. No matter what she says."

"I know." Ash's voice came from just over her left shoulder, so close the chill of him pressed against her ear, cold where breath would have been warm. The sensation raised goosebumps along her neck.

"You've said it four times."

"I'm saying it a fifth. She killed you, Ash. She's going to say things designed to make you reveal yourself."

"I can control myself."

"Can you?"

Silence.

The Hessian at the main gate waved them through without a word. Its golden face was blank, expressionless, but its sensors tracked her as she passed, scanning for weapons, for prohibited magic, for anything that didn't belong. She held her breath until they were past, half-expecting alarms to sound, brass hands to clamp down on her shoulders.

Nothing happened.

The path curved through gardens that belonged in a painting. Rose bushes in unnatural colors, deep purple and pale silver, one variety so dark a red it was nearly black. Fountains carved from white marble, water cascading in perfect sheets, and statuary of ancestors who had been dead for three hundred years, their stone faces serene and disapproving.

A carriage was pulling away from the manor's front entrance as they approached, black lacquer, drawn by two grey horses whose coats had been groomed to a metallic sheen. The Greythorn ser-pent-and-crown was emblazoned on the door in silver. Through the window, Teyra caught a glimpse of the man inside. Sixty, per-haps older, with silver-white hair swept back from a high forehead and a face that looked like it had been carved from the same stone as the statuary. Sharp and rigid, the face of a man who had never been uncertain about anything in his life.

Lord Greythorn. She knew him from the society pages, the charity galas, the Council portraits, the endless photographs of a man who cultivated the appearance of a benevolent patriarch while running the city's most powerful house. In person, even glimpsed through carriage glass, he was smaller than she'd expected. And colder. The servants on the path stepped aside for the carriage with a deference that looked like respect and more like the stillness of rabbits when a hawk passes.

The carriage passed close enough for Teyra to feel the draft. Greythorn's eyes swept the garden without pause, past the foun-tains, the roses, the necromancer in her grandmother's robes, and found nothing worth his attention.

She held onto that. The sort of man who looked through peo-ple, who made servants flinch, who had left his own estate minutes before Teyra arrived to question the woman who lived there.

That last detail bothered her. But there was no time to think about it now.

And there, at the end of the path, the conservatory.

It was obscene.

That was Teyra's first thought. Forty feet of glass and iron bolted to the side of a gothic manor gleaming in the weak afternoon sun. The structure was enormous, easily the size of her entire shop, twice over, with glass panels held together by a skeleton of wrought iron twisted into elaborate patterns of vines and flowers. The metalwork alone must have cost more than Teyra would make in ten lifetimes. The glass was clear as water, showing the vivid green within.

A jungle. In the middle of Athergard's perpetual autumn. Tropical plants pressed against the glass, their fronds and flowers fogging the panels with moisture. Heat radiated from the structure even from twenty feet away.

"She chose this place on purpose," Teyra murmured. "All glass. Nowhere to hide. She wants everything visible."

"She wants to see me," Ash said. "She wants to know if I'll show myself."

"Then don't."

"I won't."

But his voice had pulled taut. The temperature dropped around her, the cold of his presence intensifying. He was already struggling.

The doors were standing open, an invitation and a dare.

Teyra stepped inside.

The heat hit her like a wall. Wet and heavy, the air so thick with humidity that she could taste it, feel it settling on her skin like another layer of clothing. Her grandmother's wool robes, designed for Athergard's chill, became suffocating within seconds. Sweat beaded instantly on her forehead and at the small of her back. And beneath the heat, or maybe because of it, the Grave-Chill in her bones recoiled. The cold she carried from every session, every spirit, every borrowed wound contracted to a hard knot at the center of her chest, as though her body's accumulated dead were flinching from this place's aggressive, suffocating life.

The smell came next: jasmine and orchids laid over the sweet-rot stench of too much life crammed into too small a space. Flowers fighting for sunlight. Leaves decomposing in the heat. The greenhouse stink of organic matter breaking down, life and death tangled so closely you couldn't tell where one ended and the other began. The whole place felt like death masked in flowers. To Teyra's Resonance-damaged senses, the perfume was worse than honest decay—the phantom blade between her ribs flared with dull heat, Thomas's battlefield-smell pushed to the surface, and the widow's longing for cool, quiet mornings ached like a bruise. Too much alive. Her borrowed dead didn't belong here, and they were letting her know.

Teyra blinked, letting her eyes adjust. Ferns the size of small trees dominated the space, their fronds spreading like giant green hands, while palm trees stretched toward the glass ceiling, trunks wrapped in climbing vines heavy with flowers she didn't recognize. Orchids bloomed in colors that shouldn't exist, electric blue beside deep violet, and one species a red so dark it looked like congealed blood.

The floor was terracotta tiles arranged in intricate patterns, but the pattern was broken in places by creeping moss, by fallen petals that had been allowed to rot where they lay. Water trickled somewhere, a fountain or stream she couldn't see, the sound echoing off the glass walls until it seemed like the whole room was breathing.

Every plant here was imported. Every flower exotic. The heating spells required to maintain this temperature in Athergard's climate would cost more per month than Teyra's annual rent. This was wealth beyond imagination, maintained for no purpose except to prove it could be maintained.

Though in one corner, half-hidden behind a stand of bird-of-paradise, a single dark violet flower grew in a clay pot—small, plain, utterly out of place among the exotics. And there, in the center of this cultivated jungle, sat the woman who had murdered a prince.

Lady Seraphine did not stand when Teyra entered.

She was seated at a wrought-iron table, surrounded by ferns that rose above her head like green sentinels. She was pouring tea from a silver service with the unhurried movements of someone who had never been rushed in her life, who had never had to be anywhere she didn't want to be. Her left hand rested on the table, and Teyra noticed, briefly, that the fingernails were bitten to the quick. The only imperfection in an otherwise flawless presentation.

She was beautiful and knew it the way officers know their rank—a fact. Her dark hair was pinned up in an elaborate style, held in place with combs of pearl and silver. Her dress was sea-green silk that caught the light as she moved, shimmering like water, cut to emphasize the length of her neck and the sharpness of her collarbones. The fabric was so fine that Teyra could see the shadow of her arms through the sleeves.

But it was the bracelet that drew Teyra's eyes.

Gold and heavy, worked into a serpent eating its own tail. The Ouroboros. The mark of the Queen's Personal Guard. Ruby eyes glinted in the filtered light, catching the sun and throwing blood-dark reflections across the white tablecloth.

The same bracelet from the vision. The same woman in red, though today she wore green.

The temperature in the conservatory dropped three degrees. A wave of cold rolled off the empty space beside her. Ash was struggling. Already.

Don't flicker, she thought. *We just got here.*

"Miss Tepes." Seraphine's voice carried the careful warmth of a woman accustomed to delivering orders that sounded like invitations. "You're prompt. I appreciate punctuality in a tradesperson."

Tradesperson. The word stung, and it was meant to.

Teyra dipped into a curtsy, shallow enough to avoid showing deference, deep enough to avoid open insult. She performed the stiff, over-studied curtsy of a commoner who had only ever read about noble etiquette.

"Lady Seraphine. Thank you for the invitation. Though the threat to dismantle my door was a nice touch."

Seraphine's lips curved. Her eyes stayed flat above it. "Motivation helps people make appropriate decisions, don't you find? I've learned that clear consequences tend to sharpen the mind." She gestured to the chair across from her. "Please. Sit."

Teyra sat.

The chair was wrought iron, ornately decorated but designed purely for punishing aesthetics. The metal dug into her spine through the wool of her dress. The seat was cold despite the heat of the room, some kind of cooling enchantment, probably, to keep the noble posterior from perspiring.

She scanned the room while pretending otherwise. A nightmare. The glass walls let in every ray of afternoon sun, turning the conservatory into a greenhouse with nowhere to hide. Every surface lit, every corner exposed. If Ash wavered even slightly, if his control slipped for a single heartbeat, he would be visible, a shimmer in the air, a distortion in the light. That's all it would take.

And the exits. There was only one door, the massive glass doors they'd entered through. Every other wall was glass, reinforced with iron frames. Beautiful and unbreakable.

They were in a cage.

"Tea?" Seraphine asked, lifting the silver pot, its surface polished to a mirror shine. "It's a rare blend. Sun-Gold, imported from the Southern Isles. The flowers only bloom once every seven years, and they must be harvested at dawn by virgins who've never seen the sea." She poured as she spoke, amber liquid flowing in a perfect arc. Steam rose, carrying a scent of honey and citrus and something Teyra couldn't identify. "It's said to reveal hidden truths."

Teyra watched the tea swirl in the cup. Reveal hidden truths. Was that a threat? A warning? Or just noble small talk?

"I'll pass," she said. "I brew my own."

"Of course you do." Seraphine sipped from her own cup, her lips touching the rim. Perfect manners. Perfect control. "You run that little shop. The Final Steep. A whimsical name. Very..." She paused, searching for the word. "Quaint. I imagine it does well with the common folk."

Common folk. Another small cut. Teyra felt her jaw tighten.

"It serves its purpose," she said, keeping her voice level. "Someone has to help the people you consider beneath your notice."

"How noble." Seraphine set down her cup with a small click of china against saucer. "Though I notice your establishment is rather modest. The roof needs repair. The windows are warped, the sign is fading. One wonders if nobility of purpose pays the bills."

"It pays well enough." Teyra met her eyes, refusing to look away. "Though I imagine you wouldn't know much about earning your keep. Inherited fortunes must be very comfortable."

A crack flickered in Seraphine's expression. The corner of her mouth twitched, a twitch that never became a smile.

"You have teeth, Miss Tepes. I appreciate that." She leaned back in her chair, silk rustling against iron. "Most people who sit there stammer and soften themselves before they speak plainly. They stammer and grovel and tell me what they think I want to hear. It's tedious."

"I'm not most people."

"No." Seraphine studied her with eyes that were too sharp, too knowing. "No, you're not. You're the woman who anchored a Class Five specter with illegal Moonflower tea, hid him from the Crown's surveillance network for two days, and walked into my home like you belonged here." She tilted her head. "Either you're very brave, Miss Tepes, or you're very stupid. I haven't decided which."

"Can't it be both?"

That did earn a smile, small, reluctant, quickly suppressed.

"Let's dispense with the pleasantries," Seraphine said, her tone shifting. The honey drained away, leaving only the razor. "You have something of mine."

"I don't know what you mean."

To Teyra's left, a pot of white lilies turned blood red.

The transformation was instantaneous, color spreading through the petals like dye through water, starting at the base and flowing to the tips. The flowers pulsed, vivid and accusing.

"Truth Lilies," Seraphine said, watching Teyra's face. "Imported from the Jade Colonies. They respond to the magical resonance of deception. Terribly useful in conversations like this one." Her eyes hardened. "Would you like to try again?"

She was in a room rigged to catch liars, hiding a ghost she wasn't supposed to have. Every lie would turn those flowers red. Every half-truth would be exposed.

She had no choice but honesty. Or at least, carefully selected pieces of it.

"Fine." Teyra forced her voice steady. "I have a ghost. He wandered into my shop two nights ago, drawn by the Resonance of my anchor wards. He was destabilizing, minutes from poltergeist transformation. I brewed him an anchoring tea to save his life. Or his existence. Whatever the proper term is."

The lilies stayed white. Truth.

"He has no memory," Teyra continued. "Doesn't know who he was or how he died. Classic spectral amnesia, probably caused by trauma at the moment of death."

Still white.

"Amnesia." Seraphine turned the word over in her mouth, tasting it for rot. "How remarkably convenient. A ghost with no past, no identity, no troublesome memories to complicate matters. And you, a struggling necromancer in need of purpose, just happened to be the one who found him."

"I didn't find him. He found me."

"Did he? Or did someone send him to you?"

The question landed strangely. Teyra frowned. "Send him? What do you mean?"

Seraphine didn't answer immediately. She was watching the lilies, her expression unreadable. When she spoke again, her voice was softer. Almost tender in a way that didn't fit.

"Does this ghost have a name?" Her tone was light, curious—the tone of a woman who already knew the answer.

"We call him Ash."

Seraphine flinched.

It was small—a tightening of her jaw, a flicker behind her eyes, her hand going still on the teacup. But it was there. The name had struck her like a physical blow.

The mask cracked, and Teyra saw something underneath—something older than the cold commander, older than the calculating noble. A wound that had never closed.

"Ash," Seraphine whispered. She looked down at her tea, her reflection wavering in the amber liquid. "And what does Ash remember?"

Teyra leaned forward, pressing the advantage. "Fragments. A ballroom, crystal chandeliers, the sound of a waltz. A sword sliding between his ribs." She paused, watching Seraphine's face. "And a woman in a red dress who smiled while she killed him."

The temperature plummeted without warning.

One moment the conservatory was sweltering, humid, oppressive. The next, ice was forming on the inside of the glass panels. Frost webbed outward from a point just behind Teyra's left shoulder, crystalline patterns splitting the glass the way old ice splits a lake.

For a single heartbeat, Ash flickered.

She felt it rather than saw it—a shimmer in the air beside her, the shadow of a man appearing and vanishing in the space of a single breath.

He'd been fighting it the whole time, she realized. Holding himself together through sheer will while the woman who had murdered him sat five feet away sipping tea. He'd been winning.

He was losing now.

The tropical plants shuddered, their leaves curling inward against the sudden cold. A fern nearest to where Ash must be standing turned brown at the edges, frost damage spreading through the fronds.

Control it, Teyra thought. *Control it or we're dead.*

But she understood. This was the woman who had murdered him. She was sitting five feet away, sipping tea from a silver cup, wearing the bracelet she'd worn when she'd driven a blade through his heart. How could anyone hold still in the face of that?

Seraphine looked at the spreading frost. Teyra found no surprise there, only a hollowed-out recognition.

"Memory is a peculiar thing, Miss Tepes," she said quietly. "It lacks context. It shows you the knife, but never the hand that forced it. The moment of death, but never the months of anguish that preceded it." She rose from her chair, the movement graceful despite the dropping temperature. "It shows you the woman who wielded the blade, but never the woman who wept for three days afterward."

She walked toward a cluster of orchids, moving closer to where Ash was standing invisible. Too close. If he lost his grip now, if his form wavered for even a heartbeat...

But Seraphine's attention had drifted past him entirely. Her hand hovered over the orchid petals without touching them, and her perfect composure cracked. Her shoulders dropped. Her chin dipped toward her chest. She looked, Teyra realized with a jolt, like someone visiting a grave.

"I used to bring him here," Seraphine said, almost to herself. "Before. He loved the orchids. Said they reminded him of his mother's garden." Her fingers trembled over the frost-damaged petals. "I haven't been able to look at them since."

Then she remembered herself—or become someone else entirely. Her spine straightened. The mask slid back into place.

"So you admit it," Teyra said, drawing Seraphine's attention back. "You killed him."

Seraphine stopped. Her back was to Teyra, her hand resting on an orchid petal that was already beginning to wilt from the cold.

"I did what was necessary," she said. "To save the Kingdom. To prevent a catastrophe that would have killed thousands." She turned, and her eyes were bright with unshed tears. "And yes, gods help me, to save him."

"Save him?" Teyra couldn't keep the disbelief from her voice. "You stabbed him in the heart. In a ballroom full of witnesses. How is that saving him?"

"Because the alternative was worse." Seraphine's voice went flat, the toneless register of someone delivering a briefing on casualties. "He takes the throne. The curse activates. The city burns. Everyone dies." She paused. "Including him. He watches himself do it. That's what the prophecy said. That's the intelligence I was given."

"That's insane."

"It's prophecy."

The word hung in the conservatory heat, cold despite it.

"The Thornwick Prophecy," Seraphine continued. "Written in blood in the Cathedral vaults three hundred years ago. Sealed by twelve seers and confirmed by the High Priest himself. 'When a Thornwick sits upon the Athergard throne, the city shall burn and the kingdom shall fall. The crowned head shall become the destroying hand. So it is written. So it shall be.'"

The lilies stayed white. She believed every word.

Teyra's stomach sank. Seraphine wasn't lying. She wasn't justifying murder with convenient excuses. She believed she had saved the kingdom. She believed she had been the hero of this story.

And the worst part, the part that made Teyra's throat close, was that she understood. The logic underneath it. One life against a hundred thousand. The Academy taught that same cold math. The Grave-Chill method was built on it. Control the dead, don't feel for them, because if you feel for them you lose control, and if you lose control, people get hurt. Seraphine had applied that principle to its most extreme conclusion. She had cut one person out to save everyone else.

It was the Academy's philosophy with a blade instead of a textbook. And Teyra hated that she could see the logic, even as she wanted to scream at it.

Seraphine was watching her with an expression Teyra couldn't read. Closer to discomfort than triumph.

"You feel everything they feel," Seraphine said. Her voice had changed, no longer the razor-under-honey register of a woman performing control, but that of a woman who had read a great deal and remembered what she'd read. "Every spirit you anchor leaves something behind in you. You carry fragments of their final hours as a matter of course. It's physiological. Your channels absorb the emotional residue of every death you've channeled."

Teyra didn't answer. The lilies stayed a frozen, accusatory white.

"Meridia Ashworth felt everything too." Seraphine set down her cup precisely. "She wept for every spirit she touched. She was celebrated for it. And she was, by every measure the Academy kept, more gifted at your age than you are now." A pause. "I have studied her case extensively. As an intelligence report, Miss Tepes. As a strategic concern."

"I am not Meridia Ashworth," Teyra said. The words came out thinner than she intended.

"I'm not making that comparison." Seraphine folded her hands on the table, the movement so precise it looked rehearsed—or like a woman stopping herself from reaching for something she'd given up. "I'm asking a question I genuinely cannot answer. You plan to use Resonance at a larger scale than she did. You are already carrying accumulated fragments from years of channeling. You are, right now, in this room, holding the emotional imprint of a man who is standing six feet away from me." She glanced, briefly, toward where Ash must have been. "What makes you certain you won't break the same way? What evidence do you have that your compassion, which is real, which I am not dismissing, is safe at the scale you're proposing? I am not asking about courage. I am asking about evidence."

The truth lilies stayed white. Because she was asking with genuine, unsettling sincerity.

Teyra opened her mouth. Closed it. The answer she'd spent four years constructing, that the Academy was wrong, that empathy was strength and Meridia had needed guidance she'd never been given, sat in her chest like a speech written for a different room.

"I don't know," she said. The admission tasted bitter. But Seraphine wasn't asking the way the Academy had, as a verdict already reached. She was asking the way a soldier asks whether a bridge will hold.

Seraphine nodded. With what might have been relief.

"Good," she said. "If you'd had a ready answer, I would have stopped trusting anything you said."

"Prophecies can be interpreted many ways," Teyra said carefully. "They're not literal. They're symbolic, open to…"

"This one isn't." Seraphine cut her off. "It was verified. Cross-referenced with six other oracular traditions. Confirmed by blood divination and bone-casting. The Thornwick line carries a curse, Miss Tepes. A blight that activates when they take power. It's magical genetics."

"And you decided to play executioner."

"I decided to prevent the deaths of a hundred thousand people." Seraphine's voice hardened. "I decided one life, one life I loved, was worth sacrificing to save a city. I made the choice that no one else was willing to make."

"You loved him?"

The question slipped out before Teyra could stop it.

Seraphine went still.

"We were betrothed," she said quietly. "Since we were children. An arrangement between our families, political, strategic, the usual noble theater. But somewhere along the way, it became real." Her hand went to the bracelet on her wrist, fingers tracing the serpent's coils. "I was going to be his queen. We were going to rule together. And then his brother found the prophecy, and everything changed."

"Elias," Teyra whispered.

Seraphine's eyes snapped to hers. "You know about Elias?"

"We found records. At the Hall of Records. He was supposed to have died in the fire with the rest of the family. But he survived. He was adopted by House Greythorn."

"He was four years old." Seraphine's voice had gone thin. "Too young to remember his real family. Too young to understand what he was giving up. Lord Greythorn raised him as his own, kept him hidden, kept him safe."

"And when Elias came of age, when he learned to read the old texts, he found the prophecy himself."

"And told you to kill his brother."

"No." Seraphine shook her head. "Elias doesn't know. He thinks Ashen died in the fire with their parents. A tragic accident. He mourned. He still mourns." Her jaw tightened. "I'm the only one who knows the truth. The only one who carries that weight."

The wrought-iron table split down the middle with a deafening scream of tearing metal, the shriek echoing off the glass walls. The silver teapot flew off the surface, spun through the air, hit the floor with a clang that rang through the conservatory. Porcelain shards and tea spread across the terracotta like blood.

Ash materialized.

He erupted, tearing through the veil of invisibility the way he must have once torn through actual doors, with his whole body and nothing held back. The air around him cracked with the sound of splintering ice. His unstable form blurred and sharpened as blue light bled freely from his fracturing skin.

His eyes were white. White-hot, the color of lightning, of stars too close to look at.

"Liar!"

The word came out wrong. Too deep. Too resonant. His voice and a second voice underneath it, grinding together, the sound of a man speaking through a door that was already closing. It vibrated in Teyra's bones, made her teeth ache, made her want to fall to her knees.

Ice erupted across the glass walls like a living thing. The panels cracked, spiderweb fractures spreading outward from where Ash stood. The tropical plants nearest to him died instantly, leaves turning black and stems folding as the flowers hit the terracotta and shattered into dry fragments.

"Ash!" Teyra leaped to her feet, her chair clattering backward on the tiles. "Stop! You have to..."

The memory crashed into him without warning, fragmented, razor-sharp. Red dress, candlelight, her hand on his cheek—gentle, trembling. Then the blade between his ribs. She had been crying.

"You were crying," he said. The words came out broken, inhuman. "When you did it. You were crying."

The reading had shown her calm. The tea had lied, or the death had—degraded memory, five years of spectral erosion wearing the truth smooth. But Ash's body remembered what the vision couldn't.

Seraphine went pale.

"You were wearing red. Holding the crown. You were supposed to put it on my head." His form destabilized, ice spreading across the orchids. "We were going to do this together, Sera. We were going to take back everything. Why did you..."

"She's lying!" He was shaking, his form flickering in and out of visibility with each ragged breath. One moment he was solid, a man consumed, vibrating with it. The next he was transparent, a ghost unraveling at the edges. "She speaks of love and sacrifice and noble duty, but she murdered me! She looked into my eyes and she was crying and she drove a blade through my heart!"

Seraphine had stumbled backward, nearly falling. Her face was white, her composure shattered. Tears were streaming down her cheeks, cutting tracks through her careful makeup.

"Ashen," she breathed. The name tore out of her like a wound reopening. "Oh gods. Oh gods, no. You weren't supposed to come back. You were supposed to rest. To be free."

"Free?" Ash took a step toward her, and the floor cracked beneath his feet. Frost spread from each footprint, ice crystals racing across the terracotta. "I have been lost for five years! Trapped in the dark! Stripped of my name, my memories—bleeding out without even knowing why I am dead!"

He was losing himself. Teyra could see it, the man fading, the monster emerging. The edges of his form were fraying, wisps of grey smoke peeling away and dissipating into the frozen air. His eyes were glowing now, twin points of cold fire that left afterimages when he moved.

"You took everything," he snarled, the human in his voice nearly buried under something ancient and terrible. "My throne, my brother—you stole my life and you called it love."

"I saved you!" Seraphine screamed back, and the scream itself shocked her. She caught herself. Locked it down.

When she spoke again, her voice was wrecked but controlled, barely. "The curse. The prophecy. The burning. You would have been the weapon, Ashen. I gave you a clean death. That was the best I could do." Her voice flattened. "That was the only mercy available."

"There is no madness!" Ash roared. "There is only your lie, standing in front of me!"

He lunged.

It happened too fast for Teyra to stop. He crossed the ten feet between them in a single violent blur and was suddenly on top of her, his hands reaching for her throat, half-solid, a blur that couldn't decide if it was man or ghost.

Seraphine's hand came up, the one with the bracelet, and golden light blazed from the serpent's ruby eyes. A ward. A defense. Teyra saw the magic hit Ash like a physical force, throwing him backward, sending him crashing through a fern and into a glass panel that cracked but didn't shatter.

"Stop!" Teyra threw herself between them, arms spread wide. "Both of you! Stop!"

The conservatory doors burst open.

Three Gilded Hessians marched in, their clockwork gears grinding in lockstep. Seven feet of brass and oak and lethal purpose. They raised their arms in unison, and panels slid back to reveal rotating barrels. Salt-Shot Cannons, weapons designed specifically to shred spirits, to tear apart ectoplasm, to erase ghosts from existence.

"Target identified," the lead Hessian droned. "Class Five Specter. Threat level, Critical. Engage with extreme prejudice."

"No!" Seraphine shouted, stepping forward. "Stand down! I didn't summon you!"

"Override protocol engaged," the Hessian responded. "Lady Seraphine is in danger. Threat must be neutralized."

The lead Hessian fired.

The sound was deafening, a cannon blast in an enclosed space, the report bouncing off the glass walls until it came from everywhere at once. A canister of rock salt, blessed by the Church and bound with iron, exploded from the barrel. It was a shotgun blast of spiritual shrapnel, dozens of pieces of consecrated salt moving at lethal velocity, spreading in a cone of destruction.

Ash threw his hand out. The air in front of him solidified, water vapor and ectoplasm freezing into a wall of jagged ice. The salt slammed into the barrier with enough force to crack it, spiderweb fractures racing across the frozen surface.

But it held. Barely.

"Run!" Teyra screamed. "Ash, run!"

"I'm not leaving you!"

"You can't fight them like this!"

The second Hessian adjusted its aim. The third was circling, trying to flank. Ash was coming apart, his outline fraying, the poltergeist transformation threatening to consume him entirely.

Teyra's hand closed around the vial of bonemeal in her pocket, a necromancer's last defense. She yanked out the cork and flung the powder at the second Hessian's leg.

"Decay!" She shoved every ounce of necrotic power into the word.

The Grave-Chill hit her chest and kept hitting, a freezing pressure that crushed the breath from her lungs. Her vision whited out at the edges. Warmth trickled from her nose, blood, she knew without touching it. But the magic worked. The brass bloomed with green verdigris, then went dead black, oxidizing centuries in seconds. The Hessian's leg buckled, gears grinding and shrieking as it collapsed.

"Teyra!" Seraphine was shouting something, a command, a warning, but the words were lost in the chaos.

The third Hessian locked onto Ash. Its targeting sensors adjusted, calculating trajectory, preparing for the killing shot.

Seraphine lunged.

A small movement, just a hand pushing against the Hessian's brass arm, deflecting the barrel a fraction of an inch to the left.

The third Hessian fired. The shot went wide, missing Ash's chest by inches. But it caught his shoulder. Salt tore through ectoplasm and spectral flesh, and blue mist erupted from the wound like blood, glowing and dissipating in the air.

Ash howled. The sound went beyond human. It was the cry of a storm, of breaking glass, of a force that had forgotten it had ever been alive.

His form destabilized. The man vanished, replaced by a swirling vortex of grey smoke and blue lightning. He was losing his anchor. The tea's magic was breaking down under the assault.

He was becoming a monster.

The conservatory shook. The iron beams groaned. The glass walls, already cracked, splintered further.

"He's going critical!" Seraphine screamed, backing away from the vortex. "Containment protocol! Don't kill him, just contain..."

The Poltergeist-Ash didn't care about protocols. A tendril of smoke solidified just long enough to grab the split iron table. He hurled it at the damaged Hessian with inhuman strength. The heavy metal smashed into the machine's head, denting the gold mask inward, shattering optical sensors, sending sparks flying.

Teyra was freezing to death. Her exposed skin burned from the cold. The moisture in her eyes was beginning to crystallize. Her thoughts were slowing, her limbs going numb.

The roof. She looked up through streaming eyes at the glass ceiling, frosted white, made brittle by the supernatural cold.

The wards. Anchored to the structure. Weakened by the temperature change.

"Lenore!" she screamed at the sky. "Now!"

A black shape plummeted from above, a missile, an arrow shot from heaven. Lenore, who had been circling and waiting for Teyra's signal, folded her wings and dove.

The raven hit the frosted glass like a hurled stone wrapped in feathers. The weakened roof shattered, exploding inward in a cascade of deadly shards. Glass fell like rain, glittering in the afternoon light as it tumbled down.

Teyra threw her arms over her head, dropping to her knees. Glass rained around her, sharp edges slicing through her sleeves. Hot pain bloomed across her cheek, a shard cutting deep, then cold blood running down her jaw.

The wards shattered with the glass. The spells broke like snapping strings, releasing a wave of dissipating magic that washed over the room.

"Ash!" Teyra screamed, running toward the vortex. "We're leaving! Grab me!"

The storm turned. Two glowing white eyes fixed on her from within the smoke, a shape held together by a thread, caught between human and gone.

She thought him lost, consumed by the poltergeist transformation, erased forever.

Then a cold, solid hand emerged from the chaos. Fingers materialized, then a palm, then an arm.

He grabbed her waist. The touch burned like dry ice, but his grip was firm.

"Hold on," the distorted voice growled.

The swirling vortex of poltergeist energy detonated beneath them like a cannon shot, and the telekinetic shockwave launched them upward through the shattered roof. Glass and iron screamed around them. Wind tore at her hair. She clung to him with desperate strength, burying her face against his coat.

They burst through the hole in the roof, through the rain of falling glass, into the cold afternoon air.

A streak of black shot through the broken roof behind them. Lenore, wings spread wide, a shard of glass catching her left wing and sending her into a spiralling tumble. She hit the grass three seconds after they did, rolling to a stop in a heap of wet feathers.

They landed hard on the wet grass outside the estate walls. The impact knocked the breath from Teyra's lungs. They rolled, momentum carrying them down the hillside, mud soaking through her dress, grass staining her hands green.

When they finally stopped, she was sprawled on top of him, gasping like something the river had spat back.

They were alive. Somehow, impossibly, they were alive. Lenore limped out of the darkness a moment later, one wing dragging, and fixed Teyra with a look of pure, feathered outrage.

Then she heard Ash groan, and reality crashed back.

He had snapped back to himself the moment they hit the ground, the poltergeist energy bleeding away into the earth. He lay on his back, clutching his wounded shoulder. Blue mist rose from cracked ectoplasm.

Teyra scrambled over to him. "Let me see..."

The wound was spreading. Fine cracks branched out from the impact site, leaking glowing blue mist. The blessed salt was eating away at his ectoplasm like acid.

She reached for the wound instinctively, the healer's reflex, the necromancer's compulsion to touch the damage and understand it. Her fingers hovered over the cracked ectoplasm, and the Resonance channel opened before she could stop it. His pain lanced through her shoulder, bright and specific, the burning dissolution of salt in spectral flesh. She gasped and pulled her hand back, but the echo stayed. A new ache in her left shoulder that hadn't been there ten seconds ago, already settling in beside the phantom blade between her ribs and Thomas's homesickness and all the other borrowed hurts she carried.

Seven fragments now, layered behind her ribs. She wondered how many more she could hold.

"I'm fine," he gritted out, trying to sit up.

"You're not fine. That was Salt-Shot. It eats spectral flesh."

She looked back at the estate, pressing her own hand against her shoulder, his shoulder, her echo, the distinction mattering less every day. Alarm bells were ringing. The heavy thud of more Hessians mobilizing. And beneath that, the baying of hounds. Spectral Trackers.

"We have hours, maybe less, before this spreads to your core."

"Seraphine let us go," Ash said.

"What?"

"The third shot." He was staring at the estate, at the broken glass of the conservatory glittering in the distance. "She pushed the Hessian's arm. It was going for my heart. She made it miss."

He looked at Teyra, his grey eyes clouded with an emotion she couldn't untangle.

"She saved me. Again. Why would she save me?"

Teyra didn't have an answer. The tears on Seraphine's face had been real. The break in her voice had been genuine. She had killed the man she loved to save a kingdom, and five years later, she had sabotaged her own soldiers to save his ghost.

"Come on," Teyra said, helping him stand. "We can figure out her motivations later. Right now, we need to find somewhere safe."

"Where?" Ash leaned heavily on her, his cold weight pressing against her side. "We have no home. No ingredients. I'm dying."

Teyra's hand went to her pocket. Her fingers closed around an object that hadn't been there that morning—cold and sharp.

A silver pin. Shaped like a moth with spread wings.

The cut on her cheek pulled tight as she frowned, and a cold pooling settled low in her stomach. She stared at the pin in the fading light, her hand trembling, because the last time she'd seen this symbol, its owner's agents had been throwing stones through her windows. Last night. The scuffle in the shop. One of them must have slipped it into her coat pocket while she was swinging the poker. Someone who wanted to be found.

"We go underground," she said. "We find the Moth."

"The crime lord? The one who's been watching us?"

"The one who has Moonflower petals for sale." She looked at Ash, at his fading form, at the wound slowly consuming him. "We're out of options, Ash. We're out of time. The last dose I gave you is already burning out, by tomorrow you'll be fading, and the wound is going to kill you before that if we don't move."

She helped him limp toward the lower city, toward the darkness, toward a deal she already knew she'd regret.

"We're going to make a bargain with the devil," she said. "And pray we survive the price."

Behind them, the Greythorn Estate burned with magical alarm lights. The hunt had begun.

But somewhere in the wreckage of the conservatory, Lady Seraphine stood alone amid the dead flowers and broken glass, the bracelet cold against her wrist, and wept for the ghost of the man she had killed and could not stop losing.

The frost Ash had left behind was already melting in the ruined heat, but where it dripped from the iron beams, the water ran grey. The Unsettled, the residue of spiritual anguish, pooling on the terracotta tiles of the Garden District for the first time in living memory. Even here. Even in this place that money and magic had kept immaculate for three hundred years.

The drainage wards in the gutter grates outside flickered, struggled, and held. Barely.

Chapter Five

THE NIGHT MARKET

DAY FOUR: FOUR DAYS REMAIN

THE ENTRANCE TO THE underworld was behind a butcher shop in the Meat District.

The literal underworld, the sunken city beneath Athergard, the catacombs, tunnels, forgotten places where the laws of the surface didn't apply. Where the things that couldn't survive in daylight made their homes and their deals and their bloody little economies.

Teyra had heard stories. Everyone had. The Night Market was legend, half myth and half warning. Children whispered about it in schoolyards. Drunk men claimed to have been there and back. Necromancers spoke of it in hushed tones as the place where forbidden ingredients could be bought, where dark magics were traded like vegetables at a farmer's stall.

She'd never been. She'd never wanted to go.

But Ash was dying again, the salt wound slower now that he'd been still for hours but still spreading, and the Moth had Moonflower, and there was no other choice.

The Meat District was bad enough on its own.

It sprawled across the lower slopes of the city, a warren of slaughterhouses beside rendering plants and cold storage facilities that kept Athergard fed. The streets here were narrow and slick, cobblestones permanently stained rust-brown from two centuries of blood runoff. No amount of rain could wash them clean. The stench was overwhelming, raw meat layered over old blood, and beneath both the sweet-sick smell of fat being rendered into tallow. Flies buzzed in thick clouds despite the cold, and rats moved brazenly in the gutters, grown fat and bold on offal.

The grey film was running here, a slow, viscous current in the gutter channels, thick as embalming fluid, moving with a purpose that normal runoff lacked. The Meat District had been skipped entirely: no drainage wards, no bronze discs in the gutter grates, no Guild-maintained purification sigils. The dead here, animal and human alike, dissolved into the infrastructure and stayed there. The cobblestones were stained with more than blood. Two centuries of unprocessed spiritual residue had soaked into the stone so deep that it came through the soles of her boots, a low, constant hum of accumulated slaughter, layered and compressed and forgotten.

No wonder the entrance to the underworld was here. The ground felt steeped in haunting already.

Teyra's boots squelched in filth she chose not to identify. Ash leaned heavily against her, his arm draped across her shoulders. The wound in his shoulder was spreading faster now, cracks branching down his arm, blue light pulsing beneath his coat sleeve like veins filled with cold fire.

"How much further?" he managed, his voice thin and strained.

"Close." She hoped, though the directions she'd gotten from a one-eyed fence in the Tanners' Quarter had been vague at best. Behind the old Grimsby slaughterhouse. Through the killing floor. Past the bone pit. Look for the rust.

Look for the rust. What kind of direction was that? Everything here was rust.

Lenore rode on Teyra's shoulder, her injured wing tucked against her body. The raven had been uncharacteristically quiet since they'd left the Greythorn Estate, no quips, no complaints. She just watched the shadows with those bead-black eyes, her head swiveling at every sound.

"There," Lenore said suddenly. "The grate."

Teyra stopped. They were behind what had once been a slaughterhouse, the building abandoned now, windows boarded, walls blackened by a fire that had gutted it years ago. The smell here was different, older, a reek that had soaked into the stones so deeply it would never come out.

And there, half-hidden behind rotting crates and piles of discarded bones, was a rusted iron grate set into the cobblestones.

Unremarkable, at a glance. Just a drainage cover, the kind you'd find in any industrial district. But as Teyra approached, wrongness radiated from below. Magic, old and festering, the kind that had been breeding in the dark for centuries.

She shoved aside the crates. The wood was soft with decay, splintering under her hands, releasing a smell of mold and something worse; the grate beneath was corroded to lace, the iron eaten away by moisture and whatever lived in the wet dark.

When she grabbed the bars to lift it, the metal was hot.

Scalding, even. Like it had been sitting in the sun for hours, even though they were in the shadow of the slaughterhouse, even though the afternoon sky was heavy with rain clouds. The heat radiated up from below, carrying with it a smell that made Teyra's stomach clench.

Sulfur and rotting sugar, barely masking the copper-sweet tang of fresh blood.

"Second thoughts?" Lenore asked.

"Dozens." Teyra pulled the grate aside. It came up with a groan of protesting metal, revealing a shaft of absolute darkness. A rusted ladder descended into the black.

Warm air rushed up from below, fetid and thick, carrying sounds that shouldn't have been possible this far from the surface. Distant music, and laughter that echoed wrong.

"After you," Ash said.

"Hilarious."

She went first.

The ladder was slick with moisture Teyra didn't want to identify.

She counted rungs as she descended, fifty, sixty, seventy, her fingers slipping on the corroded iron, her boots scraping against metal that felt soft and organic. The air grew thicker with each step, warmer, heavier, pressing against her ears until they popped, once, twice. The darkness swallowed even her own hands.

Above her, she heard Ash struggling. His breath hitched in uneven pulls, an old reflex, and the effort of keeping himself solid was draining him. Once, she heard his boot slip through a rung with a wet sound, heard him curse, then catch himself.

"Still there?" she called up.

"Barely."

Eighty rungs. Ninety. The heat was becoming unbearable. Sweat soaked through her dress, plastered her hair to her forehead. The air tasted foul now, thick and oily, coating her tongue with a film that made her want to gag.

At one hundred and twelve rungs, her foot hit solid ground.

She stepped off the ladder into a narrow tunnel carved from raw stone. The walls were wet, glistening in a faint phosphorescent glow that came from patches of fungus growing in the cracks. The ceiling was low enough that she had to duck, the stone scraping against her hair.

The smell here was overwhelming. Rot and sulfur laced with a sweetness that should have been floral but had turned cloying, like fruit that had kept sweetening long past the point of edible. It triggered a primal alarm in the back of her brain, some ancient warning system screaming at her to run, to climb back up the ladder, to get away from whatever made that smell.

She didn't run. She couldn't. Ash was dying.

"First checkpoint," Lenore whispered. "Fifty yards ahead. I can hear it breathing."

They moved through the tunnel, Teyra in front, Ash leaning on the wall for support. The phosphorescence grew brighter as they walked, the fungus thicker, until the tunnel was lit in a sickly blue-green glow that made their skin look corpse-pale.

The breathing got louder.

The breathing came too slow, too deep for anything human. A bellows sound, like a massive chest pulling air through damaged lungs. With each exhale, the air temperature spiked, and Teyra tasted copper.

They rounded a corner and found the checkpoint.

The creature blocking the tunnel was seven feet tall and built like a slaughterhouse beam given flesh. Its skin was grey and hairless, stretched tight over muscles that shouldn't have fit on a human frame. Its face was a ruin, nose broken and healed flat, teeth filed to points, one eye milky white while the other glowed faintly red.

It wore a vest stitched from leather scraps that Teyra recognized, with a sick lurch of her stomach, as human skin. The faces were still visible in patches, a woman's eye here, a child's mouth there, sewn together in a patchwork of horror.

It held a club wrapped in barbed wire, the metal crusted with old blood.

"Toll," the creature grunted, its voice like gravel being crushed. "Three fingers or a gold sovereign."

She had no gold, the last of her coins had gone to the fence for directions, and the realization sat cold in her chest. And her fingers...

She pulled out the silver moth pin.

If this was a trap, she was walking into it with her eyes open. But they had no other leads, no other allies, and four days before Ash's anchor burned out. The only door open was the one the Moth had left unlocked.

The creature's red eye went wide. It took a step back, then another, its massive body pressing against the tunnel wall as if it were trying to disappear into the stone.

"Pass," it said, the word tumbling out fast and breathless. "Pass quickly. Don't... don't tell him I stopped you. Please. Please don't tell him."

They passed. The creature watched them go with wide, white-rimmed eyes.

"He was shaking," Ash said when they were out of earshot. "Of a pin."

"The owner," Teyra said. "He was shaking because of the owner."

The tunnels branched and split, a maze of passages carved into the bedrock of Athergard's foundations. Some were ancient, remnants of the old city that had existed before the fire, before the rebuilding, before the current age. Others were newer, rough-hewn and shored up with rotting timber.

They descended further. Down another ladder, this one rope instead of iron, the fibers fraying beneath their fingers. Through a passage so narrow they had to turn sideways to squeeze through, the stone pressing against Teyra's chest and back until she could barely breathe.

The sounds grew louder as they went, resolving into discordant violin notes from no scale Teyra knew, drums beating in tooth-aching rhythms, and laughter that never stopped.

And the smells, gods, the smells. Each turn brought a fresh horror. Here, the reek of unwashed bodies packed too close together. There, the chemical burn of illegal alchemy, potions being brewed in the dark. Around the next corner, the unmistakable stench of rotting flesh, fresh, recent, still wet.

"We're close," Lenore said. "I can feel it pulling."

"Pulling?"

"The market." The raven ruffled her feathers. "It's like a current. A tide. Drawing things in. Dead things especially. This place is a burial ground, Teyra. Thousands of years of dead layered into the earth, seeping into the stone. The ghosts here aren't just spirits. They're part of the architecture."

Ash shuddered. "I can feel it too. Something whispering. Telling me to let go. To join them."

He went translucent for a breath, then thickened back to himself. The wound on his shoulder pulsed brighter.

Teyra grabbed his arm. "Don't listen. Whatever it's saying, don't listen."

"I'm trying." The strain in his voice was audible. "It's loud, Teyra. So loud."

They pushed on.

The passage opened and Teyra stopped, because her body stopped for her.

The smell hit first. The tunnel had smelled of rot and sulfur and industrial death soaked into centuries of stone. This was different.

This smelled like longing that had curdled past the point of wanting what it had lost. Like every spirit she had ever helped who had waited too long to ask. She breathed it in and felt her Resonance channels open before she could stop them.

Hundreds, maybe thousands. The bedrock of Athergard down here was sediment. Layered and compressed. The architectural record of everyone who had come down looking for something they couldn't find above ground and never fully come back up. People who had needed things the city wouldn't give them. Help that cost more than they had. Remedies that required you to descend past the law and stay past your welcome. Three hundred years of the city's dispossessed, compressed into the rock beneath her boots, and her Resonance channels, still raw from the tunnel's accumulated animal slaughter, were drinking it in like dry earth after rain.

The cavern was vast, and it hit her all at once, the way cold runoff hits when you are already drenched through. The stalactites. The lanterns in every color imaginable, colors that had no names because they'd been made down here and never needed to be described to anyone above ground. The market filling the space the way mold fills a closed room: without asking, because this was what happened when things grew in the dark for long enough.

She had sat across from the dying before, in a velvet armchair, and helped it say goodbye. She had never stood inside it the way you stand inside a cathedral. Or a slaughterhouse. Both of those, she understood now, were the same thing at heart, a space built to hold something too large for ordinary rooms. A truth that couldn't survive daylight, with witnesses.

"First rule of the Night Market," Lenore said from her shoulder, very quietly, as if even the raven understood volume was the wrong register for this place. "Don't feel too much. The dead here don't know the difference between a sympathetic ear and a door."

Teyra thought of Meridia Ashworth. Of the ward that had been evacuated. Of eleven children waking up no longer themselves. Of the six months between the Gathering that worked and the night the bonds woke up and walked through her.

"I know," she said.

She walked in anyway. She knew exactly what the danger was called. She went in anyway. Whether that made her brave or just reckless, she'd run out of time to decide.

The stalls twisted and branched and doubled back, creating a labyrinth that would swallow the unwary.

And the crowd.

Gods, the crowd.

Bodies pressed together so tightly that Teyra couldn't see the ground beneath them. Human and otherwise, living and dead and things in between. She saw thieves in black leather, their faces hidden behind masks. Rogue mages with tattoos that glowed and writhed on their skin. Goblins with yellow eyes, a minotaur with filed horns, things with scales and too many eyes that she couldn't identify.

They moved in currents, flowing between the stalls, their voices creating a wall of sound that hit Teyra in the chest. Hawkers screamed their wares in a dozen languages. Customers bargained and begged. Somewhere, someone was crying. Somewhere else, someone was laughing, the same laugh she'd heard in the tunnels, going on and on without breaking.

The smell was indescribable. Incense and unwashed bodies, exotic spices and fresh blood, all of it layered together until her eyes watered and her throat closed.

"Stay close," she said, gripping Ash's arm. "Don't look anyone in the eye. Don't touch anything. Don't speak unless I speak first."

"You've done this before?"

"No. But I've read the stories. The rules are simple. Don't engage, don't bargain, don't trust. Anyone who approaches you wants something, and what they want is never good."

They pushed into the crowd.

The first horror found them three stalls in.

A tent of red canvas, stained dark in patches that might have been wine or might have been blood. The entrance was flanked by torches that burned with black flame, fire that gave off cold instead of heat, that cast shadows that moved on their own.

Inside, visible through the open flap, was a woman.

She sat in a chair that might have once been beautiful, carved from dark wood with velvet cushions. But the cushions were rotting now, the velvet peeling away to reveal stuffing that squirmed with maggots. The woman's face was serene, peaceful, even beautiful, with high cheekbones and full lips painted deep red.

But she had no eyes.

Where her eyes should have been were holes, actual holes, portals into something else. Darkness moved behind them, darkness with depth, darkness that went on forever. As Teyra watched, a hand emerged from one of the holes, pale and delicate and child-sized, reached out, and plucked something from the air. A moth. The hand retreated back into the woman's skull, taking the moth with it.

The woman's lips moved "Would you like to see what I see?" Her voice was coming from somewhere else, from inside Teyra's own head, from behind her, from the holes where her eyes should be. "I can show you things. Things that were. Things that will be. Things that should never be."

Her empty sockets turned toward Ash.

"I can show you how you died. Every detail. The blade. The woman who held it. The words she whispered as she watched you fall. Would you like to know what she said?"

Ash took a step forward. His face was slack, eyes unfocused, drawn toward those dark portals.

Teyra yanked him back. "Don't," she hissed. "Don't look. Don't listen."

She pulled him past the tent, past the eyeless woman, into the crush of bodies.

The second horror was worse.

A stall made of bone, actual bone, femurs, ribs, and spines fitted together with wire and sinew into a structure that looked like a ribcage turned inside out. Inside, jars lined the shelves, dozens of them, hundreds, each one filled with liquid that glowed in the colored light.

The jars contained eyes.

Human eyes, mostly, floating in preservation fluid, their irises in every color. Blue, green, brown, yes, but also colors that didn't belong on human faces. Purple and gold. One jar held eyes that were black from edge to edge, no white, no iris, just pools of absolute darkness.

They were watching.

Every eye in every jar had turned to track Teyra and Ash as they passed. They moved in their liquid prisons, rotating in their jars, following. Some of them blinked.

"Fresh eyes!" the vendor called. He was a small man with bandages wrapped around his head where his own eyes should have been. He smiled, revealing teeth filed to points. "Eyes of the dying, eyes of the dead! See what they saw! Know what they knew! I have the eyes of a hanged man who watched his children starve! I have the eyes of a priest who witnessed the face of god! I have the eyes of a child who saw what waits at the bottom of the dark!"

He held up a jar. Inside, two tiny eyes, the size of marbles, still fresh, still wet.

"These belonged to a little girl." His voice carried somehow over the din of the market. "She saw something in the basement of her home. Something that shouldn't have been there. And it smiled at her. Would you like to know what smiles in the dark? Fifty gold and a year of your life, and you'll know. You'll see."

She pulled Ash past the stall, stomach heaving, moving faster now, pushing through the crowd without apology.

The third horror stopped her cold.

It wasn't a stall. It was an open space in the market, a clearing where the crowd parted and kept their distance. A circle of bare stone, maybe thirty feet across, lit by a single hanging lantern that cast sickly green light.

In the center of the circle was a cage.

The cage was made of iron, cold iron, warded with sigils that glowed red. It was large enough to hold a man, and it did. It held a thing that had been a man, once.

The creature inside was naked, its skin pale and stretched tight over bones that had been broken and reset in wrong configurations. Its arms bent backward. Its spine curved at impossible angles. Its head was too large, its mouth too wide, filled with teeth that had grown in rows like a shark's.

But the worst part was its face.

Recognition struck before the name did.

"No," she breathed.

The thing in the cage had been Aldous Whitmore. Professor Aldous Whitmore, Department of Applied Necromancy, Athergard Academy of the Arcane. He had taught her sophomore year. He had written the textbook on spectral containment. He had been kind, one of the few professors who hadn't looked down on her for her background, who had encouraged her talent instead of dismissing it. He had been the one to first tell her about Meridia Ashworth, and he'd told it differently than Professor Grimwald, told it as a tragedy rather than a warning. "She wasn't weak," he'd said, marking Teyra's essay with careful red ink. "She was too open. There's a difference, and the Academy has never been willing to learn it."

He had disappeared three years ago. The Academy had called it a sabbatical. Teyra had always wondered. Now she knew. It sat in her like stone.

"Teyra." Ash's voice was sharp. "Teyra, we need to keep moving."

But she couldn't move. She couldn't look away. The thing in the cage, the thing that had been Professor Whitmore, had seen her. Its too-wide eyes locked onto hers, and recognition flickered in their depths.

"Teyra," it said. Its voice was ruined, wet and gurgling, the words distorted by a mouth that had been reshaped for something other than human speech. "Teyra Tepes. Talented student. Should have passed the exam. I told them. I told them she was special."

It pressed against the bars, its broken fingers curling around the cold iron.

"They wanted to know about ghosts. About what happens when you push a soul too far. They paid me to find out. They paid me, and I said yes, and now I know. I know what happens, Teyra. I know what waits on the other side. Do you want to know? What your ghosts feel when they fade?"

Teyra's throat was too tight to speak.

"Come closer," the thing that had been Whitmore whispered. "Come closer, and I'll tell you. I'll tell you what death tastes like. I'll tell you the name of the thing that lives in the space between heartbeats. I'll tell you..."

Ash grabbed her arm and pulled her away.

"Don't," he said fiercely. "Don't look back. Don't think about it. Whatever that was, it's not your professor anymore. It's bait. It's a trap."

"He remembered me." Her voice was shaking. "He knew my name."

"That's what makes it effective." Ash's grip on her arm was cold, but it was real, the most real thing she'd felt since they'd entered this nightmare. "Keep moving. We're almost there."

Teyra bit down until she tasted copper, walled the cage behind her eyes, and kept walking.

The deeper parts of the Night Market were different.

The chaos faded as they moved toward the center of the cavern, replaced by order. Control. The stalls here were larger, more elaborate, proper shops rather than the ramshackle constructions of the outer ring, some of them carved into the cavern walls, others built from materials that didn't exist on the surface.

The crowd was different too. Fewer desperate scavengers and petty criminals, more figures in expensive clothing, their faces hidden behind masks of gold and silver, and the quality of goods on display had shifted toward items of genuine power. A sword that drank light, leaving void-shaped shadows where it passed. A clock that ran backward, its hands sweeping counterclockwise through hours that hadn't happened yet, beside books bound in materials that moved when you looked at them too long.

The Silk District, Teyra realized. The part of the market where the real power resided.

The tent they were looking for stood at the center.

Black silk draped the tent, so fine it absorbed the light around it. Silver poles held up the canopy, shaped like wings, moth wings, rendered in exquisite metalwork, each scale visible. There were no lanterns here, no torches. Instead, hundreds of moths fluttered around the entrance, their wings glowing with soft bioluminescent blue.

A sign hung above the entrance, embroidered in silver thread. THE COLLECTOR.

"Ready?" Teyra asked.

Ash's face was grey, drawn. The wound on his shoulder was spreading faster now, the cracks reaching toward his neck. He had hours left. Maybe less.

"No," he said. "Let's go anyway."

They didn't get three steps.

The thing that materialized in front of the tent entrance had been human once. Maybe. It had the rough shape of a person—two arms, two legs, a head—but everything was wrong. The proportions were off, the limbs too long, the joints bending in directions that made Teyra's eyes ache. Its skin was grey and papery, stretched tight over bones that seemed to shift beneath it. Its mouth was sewn shut with silver thread.

It had no eyes. Where eyes should have been, there were moth wings, real ones, still fluttering, embedded in the sockets like living jewelry.

It said nothing, and needed to say nothing. It simply stood in the entrance and radiated a message as clear as any words. You do not belong here.

Teyra held up the silver moth pin.

The creature's head tilted, that same insectile movement she'd seen in the eyeless woman three stalls back. The moth wings in its sockets fluttered faster. It leaned forward, close enough that Teyra could smell it, formaldehyde and dried lavender, the same chemical sweetness that drifted from the tent behind it.

Then it reached out with one too-long hand and pressed a finger against Teyra's forehead.

The world went white.

It rifled through her, bypassing pockets and belongings entirely, going straight for her mind. Memories flashing past in a blur. The soldier ghost at her exam. Her grandmother's funeral. The first time she'd touched Ash and felt the void inside his skull. The silk bookmark in the Archives. *Patience.* Every secret, every hidden thing she'd tried to bury, pulled to the surface, examined, cataloged.

And the borrowed ones. It found those too.

It paused on them, on the borrowed wounds, every one, stacked behind her ribs like coins sewn into a coat lining. It examined each the way a customs officer examines smuggled goods. Contraband feelings. Hurt that didn't belong to her, lodged in her body uninvited.

The creature's moth-wing eyes fluttered faster. It tilted its head. And Teyra had the sudden, terrible sense that it was counting them, tallying the fragments she carried, measuring the weight of borrowed pain, and finding the total interesting.

It lasted three seconds. It felt like an hour.

The creature withdrew its hand. The moth wings settled. And then it stepped aside.

The pin hadn't earned the gesture, and neither had Teyra.

It was looking at Ash.

Looking at the wound on his shoulder, at the cracks spreading through his spectral flesh, at the blue light pulsing beneath his coat. Looking at him with the appraising calm of a jeweler before the cut.

It bowed. A deep, formal bow, the bow of a servant greeting its master's most expensive problem.

Then it melted back into the silk of the tent wall and was gone.

"What," Ash said, "was that."

"The price of admission," Teyra said. Her head was pounding. Her memories felt rearranged, like books reshelved in the wrong order. "He knows everything about us now. Everything."

"He already knew everything about us."

"Yes. But now he knows we know that."

The interior of the tent was larger than it should have been. Much larger. The silk walls enclosed a space that could have held a small house, filled with shelves and display cases and cabinets that stretched up toward a ceiling that seemed too far away. Magic warped the dimensions, made Teyra's inner ear rebel. Her balance shifted, caught herself on the edge of a display case.

The noise of the market vanished the moment they crossed the threshold, replaced by a silence so complete it pressed against her eardrums.

And the smell, different here. Dried lavender and old paper, and formaldehyde beneath it all. Familiar, in a way that made her skin prickle. Preservation fluid. Formaldehyde. The smell of things that had been dead a long time.

The shelves were filled with impossibilities.

A clock running backward, bone dice from the Tepeshan Empire still warm to the touch, and a jar containing a miniature thunderstorm, lightning flickering silently behind the glass. A skull carved from diamond, its eye sockets filled with liquid darkness that moved when she looked at it. A music box playing a melody she could feel in her bones but couldn't quite hear, and beside it a pair of spectacles that, when she glanced at them, showed her a flash of her own funeral, a pine box, a rainy day, no mourners.

And on the lowest shelf, almost hidden behind a stack of leather journals, a glass jar that made Teyra stop walking.

Inside wasn't a specimen or a liquid or anything she could name. It was a knot of nothing. And nothing was the closest word she had, though even darkness was too solid a comparison, an absence of light her eyes could at least process. This went further. An absence of everything. Looking at it felt like pressing her tongue against a missing tooth. Her eyes kept sliding off it, refusing to focus, her brain insisting that what she was seeing couldn't exist.

The air around the jar tasted like nothing. The jar was eating the smell out of the air around it.

She looked away quickly.

Behind an obsidian desk, in a chair that looked more like a throne, sat the Moth.

He looked like a clerk. That was what struck her first. Slim, precise, with delicate features and long fingers encased in gloves of pale kidskin. He wore a suit of grey velvet that shifted color when he moved, darker at the edges, lighter at the center. A mask of silver filigree covered his nose and mouth, the metalwork wrought into the pattern of moth wings, leaving only his eyes visible above the delicate, folded edges.

His eyes were the worst part.

They were grey, but the wrong kind of grey. Ash-grey. Dead-thing grey. A grey that had never held warmth or anything that could be called human.

He was examining something when they entered, a pocket watch, held up to a jeweler's loupe. He didn't acknowledge them, just continued his examination with the careful attention of a man who had all the time in the world.

The quiet kept thickening, acquiring a texture that sat against her eardrums.

Teyra waited. Ash shifted beside her, his wound pulsing blue, his patience visibly fraying. A minute passed. Two. The Moth continued his examination of the pocket watch, occasionally making small adjustments with a tool so fine it was almost invisible, his breathing slow and measured, his attention utterly elsewhere.

Ash's light dimmed. The cracks in his shoulder were spreading, inching toward his neck, slow but relentless. Every second they stood here was a second he was dying.

"We need..." Teyra started.

"Shh."

One syllable. He didn't look up. Just that sound, quiet, almost gentle, and Teyra's voice died in her throat. The absolute certainty settled over her that this man controlled the tempo of every room he occupied, and they would speak when he decided they could.

Another minute. Ash was gripping the edge of a display case, knuckles white, the effort of staying solid written across his face. Her own pulse was climbing, a hot, sharp pressure building against the cold in her chest.

The Moth set down his loupe. Closed the pocket watch. Placed it on the desk, and the click, in that suffocating silence, filled the room.

Then he looked up.

Those dead eyes fixed on Teyra, and she understood, suddenly and completely, that the wait had been the test. He'd been watching them the entire time, measuring their patience and their desperation. Calculating exactly how much they needed him.

"You're late," he said. He spoke softly, the sound of dry leaves skittering across stone. "But I expected worse. The Conservatory. Lady Seraphine. The Hessians." He recited the words like a list of groceries. "Quite the dramatic afternoon. I particularly enjoyed the part where you jumped through the ceiling."

"You've led an interesting life, Miss Tepes. Teyra Tepes. Failed necromancer. Tea shop proprietor. Daughter of Marcus Tepes, a mediocre accountant who drank himself to death when you were fourteen."

He tilted his head, the movement too quick, too sharp. "You owe forty-two gold sovereigns in back rent. You have eleven. You haven't paid your Academy loans in three years. The interest is considerable."

Each fact landed like a small blow. Heat rose in Teyra's face.

"You've done your research."

"I don't do research, Miss Tepes. I know. There is a difference."

His eyes slid to Ash. "And you. The lost antique. The ghost who shouldn't exist. The dead prince."

Ash straightened despite his wound. "Do you know who I am? Who I was?"

The Moth smiled behind his mask, his cheeks shifting, those dead eyes crinkling.

"Know you? I have been waiting for you for twenty-five years, Your Majesty. Since the night of the fire."

He stood, and the movement was wrong in a way she couldn't immediately place, too fluid, almost boneless, as though the fire that had taken his face had also melted the structure beneath the skin and it had set crooked, leaving him with a jointless, liquid grace that no longer answered to human rules. He walked around the desk, his grey velvet suit shifting and flowing. He stopped in front of Ash, looking up at the taller man with those flat, empty eyes.

"Ashen Thornwick. Heir to the throne. Killed by his own betrothed in a private ballroom on the eve of his coronation."

"Stop." Ash lunged. He didn't think. He just moved, his hand closing around the Moth's throat, or trying to.

But the Moth moved faster.

With a speed that blurred in the dim light, the crime lord caught Ash's spectral wrist. His gloved hand didn't pass through the ghost. It held fast, silver light flaring where skin met glove. The Moth twisted, slamming Ash's arm down onto the obsidian desk with a crack that rang off every glass surface in the room.

"I haven't finished, my lord," the Moth whispered, leaning in. His grip was iron. "I know about the prophecy your brother discovered. I know Lady Seraphine wept while she washed your blood off her hands. And I know about the throne that is currently sitting empty because you were too busy dying to claim it."

He released Ash, shoving him back. Ash stumbled, rubbing a wrist that shouldn't have been able to feel pain, staring at the Moth with wide eyes.

"You can touch me," Ash breathed.

"I can do many things." The Moth smoothed his velvet coat, unbothered. He settled back into his chair with the patience of a predator that had never needed to chase. "Now, are you done posturing? Because I know how to get your throne back."

He opened a drawer in his desk and pulled out a black velvet pouch.

"And I know that you're dying. Again. The Salt-Shot wound is spreading. You have perhaps three hours before it reaches your core and dissolves you into nothing." He set the pouch on the desk. "Moonflower petals. Fresh. Enough to anchor you for another month, perhaps two. Enough to seal the wound and stabilize your form."

"How much?" The question was out before she'd weighed it.

"Ah." The Moth leaned back in his chair. "That is the question. What is the life of a dead prince worth? What would you pay to save a ghost?"

"I have gold..."

"I don't want your gold." He waved a dismissive hand. "Gold is useful for buying bread and paying rent. For acquiring things of true value, one must trade in different currencies. Secrets. Favors. Souls, if you have one to spare." He steepled his gloved fingers. "Or services."

He let the word hang in the air.

"There is a vault," he said, "in the basement of the Greythorn Estate. Warded with blood magic. It can only be opened by someone carrying Thornwick blood, a security measure installed by the original builders, long before the family fell."

Those flat eyes fixed on Ash.

"You are going to break into the estate. Find the vault. Open it with your blood. And bring me what's inside."

"That's impossible," Teyra said. "The Greythorn Estate has Hessians, wards, armed guards…"

"It has your prince's brother," the Moth interrupted. "The Lord Elias Greythorn, né Thornwick. The man who discovered the prophecy. The man who set in motion the chain of events that led to Ashen's death." He smiled behind his mask. "Convenient. You want answers. What better way to find them than breaking into his home?"

"The Moonflower," Teyra said. Her voice came out steadier than she felt. "We need it now. He won't survive two days without it."

"No," the Moth agreed. "He won't."

He placed his gloved hand over the pouch. Almost tenderly. The way you might cover a sleeping child's hand.

"The flower is yours the moment we have an agreement. Before that, it stays where it is." His eyes moved to Ash, watching the cracks spread, watching the blue light gutter. Measuring. "Your prince is deteriorating at approximately three percent per hour. By my calculation, you have until dawn before the damage becomes irreversible." He smiled behind the mask. "Plenty of time for a conversation."

The cruelty of it sat in the air between them like a physical object. He'd put the cure on the desk where they could see it. Where Ash could smell the magic that would save his life, sitting just out of reach, while a man in a silver mask decided their fate.

Teyra's hands balled into fists beneath the desk.

"What do you want?" she asked.

Her mind was racing. It was a trap. It had to be a trap. The Moth didn't give gifts. Everything in this room had a price, and the price was never what it seemed.

"Why?" she asked. "Why do you want what's in that vault?"

The Moth regarded her. Those ash-colored eyes gave nothing away. Just emptiness, vast and patient.

"That," he said softly, "is an expensive question, Miss Tepes. Can you afford the answer?"

"I think I deserve..."

"Deserve." He tasted the word like it amused him. "You owe forty-two gold sovereigns in back rent. You have eleven. Your prince is dying in my chair. And you want to talk about what you deserve."

He leaned forward.

"I want a book. You need a cure. The arrangement is simple." He spread his gloved hands. "If you survive the heist, if you bring me what I want, and if you're still curious, ask me again. I may feel generous."

He wouldn't. They both knew it. But the door was closed, and that was that.

The Moth regarded her with those empty eyes. He didn't speak.

Then he laughed, a dry, rustling sound, like old paper curling in heat.

"I like you, Miss Tepes. You have spine. Most people who come to me are broken things, desperate and pathetic. They'll agree to anything for a crumb of what I offer. But you, you want to know why."

He leaned forward, his elbows on the desk.

"Very well. Inside that vault is a book. Leather-bound. No title. You'll know it when you see it, it will feel wrong. Heavy with magic that doesn't belong in this world."

He paused, examining his gloved fingernails with theatrical disinterest.

"What's in it?" Teyra pressed.

"That depends entirely on what you're willing to offer for the answer."

"You already told us the price. The heist."

"That's the price for the Moonflower and the key." Something glittered behind the Moth's eyes, the first sign of life she'd seen in them. "The price for knowing why you're risking your lives is separate. Information has its own currency, Miss Tepes. Surely a woman who trades in the secrets of the dead understands that."

Teyra's spine straightened. "What do you want?"

"A question answered honestly. Just one." He leaned forward, and his voice dropped to something almost intimate. "When you held that soldier's ghost at your Academy exam, when you felt everything he felt, did you let go of the summoning circle because you couldn't bear his pain? Or because you couldn't bear to command him?"

The question found the phantom blade that already lived between her ribs and pressed against it, as if Ash's death wound knew when someone was aiming for the same spot.

She opened her mouth. Closed it. The Moth waited, patient as a drainage ward, passive and always working.

"Both," she finally said. "It was both. I felt everything he felt, the homesickness, the bread his mother used to bake, and I couldn't hold the circle and hold all of that at the same time. The Academy wanted me to contain him. I couldn't contain him without commanding him, and I couldn't command him because he was seventeen years old and dying and nobody in that room cared except me."

She hadn't meant to say that much. The words had poured out the way the borrowed fragments sometimes did, unbidden, unexpected, belonging to a version of herself she usually kept locked in the back room.

The Moth smiled behind his mask, eyes crinkling, cheeks shifting.

"Honesty. How refreshing." He settled back in his chair. "The book contains something that changes the rules of the game you're currently losing. That's all you're buying tonight, Miss Tepes."

"That's not an answer."

"It's the only one you can afford." The Moth examined a gloved fingernail. "You asked what's in the vault. I've told you, a book. You asked why you should risk your lives. I've told you, Moonflower. The contents of the book are my concern. You are the delivery service. The delivery service does not need to read the mail."

Ash's jaw tightened. "You expect us to break into a guarded estate, risk our lives, and bring you something we know nothing about?"

"I expect you to weigh a certainty against an uncertainty." The Moth's dead eyes moved to the wound pulsing on Ash's shoulder. "Without Moonflower, you dissolve before dawn. Whether the book matters to you remains the uncertainty. But you'll never find out if you're dead."

He let the silence do his work for him.

"I will tell you this much." He leaned forward, and his voice dropped, the register of a man offering a single coin to a beggar. "The book is old. Older than the current monarchy. And the people who hid it in that vault did so because its contents threatened everything they'd built. Whether that's useful to you is a question you'll have to answer for yourselves. After you survive the heist."

Teyra looked at Ash. His face was unreadable, but she could see the calculation behind his eyes. A book that threatened the Greythorn power structure. Hidden in a Greythorn vault. Sealed behind blood wards that only Thornwick blood could open.

It might be nothing. It might be everything.

But the Moth wasn't going to tell them which.

"And if we refuse?" she asked.

"Then you refuse." The Moth spread his hands. "I won't force you. Forced bargains are worthless, there's no power in an agreement made under duress." He gestured toward the tent entrance. "You're free to walk out that door. Take your dying prince and leave. Find another source of Moonflower, if you can. There isn't one, of course, I've bought every petal in Athergard, but you're welcome to try."

He picked up the pocket watch again, returning his attention to it like they'd already left.

"Or," he continued, without looking at them, "you can accept a different bargain."

Teyra frowned. "Different?"

"Walk away right now, and I'll still help you." He said it casually, like he was offering her tea. "I'll hide you somewhere safe, a place where the Guard won't find you, where Lady Seraphine's Hessians can't track you."

He looked up, and there was something in those dead eyes that might have been amusement.

"I'll even clear your debt. Forty-two gold sovereigns, paid to your landlord tomorrow morning. You can keep your little shop. Keep brewing your tea. Keep helping ghosts find their way to the other side."

Teyra went still. "In exchange for what?"

"Nothing." He set down the watch. "Nothing except walking away. You disappear into the city and you never pursue this matter again. You don't break into the Greythorn Estate. You don't search for whatever's in that vault. You don't try to reclaim the throne or expose whatever conspiracy put a dead prince in your tea shop."

He smiled, and the expression made Teyra's skin crawl.

"You take the easy path. You survive. You live a quiet life, hidden away in some corner of Athergard where no one will ever find you. No answers, no justice. Just a few safe weeks while your ghost prince fades, and then you go back to brewing tea for old women who want to scold their dead husbands."

The image was vivid. Too vivid. Teyra could see it, the years stretching out, quiet, safe, and utterly empty.

Just survival. A quiet, hollow survival.

"Why?" she asked. "Why offer that?"

"Because I like to give people choices," the Moth said. "Real choices, with real consequences. Most people, faced with two doors, will choose the one marked 'Safety.' They'll take the certain thing over the possible thing. They'll trade their dreams for the guarantee of another day alive."

He leaned forward.

"I want to know which kind of person you are, Miss Tepes. Do you take the easy path? Or do you walk into the fire?"

The silence that followed was absolute.

Teyra looked at Ash. He was watching her, his face unreadable. The wound on his shoulder pulsed, blue light guttering under his coat. He had hours left. Maybe less.

And she had a choice.

Take the Moonflower. Walk away. Live a quiet life in the shadow of a truth she would never know. Watch Ash fade into a half-existence, a ghost haunting her shop forever, never knowing who had killed him or why.

Or take the heist. Risk everything. Break into a guarded estate, steal from a lord, challenge a conspiracy that reached to the throne itself. Face the real possibility of death, hers, Ash's, maybe both.

Safety on one side. Fire on the other.

Her grandmother, who had taught her everything about necromancy, who had believed the dead deserved the same dignity as the living.

Thomas, the soldier ghost, seventeen and six hundred miles from home.

Professor Whitmore in his cage, broken and remade, still remembering her name.

Ash, dying in front of her, asking why.

"I want to know," she said. "I need to know. The throne doesn't matter. Whatever's in that book doesn't matter. A good man was murdered, and the people who did it are still out there, and if I walk away now, I'm saying his life didn't count."

She met the Moth's empty eyes.

"Give me the key."

The Moth studied her for a long moment. Then he smiled, a real smile this time, something that might have been respect rather than the predatory curl she'd seen before. Beneath it, so brief she nearly missed it, something else—the exhale of a man whose long bet had just paid off.

"I knew I liked you, Miss Tepes."

He slid the wooden box across the desk. Teyra took it, feeling the weight of the black iron key inside. "It opens every lock in the estate," the Moth said, as if reading her next question. "The vault is the only door that asks for more than the key."

"The jar on the shelf," Teyra said. "The one with nothing in it."

The Moth's eyes flickered, a crack in the mask, gone as fast as it appeared.

"A sample," he said. His voice was careful now, stripped of its usual theatrical amusement. "Dug up from the lowest foundation of the Palace. Where the old wards are thinnest." He paused, selecting his words with a collector's precision. "It ate through the first three containers I tried. Glass, iron, warded crystal, and consumed them all. The current jar holds only because I convinced a dying saint to bless it."

He turned back to his pocket watch.

"It's growing, Miss Tepes. Slowly, but growing. And it is very, very hungry."

A silence. Then the Moth remembered himself, and the mask of pleasant menace slid back into place.

"The Moonflower." The Moth pushed the velvet pouch toward her. "Brew it tonight. It will stabilize him and seal the wound. You have two days to complete the heist. After that, the price changes."

"Changes how?"

"I'm sure you'd rather not find out." He stood, the audience clearly at an end. "There's a back exit through the Bone District. I'd suggest using it. You have followers."

Teyra stiffened. "Followers?"

"Someone has been tracking you since you left the Conservatory. They're very good. I only spotted them because I know what to look for." His eyes glittered. "Someone wants to know where you're going. What you're doing. Who you're talking to."

"Who?"

"Now, Miss Tepes. If I told you that, it would ruin the surprise." He gestured toward the silk curtain at the back of the tent. "Two days. Don't disappoint me. I dislike disappointment. It makes me creative."

Teyra took the pouch, feeling the magic radiating through the velvet. Heavy and warm, alive with power.

"One more question," she said.

The Moth raised an eyebrow.

"The book in the vault. Whatever it is. If it's valuable enough to orchestrate all this, why haven't you stolen it yourself?"

The Moth smiled.

"Because I can't open the vault, Miss Tepes. I'm not a Thornwick." He spread his gloved hands. "Even I have limitations. Very few, but they exist."

Teyra stared at him. The pieces were clicking together in her head, ugly, sharp-edged pieces, the kind that cut you when they fit. The Moth had known about the vault. Known about the blood-lock. Known that only a Thornwick could open it. And the moth-embroidered bookmark had appeared in the Archives the same night Ash had appeared in her shop. The Moth had sensed the ghost, or heard about it, and within hours he'd planted the bookmark where she'd find it. Twenty-five years of patience, and he'd still moved faster than she could think.

"You knew," she said. "Before he walked into my shop. Before I anchored him. You already knew a Thornwick ghost was wandering Athergard, and you were waiting to see who caught him."

The Moth's dead eyes narrowed, the first truly unguarded reaction she'd seen from him, the brief, sharp attention of a man recalculating someone's threat level.

He didn't answer.

"The fire was twenty-five years ago," Teyra continued, her voice hardening. "You've been looking for a way into that vault ever since. Twenty-five years of planning. And when Ash's ghost surfaced, the one Thornwick who could open a blood-lock from the other side of death, you planted a bookmark in the Archives where you knew I'd find it. Pointed me toward the records that would make me ask the right questions. Let me think I was investigating when I was really being steered."

Silence. The pocket watch ticked.

The Moth's voice had lost its theatrical warmth. Flatter now. More careful. "You want to know why."

It wasn't a question.

"Twenty-five years ago, before the fire, before any of this, I was a man named Aldric Vane." The Moth's eyes crinkled, maybe amusement, maybe mockery. "Aldric Vane was a scribe. A records keeper. He worked in the Cathedral archives, cataloging prophecies, copying texts, doing the tedious work that keeps civilizations running. He was nobody important. Nobody worth remembering."

"What happened to him?"

"He found a discrepancy. A prophecy that had two versions, an original and a copy that didn't quite match. Being a diligent man, Aldric brought this to the attention of his superiors. He thought they would be grateful." The Moth laughed, that dry, rustling sound. "They tried to kill him. Burned down his home with his family inside. His wife and daughter. His son, who was seven years old and dreaming of becoming a knight."

The room was silent. Even the pocket watch had stopped.

"Aldric survived. The fire took his face, his identity, his ability to feel anything the way a living man should."

Seven years old, Teyra thought. *The same age Ashen had been. The same fire.* "But it gave him something in return. Twenty-five years of purpose." Those dead eyes fixed on Teyra. "So when you say I steered you, Miss Tepes, you are correct. But perhaps you understand now that the hand on the wheel has been shaking the entire time."

"I found your prince," the Moth said, quieter now. "Ashen. When he was grown, when he came back to the city and began asking questions about the fire. I was building toward the moment when he could act."

A pause. "Greythorn moved first. I was one day behind. I have been one day behind for twenty-five years."

He waved a hand, tired now rather than dismissive.

"Two days, Miss Tepes. The clock is ticking."

The silk curtain fell closed behind them, cutting off the sound of his dry, rustling laughter.

The back exit led through tunnels that were older than anything Teyra had seen in the market, carved stone worn smooth by water and time, the walls covered in carvings that predated the current age.

She didn't look at the carvings. They made her eyes hurt.

Ash walked beside her, stronger now that they were away from the market's spectral pull. His wound was still spreading, but slower, the presence of the Moonflower in her pocket seeming to calm it, the magic radiating outward like a gentle tide.

"You didn't have to do that," he said.

Teyra didn't answer.

"The other option. The safe one. You could have taken it. Lived a quiet life. Watched me haunt your shop for the rest of your days." He was looking straight ahead, his face unreadable. "Why didn't you?"

"Because it wouldn't be a life," Teyra said. "It would be hiding. Waiting around pretending that everything was fine while the truth rotted away in some vault somewhere."

She stopped walking. Turned to face him.

"You deserve to know who killed you. You deserve to know why. And I..."

She hesitated.

Ash was watching her with eyes that had seen his own death, that had watched the woman he loved drive a blade through his heart.

"You're not soft," he said. "You're the strongest person I've ever met."

A shift in her chest, warm and sharp and completely undeniable.

She didn't clear her throat. Didn't reach for a cup of something. Didn't deflect into business or bravado or the comfortable fiction that she was only here because he needed her help.

She let it sit. The wanting. Her, alive. Him, borrowed time. Four days.

She didn't look away.

"Teyra."

Roughness had crept into his voice. His eyes held hers, and she saw it in him too, the same recognition, the same doomed wanting.

"Thank you," he said. "For choosing the hard path. For believing I was worth saving in the first place."

A week ago, she would have deflected. Said something cutting and clever and wrong.

"You are," she said. Nothing else. No joke to soften it.

They stood in the dark tunnel with the Moonflower warm in her pocket and the weight of everything unsaid between them, and for once, the silence wasn't uncomfortable. It was just honest.

So that was the shape of it. The Moth had given them the Moonflower to save Ash and a key to enter the vault. The price was the book inside, proof of a conspiracy that had killed a royal family and corrupted a kingdom. Two days to steal it.

"We still have a heist to plan," she said eventually. But the words were soft. An acknowledgment that the world was still there, waiting, and they owed it their attention even if they'd rather stay in this moment a little longer.

They walked on through the tunnels, the black iron key heavy in her hand.

Behind them, somewhere in the dark, a presence was watching.

A presence that smiled in the shadows and took notes and waited for its moment.

Cold night air hit Teyra's face like a splash of graveyard rain. They were aboveground, standing in a mausoleum in the Greymarch Cemetery, ivy-choked and forgotten, a fitting place for a necromancer and a ghost to crawl out of. The storm had broken while they were below. Athergard spread out before them, wet and glittering, the gas lamps of a thousand streets flickering to life in the dusk.

But the city looked different from up here. The divide was visible, and from this height she could see it rather than merely feel it. The Garden District gleaming clean on the upper slopes, its rooftops sharp against the pale sky. And below it, the lower city sitting in a haze that was somewhere between fog and smoke, the grey film risen to a mist, hovering over the rooftops of Hollow Stair and the Tanners' Quarter like a low ceiling. The Unsettled, visible from a distance in a way she'd never noticed before. From up here, it looked like the lower city was slowly being smothered.

They had the Moonflower. They had their lives, barely. Everything else was gone.

"Where do we go?" Ash asked.

Teyra considered. They couldn't go back to the shop, Seraphine's people would be watching it. They couldn't go to any of her usual contacts, the Moth had made it clear they were being followed.

"I know a place," Lenore said. The raven had been silent through most of the market, but now she stirred on Teyra's shoulder, ruffling her injured wing. "A safe house, old and abandoned. Almost no one knows about it. The old underground knew, it belonged to one of Whitmore's colleagues, but that was before the purges."

"Where?"

"The Tanners' Quarter. There's a building, used to be a leather works, before the fire. Built with features. Hidden rooms. Warded spaces. It's been empty for twenty years, but the wards still hold."

Teyra nodded. It would do. It would have to do.

"Lead the way."

They moved through the cemetery, past headstones slick with rain and monuments to the dead. The last light was bleeding out of the sky, painting the western clouds in shades of bruised purple and fading gold.

Two days. They had two days to plan a heist, break into a guarded estate, steal a book from a blood-locked vault, and escape with their lives.

And somewhere in the city, their followers were out there. Watching. Waiting.

"Ash," Teyra said as they walked. "When we get to the safe house, I need to brew the Moonflower. It's going to hurt. The magic is strong, stronger than anything I've worked with before."

"Will it heal the wound?"

"It should. If we're lucky." She paused. "But that's not what I wanted to tell you."

He looked at her.

"While I'm brewing, you need to rest. Really rest, the kind ghosts don't usually allow themselves. Actual dormancy. Let your form go still. Stop fighting to stay solid."

"And if I can't wake up?"

"Then I'll wake you." She met his eyes. "I promise."

He held her gaze. Then he nodded.

"I trust you," he said.

Three words that shouldn't have meant anything.

But coming from a man who had been murdered by the woman he loved, who had spent five years lost in the dark, who had every reason to never trust anyone again, they meant everything.

Teyra turned away before he could see her face.

"Come on," she said, her voice rougher than she intended. "We're burning daylight."

But she didn't move. Not yet.

They sat on the steps of the mausoleum instead, a necromancer and a ghost, perched on the threshold of someone else's death, watching the city settle into night. The stone was cold. The ivy smelled green and alive. Somewhere below them, a church bell tolled eight times, each note hanging in the wet air like something you could touch.

Ash's shoulder was almost touching hers. The gap between them felt smaller than it used to.

"I've never hidden in a graveyard before," he said.

"You're a ghost. This is basically your natural habitat."

"That's offensive."

"You're literally dead."

"Rude." But the corner of his mouth twitched. "I expected more sympathy from a medical professional."

"I'm a necromancer, not a therapist."

"The line between those two things seems thinner every day."

She almost laughed. Almost. The sound caught somewhere in her chest and turned into something else, something caught between a sob and a laugh. Just the sheer stupid relief of being alive and tired and sitting next to someone who mattered.

"Ash."

"Mm."

"When this is over, if we survive, I'm going to sleep for a week."

"Only a week?"

"Fine. A month. I'm going to close the shop and sleep for a month and not talk to a single dead person."

"Present company excluded?"

She looked at him. At the the fading edges and the stubborn, impossible solidity of a man who refused to stop existing.

"Present company excluded," she said.

The bell tolled again. The city below them was filling with smoke and noise and the ordinary business of being alive. They had two days. They had no plan. They had each other, which was either everything or nothing, depending on how the next forty-eight hours went.

They walked on toward the Tanners' Quarter, toward the safe house, toward whatever came next.

And behind them, in the shadow of a mausoleum, a presence that was neither human nor ghost watched them go.

It had been following them since the Conservatory.

It had been watching. Listening. And it had learned enough.

And now, finally, it knew where they were going.

It smiled, a thin, cold smile, and melted back into the shadows.

The hunt was just beginning.

Chapter Six

THE SPACE BETWEEN HEARTBEATS

DAY FOUR, NIGHT: FOUR DAYS REMAIN

T HE SAFE HOUSE SMELLED like old leather and forgotten things.

It had been a tannery once, Lenore was right about that. The building sat in a narrow alley in the Tanners' Quarter, squeezed between a chandler's shop and a tenement so decrepit it was held together by stubbornness alone. The facade was unremarkable. Warped wooden siding with windows boarded over, a door that hung slightly crooked on its hinges.

But inside, past the first room full of dust, cobwebs, and the desiccated corpse of a cat that had died sometime during the previous century, was another place altogether.

The hidden door was behind a false wall in the old curing room, and Lenore had to show them the pressure point, a brick that looked identical to every other brick until you pushed it and heard the soft click of a mechanism older than the current monarchy. The wall swung inward on silent hinges, revealing a staircase that descended into the earth.

The space below was surprisingly livable

A single large room opened before them, maybe thirty feet by twenty, carved from the bedrock beneath the city. The walls were stone, smoothed by hand and covered in wards that glowed when Teyra crossed the threshold, protective magic still active after all these years. There was a fireplace built into one wall, the chimney hidden somewhere in the building above. A bed with a mattress that was old but clean, the sheets wrapped in preservation charms. A table and two chairs. A small kitchen area with a pump that, miraculously, still produced water when Teyra worked the handle.

"The previous owner had built the place with paranoia in every wall," Lenore explained, settling onto a dusty bookshelf. "He'd survived three assassination attempts before he built this place. Said he needed somewhere to vanish."

"What happened to him?" Ash asked.

"Fourth assassination attempt."

"Ah."

Teyra set her bag on the table and began unpacking. The velvet pouch of Moonflower. The black iron key in its wooden box. Her portable brewing kit, copper pot, bone stirrer, measuring spoons worn to nothing at the edges. Her hands moved automatically, the familiar motions soothing in their repetition.

"I need to brew the tea," she said, without looking at Ash. "It'll take about an hour. You should rest."

"I'm fine."

"You're dying." She finally looked at him, and her chest tightened at the sight. He was standing in the center of the room, his coat still torn at the shoulder, the wound beneath pulsing with that sickly blue light. The cracks had spread further while they'd traveled, reaching toward his collarbone now, thin lines of cold fire tracing patterns beneath his spectral skin. "You've been dying since the Conservatory. The only reason you're still standing is stubbornness."

"It's a family trait."

"Sit down, Ash."

He sat.

Teyra lit the fire, using kindling stacked beside the hearth, dry despite the years, another gift from the paranoid necromancer who'd built this place. The flames caught quickly, filling the room with warmth and dancing shadows. She filled the copper pot with water from the pump, set it over the flames, and began preparing the Moonflower.

The petals were beautiful, pure white and luminescent, each one cut with the same cold precision as frost. They smelled of rain and midnight, stirring a deep, recognizing frost in her bones. Death magic, concentrated and refined. And when she held them, her collected fragments stirred too, the phantom blade between her ribs, the shoulder ache from the Salt-Shot, Thomas's homesickness, all of them shifting and settling like sleeping animals disturbed by a sound they half-recognized. The Moonflower was speaking their language. The dead things inside her were listening.

"You've done this before," Ash said. "Brewed illegal tea for dying ghosts."

"No." Teyra measured out the petals with careful precision, ignoring the way her hands wanted to tremble. "I've brewed anchoring tea. Standard formulas, approved by the Guild This..." She held up a petal, watching the light shine through it. "This is something else. What I gave you before was two-year-old dust, barely three days' worth. This is fresh, and there's enough of it. The Moonflower only grows in places where violent death has soaked into the soil. Battlefields, execution grounds, massacre sites. It absorbs the death magic and concentrates it."

"That sounds horrifying."

"It is. And the Moth's wrong about the timeline." She said it carefully, wishing it weren't true. "A month, he said. Maybe two. But that's not how anchoring works. The first brew, the one I made the night you walked in, that set the tether. Seven days. That's the ceiling. The original anchor determines how long the spirit can exist in the physical world, and no amount of fresh Moonflower changes that." She held his gaze. "What the fresh petals do is give you strength within those seven days. Stability. Enough power to survive what's coming. But the clock doesn't reset. We still have four days."

Ash was quiet for a moment. "Then why did the Moth say a month?"

"Because the Moth trades in secrets, and anchor decay is outside his expertise. Or because he wanted us to take the deal without asking too many questions." She dropped the petal into the water.

The liquid immediately darkened, turning from clear to silver to a deep, iridescent black. The moment the petal touched the surface, Teyra felt a pull, something old and wordless. The Moonflower was drawing on her Resonance channels, feeding on the borrowed fragments as though they had been laid aside for it. She could feel Thomas's homesickness feeding the brew, the widow's loneliness deepening the color, the little girl's winter-cold sharpening the magic's edge. She was the conduit, and the borrowed dead were the current flowing through her.

No wonder the Academy banned this. No wonder Meridia had broken. The magic used everything you carried, not just you but every fragment lodged in your channels.

"But it's also the only thing that will save your life. Or your existence. Whatever."

Ash watched her work in silence. The fire crackled. The water hissed, heating. Outside, somewhere far above them, the distant sounds of the city drifted down to them, a cart rattling over cobblestones, a dog barking, the low murmur of voices from the tenement next door.

The ordinary noise of a world that didn't know two fugitives were hiding beneath it, brewing forbidden magic in a dead man's sanctuary.

"Teyra."

She looked up.

"Thank you," Ash said. "For all of this. For saving me. For choosing the hard path." He stopped, struggling for words. "For not giving up on me."

"Don't thank me yet. We still have to survive the heist."

"I know. But even if we don't, even if this all goes wrong and we die in that vault, I want you to know that these days have been..." He trailed off, his eyes reflecting the firelight. "I don't remember my life. My family, my home, the people I loved. But I'll remember you. Whatever happens, I'll remember you."

She turned back to the pot, stirring the blackening liquid with her bone stirrer, her throat tight. "The tea needs to steep for forty minutes. After that, you drink it, and then you sleep. Real sleep, the kind ghosts don't usually allow themselves. Your body, your form, needs time to integrate the magic."

"And what will you do while I'm sleeping?"

"Watch over you." She said it without thinking, and then felt heat rise in her cheeks. "I mean, someone needs to make sure the magic takes properly. If there's a reaction, if something goes wrong..."

"You'll be here."

"Yes."

Ash smiled. It was a small thing, barely a curve of his lips, but it transformed his face. Made him look younger. More human. "Then I'll sleep well."

She watched the pot in silence, counting the seconds as her grandmother had taught her. When the liquid turned the color of a moonless night, so dark it seemed to absorb the firelight, she knew.

Teyra poured it into a ceramic cup she'd found in one of the cupboards, plain white, chipped at the rim, probably older than she was. The steam smelled of graveyards and winter nights, laced with an unsettling sweetness underneath.

She held it out to him. "Slowly. Don't gulp. The magic needs time to spread through your system."

Ash took the cup with both hands. His fingers overlapped hers for a moment, just a moment, and she felt the cold of him, the strange not-quite-solidity of a ghost made flesh. His eyes met hers over the rim.

"Will it hurt?"

"Probably." She couldn't lie to him. "Healing magic always hurts. You're essentially forcing your body, your form, to rebuild itself. The Grave-Chill will hit you hard. You might feel like you're freezing to death. You might feel like you're dying all over again."

"Wonderful."

"But when you wake up, the wound will be sealed. The cracks will be gone. You'll be solid again, really solid, the kind of solid you haven't managed since the Conservatory."

He looked at the dark liquid, then back at her. "Will you stay? While I drink it?"

"Of course."

He raised the cup to his lips and drank.

His eyes went wide. His back arched. A sound came out of his throat, caught between a scream and a gasp, and blue light blazed from the wound on his shoulder, bright enough to make Teyra shield her eyes.

She grabbed his arm, steadying him. The cold that radiated from his skin was worse than anything she'd felt before, worse than the moment they'd met, worse than the Conservatory. It burned her fingers, sent needles of ice racing up her arm to her elbow.

She didn't let go.

"I've got you," she said, her voice steady despite the pain. "I've got you. Breathe through it."

"Can't…" He was shaking violently, the cup falling from his fingers, breaking on the stone floor. The dark liquid spilled out, absorbed immediately by the warded stone. "Can't breathe…"

"Don't fight it." She moved closer, supporting his weight as he slumped forward. Her hands were going numb from the cold, but she didn't care. "Just hold on. The worst part will be over soon."

The blue light pulsed twice, then faded. The cracks in his skin knit together with a sound like ice forming on a lake, the fractured lines sealing shut one by one. The wound on his shoulder closed, the torn ectoplasm smoothing over until there was nothing left but unmarked spectral flesh.

Ash collapsed against her.

For a long moment, they stayed like that, his head on her shoulder, her arms around him, his cold weight pressing into her warmth. She could feel his form settling, becoming more real with each passing second. The instability that had plagued him since the Conservatory was gone, replaced by wholeness.

"Better?" she asked.

"Better." The word came out scraped raw. "I feel heavy. Like I actually exist."

"You do exist. You always existed." She helped him to the bed, lowering him onto the mattress. His eyes were already closing, the healing magic pulling him toward sleep. "Rest now. I'll be here when you wake up."

"Promise?"

"Promise."

His eyes closed. The tremor in him eased, his form settling into stillness. Within seconds, he was asleep.

Teyra sat on the edge of the bed, watching him. The firelight played across his features, softening the sharp angles of his face. He looked peaceful. Young.

Then, twenty minutes later, the cold came.

This was deeper, wronger than anything she'd felt sleeping near a ghost. The room temperature plummeted in seconds, and frost began crawling across the stone floor in patterns she'd never seen. Nothing like the crystalline webs of Ash's emotions or the random scatter of spectral cold. These were concentric spirals, moving inward toward the center of the room, toward the bed where Ash lay.

His form was almost transparent, pulsing in and out of visibility like a candle in a draft. And his lips were moving. Whispering words in a language she didn't recognize, words older than Athergard, older than the monarchy, older than anything that belonged in a human mouth.

"Ash." She shook him. His skin was ice, a cold that burned beyond his usual chill. "Ash, wake up."

His eyes opened. For one terrible heartbeat, they were empty. Void-dark, holes in his face where eyes should have been, and behind them a depth that went down and down and down forever.

Then he blinked, and he was himself again. Grey eyes. Human eyes. Wide and shaken.

"I was dreaming," he said, the words unsteady. "I was somewhere dark. Somewhere deep. And something down there was calling me home."

He sat up, running his hands over his face. The frost on the floor was already melting.

"It knew my name, Teyra. It knew my name."

She didn't know what to say. She took his hand instead, and held it until the shaking stopped.

Four days. Had it only been four days? It felt like a lifetime.

Her hand hovered over his cheek. She wanted to touch him, to feel him under her fingers, solid, proof that he was here and that any of this was happening.

But she remembered the rules. Strong emotions disrupted the anchor. If she touched him now, with the nightmare still hanging in his eyes, with him this raw...

She pulled her hand back.

"Idiot," she muttered to herself. "Absolute idiot, Teyra Tepes."

She stood up, moving to the table, and began cleaning up the spilled tea and broken cup. Her hands were still numb from the cold, tingling as feeling returned. Her head ached, the familiar pulse of frost settling behind her eyes.

The brewing had cost her. It always did. But this time, it was worth it.

Ash slept for five hours.

Teyra spent the first two cleaning the safe house. It was busy work, sweeping dust and checking wards, organizing the meager supplies they'd brought, but it kept her hands occupied and her mind from wandering to dangerous places.

The third hour, she tried to sleep herself. The bed was large enough for two, she could have curled up on the far edge, put distance between them, but she couldn't bring herself to do it.

Instead, she dragged one of the wooden chairs to the bedside and sat there, watching him breathe.

Watching over him. Like she'd promised.

By the fourth hour, she was too restless to sit still. She found a deck of cards in one of the cupboards, old, the edges worn soft, the backs decorated with a pattern of moons and stars that had faded to near-invisibility. She shuffled them absently, the familiar snap and whisper of cardstock soothing her nerves.

Ash woke during the fifth hour.

He came awake slowly, like someone climbing the last rungs of the ladder they'd descended hours ago. His eyes opened and blinked, then focused on the ceiling of the safe house. Then he turned his head and saw her.

"You're still here," he said, his voice rough with sleep.

"I promised."

He sat up slowly, testing his body, his form. He looked at his shoulder, at the place where the wound had been. Nothing but smooth, solid flesh. He flexed his fingers, made a fist, opened it again.

"It worked," he breathed. "I feel whole."

"The Moonflower is powerful stuff." Teyra set down the cards, trying to look casual despite the relief flooding through her. "How do you feel otherwise? Any pain? Dizziness? Uncontrollable urge to destroy furniture?"

"No." He swung his legs over the side of the bed, sitting up fully. "I feel good. Better than I've felt since I woke up." He looked at her, his grey eyes warm in the firelight. "Better than I've felt in twenty years, probably."

"You don't remember the last twenty years."

"True. But I imagine they weren't great." He noticed the cards on the table. "What's that?"

"Found them in a drawer." Teyra picked up the deck, shuffling it again. "I used to play with my grandmother, When I was little. She said it helped with focus, keeping track of the cards, reading the patterns. Good training for a necromancer."

"What game?"

"Lots of them. Gin rummy. Poker. A thing she called Graveyard Patience, which I'm pretty sure she made up because it involved laying out cards in the shape of a coffin." Teyra smiled at the memory. "She was odd. I loved her."

"Will you teach me?"

The question caught her off guard. "What?"

"Teach me." Ash gestured at the cards. "I can't remember if I knew how to play. Can't remember much of anything. But I'd like to learn. If you're willing."

Teyra looked at him, at this man, this dead prince, this ghost who had stumbled into her life and turned it upside down. He was asking her to teach him a card game. In a hidden safe house beneath the city. While they waited to commit a heist that would probably kill them both.

It was absurd. It was exactly what she needed.

"Alright," she said. "But I warn you, I cheat."

"I'd expect nothing less."

Ash picked up the deck, his movements fascinatingly clumsy for a man who could catch a falling woman in mid-air. He fumbled the shuffle, the cards whispering against each other with a soft, friction-heavy sound that was too loud in the quiet room. He was reveling in it, the simple tactile resistance of paper against skin that he had been denied for five years.

"It's strange," he murmured, abandoning the shuffle to spread the cards across the scarred wooden table. "I remember the strategy. I remember the rules of Whist, Rummy, and Bridge, but I couldn't remember the texture. It feels dry and rough. Like holding a handful of dried leaves."

Teyra watched him, the firelight catching the concentration in his furrowed brow. The damp walls of the tannery and the Hessians felt a thousand miles away, pushed back by the simple, domestic reality of a ghost learning to use his hands again.

For two hours they played.

Teyra taught him gin rummy first because it was simple, quick to learn, and good for building the rhythms of play. Ash picked it up quickly, his sharp mind grasping the patterns faster than she expected, and by the third hand he was winning.

"You're a natural," she said, grudgingly impressed. "Or you're cheating."

"I thought you said cheating was allowed."

"I said I cheat. I didn't say you could."

He laughed, a real laugh, unguarded and warm. The sound made her chest flutter.

She caught herself memorizing the way his face changed when he laughed—the crescent scar lifting, the grey eyes losing their storm. Three days from now he might not exist. She wanted to remember this.

They moved on to poker. This was harder, bluffing required reading faces, and Ash's expressions were still learning how to be human again. But he was a quick study, and by the fifth hand, he'd figured out her tells.

"You touch your ear when you're bluffing," he said, laying down a winning hand. "And you shuffle the cards faster when you have a good hand."

"Damn." Teyra tossed her cards onto the table. "My grandmother would be ashamed."

"Your grandmother sounds like she was remarkable."

"She was." Teyra gathered the cards, stacking them neatly. "She's the one who taught me necromancy. The Academy just gave me four years of theory and a Second Class license. She taught me the real stuff. The heart of it."

"What's the heart of it?"

Teyra considered. The fire had burned low, casting long shadows across the room. Outside, the city had gone quiet, deep night, the hours when even Athergard slept.

Her grandmother's hands came back if she closed her eyes. Broad hands, flour-dusted more often than not, because Maren Tepes had believed baking and necromancy ran on the same principles—patience, warmth, and knowing when to let the fire do its work, you put warmth into something and trusted it to rise. She'd smelled of bread and dried sage, and she'd brewed her teas humming tunelessly, and when Teyra was small and frightened of the ghosts that whispered in the shop walls, Maren had pulled her into her lap and said, They're just lonely, love. Loneliness sounds like that. And then she'd sing the old rhyme, the one every Hollow

Stair child knew: *Leave a cup and shut the latch, the dead don't knock if you leave their match.* Teyra hadn't understood it then. She understood it now.

She'd died in the chair by the window. Quietly. The way she'd done everything, without fuss, without asking anyone to carry her weight. Teyra had come downstairs one morning and found the tea still warm and her grandmother still smiling and Lenore sitting on the back of the chair, silent for the first and only time in her life.

"Compassion," she said finally. "She used to say that death was just a door. A transition. And a necromancer's job was to help people through that door. To give them dignity. To give them peace."

"That's not what they taught at the Academy."

"No. The Academy taught control. Domination. The dead are tools, they said. Resources to be used." Teyra's chin lifted. "My grandmother disagreed. She said the dead were people. Scared, confused people who didn't understand what had happened to them. They deserved kindness."

She looked at Ash.

"That's why I helped you. You weren't a prince to me, and I didn't care about conspiracies or adventure. You were lost, and you deserved better than to fade away alone in my shop."

Ash was silent. The firelight flickered across his face, picking out the silver threads in his dark hair, the sharp line of his jaw.

"You try to hide it," he said. "The sarcasm. The practicalities. The way you pretend it's all just business." His grey eyes caught the firelight. "But you can't help yourself. You care about everyone. Strangers and ghosts. People you've never met."

"It's a character flaw."

"It's the best thing about you."

The space was suddenly smaller.

Ash reached out.

His hand stopped an inch from her cheek, the same distance as always, the Touch Barrier they'd learned to live around. His flickering was instability, his anchor losing grip. This was deliberate resistance, as if the magic itself had drawn a line between the living and the dead and refused to let them cross it. But this time, his fingers trembled. This time, his eyes were fixed on hers with an intensity that made her breath catch.

"I want to touch you," he said, his voice rough. "More than I've wanted anything since I woke up. More than answers." His hand hovered there. The cold radiating from his skin prickled against her cheek. "But I'm terrified that if I do, if I let myself feel this, I'll flicker out. And I'll hurt you."

Teyra's heart was pounding so hard she was sure he could hear it.

"What if you don't?" she whispered. "What if the Moonflower made you stable enough? What if..."

"What if it didn't?"

She didn't have an answer. She didn't know. The magic was unpredictable, the rules unclear. He might be solid enough to withstand strong emotion now. Or he might not. There was only one way to find out.

She reached up and closed the distance between them.

Her fingers touched his cheek.

The cold was immediate but different than before. The first time she'd touched him, in the shop, it had burned like frostbite. Now it was deep and strange, like pressing her hand against winter glass, but bearable. Almost warm, if she focused on the pressure of his skin rather than the chill.

She understood, dimly, what was happening. The Barrier existed because Teyra was different from a railing or a table or Seraphine's arm. The Resonance bond between them turned every touch into a channel, her life energy flowing into his death, his weight flowing into her warmth, and the Barrier regulated that exchange. It kept the living and the dead from pouring into each other until there was nothing left to distinguish them.

His skin settled under her hand, rough with stubble, all sharp cheekbone and impossible reality. Real and solid and here.

He gasped, a sharp intake of breath that he didn't need, and his eyes went wide.

But he didn't flicker.

His form held. The anchor held. He was solid and real and present, and she was touching him, and nothing was breaking, nothing was falling apart.

His hand came up to cover hers. His fingers intertwined with hers, pressing her palm against his cheek. His skin was cold, but his grip was warm somehow, desperate and gentle at the same time.

"Teyra," he breathed.

And then there was a pounding on the door.

They were on their feet in seconds.

The pounding came again, urgent and desperate, the sound of fists hitting wood with more force than precision. Someone was at the entrance to the safe house. Someone who knew where to find the hidden door.

"Stay here," Teyra hissed, grabbing the poker from the fireplace. "If it's Hessians..."

"If it's Hessians, I'm not letting you face them alone."

"Ash..."

"Not negotiable."

The pounding stopped. A voice came through the door, muffled by the stone, but recognizable.

"Tepes. I know you're in there. Open the door before I bleed out on your threshold."

She knew that voice.

"It's Seraphine," she breathed.

Ash's face went hard. The warmth of the moment before vanished, and a cold, dangerous edge took its place. His hands clenched into fists at his sides.

"Don't open it."

"She said she's bleeding..."

"She murdered me, Teyra. She drove a blade through my heart and smiled while she did it. Whatever's happening to her, she deserves it."

"For what it's worth," Lenore said from the bookshelf, her voice unusually quiet, "I've never seen a trap bleed quite that convincingly."

"Ash." Teyra grabbed his arm, forcing him to look at her.

"I'm not saying we trust her. I'm not saying we forgive her. But if she's dying on our doorstep, if we let her die when we could have helped, what does that make us?"

"Survivors."

"Monsters."

He recoiled from the word, something flickering behind his eyes, the ghost of a man who hadn't always been made of what he'd become.

Teyra turned and walked to the door.

Seraphine looked like death, and the ugly kind at that, the real kind. Her sea-green dress was ruined, torn in a dozen places, soaked through with blood that was still spreading. Her dark hair had come loose from its elaborate pins, hanging in matted tangles around a face that was grey with blood loss. Her eyes, when they met Teyra's, were glazed with physical effort.

The Ouroboros was still on her wrist, the gold dulled with blood, the serpent's ruby eyes dark for the first time. Whatever power the bracelet carried, it had been spent getting her here.

She was leaning against the doorframe, one hand pressed against her side, blood seeping through her fingers.

"Surprised?" she managed, her voice barely above a whisper. "One of the Moth's watchers found me. He sells to everyone, you know." She winced, shifting her weight. "The Hessians turned on me. Apparently there were new orders. After the Conservatory."

"New orders from who?"

"Take a guess." Seraphine laughed, a wet, rattling sound. "Greythorn always was efficient. The moment I interfered with the kill shot, I became a liability. Loose ends... he doesn't tolerate loose ends." She paused, breathing through what was clearly a fresh spike of agony. "Two of them were waiting in my quarters. I killed the first with the maintenance override, the shutdown phrase I'd memorized when I was still Commander. The second one got close enough to fire. Salt-Shot Cannon, point-blank. The chassis exploded when I put my sword through its boiler." She looked down at the blood seeping through her fingers. "I was already down when the third found me. I killed it from the floor. Don't ask me how. After that it was just walking. Walking and bleeding and trying to remember how the streets connected."

She swayed. Teyra caught her before she could fall, her arms going around the taller woman's waist. Seraphine was heavier than she looked, all that muscle beneath the silk, all that training, all that deadly grace, and her blood was soaking into Teyra's dress, warm and smelling of copper.

"Ash," Teyra called over her shoulder. "Help me get her inside."

Silence.

"Ash."

He appeared in the doorway, his face unreadable. For a long moment, he just stood there, staring at the woman who had killed him. The woman who had been his betrothed. The woman who had destroyed his life and was now bleeding out on the threshold.

His eyes dropped to the wound. Ragged, torn—shrapnel, not a blade. Hessian damage. He'd smashed an iron table into one of those machines at the Conservatory, and the thought settled into him like cold water. Had that been the one that turned on her?

The people who had ordered his death had just tried to kill her too.

His jaw set. The enemy of my enemy.

Then, slowly, he reached down and took Seraphine's other arm.

Together, they carried her inside.

As they lowered her through the doorway, Seraphine's hand brushed against Ash's arm, the first time they had touched since the night she'd killed him. She flinched as if burned, and when Teyra looked at her face, she saw tears cutting tracks through the blood and grime.

"I'm sorry." Seraphine said it once. Once, and only once, without elaboration. She said it as she'd file a report, factual and final and nowhere near enough.

Ash said nothing. But his grip on her arm didn't loosen.

They laid her on the table, the only surface large enough, the bed still rumpled from Ash's healing sleep. Blood immediately began pooling beneath her, dripping onto the stone floor. Her breathing was shallow, rapid, the sound of lungs trying to remember a rhythm they'd lost.

"You want to know why," Seraphine said. Her eyes were on the ceiling, glassy with the effort of staying conscious, but her voice was steady, the voice of a woman who had rehearsed this in order to survive saying it.

"We know why," Ash said. "The prophecy. The curse."

"No. You know the excuse. The official intelligence assessment. The briefing I was given." She coughed, wet and rattling, and blood flecked her lips. "You don't know that I went back, three months ago. I went to the Cathedral vaults myself and found a protected partial copy—enough to compare it against the version the Greythorns gave me, enough to see they did not match." Her hand found Teyra's wrist, gripping with surprising strength. "What they told me it said and what it actually said were two very different things."

The room contracted around the silence.

"The real prophecy doesn't say a Thornwick king will destroy the kingdom. It says a Thornwick king will open the door between worlds. That's all. Open the door." Her breath hitched. "The Greythorns added the rest. The burning. The destruction. They rewrote a prophecy to turn a key into a threat, and I believed them because I was twenty-two and in love and unable to see past what losing him would mean."

"You killed me because of a forgery," Ash said. Something in his voice had worn through to nothing.

"I killed you because I thought your coronation would end the world. And I have spent every day since learning that I was wrong." She closed her eyes. "The door was always going to open. The Thornwicks were the cure, the only bloodline that could open the door and close it again. And I removed them from the board."

"Then the breach..." Teyra started.

"Is my fault." The words came out clean and precise, a blade laid on a table. "Every void-creature. Every death. Everything that's coming. I did that. Because I was right about the wrong thing, and by the time I understood, it was too late to undo it."

She opened her eyes and looked at Ash. She was offering something rawer than forgiveness or understanding. Just letting him see, a woman who had destroyed the thing she loved to save a world she'd accidentally doomed.

"So when I say I'm sorry," she whispered, "I don't mean for the murder. I mean for all of it. For everything that comes after."

Ash stared at her for a long time. Recognition moved behind his eyes. Maybe. The terrible recognition that his killer had been suffering too.

He didn't speak. He turned away.

Teyra let the silence hold. There was nothing to say that wouldn't diminish it.

"The wound," Teyra said, pulling away the ruined fabric of Seraphine's dress. "Let me see."

It was bad, worse than bad. A gash across her side, just below the ribs, deep enough to see the white gleam of bone, wide enough that Teyra could have fit three fingers inside. The edges were ragged, torn by shrapnel.

"Hessian," Seraphine confirmed through gritted teeth. "Salt-Shot Cannon. Point-blank range. The chassis exploded when I destroyed it. Shrapnel."

"You destroyed a Hessian?"

"I destroyed three." A ghost of her old arrogance surfaced across her pain-twisted face. "I was Commander of the Guard. I know their weaknesses."

"You're also dying." Teyra was already pulling supplies from her bag, bandages, antiseptic, the small kit of emergency tools she always carried. "This needs stitches. Possibly surgery. I'm a necromancer, Seraphine. I work with the dead."

"Then use what you know." Seraphine grabbed Teyra's wrist with surprising strength. "Necrotic healing. I've seen it done. You can seal the wound."

"That's... no. That's forbidden. The cost..."

"The cost is yours to pay." Seraphine's eyes were fierce despite the agony etched across her face.

Teyra's hands were already moving, reaching for the wound, positioning themselves the way her grandmother had taught her in the quiet hours after the shop closed, the knowledge passed down like a family recipe the Academy would have burned.

"Buy me a few hours. That's all. Enough to tell you what I know. Enough to help you survive what's coming."

"Help us?" Ash's voice was cold. He was standing at the foot of the table, arms crossed, his face carved from ice. "You murdered me. You destroyed my family. And now you want to help us?"

"I want to atone." Seraphine turned her head to look at him. Her eyes were wet, but her voice held by a thread. "You should hate me. That's rational. That's earned." She swallowed. "I can't undo the blade. I can give you intelligence. Layouts, ward sequences, guard rotations—everything I have."

"Five years?" Teyra frowned. "The fire was twenty-five years ago."

"The fire was twenty-five years ago. Ash's death was five." Seraphine was quiet for a long time. When she spoke, her voice gone flat, stripped of inflection and performance. Like dictating an after-action report to an empty room.

"I was fifteen when they sent me north. House Welden had him in a barn in the provinces. Skinny kid. Too-serious eyes. Practicing swordforms like his life depended on it." She paused. "I pressed a flower into a book the week before I left. Violet, from my mother's window box. Stupid, childish thing to keep." She stopped. "I don't remember when I stopped carrying it." She stopped. Started again. "It did depend on it. I just didn't know that yet."

She stared at the ceiling.

"Margit Welden. That was the woman who kept him. A minor house, no army, no title worth mentioning. She'd served the Thornwick queen before the fire and she'd sworn an oath and she was too stubborn to break it." A pause, flat as a filed blade. "When I arrived in uniform, she stepped between me and the door and told me if I'd come to take him, she'd kill me with her hands. I believed her." Another pause, and this one cost her more. "Her son was the same age. They trained together in the yard every morning. When I rode up, the two of them were sitting on a fence sharing an apple, and the Welden boy had given Ash the bigger half." Her eyes moved to Ash's face, to the scar above his left eyebrow. "Her husband's practice blade did that. You were twelve. Bled everywhere. Margit stitched it herself and told you that if you cried, she'd make you run the hill twice."

"Half my life in uniform. I can give you the operational summary or I can give you the version where I fell in love with him at sixteen and spent every year after that planning a future we were never going to get." A pause. "Five years since the blade. Some mornings I can't remember which number is worse."

Ash's expression didn't soften, but something shifted behind his eyes. "The blade. The one you used. It wasn't ordinary."

"No." Seraphine's gaze went to the wall. "Greythorn weapons division. They called it a severance. Designed to cut the soul's tether. No ghost. No afterlife. Total erasure." The words came out like items on an inventory list. "It was supposed to be clean. Five years, I believed it was."

She stopped.

"Then you walked into a tea shop in Hollow Stair." Her voice changed, just enough to hear the discipline crack. "And I realized the blade hadn't erased you. It had trapped you. Five years in the dark."

"You can't make it right. I'm dead."

"I know." Her voice cracked. "And I'm sorry. I'm so sorry, Ashen. I know those words mean nothing. I know they can't undo what I did. But I need you to hear them. I need you to know that I didn't do it because I wanted power or position or safety. I did it because I loved you, and I was unable to see past my own certainty, and I believed, I truly believed, that I was saving you from something worse."

Ash went rigid. His hands clenched at his sides.

Teyra watched him, her chest aching. She could see the war inside him written across his body, the tension in his shoulders fighting against the part of him that remembered loving this woman, the part that wanted to uncurl toward forgiveness even though forgiveness felt impossibly far.

Then Ash said finally, his voice flat, "Do it. Heal her. I want to hear what she has to say."

Teyra nodded. She pushed up her sleeves, took a deep breath, and placed her hands over Seraphine's wound.

Necrotic healing was the opposite of healing. It forced the wound shut through sheer death magic, brutal and scarring. And it cost the healer dearly.

Teyra closed her eyes and reached for the cold inside her.

It was always there, that frozen core at the center of her being, the price she paid for her gift. But it had become a chorus. Thomas's battlefield frost. The little girl's blizzard. Ash's void-deep chill. Every spirit she'd ever channeled had left a different temperature inside her, and when she reached for the death magic now, all of them answered at once.

The cold hit her the way the Grave-Chill had the first time, years ago, except deeper and with no promise of warming.

Her teeth chattered. Frost formed on her eyelashes, on her lips, on the tips of her fingers where they pressed against Seraphine's torn flesh. Her vision narrowed to a tunnel, darkness creeping in at the edges. She felt the fragments burning as the magic consumed them, drawing on them the way a lamp draws on oil. Thomas's homesickness thinned. The widow's loneliness dimmed. The phantom blade between her ribs went cold-hot, then numb. The magic was feeding on her borrowed pain, converting it into raw necrotic force.

She pushed the magic into the wound.

Seraphine screamed.

It was a terrible sound, raw and animal, the sound of someone being burned alive from the inside. Her back arched off the table, her hands clawing at the wood, her heels drumming against the surface. Blood bubbled up around Teyra's fingers, black now instead of red, carrying the death magic into the wound.

"Hold her down!" Teyra shouted, her voice cracking with cold.

Ash grabbed Seraphine's shoulders, pinning her to the table. His face was pale, his eyes wide, watching the woman who had murdered him writhe in agony while Teyra's skin turned grey with channeled death.

The wound closed.

The edges of the gash pulled together, fused by magic that didn't care about tissue or muscle or the natural order of things. The flesh knit itself shut with wet, tearing sounds, new scar tissue forming in seconds instead of weeks.

Teyra's nose bled.

Red drops fell onto Seraphine's ruined dress, stark against the sea-green silk. Her hands were shaking, from cold rather than effort. Her fingers had gone white, then blue, the color draining from them as the cold consumed her warmth. And inside her chest, where the fragments usually sat like a collection of stones, a terrifying lightness opened in her chest, as though the magic had spent some of them. The magic had thinned the collection. Used the borrowed weight as currency and left her with less.

Relief and unease sat in her chest at the same time, impossible to separate. The fragments hurt. They always hurt. But they were hers now, the dead who'd trusted her with their feelings, the pain she'd chosen to carry. Spending them felt like a betrayal.

"Almost..." she gasped. "Almost..."

The wound sealed.

Teyra pulled her hands back and collapsed.

She hit the floor hard, her legs giving out beneath her. The world was spinning, tilting, the safe house walls swooping around her like birds. She was so cold. Colder than the moment she'd touched Ash for the first time, colder than she'd thought a living body could get.

"Teyra!" Ash was beside her in an instant, his cold hands on her face, but his cold was nothing compared to the ice in her veins, nothing compared to the frost that had consumed her from the inside out. "Teyra, look at me. Stay with me."

"'M fine," she slurred. Her tongue felt thick, clumsy. "'S just cold. So cold."

He pulled her against him, wrapping his arms around her, pressing her body against his chest. It should have made her colder, he was a ghost, a creature of death and frost, but against all logic, warmth bloomed inside her, sparked by the ferocity with which he held her.

"Don't you dare," he said fiercely, his lips against her hair. "Don't you dare fade on me, Teyra Tepes. Not after everything."

"Not fading," she managed. "'M just resting. Eyes. Resting my eyes."

She didn't remember closing them.

When she woke, she was in the bed.

Someone had moved her, Ash, presumably, and covered her with blankets. The fire had been built up, blazing warmth into the room. She was still cold, but the killing frost had receded, replaced by a manageable chill that passed for normal.

She did a quiet inventory. The phantom blade was still there, duller now, a faded ache instead of a sharp pulse. Thomas's homesickness remained, but thinner, like a photograph left too long in the sun. The little girl's winter-cold was nearly gone. Nearly. A whisper where there had been a voice.

The necrotic healing had spent them. The shapes of what they'd been were still there, like indentations in a cushion after someone stands. But the intensity was halved. The magic had taken the loudest notes and left her with an echo.

Lighter. She hated it.

She sat up, her head pounding, to find Ash sitting beside the bed, watching her with an expression of coiled tension, every line of his body drawn tight.

"You're awake," he breathed. "Thank the gods. You were out for two hours. I thought…" He stopped, his jaw tightening. "Don't ever do that again."

"I'm a necromancer. It's what I do."

"Nearly killing yourself is what you do?"

"Saving people is what I do." She looked past him to the table, where Seraphine was now sitting upright, her ruined dress pulled closed over the fresh scar on her side. The woman looked pale, exhausted, but alive. "Did it work?"

"It worked." The roughness in Seraphine's voice had steadied. "The wound is sealed. I'll have a scar the size of my hand, but I'll live." She paused. "Thank you."

"Don't thank me yet." Teyra's voice came out thin, scraped hollow by the cold. "Necrotic seals aren't real healing. The tissue is fused, held shut by death magic instead of by your own body. If you push too hard, move too fast, take a bad hit, the seal can crack. And if it cracks, it won't reseal. Not without another round of what I just did."

She swung her legs over the edge of the bed, ignoring Ash's protests, and stood on shaky feet. The room swayed for a moment, then steadied.

"You said you had information," she said, walking toward the table. "Something that would help us survive what's coming. Talk."

Seraphine looked at Ash, a long, searching look that held a lifetime of what she'd done and what she'd give to undo it.

"The prophecy," she said. Her voice held nothing but fact. "The one I killed you for. The one that says a Thornwick on the throne will bring the End of Days." She took a shaky breath. "It's a lie."

The revelation hung in the air between them, heavy and poisonous.

"A lie," Ash said flatly. "You killed me for a lie."

"Let me explain. Please." Seraphine raised a hand, forestalling his response.

She stood, wincing as the movement pulled at her new scar. She walked to the fire, her back to them, her shoulders tense.

The firelight threw her shadow against the stone wall behind her, and the shadow was wrong. Too large, too still, the shape of everything she carried projected in silhouette, bigger than the woman casting it.

"Lord Greythorn gave me the briefing himself." Seraphine's voice was flat, factual, the voice of someone who had rehearsed this in order to survive saying it. "The intelligence assessment. The prophecy text. The order. He told me you would destroy the kingdom if you took the throne.

"He told me there was no other way. That someone had to carry what his grandfather had built, that the lie was the only thing holding the walls up, and that stopping would mean admitting something that could never be admitted. And the prophecy he showed me seemed to confirm it, sealed by twelve seers, confirmed by blood divination, every test saying the same thing. Real. Inevitable. And your fault."

"But?" Teyra prompted.

"But the prophecy he showed me wasn't the original." Seraphine turned to face them. "It was a copy. And copies can be edited. Altered. Made to say things the original never said." She paused. "What I didn't know, what none of us knew, was that when Elias came of age and began studying the old texts, he had found the same falsified copy in the Estate archives. And reached the same conclusion. He thought it was real too. Greythorn had planted it there for exactly that reason."

"Someone changed the prophecy," Ash said.

"Someone removed the second half." Seraphine's eyes were bright with unshed tears. "The version I was shown said the Thornwick bloodline would destroy the kingdom. That the curse was in the blood. That killing you was the only way to stop it." Her voice cracked on the last word, recovered.

"Three months ago, I got access to a partial copy of the original. Enough to see that entire clauses had been cut. Enough to know the prophecy I'd been given was gutted and rewritten to justify exactly what I did." She drew a ragged breath. "I don't have the full original. Greythorn keeps it in the blood-vault beneath the estate, locked behind wards only Thornwick blood can open. He kept it as insurance, proof of his own family's manipulation, too dangerous to destroy and too incriminating to leave where anyone could find it. The full truth is in that vault. That's why we need to get inside."

"And you didn't know this when you killed me."

"I didn't know." Her voice cracked. "I found out three months ago. A contact in the Scribes' Guild, someone who'd seen the original prophecy before it was sealed, told me what had been removed. He told me the truth, and I realized what I'd done. What I'd been made to do."

"Three months." Teyra's voice turned to ice. "You've known for three months and done nothing?"

"Done nothing." Seraphine repeated it without the question mark, a flat correction rather than a defense. "I've been under surveillance since the coronation night. Quarters watched. Correspondence intercepted. Hessian tracking detail, three units, rotating shifts." She reeled off the details the way she'd once recited guard rotations. "The moment I confirmed the intelligence about the prophecy, I initiated a search. Every cemetery, every known haunt, every necromancer willing to take a bribe. Three months. Zero results."

"The severance blade," Ash said. "It was supposed to unmake me completely."

"Yes. And I thought it had." Seraphine met his eyes. "Until four days ago, when my informants told me a ghost matching your description had walked into a tea shop in Hollow Stair. A ghost no one should have been able to call back from where that blade sends souls."

She looked at Teyra.

"I don't know how you did it. I don't know what kind of magic pulled him out of that darkness. But the moment I heard he was alive, I knew I had one chance to make this right. One chance to tell the truth before Greythorn silenced us both."

"Made?" Teyra cut in, her voice softer now. "By whom?"

Seraphine met her eyes.

"Lord Greythorn. Elias's adoptive father. The man who took him in after the fire. The man who raised him, educated him, shaped him into what he is today." Her voice hardened. "He's been planning this since before the fire. Twenty-five years of building on his grandfather's work. Since before any of us were born."

"Planning what?"

"To put a Greythorn on the throne." Seraphine laughed, and the sound was wet and hollow. "The Thornwick line stood in his way, the rightful heirs, beloved by the people. So he manufactured a threat. He altered the prophecy to make them seem dangerous. He arranged the fire that killed the king, queen, and heirs. And when Ashen survived, when he grew up and came of age and threatened to reclaim what was his..."

"He used you to kill me," Ash finished.

"He used me." Seraphine said it the way you'd report an equipment malfunction. Then the composure cracked, and it kept going. Her jaw locked. Her eyes filled. She didn't wipe the tears. Didn't acknowledge them.

"I believed the briefing," she said. "I executed the order. I..."

She stopped. The sentence she couldn't finish said more than any speech.

Ash stood very still.

This was the moment. This was the choice. He could let the poltergeist energy consume him and tear this woman apart. She had killed him. She had destroyed his life. And she was laying herself open for whatever he decided to do.

But Seraphine had come with something other than a plea for forgiveness. She was offering the truth. The whole truth, finally, after twenty years of lies and silence. She was leaving the judgment to him.

"The vault," Ash said finally, quiet and controlled. "The Moth said there's a book in the Greythorn vault. If what you're telling us is true, if the original prophecy is in there, with the clause they removed, then that book is proof. Proof of everything."

Seraphine nodded. "It's there. Greythorn kept it as insurance, proof of his manipulation, in case he ever needed to blackmail the seers who helped him. I've seen it. I know exactly where it is."

"Then you're going to help us steal it."

Seraphine searched his face for condemnation, for the hatred she expected to find.

What she found was different.

"I'll do more than help," she said. "I'll get you inside. Greythorn held the operational briefings at the estate, I've walked those halls a dozen times. I know the ward sequences, the guard rotations, the secret passages. I know which Hessians can be disabled and where he keeps his private quarters."

She straightened, and the Commander surfaced, cold and precise.

"Twenty years of service to a hostile asset. I didn't know. Now I do. I'm going to dismantle his operation. Completely."

Silence. The fire crackled. Rain tapped against the stone above their heads.

Then Ash spoke.

"Teyra. A word."

He walked to the far side of the room. Teyra followed, leaving Seraphine at the table with her fresh scar and her offered alliance.

Ash kept his voice low. "She killed me once. On someone else's orders. With tears in her eyes and a speech about how sorry she was." His jaw was iron. "What if this is the same thing? Greythorn sends her bleeding to our door. We feel sorry for her. We trust her. She leads us straight into the vault, and the door locks behind us."

Teyra didn't answer immediately. She'd been thinking the same thing. Had been thinking it since the moment Seraphine had said *the Moth told me where you were going*. How had the Moth known about the safe house? How had Seraphine found them? A wounded woman, alone, navigating a city under martial law, straight to a hidden door that only Lenore was supposed to know about?

The math didn't add up. But Teyra had watched the Moth track their movements since the Archives. He'd had agents on the street outside her shop. He'd known they were at the Night Market before they'd arrived. A man with twenty-five years of surveillance infrastructure didn't need Lenore's address, he just needed to follow the necromancer who left his tent carrying Moonflower. And if he'd sold that information to Seraphine, it was because he'd already decided she was more useful to them alive than dead.

"You might be right," she said. "She might be lying. She might be another layer of the trap."

"Then why are we doing this?"

"Because we're out of Moonflower. We're out of time. We don't know the estate layout, the ward sequences, or the guard rotations. She does." Teyra met his eyes. "If she's telling the truth, she's the only reason we survive tomorrow. If she's lying, we were dead anyway."

Ash stared at her. Then, slowly, something like dark humor crossed his face.

"That's the worst reason to trust someone I've ever heard."

"I know."

"If she betrays us..."

"Then I was wrong about her, and we die in a vault instead of a safe house. At least the scenery will be different."

His mouth nearly twitched into a smile. It was the saddest near-smile she'd ever seen.

"Fine," he said. "But I'm watching her. Every second. And the moment something feels wrong..."

"We run."

"We run." Ash's echo was quieter. A vow rather than a plan.

They walked back to the table. Seraphine hadn't moved. She was looking at her hands, at the blood still drying beneath her fingernails, at the calluses from twenty years of swordwork, and Teyra couldn't tell if the expression on her face was calculation or patience. Both looked the same on a woman who'd spent her life performing.

"You're coming with us," Teyra said. Not a question.

"We leave before dawn," Teyra said. "Get some rest. You're going to need it."

Seraphine nodded. If she'd heard their whispered conversation, she gave no sign. But Teyra noticed she didn't ask them to trust her. Offered no reassurance, none of the comforting words a liar would have prepared.

That, more than anything, made Teyra think she might be telling the truth.

Chapter Seven

THE ARITHMETIC OF TRUST

DAY FIVE, PRE-DAWN: THREE DAYS REMAIN

THEY LEFT THE SAFE house at the darkest hour of the night, Teyra's bag slung across her body with the key and what remained of her supplies.

The city was different now. It hit her the moment they emerged from the hidden door behind the tannery, a tension in the air, a wrongness that settled into her bones and wouldn't leave. The streets were too quiet. The gas lamps had been turned down to half-brightness, casting weak pools of yellow light that didn't reach the cobblestones, and shadows pooled thick and deep in every doorway, every alley, every space between buildings.

And the grey film was glowing.

She hadn't expected that. In daylight, the Unsettled residue was a dull, grimy sheen, visible only if you knew to look for it. But in the dead of night, with the gas lamps dimmed and the living driven indoors by martial law, it phosphoresced. A faint, sickly luminescence in every gutter, every crack, every low-pooling hollow, the spiritual runoff of an entire district, shimmering like foxfire in the dark. Without the living to walk through it, to scrub it, to pretend it wasn't there, the dead were the most visible thing on the streets of Hollow Stair now, the city's unfinished business glowing in every gutter.

And in those shadows, things moved.

"Martial law," Seraphine murmured, pulling her hood lower over her face. She was wearing a cloak Teyra had found in the safe house, dark wool, moth-eaten at the hem, but serviceable. It hid the bloodstains on her dress, hid the fresh scar that pulled at her side with every step. "Greythorn must have declared it after the Conservatory incident. The Guard will have orders to detain anyone out after curfew."

"Detain," Ash repeated. "Is that what they're calling it now?"

"The polite term, yes." Seraphine's mouth thinned. "The reality is less polite."

She moved ahead of them, checking a corner before waving them forward.

In the weak lamplight, Teyra saw something she hadn't noticed before, how Seraphine flinched every time she looked at Ash. The expression of someone who had done the math on their worst decision and kept arriving at the same unbearable answer, that the door would have opened whether she'd killed him or not, and she'd destroyed a man she loved for nothing.

She hadn't said it in those words. She didn't need to. Her body said it every time she put herself between Ash and danger, every time she offered tactical information without being asked, every time she moved through the city like a woman walking toward her own execution and finding the pace too slow.

Teyra recognized the posture. The locked jaw, the operational flatness, Seraphine compressing five years of accumulated weight into clipped tactical sentences, it was the same discipline the Academy taught. Compartmentalize. Detach. Do the job without feeling the patient. Seraphine had been trained to kill the way Teyra had been trained to contain, by sealing the feeling in a box and pretending the box didn't exist. The difference was that Teyra's box had always leaked. Seraphine's hadn't, until the night she'd used a severance blade on the man she loved, and the box had shattered, and five years of compressed anguish had been sitting in the wreckage ever since, with nowhere to go.

They moved in single file. Seraphine in front, her knowledge of the city's patrol routes invaluable despite her injuries; Teyra in the middle, her necromancer's senses stretched to their limit, feeling for the cold spots that would indicate Hessian patrols. Ash bringing up the rear, fading in and out like a signal losing its frequency—the martial-law wards were burning through the Moonflower's gains faster than Teyra had expected, the city's heightened defenses treating him as a threat to be erased.

The Greythorn Estate was across the city, in the Old Quarter where the noble families had kept their townhouses for three hundred years. To get there, they would have to cross through the Merchant District, skirt the edge of the Temple Ward, and navigate the narrow lanes of the Scholars' Row, all without being seen or stopped or killed.

Impossible. But they were going to do it anyway.

They were three blocks east of the safe house when Teyra felt it.

A cold spot. Fresh, the raw, bewildered chill of someone who had died minutes ago and hadn't understood it yet.

She kept walking.

The ghost was in a doorway ten feet off their path. She didn't look. The confusion poured off him, the frantic reaching for a world that wouldn't reach back. A man. Middle-aged, from the weight of the presence, and the Hessian salt-round had been recent—the spirit still smelled of gunpowder and disbelief.

Everything in her screamed to go to him. Her hands ached with the old gestures, the calming patterns, the ones that said *you are seen, you are known, you are not alone.*

She kept walking.

Seraphine glanced at her. Said nothing. Ash's cold hand found hers and squeezed once, an apology for a choice he knew she'd already made.

The ghost's presence faded behind them. Teyra added his face, the face she hadn't looked at, the face she hadn't looked at and would therefore have to invent, which was always worse, to the list of costs. The list was getting long.

And as the ghost's cold receded behind her, she felt a shift inside her chest. A stirring. The fragments she'd spent healing Seraphine, the ones that had been thinned and dimmed and nearly emptied by the necrotic magic, were waking up. The old ones were still faded echoes, shapes without weight. But the ghost in the doorway had left a residue behind without Teyra even touching him, his bewilderment, his gunpowder-sharp disbelief, settling into her damaged

Resonance channels like dust in cracked plaster. She hadn't opened the channel. She hadn't invited it. Her scarred pathways were simply porous now. Leaking inward. The city's crisis was pressing its dead into her whether she consented or not.

The collection was rebuilding. And this time, she wasn't the one filling it.

A necromancer commands the dead, Miss Tepes. She does not weep for them.

No. But she could carry them while she ran. And the dead could settle into her whether she stopped or not.

"First checkpoint," Seraphine whispered, stopping at the mouth of an alley. "Hessian patrol. Four units. They're circling the fountain in Merchant Square every eight minutes."

Teyra peered around the corner. The square opened up before her, a wide expanse of rain-slicked cobblestones, dominated by a massive marble fountain in the center. The fountain depicted some long-dead king wrestling a serpent, the stone worn smooth by centuries of weather. Water still flowed from the serpent's mouth, splashing into the basin below, too loud in the silence.

And there, marching in perfect formation around the fountain's edge, were the Hessians.

Four of them. Identical. Seven feet of brass and oak, their golden masks blank and expressionless, their joints hissing softly as they moved. Their footsteps rang against the stone in perfect synchronization, left, right, left, right, the rhythm of machines that never tired, never slept.

"Eight minutes," Seraphine repeated. "They complete a circuit, pause for thirty seconds at the north corner to scan, then begin again. We have a window of maybe forty-five seconds to cross while they're at the south end."

"Forty-five seconds." Teyra measured the distance with her eyes. The square was at least a hundred yards across. They would be exposed the entire time, three figures in dark cloaks, running across open ground in the middle of martial law. If the Hessians spotted them, if their sensors picked up movement...

"I can create a distraction," Ash said.

"No." Seraphine's voice was sharp. "Your spectral signature will light up their sensors like a bonfire. The moment you manifest, every Hessian in a six-block radius will know exactly where we are."

"Then what do you suggest?"

Seraphine was quiet for a moment, her eyes tracking the patrol's movement. Left, right, left, right. The Hessians reached the north corner, stopped, turned their golden heads in a slow arc. Scanning, processing.

"There's a maintenance tunnel," she said finally. "Runs beneath the square. The entrance is in the basement of the chandler's shop on the east side. It comes out near the Old Quarter."

"A tunnel?" Teyra frowned. "Why didn't you mention this before?"

"Because it's flooded. The pumps failed three years ago, and the city never bothered to fix them. The water will be waist-deep, possibly higher." Seraphine's mouth was set in a hard line. "And there are things living in that water. Things that crawled up from the deeper tunnels during the last flood and never left."

"What kind of things?"

"The kind that eat anything that moves." Seraphine's hand went to the knife at her belt, a blade scavenged from the safe house's armory cache, since her own weapons had been lost in the fight with the Hessians. "We'll be vulnerable, slow, making noise with every step. If they find us..."

"If they find us, we fight." Ash's voice was flat. "I'd rather face monsters in the dark than clockwork soldiers in the open."

Teyra looked at him, at the strain in his face, at the way his edges blurred and sharpened with each breath. He was barely holding on. The hostile magic saturating the city was pressing against his anchor, trying to tear him apart.

"The tunnel," she decided. "We take the tunnel."

The chandler's shop was locked, but Seraphine knew the back entrance, a window with a broken latch that the owner had never bothered to fix. They slipped inside, moving through racks of half-made candles and barrels of rendered tallow, the smell of beeswax and animal fat thick enough to taste.

The basement stairs were narrow, the wood rotting in places. Teyra went first, testing each step before putting her weight on it. The darkness was absolute, she couldn't see her hand in front of her face, but she could feel the cold emanating from below. Something older and deeper than death magic. The cold of places that had never known sunlight.

"Here," Seraphine said, her voice barely above a breath. "The grate."

Teyra heard metal scraping against stone. Then a rush of air that smelled of stagnant water and things that had been rotting for too long.

"I'll go first," Seraphine continued. "I know the layout. Stay close, stay quiet, and for the love of all gods, don't splash."

She lowered herself through the opening. Teyra heard a soft splash, then a hissed curse.

"Waist-deep," Seraphine confirmed. "Colder than I remember. Come on."

Teyra followed.

The water was a shock, viscous and cold, thick with sediment and things she didn't want to identify. It soaked through her dress instantly, dragging at her legs like hands trying to pull her down. The bottom was slick, covered in some kind of slime that made every step treacherous.

She bit down on her gasp, forcing herself to breathe slowly, quietly. Sound carried in tunnels. Sound attracted attention.

Ash came last. She heard him descend, heard the splash as he hit the water, and heard something else. A flicker. A buzz of disrupted magic.

"Ash?" she whispered.

"I'm here." His voice came through strained, distorted. "The water is affecting my anchor. Hard to stay solid."

"Can you make it?"

A long pause. Then, "I don't have a choice."

They moved.

The tunnel was narrow, tight for two people to walk abreast, the ceiling low enough that Teyra had to duck in places. The walls were old brick, crumbling in spots, covered with growths that glowed in shades of green and blue. Bioluminescent mold. It gave just enough light to see the shape of things, but never enough to see them clearly.

The water came up to Teyra's waist in places, her chest in others. Every step required effort, lifting her leg against the drag, finding stable footing, pushing forward through the resistance. The cold seeped into her bones, making her muscles stiff and clumsy, and her teeth wanted to chatter, but she clenched her jaw, refusing to make a sound.

Seraphine moved ahead, her knife out, her movements careful and deliberate. Even wounded, even exhausted, she moved like a predator, weight balanced, steps silent, eyes constantly scanning the darkness ahead. But Teyra was close enough to see what the darkness hid. The way Seraphine's left arm stayed pressed against her side, guarding the sealed wound. How she favored her right leg when the water rose above her waist. Once, climbing over a collapsed section of brickwork, her foot slipped and she caught herself on the wall with a sharp, bitten-off sound that she swallowed before it became a gasp. When she pulled her hand away from her side a moment later, Teyra saw the faintest dark stain on her palm. The seal was holding. But it was unhappy about it.

"Something's watching us," Lenore whispered from Teyra's shoulder. The raven had been silent since they'd entered the tunnel, her feathers pressed flat against her body, though the injured wing had at least closed since the conservatory and she'd stopped favoring it somewhere between the safe house and the sewer grate.

"I can feel it. Multiple somethings. They're curious."

"Curious is good," Teyra breathed back. "Curious means they haven't decided to attack yet."

"Yet."

They reached a junction, three tunnels branching off in different directions, each one identical, each one swallowed by darkness. Seraphine stopped, orienting herself.

"Left," she said. "The left passage leads toward the Old Quarter and the estate. The right goes up." She hesitated. "The right connects to a Greythorn service exit. It comes out behind the stables on Alderman's Row, where the air is clean and there are no wards or creatures."

Nobody spoke. The dripping of the tunnel water suddenly sounded deafening.

"That's your way out," Ash said quietly.

Seraphine met his eyes. In the faint glow of the mold, her face was unreadable.

"Yes."

"You could take it. Right now. Walk out into clean air, disappear into the city. Greythorn thinks you're already dead. You could be on a coach to the provinces by morning."

She held his gaze, steady, without flinching, without performing indignation or wounded loyalty.

"I could," she said.

She turned left.

Ash watched her back as she waded deeper into the dark, toward the Old Quarter, toward the estate, toward the man who'd ordered both their deaths.

And Teyra saw something cross his face that she didn't expect. Brief and precise, a general's satisfaction at confirming an asset's loyalty. He'd offered the exit the way a general offers a soldier leave on the eve of battle—a test dressed as generosity. If Seraphine had taken the right tunnel, he would have let her go without a word. And he would have written her off.

The expression lasted less than a second. Then it was gone, replaced by a look she couldn't name.

But Teyra had seen it. The calculation underneath the composure. The prince underneath the ghost, sorting people the way princes did.

You didn't walk toward the danger when the exit was right there unless you meant it.

"The center tunnel," Ash said to Teyra as they followed. "What's down it?"

"The Bone Pits." Seraphine's voice floated back without turning. "Where the city used to dump its dead before the crematoriums were built. A hundred years of corpses, rotting in the dark."

"Let's not go there."

"Agreed."

The tunnel narrowed. The water grew deeper, up to Teyra's chest now, cold enough that she couldn't feel her legs. Every breath was an effort, the air thick with rot and minerals and a wrongness she couldn't place, metallic and alive.

Then she heard it.

A ripple. From somewhere ahead, the sound of water being displaced by something moving beneath the surface.

Everyone froze.

Teyra strained her eyes, trying to pierce the darkness. The bioluminescent mold gave her glimpses, a curve of brick, a patch of slime, the surface of the water smooth and black as oil.

And then, twenty feet ahead, the surface broke.

It rose slowly. A shape. A head, if you could call it that. Pale and bulbous, covered in what looked like warts or barnacles or possibly eyes. A mouth opened, vertical instead of horizontal, lined with teeth that looked like needles, hundreds of them, catching the faint glow of the mold and gleaming.

It made a sound. A clicking. Wet and rapid, like someone tapping bones together underwater.

More clicking answered from behind them.

"Don't move," Seraphine breathed. "Don't breathe. Don't make a sound."

The thing's head swiveled. Those barnacle-growths were eyes, Teyra realized, dozens of them, clustered across the pale flesh like blisters on proved dough. They swiveled independently, scanning, searching.

Looking for prey.

Every nerve in Teyra's body screamed at her to run. Her lungs burned, she'd been holding her breath without realizing it, but she didn't dare exhale. Didn't dare move.

The clicking intensified. The thing moved closer, its body rising further from the water. More of it was visible now, a neck, if you could call that twisted column of pale flesh a neck. Shoulders, maybe. Arms that were too long, jointed in too many places, ending in hands that were all fingers, all claws.

It was close enough that she could see the individual needles of its teeth. Close enough to touch.

The clicking stopped.

The thing's head turned, slowly, horribly, until it was facing directly toward Ash.

Understanding hit her at once, sick and heavy in her chest. Of course it could sense him. He was a ghost, a beacon of death energy in a tunnel full of darkness. His anchor was thinning, his presence bleeding into the water, calling to every predator that fed on the dead.

The thing lunged, but Ash moved faster, his form detonating outward as pure, blinding concussive force. A wave of cold energy blasted from his body, hitting the water and the creature and the tunnel walls with enough power to send Teyra staggering backward. The thing shrieked, a sound like glass being shattered inside a throat, and recoiled, its pale flesh blackening where the cold had touched it.

"Run!" Ash roared, his voice doubled and distorted, the poltergeist bleeding through. The more of himself he threw into the blast, the less of him would be left.

They ran.

The water dragged at them, fought them, tried to pull them down. Behind them, the clicking multiplied, more creatures, drawn by the commotion, answering the call of wounded prey. Teyra couldn't see them, but she could hear them. Splashing and clicking, getting closer.

Seraphine was ahead, moving with desperate speed despite her injury. The necrotic seal was splitting, Teyra could smell the blood seeping through the bandages, copper-sharp over the rot, and she knew the creatures could smell it too.

Light ahead. Faint, but real. A grate, set into the ceiling, starlight filtering through the bars.

"There!" Seraphine gasped, reaching up. Her fingers found the bars and pulled. The grate didn't move.

"It's stuck, rusted shut..."

A hand grabbed Teyra's ankle.

She screamed, couldn't help it, as claws dug into her flesh, yanking her backward, pulling her under. Water rushed into her mouth, her nose, her lungs. Darkness swallowed her. She couldn't see, couldn't breathe, couldn't think—then a blast of cold so intense it burned, searing through the water, through her flesh, into her bones. The claws released her. She surged upward, gasping, coughing, spitting water that tasted like death.

Ash was beside her, his arm around her waist, pulling her toward the surface. His form was barely there, closer to light than substance, closer to cold than warmth, but his grip held. Real.

"The grate!" he shouted at Seraphine. "Now!"

Seraphine didn't hesitate. She drew her knife, shoved it into the gap between grate and stone, and wrenched with all her strength. Metal screamed. Rust crumbled. The grate tore free.

They scrambled through, Seraphine first, then Teyra, Ash last. He pulled himself up with arms that flickered at the edges, his form guttering like a candle in a hurricane.

And then they were out. On the surface. In the rain.

The grate slammed shut behind them. Below, the clicking faded into the distance, the creatures retreating from the light.

No one spoke. They lay on the wet cobblestones, gasping, bleeding, broken in a dozen different ways.

Then Seraphine laughed.

It was a ragged sound, half-sob, half-hysteria. "Well," she managed between gulps of air. "That could have gone worse."

"Could it?" Teyra croaked. Her throat was raw from the water, from the screaming, and her ankle throbbed where the claws had gripped her.

"We're alive, aren't we?"

Teyra supposed it was true. Though looking at Ash, at his fading form, at the exhaustion carved into features she could hardly see, she wasn't sure for how much longer.

"How far?" she asked.

Seraphine sat up, wincing, and looked around, orienting herself. They were in a narrow alley somewhere in the Old Quarter, and Teyra could see the iron gates of the noble estates rising above the rooftops, black against the pre-dawn sky.

"Three blocks," Seraphine said. "We're close. So close."

Teyra looked at the gates. They loomed over the surrounding buildings, guarding secrets that had been kept for centuries.

"Then we keep moving."

The Greythorn Estate was a fortress dressed as a mansion.

Fifteen-foot black iron walls surrounded it, topped by spikes gleaming in the rain. The architecture was old, older than the current monarchy, older than most of the city, built in the severe style of the founding families, all sharp angles and narrow windows and stone the color of dried blood. Gargoyles crouched at every corner, their faces worn smooth by centuries of weather, their eyes seeming to track movement even though they were carved rock and nothing more.

The main entrance was a pair of massive iron gates, decorated with the Greythorn family crest, a serpent coiled around a crown, its mouth open to swallow. They were beautiful. They were also locked, reinforced with wards that glowed in the darkness, and guarded by three Hessians who stood motionless beneath the portico, their golden masks gleaming in the light of oil lamps that burned in alcoves on either side.

"We're not going through the front," Seraphine said. They were huddled in the shadow of a tenement building across the street, watching the guards. "There's a service entrance on the north side. Deliveries, maintenance, that sort of thing. It's how the household staff gets in before dawn."

"Guards?"

"One Hessian. Possibly two during high alert."

"Can we get past them?"

Seraphine considered this. Then, "We can try."

They circled around, keeping to the shadows, moving through alleys that smelled of garbage and human waste. The rain had picked up again, a steady drizzle that soaked through their already-wet clothes and turned the cobblestones treacherous.

The service entrance was exactly where Seraphine had said, a small door set into the north wall of the estate, easily overlooked, marked only by a faded brass plaque that read DELIVERIES. A single Hessian stood guard, its back to the wall, its sensors scanning the empty alley in slow sweeps.

"One. I can take one," Ash said.

"You can barely stand."

"I can take one Hessian." Iron had crept into his voice. "I've taken three."

"And nearly destroyed yourself in the process." Teyra touched his arm, or tried to. Her fingers passed through his sleeve, cold biting into her skin. "You're coming apart, Ash. One more burst of power and you might not come back."

"Then what do you suggest?"

Teyra looked at the Hessian. A complicated machine, but still a machine. And machines had weaknesses.

"Bonemeal," she said. "I used it at the Conservatory. Accelerated decay. Turned brass to rust in seconds."

"You collapsed after one dose," Ash pointed out. "And you've already nearly killed yourself once tonight."

"I don't need to destroy it. Just disable it. Jam the joints. Blind the sensors." She was thinking out loud now, the plan forming as she spoke. "A small dose. Targeted. The Grave-Chill won't be as bad if I focus."

"Teyra..."

"We don't have another option." She met his eyes, or where his eyes would be, if she could see them clearly. "Let me do this. Let me help."

Ash was silent. Then he nodded.

The approach was the hardest part.

Teyra moved alone, keeping to the shadows, her footsteps as quiet as she could make them on the rain-slicked stone. Her blood was loud in her ears, a sharp taste at the back of her throat, but she kept her breathing slow, controlled.

Twenty feet from the Hessian. The brass joints, the wooden panels, the spinning gears visible through gaps in its chassis.

Its head was turning in that slow, mechanical sweep. Left, right, left, right.

Fifteen feet.

She reached into her pocket. The vial of bonemeal was cold against her fingers, colder than it should have been, colder than the rain. The powder inside pulsed with its own dark energy.

Ten feet.

The Hessian's head paused. Its sensors locked onto something. Teyra froze, pressing herself against the wall, holding her breath.

A rat. Just a rat, scurrying across the alley, its wet fur glistening in the lamplight. The Hessian tracked it for a moment, then dismissed it. Its head resumed its sweep.

Five feet.

Teyra was close enough to see the rivets in its armor, the scratches in its golden mask, the faint glow of its optical sensors. Close enough to smell the machine oil and heated metal. Close enough to touch.

She uncorked the vial.

The smell hit her instantly, old graves, turned earth, things that had been dead too long. The cold stirred in her chest, recognizing kinship.

She threw the powder.

It hit the Hessian's face in a grey cloud, coating the golden mask, seeping into the gaps around its optical sensors. For a moment, nothing happened.

Then the brass corroded.

It started at the edges, green oxidation spreading like frost on a window, eating into the metal, turning gleaming brass to crumbling rust. The Hessian's optical sensors flickered, sparked. Its head jerked, a broken, stuttering movement, as the corrosion reached the delicate mechanisms inside.

"Target... target... target obscured..." Its voice was glitching, distorting. "Malfunction detected. Malfunction... malfunction..."

The Hessian took a step forward and its leg gave out. The knee joint, corroded through, collapsed under its weight. It went down with a crash of metal on stone, its arms flailing, its voice cutting out mid-word.

Teyra was already running.

She grabbed the door handle, locked, of course, but the Moth's skeleton key was already in her hand. She shoved it into the keyhole, felt the wards resist for a moment, then yield.

The door swung open.

"Now!" she hissed.

Seraphine and Ash materialized from the shadows, moving fast despite their exhaustion. They slipped through the door as the Hessian behind them convulsed, its damaged systems sending distress signals that would bring reinforcements within minutes.

Teyra slammed the door shut behind them.

Lenore was off her shoulder before the lock clicked, a black shape arrowing down the corridor, silent as a thrown knife. Three seconds, five. She vanished around a corner and the darkness swallowed her.

Teyra counted her heartbeats. At twelve, the raven reappeared, landing on a wall sconce with a soft click of talons on brass.

"Corridor's clear for sixty feet," Lenore reported, her voice barely a whisper. "Two doors on the left, one on the right, all closed. No Hessians. But there's a ward-line at the far end. I can feel it humming."

"You flew through the wards?" Seraphine's eyes narrowed. "The estate's blood protections should have stopped you."

"Should have," Lenore agreed, preening a wing feather with elaborate unconcern. "Didn't."

Seraphine looked at Teyra. Teyra shook her head. Later.

The inside of the estate was vast and silent.

They were in a service corridor, narrow, utilitarian, lit by oil lamps that cast flickering shadows on whitewashed walls. The air smelled of furniture polish and old wood, but the taste on her tongue was iron. It made her skin prickle with recognition.

"The blood wards," she breathed.

Layers of protective magic pressed through the very stones of the building, pushing against her necromancer's senses like heat from a fire, warning her away, telling her she didn't belong here.

Ash stumbled.

He stuttered in and out of existence, flickering, his face contorted. He grabbed the wall for support, but his hand passed through the stone and he nearly fell.

"The wards," Seraphine said grimly. "The estate is blood-bound. Every stone, every beam, every inch of this place has been keyed to the Greythorn bloodline for three centuries. For the living, the wards simply watch. For the dead..."

"They reject me," Ash finished, the words almost soundless. "I can feel it. Burning, trying to unmake me. The wards see me as an intruder, something dead that was never given permission to be here."

The tightness in Teyra's chest was immediate. The Moonflower was supposed to keep him strong through the remaining three days, stable and solid, powerful enough to survive whatever they found in the vault. The blood wards were burning through that strength like a furnace through kindling, devouring the reserves that should have carried him to the end. Every step he took inside these walls cost him hours of stability he couldn't afford to lose.

Teyra was at his side in an instant. "How bad?"

"The wards are strong." He looked at her, eyes tight with strain. "Stronger than anything I've felt. Every step feels like erasure."

"Then we go faster." Teyra looked at Seraphine. "The vault. Where is it?"

"Below. In the ancestral crypts, beneath the oldest wing." Seraphine pointed down the corridor. "Through the servant's wing, down the family stairs, past the old tombs. The vault is at the very bottom, built on the foundations of the original Greythorn manor, before the estate was expanded."

"How far?"

"Three levels. Maybe four hundred feet." Seraphine hesitated. "But there are more wards. Each level has its own protections. And the closer we get to the vault, the stronger they become."

Ash made a sound that might have been a laugh. "Of course they do."

"Can you make it?" Teyra asked again.

He looked at her. His form steadied, whole, real, the man she'd come to know over these harrowing days.

"For you?" The word was barely there. "I'll make it wherever I have to."

The servant's wing was dark.

Rows of uniforms hung on wooden racks, their fabric catching the light from Teyra's small lantern. Silver serving pieces sat on shelves, gleaming in the dim light. The air was thick with the smell of starch and cleaning solutions and the faint, lingering traces of old meals.

Teyra moved carefully, avoiding the ceremonial objects, keeping to the center of the room. The wards here were stronger, they pressed against her skin, sat bitter in the back of her throat. Iron and old blood. Ancestral power turned into a weapon.

Ash was struggling. He dimmed with every step, his outline blurring, his features bleaching like a photograph left in the sun. The blood wards were tearing at him, recognizing him as dead, as uninvited, as something that had no right to exist within these walls.

Lenore hopped from Teyra's shoulder and flew ahead again, banking around a corner, disappearing for ten seconds before returning.

"Two more Hessians at the end of the next corridor," she said, landing lightly on a shelf of folded linens. "Stationary. Facing the main hall."

"The distress signal," Seraphine said quietly. "They repositioned to intercept anyone coming up from the service entrance. Which means the pantry is clear."

"If we go through the pantry, we can bypass them."

Teyra stared at the raven. The wards were pressing against her own skin like sunburn, making Ash waver and gasp, and Lenore had just flown through three rooms of blood-bound stone without so much as ruffling a feather.

"Lenore. How are you doing that?"

The raven tilted her head. The performative tilt, the one-eyed assessment she used when she was buying time.

"Doing what?"

"Ignoring wards that are designed to reject anything that isn't Greythorn blood. Ash is being erased. You're flying through walls like they're scenery."

A long pause. Lenore's feathers settled flat, the way they did when she was uncomfortable rather than performing discomfort for comedic effect.

"The wards are looking for things that are alive," she said carefully. "Or things that are dead. I'm neither."

"You're..."

"I'm a familiar, Teyra. I'm bound to your bloodline. I don't have a soul for the wards to read. I don't have a life force for them to reject. I'm outside their system." She clicked her beak. "It's like asking a lock to stop a shadow. The lock works fine. I'm just the wrong kind of thing for it to catch."

Teyra opened her mouth. Closed it. Added it to the growing list of *Things Lenore Has Never Told Me*.

"We'll talk about this later."

"We absolutely will not."

Seraphine held up a fist. Stop.

They pressed flat against the wall as footsteps passed overhead, a servant on the upper landing, the soft scuff of slippers on wood, then silence. Seraphine counted to thirty under her breath before motioning them forward.

The corridor turned. And there it was. A door, slightly ajar, warm light spilling across the floorboards in a thin gold line.

Seraphine went rigid.

"That's his room," she breathed.

She didn't need to say whose.

Ash's form solidified. Whatever was holding him together now was stronger than the wards trying to pull him apart. He moved toward the door before Teyra could stop him.

"Ash," she whispered. "We can't."

He didn't answer. He stood at the gap in the door and looked through.

Teyra looked too. She couldn't help it.

The room was modest by estate standards, a cluttered study lined with bookshelves and half-unrolled maps and loose papers. A fire had burned low in a small grate, painting everything in amber and ash. And there, slumped in an armchair with an open book across his chest, was a man.

He'd fallen asleep reading. His head was tilted back, his mouth slightly open, one hand dangling over the armrest. He was younger than Teyra had expected, late twenties, close to the age Ash had been when he died, with the same dark hair, the same sharp jaw. But softer. Rounder in the cheeks. The version of a Thornwick who'd been fed and housed and told he was loved, even if the love was a leash.

The resemblance hit her like a Grave-Chill spike through the sternum.

Ash made a sound beside her. Barely audible. Barely human. A breath drawn through teeth that didn't need air.

On Elias's wrist, she noticed a band of dull iron, too thick for jewelry, too plain for decoration. Inscribed with ward-sigils that pulsed against his skin even in sleep, timed to his heartbeat. Monitoring him. Tethering his blood to the estate's defenses.

A battery. A living key.

He didn't even know what it was.

Ash's hand rose. His fingers drifted toward the gap in the door, toward his brother, toward the only blood he had left in the world. The cold radiating from his palm made the fire gutter, the embers dimming, and Elias stirred in his chair. Shifted, murmured something that might have been a name.

Seraphine caught Ash's wrist. Her grip was iron.

"If you wake him," she said, barely audible, "he screams. The wards respond. Every Hessian in the building activates." She swallowed. "And he won't know you. He was four years old, Ash. He'll see a ghost in his doorway, and it will be the worst moment of his life."

"He's my brother." Ash's voice was wrecked. A thread. "He's right there."

"I know." Seraphine's eyes were wet. "But we get the book first. We prove what was done to both of you. And then you come back to him as a king with evidence, not a ghost in the dark. You give him the reunion he deserves."

Ash stood at the door for what felt like hours. Teyra counted his breaths, the ones he didn't need to take but couldn't seem to stop. Five, ten, fifteen.

Then he lowered his hand.

"When this is over," he said quietly, "I'm coming back for him."

"When this is over," Teyra said, "we both are."

He turned from the door. His form lost shape as the feeling crested, the wards seizing the moment to tear at him harder, and then locked back into steel. Harder than before. With teeth.

He didn't look back.

"Here," Seraphine said, stopping at a door at the end of the corridor. She didn't meet anyone's eyes. "The family stairs."

The name was apt.

The staircase spiraled downward, carved directly into the bedrock beneath the estate. The walls were lined with portraits, generations of Greythorns staring down with cold, painted eyes. Some of the faces had been scratched out. Some of them had been burned. The erased heirs. The disowned. The ones the family had decided never existed.

Lenore went first, dropping into the dark like a spent candle stub into deep water. Teyra listened to the diminishing click of talons on stone, counting seconds. At eight, the raven's voice echoed up from below, distorted by the spiral.

"Stairs are clear to the first landing. No guards. But the ward gets thick about forty steps down. Even I can feel it, and I'm supposedly invisible." A pause. "There's also a smell. Old and wrong. Like a butcher's shop that's been locked for a century."

The bone chamber. They weren't far now.

Teyra descended after her, lantern held high. The light only reached a few feet ahead, the darkness below absolute. The steps were worn smooth by centuries of feet, each one slightly concave in the center where countless family members had walked.

The smell changed as they went deeper. Less furniture polish, more earth. Less cleaning solution, more decay. The smell of things that had been buried and forgotten.

"The first ward is ahead," Seraphine said, her voice dropping. "It's designed to turn back anyone without Greythorn blood. Anyone who doesn't belong to the family will feel it like a wall."

Teyra felt it before she saw it.

A pressure, building in her chest. A sensation of wrongness, of rejection, of a power that did not want her here. She pushed forward, one step at a time, and the pressure intensified, a hand pressing against her sternum, trying to push her back up the stairs.

"Keep going," Seraphine urged. "The ward isn't lethal to the living. It's just persuasive."

Persuasive was one word for it. Teyra gritted her teeth and pushed forward, each step an act of will. The pressure peaked, unbearable for a moment, like being squeezed in a giant fist, and then suddenly released.

She stumbled forward, gasping.

"One down," she panted. "How many more?"

"Two. Maybe three." Seraphine was already moving past her. "The second ward is worse. It burns."

"Burns?"

"Blood fire. Anyone without Greythorn blood in their veins will feel like they're being immolated." Seraphine said it the way she said everything now, scoured clean of inflection. "I had clearance before. A commander's exemption, keyed to my sigil ring. Greythorn revoked it the moment I deflected that kill shot. The wards won't know me anymore."

Teyra looked back at Ash. He was barely visible now, suggestion rather than form, cold rather than substance.

"Can you...?"

"I don't have a choice." His voice came from everywhere and nowhere. "Keep going. I'll be right behind you."

The second ward was everything Seraphine had promised.

Teyra felt the heat before she reached it, a dry, scorching warmth that radiated from the walls, from the floor, from the air itself. By the time she could see the threshold, a line of dark iron embedded in the stone, glowing with reddish light, she was sweating despite the underground cold.

"Now," Seraphine said. "Move quickly. Don't stop, no matter what."

Teyra ran.

The fire hit her the moment she crossed the threshold. Nothing was burning, nothing was actually hot, but her nerves screamed anyway, convinced they were being consumed. She felt her skin blistering, felt her hair catching flame, felt the fat beneath her flesh beginning to render.

She screamed.

She kept running.

Ten feet. Twenty. Thirty. The iron line at the end of the passage seemed impossibly far, receding as she approached, the fire growing hotter with every step.

Forty feet. Fifty.

She crossed the second threshold and collapsed.

The fire vanished. She lay on the cold stone, gasping, her hands pressed flat against the floor, convincing herself she was still alive, still whole.

"Teyra." Seraphine's voice, close by. "You're through. You made it."

Teyra looked up. Seraphine was kneeling beside her, her face pale, her bandages dark with fresh blood. The sprint through the fire had cracked the necrotic seal further, Teyra could see it in the way Seraphine held herself, one arm locked against her side, her breathing shallow and careful. She'd run through the fire on a wound that was reopening with every step.

"Ash?" Teyra croaked.

Silence.

She turned to look back at the passage.

He wasn't there.

"Ash!" She scrambled to her feet, staring into the red-lit corridor. Empty—no pale shape, no cold presence, nothing but the glow of the ward and the darkness beyond.

"ASH!"

A faint sound, coming from inside the ward itself.

He was still in there.

Teyra didn't think. She ran back into the fire.

The second time was worse, or maybe she was just more aware of it, knowing what to expect, feeling every imaginary flame licking at her skin. She pushed through, her eyes streaming, her lungs burning, her voice screaming his name.

She found him twenty feet in.

He was on his knees, his form almost completely transparent, his hands pressed flat against the floor. Blue light was pouring from his skin, something being burned out of him. Being purged.

The ward was destroying him.

"Ash!" Teyra dropped to her knees beside him. The fire was scorching her, cooking her from the inside out, but she didn't care. "Ash, look at me. Look at me!"

His eyes found hers. They were almost visible, just the faintest suggestion of grey in a face that was mostly light and shadow.

"Can't," he gasped. "The ward. It's too strong. I have no blood. No permission. It sees me as an intruder and nothing else. I can't..."

"You can." She grabbed for his hands, and the cold met the fire in her body like two wounds colliding. "You told me you could make it anywhere for me. You promised. You don't get to break that promise."

"Teyra..."

"Hold on to me."

She reached again, and this time, against everything—the Moonflower tether still burning between them like a thread refusing to snap—she caught him.

Her hands closed around his wrists. The cold was agonizing, the fire was agonizing, everything was pain that was both heat and cold at once and she didn't care, she didn't care, she just needed him to survive.

She pulled.

He came with her. They stumbled through the fire together, his body thinning to smoke with every step, her body screaming with every nerve, neither of them stopping, neither of them letting go.

They crossed the threshold.

They collapsed in a heap of tangled limbs and gasping breaths and tears that neither of them acknowledged.

"You're an idiot," Ash whispered.

"I know." Teyra's voice was raw. "I don't care."

"You could have died."

"I know." She looked at him. He was still barely there, more ghost than man, but he was here. "It was worth it."

His hand found hers. Cold, so cold, but there. Real.

"Thank you," he breathed.

"Don't thank me yet." She helped him sit up, looking around. They were in a chamber, the tomb level, she realized. Ancient sarcophagi lined the walls, their stone lids carved with the faces of long-dead Greythorns. The air was thick with dust and old death. "We still have one more ward to pass."

"One more?"

Seraphine was standing at the far end of the chamber, before a massive iron door covered in chains, locks, and sigils that glowed with a light that hurt to look at.

"The vault ward," she said. "The strongest of them all. It's designed to kill anyone who tries to pass without proper authorization."

"Can we break it?" Teyra asked.

Seraphine shook her head. "The ward is tied to the bloodline. Only Thornwick blood can deactivate it."

She looked at Ash.

"Your blood, specifically. The Greythorns built this vault on Thornwick foundations. The original owners' blood is still the key."

Ash stared at the door. At the chains, the locks, the glowing sigils. At the last barrier between them and the truth.

"Go back up," Teyra told Lenore quietly. "Wait at the top. Whatever's in there, I don't need you in the middle of it." Lenore regarded her for a moment with one bright eye. Then she lifted off without argument, her wingbeats swallowed by the dark above.

"Then let's finish this," he said.

He walked to the door, his edges still fraying, his steps unsteady. Seraphine handed him her knife, the blade still stained with rust-colored blood from her wound.

Ash pressed the blade to his palm. Ghosts didn't bleed, at least not really, but the Moonflower tea had given him substance, had given him form.

The blade bit into spectral flesh.

Blue light welled up, ectoplasm, the closest thing he had to blood. He pressed his hand against the door, against the central sigil, and waited.

Nothing happened.

"It should be working," Seraphine said, her voice tight. "The ward should recognize..."

The outer sigils flared. Then stopped. The chains shuddered but held. The locks clicked once, twice, then went still.

"There's a secondary sequence," Seraphine said. "A private ward. Built into the inner lock. I never found the combination, it wasn't in any of the records I accessed."

Ash's hand was still pressed to the door.

His other hand had risen without his knowing it.

His fingers were moving. Index, middle, ring, thumb. Index, middle, ring, thumb. Pressing against the iron surface in the sequence Teyra had watched him trace on a counter in the grey light of early morning, the one he hadn't been able to name, the one his hands had been practicing in the dark for five years without him.

He didn't look at his hand. He was staring at the door with an expression she had never seen on him before. Something quieter than anything she could name. The recognition of a thing his body had known before his mind caught up.

Four beats, repeating. Then the inner lock clicked.

"Ash," Teyra said. Her voice came out wrong.

"I know." He didn't move his hand. "I didn't know I knew it. But I knew it."

The ward recognized Ash as rightful blood and rightful memory both.

Light exploded outward, white and gold and blinding, and Teyra couldn't see anything, couldn't hear anything, couldn't feel anything but the shockwave of magic being released.

Then, slowly, the light faded.

The chains fell away, the locks clicked open, and the sigils dimmed into nothing.

The vault door swung open.

Beyond was darkness. Deep, absolute darkness, darkness that had never known light, that had been waiting in the belly of the earth since before the estate was built.

But in that darkness, Teyra could feel something A pull. A presence.

The book. The original prophecy. The truth that had been hidden for half a century.

"We're in," Ash breathed.

They stood together at the threshold, a necromancer, a ghost prince, and a traitor who was trying to be a hero, staring into the darkness that held all the answers.

Seraphine retrieved the knife from where Ash had dropped it by the lock. Then they stepped through, and the door closed behind them.

Chapter Eight

THE TOMB OF TRUTH

DAY FIVE, PRE-DAWN, CONTINUED: THREE DAYS REMAIN

T HE DOOR CLOSED BEHIND them with a sound like a coffin lid settling into place.

No echo. No reverberation. The darkness swallowed the noise whole, absorbed it into itself, and left nothing behind but a silence so complete it pressed against Teyra's eardrums like water at depth. She stood motionless, hand still outstretched toward where the door had been, fingers touching nothing but cold air.

"Light," she whispered. The word came out strange, flat and muted, as if the darkness was eating the sound before it could travel.

She fumbled for her lantern. The flint sparked, caught, and a small flame guttered to life.

It didn't help much.

The light extended perhaps five feet in every direction before the darkness defeated it, actively pushing back, as if the darkness itself resented illumination. Teyra could see the floor beneath her feet, stone, ancient, worn smooth by time alone, untouched by any foot, and the vague shapes of walls on either side, too far apart to touch, carved with symbols she didn't recognize. Nothing else.

The ceiling was invisible, and so was the far end of the chamber. They might have been standing in a room or a cavern or the belly of some vast dead thing, and there was no way to tell.

"I can't see anything," Seraphine said. Her voice was wrong too, flattened and small. She was leaning against the wall, one hand pressed to her side where the bandages were soaking through again. In the dim light, her face had gone the color of old mortar, sheened with sweat. "The vault should be ahead. Somewhere."

"Can you walk?" Teyra asked.

"I can walk." Seraphine pushed herself off the wall, swayed, caught herself. "I can walk until I can't. That's the only option."

Ash was silent.

Teyra turned to find him, and the words died in her throat.

He was glowing.

The sickly blue of his wound was gone. Whatever had been failing in his anchor had caught and held, steadied into something new. A soft, silver luminescence outlined his form in the darkness, until he looked closer to something carved from moonlight than any ghost she'd seen. His edges were sharper than she'd ever seen them, his features clearer, his presence more substantial.

The catacombs were feeding him.

Of course they were. This place was saturated with death, three hundred years of Greythorn dead, their bones and their memories and their unfinished business soaked into every stone. For a necromancer, it was overwhelming, a pressure against her senses that made her teeth ache. For a ghost, it was sustenance.

"I can feel them," Ash said. He sounded steadier than he had since the Conservatory, stronger, clearer, almost alive. "The dead. They're everywhere. Hundreds of them. Watching."

"Watching what?"

"Us." He turned to look at her, and his eyes were brighter too, the grey gone silver in the strange light. "They've been waiting. For a very long time. For someone to come and listen."

A chill passed through her that had nothing to do with the temperature. She felt them too, though less clearly than Ash, as a pressure rather than individual presences. A hum beneath her awareness, like a crowd pressed against the other side of a wall. Hundreds of voices, compressed into a single feeling. *We are here. We have always been here.*

She thought, absurdly, of the Academy exam. Of the soldier boy whose overwhelming presence had broken her because she'd opened the channel too wide. One spirit had nearly ended her. What would hundreds do?

She pushed the thought away.

"Then let's not keep them waiting," she said.

Her ankle throbbed where the tunnel creature had clawed it, but she set her weight on it anyway and started walking. The passage stretched on far longer than it should have. Teyra counted steps automatically, a hundred, two hundred, three hundred, but the numbers felt meaningless. Distance didn't work properly in this place. The walls seemed to breathe, contracting and expanding in her peripheral vision, always the same when she looked straight at them but somehow different when she looked away. The carved symbols shifted, rearranged themselves, spelled out words in languages that had been dead for a thousand years.

She tried not to read them. Instinct told her that reading them would be a mistake.

Seraphine was flagging. Her steps had grown uneven, breathing labored. The blood seeping through her bandages was darker now, thick and slow, the bleeding of a body that had stopped pretending it could heal. She kept walking, one foot in front of the other, jaw set in a line of pure stubbornness, without complaint, without pause.

Teyra moved closer to her, ready to catch her if she fell.

"The wound is opening," she murmured. "The necrotic seal is breaking down."

"I know." The words barely carried. "The magic of this place is interfering. Too much death energy. It's eating the healing."

"You need to rest."

"I need to finish this." Seraphine met her eyes, and there was something fierce in her gaze, beyond exhaustion. "I've spent my whole life serving a lie. I need to know the truth. I need to see it with my own eyes. Then I can rest."

She paused, and her expression shifted, the mask slipping again. "Do you know what the worst part is? I still remember how it felt. Being happy. Planning our wedding. Believing we would grow old together." Her voice cracked. "I remember the exact moment I decided to destroy all of it. I was brushing my hair. Looking in the mirror. And I told myself I was being brave."

She laughed, a hollow, broken sound.

"I wasn't brave. I was a coward. Too afraid to question. I took the easy path and called it sacrifice."

Part of her wanted to grab Seraphine by the shoulders and force her to sit. But she understood. She understood. She'd felt it herself, every time she'd reached across the veil.

"Just a little farther," she said instead. "We'll find somewhere to stop."

The passage opened into a chamber.

It was a cathedral of bone.

The ceiling soared into darkness, supported by columns of fused human remains rather than stone. Femurs and tibias stacked in intricate patterns, mortared together with something that gleamed wetly in the lantern light. Skulls formed the capitals, hundreds of them, their empty eyes staring down at the intruders below. The walls were the same, bones fitted together with geometric precision, creating patterns that might have been decorative or might have been ritual.

And Teyra's porous channels, the ones that had been involuntarily absorbing the city's dead since the ghost in the doorway, opened like floodgates.

The bones were anonymous to the eye and nowhere else. The skulls, the femurs, the ribs fitted into these walls had all belonged to someone, and those people were still here, compressed into a residue of identity, three centuries of silenced people mortared into the architecture of a rich man's secret. Workers and servants, the people who had dug the vault and carved the passages and fitted the bones into place. They hadn't left when the job was done. They hadn't been allowed to leave. The Greythorns had entombed them inside their own construction the way you'd mix gravel into cement, as material rather than people. Filler for the walls.

Their collective weight hit Teyra's Resonance channels like a wave, a three-hundred-year old scream of *we were here, we built this, we died for this, and no one remembers our names.* It poured into the cracks the necrotic healing had left, filling her with a weight older and heavier than anything she'd carried before. Her hands trembled, her vision blurring with it. She tasted mortar dust and sweat and the knowledge of a person realizing they will never see daylight again.

She added it to the collection. It was the heaviest thing she'd ever carried.

The floor was different. Black marble, polished to a mirror shine, inscribed with a single massive sigil that Teyra recognized from her Academy training, though the textbooks dated it to the Founding Age, centuries before even the first Thornwick king, when the Veil-builders had raised Athergard over the place where the world was thinnest.

A summoning circle. Bigger than any she'd ever seen, big enough to summon something that shouldn't exist.

"Gods," Seraphine breathed.

"This isn't a vault," Ash said. His voice echoed strangely in the space, multiplied by the bones until it came from everywhere at once. "This is a prison."

He was right. Teyra could feel it now, the weight of the wards pressing down from every direction, the magical pressure wholly different from death—this was containment, pure and deliberate. A force had been locked in here. Powerful enough to require three hundred years of Greythorn blood to keep it bound. And three hundred years of anonymous dead to reinforce the walls.

"The prophecy," she said. "The original prophecy. What if it wasn't predicting the future? What if it was describing something that already existed? Something they were trying to control?"

"Then the entire foundation of my murder was a lie," Ash said flatly. "But we already knew that."

He walked toward the center of the chamber, his silver glow casting long shadows across the bone walls. The summoning circle pulsed faintly as he approached, recognizing him, Teyra realized. Responding to Thornwick blood the same way the vault door had.

In the center of the circle, on a pedestal of black stone, sat a book.

It was exactly as the Moth had described. Leather-bound, no title, ordinary-looking except for the way the air bent around it. The leather was cracked with age, the pages yellowed, the spine broken in places where someone had opened it too many times. It looked like something you might find in a used bookshop, discarded and forgotten.

Wrongness poured off it with the steady pressure of an open furnace.

"That's it," Seraphine said from the edge of the circle, where she had stopped, unwilling or unable to cross. "The original prophecy. The one Greythorn hid."

Ash stood before the pedestal, looking down at the book. He didn't touch it. His hands were clenched at his sides, his voice low.

"What happens when I open it?" he asked.

"I don't know." Seraphine's voice was hollow. "I've never seen it opened. I only knew it existed because I overheard Greythorn speaking of it once, years ago. He said it contained 'the truth that broke the world.'"

"Comforting."

Teyra stepped into the circle. The magic pressed against her, questioning rather than hostile, trying to determine if she belonged. She felt it probe her blood, her magic, her intent. Then, as though reaching a decision, the pressure eased.

She stood beside Ash, looking down at the book.

"Whatever's in there," she said quietly, "we go into it together."

He looked at her. His eyes were bright, and she couldn't separate what she saw there into its parts, only that everything was present at once and all of it real.

"Together," he agreed.

He reached out and opened the book.

The world inverted.

Through her blown-wide Resonance channels, still raw from the bone walls, still saturated with three centuries of compressed weight, Teyra felt herself dragged along in his wake, falling spiritually rather than physically, her consciousness ripped from her body and hurled backward through time. Colors blurred. Sounds distorted. The bone chamber dissolved into streaks of grey and gold, reforming around her into something else, somewhere else, somewhen else.

A ballroom.

She was standing in a ballroom, though as a witness, present but unable to act. A ghost watching ghosts. The room was magnificent, crystal chandeliers dripping with candlelight, walls covered in gilt mirrors that reflected infinity, a ceiling painted with clouds, angels, and a sun that seemed to glow with its own light. The smell of roses and expensive perfume hung thick in the air, undercut by the sharper scents of champagne and roasted meat.

Music played, a waltz, the strings sweet and melancholy, the rhythm steady and hypnotic. Couples spun across the floor in elaborate gowns and tailored coats, their faces blurred, their laughter echoing strangely.

But the dancers were not the point.

In the corner of the room, near a door that led to a private balcony, three people stood in conversation. Two men and a woman, their heads bent close together, their voices too low for the dancers to hear.

Teyra drifted closer. The vision placed her within arm's reach of the conspirators.

They were clear now.

The first man was old, seventy at least, with white thinning hair and a face lined by a lifetime of power. He wore the robes of a high official, heavy velvet embroidered with silver thread, a chain of office around his neck. His eyes were cold and calculating, the eyes of someone who had long ago stopped seeing people as anything other than pieces on a board.

Lord Casimir Greythorn. The current Lord's grandfather. The architect of everything that followed.

The second man was younger, perhaps forty, with the sharp features and intense eyes of a scholar. He wore simpler clothes, black robes without ornamentation, but carried himself with the quiet confidence of someone who knew secrets that others didn't. His hands were ink-stained. His gaze never stopped moving.

Brother Matthias. High Seer of the Order of the Blind Eye. The man who had written the prophecy.

The woman was beautiful. Dark hair, pale skin, a gown of midnight blue that caught the light like a starfield. She couldn't have been more than twenty-five, but there was something ancient in her eyes, a weariness that didn't match her youth, a weight that bend her shoulders even as she stood straight.

Lady Evelyn Thornwick. Ash's grandmother. The queen who would never be.

"It must be done tonight," Greythorn was saying. He spoke in a rasp, the sound of parchment being torn. "The boy is nearly old enough. Once the blood-right awakens in him, the throne passes beyond our reach. We'll lose our chance."

"The prophecy is ready," Brother Matthias said. "I've altered it as you requested. The escape clause has been removed. When the seers confirm it, they'll find exactly what we need them to find, a doom that can only be averted through the extinction of the Thornwick line."

"And you're certain it will hold?" Greythorn pressed. "The magic must be undetectable. If anyone discovers the alteration..."

"They won't." Matthias smiled, and there was no warmth in it. "I've spent thirty years mastering the arts of prophetic manipulation. The false version will read as authentic to any examination. Even the blood divination will confirm it. The original will be hidden here, in the vault you've prepared, sealed away where no one will ever find it."

Lady Evelyn spoke for the first time. Her voice was soft, musical, utterly empty of feeling.

"And my son? What becomes of him?"

"The fire will take care of that," Greythorn said dismissively. "An accident. A tragedy. The entire Thornwick line, wiped out in a single night. The throne will pass to the nearest eligible house, which, by remarkable coincidence, will be mine."

"All of them." Evelyn's eyes were fixed on something in the distance, through the ballroom doors, Teyra realized, where a small boy was playing with a wooden sword, laughing as a nursemaid chased him around a fountain. "My grandson Elias. The younger one. You promised he would live."

"He will live," Greythorn confirmed. "Adopted into my house. Raised as my own. He'll never know his true heritage. He'll grow up believing the story we tell him, that his family died in a tragic accident, that I saved him from the flames out of the goodness of my heart." His smile was reptilian. "By the time he's old enough to matter, he'll be more Greythorn than Thornwick. A useful piece. A living symbol of my family's generosity and compassion."

"And the older boy? Ashen?"

Silence.

Greythorn's expression didn't change. "Ashen is the heir. He carries the blood-right. He cannot be allowed to survive."

"He's seven years old."

"He's a threat." Greythorn's voice was flat, final. "I've worked too long to let a child destroy everything. The prophecy will justify his death. The people will believe we had no choice, that we sacrificed him to save the kingdom. They'll mourn him as a martyr. They'll never know the truth."

Lady Evelyn closed her eyes. A single tear tracked down her cheek.

"And what is the truth, Lord Greythorn? Remind me. I seem to have forgotten."

"The truth is power," Greythorn said. "The Thornwicks have held the throne for three hundred years. Three hundred years of incompetence, of weakness, of kings who cared more about poetry than politics. Alaric's father opened the drainage wards to Hollow Stair for free, did you know that? Free ward maintenance for the lower city, paid for from the Crown's purse. Bankrupting the treasury to give the poor clean rain." He said it like a curse. "The kingdom is rotting from the head down. Someone must cut out the infection. Someone must seize control and restore order."

"And that someone is you."

"That someone is my family. For generations. Forever." Greythorn's eyes glittered with a fervor that bordered on madness. "The Greythorns will rule this kingdom until the sun burns out. And we will do what must be done to ensure that future, no matter how many children must burn."

The ballroom dissolved into ash and smoke, reforming around her.

Now Teyra was somewhere else, a bedroom, richly appointed, filled with the golden light of morning. A small boy sat on the edge of a massive bed, his feet dangling, too short to reach the floor. He was perhaps seven years old, with dark hair that fell into his eyes and a face that Teyra recognized with a pang like a Resonance spike behind her ribs.

Ash. The child who would become the ghost who would become the man she loved.

He was crying. Silent tears that he kept wiping away, trying to hide them, trying to be brave.

A woman sat beside him, someone younger and softer than Lady Evelyn, with kind eyes and gentle hands. A nursemaid, perhaps, or a beloved aunt. She was stroking his hair, murmuring comfort.

"I don't want to go," the boy whispered. "I don't want to be king. I want to stay here with you and Elias and the horses."

"I know, sweet boy. I know." The woman's voice cracked. "But some things aren't for us to choose. You were born to a duty, and duty must be served."

"Father says kings have to be strong. That they can't cry. That they can't love things too much because everything they love becomes a weapon their enemies can use against them." The boy looked up, his eyes, grey, storm-grey, Ash's eyes, filled with a bewilderment too vast for his young mind. "But I love everything. I love you. I love Elias. I love my horse and my books and the garden where the roses grow. Does that mean I'm going to be a bad king?"

"No, my darling." The woman gathered him into her arms, holding him tight. "That means you're going to be the best king this kingdom has ever had. Because you'll rule with love, not with the thing your father's afraid of. And that's the rarest gift of all."

Time lurched forward, violent and dizzying. Night now. Fire.

The Thornwick manor was burning.

Teyra stood in the courtyard, surrounded by chaos. Flames roared from every window, painting the sky orange and black. People ran screaming, servants, guards, and nobles fleeing in their nightclothes. Horses shrieked in the stables. The heat was unbearable, scorching her skin even though she knew she wasn't really here, knew this was just a memory playing out before her eyes.

And there, in the center of the courtyard, was the boy.

He was alone. Separated from the rest, standing frozen in the middle of the chaos, his eyes fixed on the upper windows where someone was screaming his name. His mother, Teyra realized. His mother was trapped in the flames, calling for him, begging him to run, to save himself.

He didn't run.

He ran toward the fire.

A man caught him, a guard, maybe, or a servant, lifted him bodily off the ground, carried him away from the burning building despite his screams, despite his struggles.

"Mother! Mother, I'm coming! Mother..."

The vision froze.

The fire stopped. The screams stopped. Everything stopped, caught in a single moment of perfect stillness.

And then a voice spoke. A voice that came from everywhere and nowhere, that vibrated in Teyra's bones and made her teeth ache.

"This is the truth they hid."

The vision pulled her forward one last time, settling the way sediment drops through cold tea, slow and irreversible.

She was back in the ballroom, but later now, years later. The child had become a tall, handsome man, dressed for coronation.

He stood before a mirror, adjusting his collar, his face calm but his hands trembling slightly.

A door opened behind him. A woman entered.

She was beautiful. Dark hair, pale skin, a gown of dark red that caught the light like liquid fire. On her wrist, a gold bracelet, the Ouroboros, the serpent eating its tail.

Seraphine.

This was not the wounded, desperate woman Teyra knew. This Seraphine was young, radiant, her eyes soft as she looked at the man who would be king.

"Nervous?" she asked, smiling.

"Terrified." Ash, the adult Ash, the prince, turned to face her. His smile was warm, genuine, the smile of a man who had learned that some things survived the wreckage. "Tomorrow I become king. Tomorrow everything changes."

"Everything has already changed." Seraphine moved closer, took his hands in hers. "We've been betrothed since we were children. I've loved you since I was old enough to know what love meant. Tomorrow, we make that official. Tomorrow, we begin our life together."

"If the prophecy allows it."

A shadow crossed Seraphine's face. "The seers confirmed it today, Ash. All twelve of them. Greythorn showed me the blood divinations himself. 'When a Thornwick sits upon the throne, the city shall burn and the kingdom shall fall.' It's been verified. Cross-referenced. Confirmed."

"Greythorn is an old man clinging to ancient superstitions to maintain his influence." Ash's voice was gentle, dismissive. "I won't let a dusty scroll dictate our future."

"It's a prophecy sealed by twelve seers and confirmed by blood divination." Seraphine's voice cracked. "What if they're right? What if the coronation triggers the curse? What if I lose you?"

"You won't lose me." He squeezed her hands. "After tomorrow, we'll have all the time in the world. The prophecy is political theater. Greythorn has reasons of his own for wanting me afraid."

"Promise me you'll be careful tonight." Her eyes searched his face. "Promise me. Something feels wrong. I can't explain it, but something feels terribly wrong."

Ash lifted her hands to his lips, kissed her knuckles gently.

"I promise," he said. "Tonight, let's just dance."

The vision jumped forward.

The coronation ball. The same ballroom where the conspiracy had been born, now filled with celebrating nobles, the music triumphant, the champagne flowing freely. Ash stood at the center of it all, resplendent in his coronation robes, a crown of gold and sapphires gleaming on his brow.

He was dancing with Seraphine. Spinning her across the floor, laughing, his face alight with the moment.

And then.

The music stopped.

The dancers parted.

Seraphine's hand moved, quick and practiced, the movement of someone who had trained for this moment, and suddenly there was a blade in her grip. Slim, dark-metaled, wickedly sharp. A severance blade.

Ash didn't see it coming.

She drove the blade between his ribs, angling upward, piercing his heart with surgical precision. Her face was wet with tears, her lips moving, whispering something only he could hear.

"I'm sorry. I'm so sorry. They showed me the prophecy. If you take the throne, the city will burn. I can't let you become a monster. I love you. I love you. Please forgive me…"

He looked at her. His eyes were wide with shock, and then, slowly, with understanding.

"Seraphine," he whispered.

And then he fell.

The vision shattered.

Teyra came back to herself with a gasp, her body jolting like she'd been dropped from a height.

She was on her knees on the cold marble floor of the bone chamber, her hands pressed flat against the stone, her breath coming in ragged sobs. The book lay open before her, the glowing ink faded to mundane script, whatever power it had contained expended in the vision.

But the vision had left something behind, and it wasn't in the book. It was in her. The scribe who'd copied the altered prophecy. She could feel him now, the way she felt all the others, an old man's weight, the tremor of a quill in an ink-stained hand, the knowledge that he was forging a lie that would kill children. He had wept while he wrote. She could feel the tears, his tears, three centuries old, still wet behind her eyes. The book had given her its last secret. The man who'd been forced to write the words, and how it had felt in his hands.

Another weight for the pile.

Ash was beside her.

He was standing in the center of the summoning circle, his form blazing with silver light, his face twisted into something that hurt to look at. The air around him had dropped forty degrees in seconds. Frost was spreading across the floor, racing outward from his feet, climbing the bone walls, coating the skulls in a rime of ice that crackled and popped.

"It was a lie," he said.

His voice had broken open, the sound of a man who had just watched everything he believed crumble to dust, who had died for a prophecy that didn't exist.

"It was all a lie. There was no curse. There was no doom. Greythorn made it up. He fabricated the entire prophecy to steal my throne, and Seraphine..."

He turned toward Seraphine, and the temperature dropped another ten degrees.

She was on her knees at the edge of the circle, her face pale as death, her hands pressed over her mouth. She was shaking, and the shaking came from somewhere deeper than the cold, somewhere inside her that was coming apart with every breath.

"I killed you," she whispered. "I killed you for a lie."

"You killed me because Greythorn told you to." Ash's voice was ice. "You killed me because you believed him. Because you trusted him. Because you thought you were saving the world."

"I thought... I believed..." She was crying now, tears streaming down her face, mixing with the blood that had started seeping from her wound again. "They showed me the prophecy. They showed me the confirmations. Twelve seers, all agreeing. How was I supposed to know? How was I supposed to know it was all a fabrication?"

"You were supposed to trust me!"

The words came out as a roar, and the bone chamber shook. Skulls rattled in their places. The columns groaned. The frost spread faster, thicker, climbing toward the invisible ceiling.

Ash was losing control.

Teyra pushed herself to her feet, her legs shaking.

Ash was about to tear the world apart.

"Ash," she said. Her voice came out steady, somehow. The calm she'd learned from years of dealing with angry spirits, the composure that had kept her alive a dozen times over. "Ash, look at me."

He turned.

His eyes were white, pure white, blazing with the cold fire of a poltergeist on the edge of transformation. The man was disappearing. The monster was emerging.

"Look at me," Teyra repeated. She stepped into the circle, into the blast radius of his power, close enough to touch if either of them dared. "I saw it too."

"They took everything from me." His voice was splitting, doubling, the human tone warring with something older and colder. "They took my family, my throne, my whole life, and they called it mercy. They called it saving the kingdom."

"I know."

"For two generations, my family has been blamed for a curse that never existed. For two generations, the Greythorns have ruled on a foundation of murder and lies. And Seraphine..."

He turned back toward her, and the air between them crystallized into a blade of ice.

"Seraphine was their weapon. Their fool. Their murderer in a red dress."

"Yes." Teyra moved between them, putting herself in the path of his power. "She was. She was manipulated and deceived and used. Just like you were. Just like your family was. Just like everyone who ever believed that prophecy."

"That doesn't excuse what she did."

"No. It doesn't." Teyra met his eyes, those terrible white eyes, without flinching. "But killing her won't bring you back. Destroying this place won't undo what happened. The only thing that can give you justice now is the truth."

She pointed at the book.

"We have it. The original prophecy. The proof that Greythorn fabricated everything. With this, we can expose him. We can show the world what he did. We can make sure that everyone knows the Thornwicks were murdered for a lie."

Ash was shaking. The white was beginning to fade from his eyes, replaced by grey, by exhaustion written into every crack in his spectral skin.

"And Seraphine?" he asked quietly.

Teyra looked at the woman kneeling on the floor, broken, bleeding, weeping for the man she had killed and the life she had destroyed.

"That's not for me to decide," she said. "That's between you and her."

Ash turned.

He walked toward Seraphine with slow, deliberate steps. The frost crackled beneath his feet. The temperature dropped with each step, until the breath he didn't need misted in the air before him.

He stopped before her.

She looked up. Her face was a ruin of tears and blood and five years of debt finally collected.

"Kill me," she whispered. "If that's what you need. Kill me, and maybe I can finally rest."

Ash looked at her for a long moment.

Then he said, "No."

Seraphine flinched as though he'd struck her.

"I spent five years dead because of you. Five years in the dark, with no memory, no identity, no understanding of why I was suffering. I have every right to hate you. Every right to destroy you."

He crouched down, bringing his face level with hers.

"But I remember now. I remember everything. The boy who loved too much. The man who wanted to be a good king. Holding your hands and promising to watch my back."

His voice cracked.

"And I remember the way you looked at me when you drove that blade into my heart. You were broken. You were destroying the thing you loved most in the world, and it was killing you as surely as you were killing me."

He reached out, slowly, carefully, and touched her face. The effort of holding solid showed in the faint tremor at the edges of his form, his fingers flickering once before steadying against her skin. They were freezing, cold enough to burn. But she didn't flinch. She leaned into his touch, desperate for the contact, desperate for something she had no right to ask for.

"I don't forgive you," Ash said quietly. "I may never get there. But I understand. And I won't become the monster they wanted me to be."

Teyra's chest ached. She was watching a man become the king he was supposed to be.

"I won't let their lies turn me into something worthy of the curse they invented."

He stood up.

"Now get up. We're not done yet."

Seraphine stared at him. Then, slowly, painfully, she pushed herself to her feet.

"The book," she said, her voice raw. "We need to take it. Show the world..."

A sharp, metallic click echoed from deep inside the bone walls.

Everyone froze.

Then another, and another, the sound of tumblers falling into place, multiplying until the chamber rang with it.

The walls were waking up. The wet, grinding sound of bone sliding against bone filled the chamber.

The recognition landed cold and sudden.

"The wards," she breathed. "The vault was protected. When we opened the book, when the truth was revealed..."

"We triggered a failsafe," Seraphine finished. Her face had gone pale. "Greythorn. He knew someone might find this place someday. He prepared for it."

The sounds were multiplying, echoing through the bone walls.

The bone walls were shifting, rearranging, revealing hidden compartments and sealed chambers.

And from those chambers, things were emerging.

These were older than Hessians. Older than guards. Constructs that had been waiting in the dark for three hundred years.

"We need to leave," Teyra said. "Now."

She grabbed the book—cold, heavier than it should have been—and shoved it into her bag. Grabbed Ash's arm—whole now, blessedly whole—and pulled him toward the passage they'd entered through.

The passage wasn't there anymore.

Where the entrance had been, there was only bone. Smooth, seamless, as if the doorway had never existed.

The clicking was closer now, louder, wet bone grinding against dry bone while tumblers fell in sequence and the walls rearranged themselves around them.

"Seraphine," Teyra said, her voice tight. "Please tell me there's another way out."

Seraphine was staring at the bone walls, her face blank with dawning understanding of what they'd walked into.

"There was," she said. "But Greythorn sealed it. Years ago. When he realized I was asking too many questions about the vault."

"So we're trapped."

"We're trapped."

Greythorn had known. He'd known Seraphine would come back here eventually, and he'd sealed her exit years before she'd even decided to betray him. The man was always three moves ahead.

One last click, quiet, precise, almost delicate, and the wall beside them split open like a wound.

The first of the things emerged.

It was made of bone.

Chapter Nine

WHAT THE BONES REMEMBER

DAY FIVE, DAWN: THREE DAYS REMAIN

THE THING THAT EMERGED from the wall was nothing like a skeleton.

Skeletons were dry, fragile, dead; this thing had been made. Something assembled in the dark over three centuries, patient and hungry and very, very awake.

It pulled itself from the bone wall one joint at a time, his form dragging against the marble as though the floor were trying to keep him, first a hand, fingers splayed, each one a different bone from a different body, fused together at wrong angles. Then an arm, a shoulder, and finally the head. The head was the worst. It was made of seven skulls, melted and merged into a single mass, eye sockets overlapping, jaws fused at grotesque angles, teeth jutting out in rows like a shark's mouth turned inside out.

It had no eyes. But it could see. Teyra felt its attention fix on her like a weight, like a hand closing around her throat.

And beneath the animation matrix, beneath the cold mechanical spell that moved the bones, she could feel the rage she'd absorbed in the bone chamber. The workers. The entombed builders. Their three-hundred-year-old fury was the *fuel* for these constructs, as her collected fragments had fueled the Moonflower brew. The Greythorns had gone further than burial. They'd harvested the workers' anger, wound it into the ward-magic, used the trapped dead to power the guardians that protected the secrets that had killed them. Even in death, the workers served. Even in death, they had no choice.

More clicking. More movement. More of them emerging from the walls, three, five, eight, a dozen. They came in different shapes and configurations of stolen bones. Some were humanoid, walking on legs made of spines and arms made of ribs. Some were quadrupeds, scuttling across the floor on hands and feet that bent the wrong way. One was a serpent, a ribbon of vertebrae thirty feet long, its head a pelvis with teeth grafted into the hip sockets.

But one of them was different.

It was smaller than the others, a hunched, vaguely human shape assembled from a child's worth of bones. It moved slower, almost hesitantly, as if it wasn't entirely sure it existed. And where the other constructs were white bone and red ward-light, this one was threaded with something else. Patches of absence, like holes in its own structure, places where the bone simply stopped and nothing took its place. Teyra's eyes slid off those patches the same way they'd slid off the jar in the Moth's tent.

The same nothing. Down here. In the walls.

Ash made a sound, low, involuntary, almost a moan. His spectral form destabilized, and she saw him take a step backward. He'd recognized it without knowing how.

"Don't let that one touch you," he said. His voice came out cracked and urgent, carrying a certainty that bypassed logic entirely. "It's hollow. It's wrong."

The bone constructs moved in perfect silence, their joints clicking softly as they advanced.

"Back to back," Seraphine hissed, drawing her knife. She was swaying on her feet, face grey, wound bleeding freely now, but her eyes were clear and her grip steady. Twenty years of combat training taking over where her body was failing. "Don't let them flank us."

Teyra pressed her back against Seraphine's, facing the constructs on the opposite side of the circle. Her mind was racing, trying to remember everything she'd learned about animated bone. They had no soul inside them, no consciousness to banish. They were constructs, puppets, held together by magic woven into their very structure.

Which meant the magic could be disrupted.

"Ash," she called out, her voice tight. "Can you feel them? The animation matrix?"

"I feel everything in this room." His voice came from everywhere at once, he had dispersed partially, spreading his presence across the chamber, filling the space with cold. "The magic is old. Three hundred years old. Woven into the bones during the original binding."

"Can you break it?"

"I'm trying." There was strain in his voice. "But the wards, the blood wards, they're fighting me. Every time I push, they push back. It's like trying to move through fire."

The first construct lunged.

It moved faster than something made of bone should move, a blur of fused skulls and reaching claws, crossing the distance in a heartbeat. Teyra threw herself sideways, felt the wind of its passage as it swept past her, heard the crack of bone on stone as its claws gouged furrows in the marble floor.

She came up rolling, her hand already in her pocket, fingers closing around the last of her bonemeal. Maybe enough to slow it down.

The construct turned, reoriented, came at her again.

Teyra threw the powder.

It hit the thing's fused skull-head, coating the bone in grey dust. She pushed her magic into it, just a weakening blow, enough to slow but not to kill. Accelerated decay, targeting the joints, the places where different bones had been fused together.

The construct's left arm fell off.

It didn't slow down.

The thing compensated for the missing limb, adjusted its balance, and kept coming, its remaining arm sweeping toward her in a wide arc, claws extended, aiming for her throat.

Teyra dropped flat. The claws passed over her, close enough to tug at her hair. She rolled onto her back, kicked upward with both feet, caught the thing in what would have been its chest. Bones cracked. The construct staggered.

She scrambled backward, putting distance between them, gasping for breath. Her vision was starting to blur at the edges, the Grave-Chill taking its toll, the magic draining her faster than she could recover.

Then the hollow construct found her.

It didn't lunge. It walked toward her with that slow, uncertain gait, the hesitant movement of something that wasn't sure it wanted to exist. Up close, it was worse than she'd thought. The bones were small. Too small. A child's femurs. A child's ribs. Tiny finger bones fused into hands that opened and closed in a rhythm that looked, horribly, like grasping.

And Teyra felt it.

The animation matrix was mechanical, cold, a spell wound through dead calcium like wire through a puppet. This was underneath the spell. Deeper, older. A residue that shouldn't have existed in a construct, because constructs didn't have souls.

But this one had a memory of one.

It hit her like a wave, pure and unprocessed and ancient. A child's bewilderment at being taken apart and put back together wrong. The bones remembered the body they'd belonged to, and the body remembered being small, and scared, and asking for its mother in a language that had been dead for three hundred years.

Help me, the feeling said. The wordless plea of something that didn't know what it was anymore.

Teyra's hand came up. To reach. To touch, with open hands.

The necromancer in her, the real necromancer, the one who had broken her Academy exam because she couldn't stop caring, overrode everything else. Training, logic, the twelve constructs still converging. The fact that Seraphine was fighting alone behind her, wounded, holding a knife against a tide of bone.

All of it vanished. All she could see was a child's skeleton, assembled wrong, hurting in a way that constructs weren't supposed to hurt, and she was reaching for it the way she'd reached for Thomas in that exam room, reaching to comfort rather than command.

"It's all right," she whispered. Her fingers brushed the construct's fused skull. The bone was ice-cold and impossibly smooth. "I can feel you. I know you're scared. I'm going to..."

The construct's hand closed around her wrist.

It wasn't attacking. It was clinging.

Tiny bone fingers wrapping around her arm with the strength of a child clinging to the only person who'd acknowledged it in three centuries. The void-patches in its structure pulsed, and Teyra felt the nothing press against her skin, profoundly wrong, like pressing her hand against a hole in the world.

She couldn't move. The construct held her, and the feeling held her harder, wave after wave of trapped suffering, of bewildered consciousness ground down to its barest residue and still, somehow, aching.

Behind her, Seraphine screamed.

The sound cut through the empathic fog like a blade. Teyra wrenched her head around and saw it. While she'd been communing with a dead child's echo, a quadruped construct, the one that scuttled on wrongly-bent hands and feet, had flanked Seraphine's unprotected side. Its claw was buried in her abdomen, hooked into the edge of the existing wound and tearing downward, ripping through the necrotic seal, through the scar tissue that had been holding her together for the last six hours, and into the fresh flesh beneath.

What had been a sealed gash was now an open wound from hip to ribs, a single ragged line deep enough to show the white gleam of bone.

Seraphine's knife clattered to the floor. Her knees buckled. Blood, dark, arterial, too much, poured from between her fingers as she pressed both hands to her stomach. The grey pallor of exhaustion was replaced by the white of genuine shock.

She was dying, and the timeline had collapsed from eventually to now.

Ash materialized between Seraphine and the construct, his power detonating in a blast of frost that sent the thing skidding across the marble in pieces. But the effort tore a scream from him, the blood wards retaliating, red fire crawling across his spectral skin, cracking him like porcelain. He dropped to one knee, gasping.

Teyra yanked her wrist free of the hollow construct's grip. The tiny bone fingers broke with a sound like snapping twigs, and the feeling cut off, sudden, total, leaving a ringing emptiness in her chest.

She ran to Seraphine.

The wound was bad. Worse than bad. The quadruped's claw had torn through the necrotic seal she'd placed on the original injury, ripping open the partially healed tissue beneath. Blood was pooling on the marble faster than Seraphine could press it back.

"Pressure," Teyra said, her hands joining Seraphine's over the wound. "Keep pressure. I can..."

"Don't." Seraphine's voice was thin, threaded with strain, but her eyes were clear. Horribly clear. "Don't waste the magic. You'll need it to get us out."

"I can seal it again. I just need,,,"

"You need to stop."

It wasn't Seraphine who said it.

Ash was on his feet again, barely, his form phasing between solid and transparent. The red cracks from the ward-fire were still glowing across his skin. He was looking at Teyra with an expression she'd never seen on his face before.

Worse than anything he'd shown her yet.

"She is dying," he said, voice raw, "because you turned your back on a fight to hold a dead child's hand."

The words hit like a slap. Teyra looked at her hands, covered in Seraphine's blood, still tingling from the construct's touch.

He was right.

He was right. The Academy had been right, and every professor who'd told her that empathy was a liability in the field had been right. She had felt a dead child's pain and it had swallowed her whole, and while she'd been drowning in someone else's hurt, a living woman had been gutted three feet behind her.

A necromancer commands the dead, Miss Tepes. She does not weep for them.

The old words rose up unbidden, and for the first time in her life, they didn't feel cruel. They felt like a warning she should have listened to.

"I know," she said, the words small and bare. "I know."

Ash's expression shifted, the hardness cracking, revealing what it had been protecting. The words had cost him as much as they'd cost her.

"We can argue about it later," Seraphine said through gritted teeth. Her hands were slick with blood, her face the color of old wax. "Assuming there is a later. The constructs are still coming, I'm running out of blood to lose, and whatever you felt in that thing..." She jerked her chin toward the hollow construct, which had re-assembled its broken fingers and was swaying in place, still radiating its trapped, awful weight. "It's been here for three centuries. It can wait."

Teyra pressed harder on the wound. Felt the wet heat of Seraphine's blood between her fingers.

The constructs were regrouping. The hollow one was watching her. What it radiated hadn't stopped, she could still feel it, pressing against her senses like a hand against a window.

She chose to let it hurt, and she chose to keep fighting anyway.

"The small one," Ash said, voice cracked from the ward-fire. "The hollow one. It dissolved Seraphine's knife. My frost didn't touch it. The void-patches just ate it."

"I felt it too," Teyra said. "When it grabbed me. The nothing. Same signature as the jar in the Moth's tent."

Seraphine looked between them, pressing one blood-soaked hand against her wound. "You're saying the void is leaking into the constructs. Into the estate's own defenses."

"Into the foundations," Teyra said. "The containment below us is failing. The Moth said it was growing. He was right." She met

Ash's eyes. "If it's already reaching the constructs three hundred years after the seal was set, how long before it reaches the surface?"

No one had an answer. No one wanted one.

But there were too many.

For every construct Seraphine destroyed, two more emerged from the walls. For every bone that fell, another rose. The chamber was filling with them, a tide of stolen skeletons, pressing inward, tightening the circle.

"We can't hold them!" Teyra shouted.

"I know!" Seraphine was slowing down, blood loss catching up with her, her movements becoming sluggish, her reactions delayed. A construct's claw caught her shoulder, tore through fabric and flesh. She cried out, stumbled.

A bone serpent reared up behind her, jaws gaping, ready to strike.

Ash materialized between them.

He was blazing, silver light pouring from his form, bright enough to cast shadows, bright enough to make the bone constructs hesitate. He caught the serpent by its vertebrae-throat, and frost exploded outward from his grip, racing down the length of the thing's body, freezing the magic that animated it.

The serpent shattered. Fragments of frozen bone rained down like hail.

But the effort cost him.

Ash screamed, a sound of pure agony, as the blood wards retaliated. Teyra saw red light flare across his skin, saw cracks appear in his spectral flesh, saw the silver glow gutter and dim. The wards were designed to reject the uninvited dead. Every time he used his power, they burned him from the inside out.

"Ash!" Teyra started toward him.

"Stay back!" He threw out a hand, and a wall of ice erupted from the floor between them, blocking her path. "I can hold them. Get Seraphine. Find another way out."

"There is no other way out!"

"Then make one!"

He turned back to the constructs, and the temperature in the chamber dropped thirty degrees in a second. Frost raced across the floor, up the walls, coating the bone columns in a rime of ice. The constructs slowed, their joints stiffening, their movements becoming jerky as the cold interfered with their animation.

But the wards fought back. Red light flared through the ice, melting it, pushing back against Ash's cold. The chamber became a battlefield of fire and frost, the two magics warring for dominance while the bone constructs continued their relentless advance.

Teyra grabbed Seraphine, pulled her toward the far wall. The woman was barely conscious now, too much blood loss, too much damage, her body finally surrendering to wounds that should have killed her hours ago.

"Stay with me," Teyra hissed, slapping Seraphine's cheek. "We're not dying in a bone pit."

"The walls," Seraphine mumbled, her eyes unfocused. "The walls... there's a... service passage. Behind the... the big column. For removing... bodies..."

A corpse chute. Of course. Even ancient noble families needed a way to dispose of the dead without carrying them back up through the main halls. It would be narrow, cramped, probably filled with three centuries of accumulated filth, but it would lead out.

Teyra looked at the column Seraphine had indicated, a massive pillar of fused femurs and tibias, rising up into the darkness. Behind it, half-hidden by the chaos of combat, she could see a darker shadow. An opening.

Between them and that opening stood a dozen bone constructs.

And Ash, fighting alone, burning alive from the inside.

Teyra made a decision.

She lowered Seraphine to the floor, propped her against the wall, and turned back toward the battle. Her hands were shaking. Her vision was blurring. The cold had settled into her bones like runoff from a Grave-Chill, making every movement an effort.

She had maybe one more spell in her. Maybe two if she was lucky. After that, she would collapse, and everything they'd fought for would be lost.

She had to make it count.

"Ash!" she shouted over the sound of cracking ice and clicking bones. "I need you to clear a path! The big column, there's an exit behind it!"

He turned toward her, his face a mask of strain and determination. The cracks in his spectral skin had spread further, the glow of the wards burned through him from the inside. He was dying again. And still fighting.

"On my mark!" she called. "Drop everything you have! One massive push!"

"If I do that..." His voice cracked. "The wards will..."

"I know! Do it anyway!"

She saw the moment he understood. The moment he accepted what she was asking. He met her eyes across the chaos, and she saw everything there at once, more than she could name and all of it real.

"On three," she said.

He didn't wait for three.

He turned back to the constructs. Drew in a breath he didn't need. And unleashed everything.

The cold that exploded from his form was beyond anything Teyra had ever felt. It was death itself, the fundamental cessation of movement and warmth. It washed over the chamber like a tidal wave, freezing everything it touched. Constructs stopped mid-motion, encased in ice. The floor cracked beneath the pressure. The bone walls groaned and popped as moisture in the ancient calcium crystallized and expanded.

For one perfect moment, everything was still.

Then the wards struck back.

Red fire erupted from the walls, from the floor, from the air itself. It slammed into Ash with the force of a physical blow, drove him to his knees. His scream echoed through the chamber, a sound of pure, overwhelming agony. The silver light of his form guttered, dimmed, faded.

Teyra ran.

She grabbed Seraphine, hauled her upright, and dragged her toward the column. The ice was already cracking, the constructs snapping into violent, rigid spasms as the animation magic seized their joints. They had seconds. Maybe less.

The opening behind the column was exactly what Seraphine had described, a narrow shaft, barely wide enough for a single person, descending into darkness. A corpse chute, designed to drop bodies into some deeper pit where they could decompose in peace.

"Go," Teyra hissed, shoving Seraphine toward the opening. "Slide. I'll be right behind you."

"Ash..."

"I'll get him. Go!"

Seraphine didn't argue. She couldn't have if she'd wanted to; her jaw was locked, her breath coming in short, controlled bursts, the discipline of a soldier managing pain that had passed beyond screaming. Teyra half-pushed, half-lowered her into the shaft. Seraphine's fingers found the edges, slipped, found them again. Her legs went over. Gravity took her, but Ash threw out a hand from across the chamber, and Teyra felt a pulse of telekinetic cold wrap around the falling woman, slowing the descent, cradling the open wound away from the filth-slicked stone. The effort cost him, she heard him cry out as the wards punished him, but Seraphine's landing, when it came, was a dull, heavy thud that shook through the burial shrouds beneath her.

She turned back.

Ash was on his hands and knees in the center of the chamber, all but lost in the red fire that wreathed his form. The constructs were converging on him, drawn by his power, by the death energy bleeding from his failing form. In moments, they would tear him apart.

Teyra did the only thing she could think of.

She reached into the deepest part of herself, past the cold, past the exhaustion, and grabbed hold of the magic that made her a necromancer. The raw, primal power that had been in her blood since birth. The Command Word, the older one, the one her grandmother had known rather than the Academy's formalized version she'd never been certified to use. And the fragments answered the call.

Every one of them. The ghost in the doorway's bewilderment. The entombed workers' three-hundred-year-old fury. The scribe's weight. The faded echoes of the old collection, every borrowed hurt she'd carried since Weaver Street, thinned by the Moonflower healing but still present. All of them, faded and new alike, surging toward the surface of her consciousness like air bubbles rising through dark water. She felt them gather, felt them compress, felt them offer themselves as fuel, the same mechanism as the Moonflower brew, the same mechanism as the necrotic healing, but at a scale that made her vision go white.

She spoke a word.

It came from somewhere older than any human language, a sound that predated speech, that came from the time when death itself was young. A word of command. A word of authority. A word that said, *These bones are mine.*

The constructs stopped.

Every single one of them. Stopped mid-motion, frozen in place, their empty skulls turning toward her in what could only be described as surprise.

The word burned through her like fire, and she felt the fragments burn with it. Each one igniting, flaring, and being spent.

Thomas's homesickness died screaming in the back of her mind. The widow's yearning for mornings evaporated. The sailor's loneliness, the cold ache for open water she'd carried so long she'd mistaken it for her own, guttered out. The little girl's winter-cold, the one who'd been with her since she was twelve, the first ghost who'd ever left a mark, guttered once and was gone. Gone. The workers' fury was spent in a single flash of heat. The scribe's weight dissolved. The phantom blade between her ribs, Ash's death, the wound she'd carried since the tea-reading on Weaver Street, finally, mercifully, stopped hurting.

Because it was gone. They were all gone.

She felt blood pour from her nose, from her ears, from the corners of her eyes. Her vision went red, then black, then red again, and her legs buckled.

But the constructs stayed still. And inside Teyra's chest, where the collection had lived, where the fragments of borrowed hurt had accumulated, one by one, day by day, since a rainy morning in a tea shop on Weaver Street, there was silence. Absolute silence. The silence of a house with every room emptied, a body with nothing left to give.

"Ash," she gasped, the word a thread of sound. The room tilted. Her vision was wrong, doubled, everything edged in red. "Move. Now."

He moved.

He dragged himself across the floor, leaving a trail of frost and fading light. The red fire followed him, burning, punishing, but he kept going. He reached the column, reached the shaft, looked back at her with eyes that were more white than grey.

"Teyra…"

"I'm coming."

She released the word.

The backlash hit her like a hammer. She felt a rupture inside her, deep in the non-physical architecture of her gift, some fundamental part of her necromancy shredding under the strain. The channels that had carried the fragments were scorched, the pathways that had connected her to the dead blackened and raw. The constructs lurched back into motion, their momentary pause ended, their attention snapping toward her with renewed purpose.

She ran.

Three steps to the column. Two more to the shaft. A construct's claw caught her ankle, tearing through boot and flesh and driving hot pain up her leg. She kicked free, threw herself into the opening, felt the darkness swallow her as she fell.

The slide was steep and slick with something she didn't want to identify. She plummeted through absolute blackness, her body bouncing off stone walls, her hands scrabbling for purchase and finding none. The construct's claw marks burned on her ankle. Her head was spinning from blood loss and magic drain.

Then she hit bottom.

The impact drove the air from her lungs. She lay stunned on a pile of something soft and yielding, old cloth, she realized distantly. Burial shrouds. The accumulated detritus of centuries of bodies dumped down this shaft.

"Teyra!" Ash's voice, somewhere above her. "Are you alive?"

"Define alive," she croaked.

Hands grabbed her, cold hands, Ash's hands, pulling her upright. Seraphine was there too, propped against a wall of rough-hewn stone. Her eyes were open but unfocused, tracking movement without processing it, the look of someone whose body was still running on training while everything else had shut down. One hand was pressed against her side. The other lay palm-up on the stone, fingers curled loosely around nothing. The bandages were gone. The wound was a dark, wet line that Teyra couldn't look at directly.

And there was light ahead. Real light. Grey and dim, but unmistakably natural.

"Surface," Seraphine said. The word came out flat, mechanical, a status report from a system running on emergency power.

The passage led upward through a maze of ancient tunnels.

Teyra had lost all sense of direction, all sense of time. She moved on autopilot, one foot in front of the other, her arm around Seraphine's waist, supporting the dying woman's weight. Ash walked ahead, silver glow lighting the way, his form thinning with every step until she could see the tunnel walls through his chest.

The blood wards had nearly destroyed him, and they weren't the only thing. The ice blasts in the bone chamber, the poltergeist bursts, the telekinetic cushioning of Seraphine's fall, the effort of holding solid while the wards tried to unmake him, each had burned through the Moonflower's reserves like a month of normal existence compressed into minutes. She could see the damage, cracks running through his spectral flesh, patches of transparency where his form had given up, the silver light dimming with every step. The fresh Moonflower that should have kept him strong through the final three days was nearly spent. He was holding himself together through sheer will.

They all were.

The light grew brighter as they climbed. The air grew fresher, still damp, still heavy with the smell of earth and old death, though the air had thinned, carrying rain and cold and the open world above.

They emerged through a broken grate into a graveyard.

The Greythorn family cemetery, Teyra realized. Rows of headstones stretched away into the pre-dawn gloom, ancient markers worn smooth by centuries of weather. Mausoleums loomed like miniature temples, their doors sealed, their windows dark. The rain had stopped, but the sky was still heavy with clouds, the first grey light of dawn barely touching the eastern horizon.

They were out.

Teyra took three steps into the graveyard and collapsed.

Her legs stopped working. She hit the wet grass face-first, body refusing another inch. The channeled death had consumed her, it was in her bones, in her blood, in the empty space where her magic should have been. She had given everything. There was nothing left.

"Teyra!" Ash was beside her, his cold hands on her face, his voice cracked. "Teyra, stay with me. Don't close your eyes."

"Tired," she mumbled. The word came out slurred, distant. "So tired."

"I know. I know. But you can't sleep yet. We're not safe. We're still on Greythorn land. We need to move."

"Can't."

"You can." His hands found hers, squeezed hard. The cold burned, but she was too exhausted to care. "You carried me out of the conservatory. You carried me through the blood fire. You held a word of command long enough for me to escape. You are the strongest person I have ever known, Teyra Tepes. You can do this. You can stand up. You can walk."

She opened her eyes.

His face was inches from hers, pale, cracked, barely holding its shape, but his eyes were steady. Grey now, the white faded, the poltergeist burned away. He looked at her like she was the only thing in the world that mattered.

"Help me," she whispered.

He pulled her upright. Her legs screamed in protest, but they held.

They stood there swaying, holding each other up in a graveyard full of the enemy's dead. The dawn was coming. Lenore was still inside—still at the top of those stairs, or already gone, because Lenore always found her way out. She had to believe that. She could smell wet grass and turned earth and the clean, cold promise of rain that hadn't fallen yet. A bird, just one, was singing somewhere in the dark beyond the cemetery wall.

And inside her chest, nothing. The place where Thomas's homesickness had lived for four years was a burned-out room. The little girl's winter-cold, carried since she was twelve, gone. She pressed her hand flat against her sternum, feeling for the familiar ache between her third and fourth rib, and found only her own heartbeat, solitary and strange. She didn't have time to understand it. Not yet.

Seraphine was a few feet away, slumped against a headstone, her eyes closed, her breathing shallow. Her left shoulder was torn where a construct's claw had caught her, a shallow wound, almost trivial next to the ruin of her side. The bandages there were gone, torn away by the construct's claw, the wound beneath open and raw, the necrotic seal Teyra had placed hours ago shredded beyond repair.

The blood had slowed to a thick, dark seep, which was worse than fast bleeding. It meant there wasn't much left to lose. She needed a healer. She needed a hospital. She needed a miracle.

"We can't carry her," Teyra said. The words scraped out of her. "We can barely walk ourselves."

"Then we drag her." Ash moved to Seraphine, crouched down, tried to pull one of her arms over his shoulders. His hand phased through her wrist, too exhausted to maintain contact. He tried again. This time he held, barely, the cold of his touch making Seraphine flinch even in unconsciousness. Her head lolled. A thin line of blood ran from the corner of her mouth, from somewhere inside rather than any wound Teyra could see. Something had torn, or was tearing, and there was nothing any of them could do about it in a graveyard at dawn.

"The estate wall is a hundred yards that way. Beyond it is the street. There will be people. Help."

"Or Hessians."

"Then we deal with Hessians." He met her eyes. "We have the book, Teyra. We have the truth. Everything Greythorn built, the lies, the conspiracy, the stolen throne, it all ends when we show the world what's in those pages. We just need to survive long enough to show them."

Teyra looked at the bag slung across her body, battered, stained, but intact. Inside was the original prophecy. The proof. The weapon that would destroy the Greythorn deception, every lie, every forged document, every murdered heir.

She had fought through monsters and wards and her own failing body to get it. Watched Ash nearly die. Used magic that might have permanently damaged her ability to touch death.

She was not going to let it be for nothing.

"A hundred yards," she said.

"A hundred yards."

She took Seraphine's other arm, draped it over her own shoulders. Together, she and Ash lifted the unconscious woman between them, a necromancer and a ghost, carrying the assassin who had started all of this, stumbling through a graveyard toward the promise of dawn.

They made it fifty yards before the first shout.

"Halt! In the name of Lord Greythorn!"

Guards. Four of them, emerging from behind a mausoleum, their uniforms bearing the Greythorn serpent. Flesh and blood men, probably the night watch, probably confused by three blood-soaked figures staggering through their master's cemetery at dawn.

Teyra didn't have enough magic left to light a candle. Ash was too faded to cast a shadow. Seraphine was unconscious.

They were going to be caught. After everything, they were going to be caught.

And then a voice spoke from the darkness behind the guards.

"I wouldn't do that if I were you."

A figure stepped out of the shadows between two headstones, slim, elegant, wearing a suit of grey velvet that seemed to shift color in the pre-dawn light. A mask of silver filigree covered his nose and mouth.

The Moth. Outside the blood wards, the cemetery perimeter sat beyond the estate's interior protections. Of course he'd known exactly where the boundary fell. He'd probably had people at every exit beyond the ward line, waiting to see which one they stumbled out of.

"These three are under my protection," he said. His voice was soft, conversational, utterly devoid of threat. "I suggest you forget you saw them, return to your posts, and never speak of this night again."

"Who the hell are you?" one of the guards demanded, raising his sword.

"Nobody important." The Moth tilted his head, and his dead eyes caught what little light there was. "But I know things, gentlemen. I know that Corporal Hendricks has been stealing from the wine cellar for three years. I know that Sergeant Marsh has a mistress in the Tanners' Quarter that his wife doesn't know about. I know that Private Collins owes a significant debt to a very unpleasant man in the Night Market."

He smiled behind his mask.

"I know everything. And if you don't lower your weapons and walk away in the next ten seconds, your wives, your employers, and your creditors will know everything too."

The guards looked at each other. Then they lowered their weapons.

"Smart choice," the Moth said. "Now run along. And remember, we never met."

The guards fled.

The Moth turned to face Teyra, Ash, and the unconscious Seraphine. His dead eyes swept over them, taking in the blood and the exhaustion and the grip they had on each other and their cargo.

"You got the book," he observed.

"We got the book," Teyra confirmed.

"And nearly died in the process, by the look of you." Satisfaction edged his voice more than concern did. "The woman needs a healer. Badly. There's a clinic in the Dockside District, ask for Dr. Croft. She doesn't ask questions."

"Why are you helping us?"

"I told you before, Miss Tepes. I've been waiting twenty-five years for someone to open that vault." The Moth spread his hands. "You've given me what I wanted. The least I can do is make sure you survive long enough to use it."

He turned to walk away, then paused.

"Oh, and Miss Tepes? The heist you performed for me? Consider the debt paid. The book is yours now. Do with it what you will."

He stepped back into the shadows between the headstones and vanished.

Teyra stared at the space where he'd been. Then she looked at Ash.

"Did that just happen?"

"I think so."

"The Moth just saved our lives and cleared a debt."

"Apparently."

Teyra laughed. It was a broken sound, more sob than humor, but it was the best she could manage.

"I hate this city," she said.

"I know." Ash adjusted his grip on Seraphine. "Come on. Let's find this doctor. We can hate the city once we've stopped bleeding."

The clinic was exactly where the Moth had said, a cramped building wedged between a fishmonger and a rope-maker, its windows dark, its door unmarked. Dr. Croft was a grey-haired woman with steady hands and no curiosity about the three battered figures who appeared on her doorstep at dawn.

She took one look at Seraphine and went to work. Through the thin walls, Teyra could hear the sounds, the clink of surgical instruments, the tear of gauze, Dr. Croft's clipped voice calling for saline, then blood, "I keep a supply for the dockworkers, don't ask where it comes from." The sharp smell of antiseptic seeped under the door like a living thing. At one point, Seraphine screamed, a short, raw sound, cut off by what Teyra hoped was sedation rather than unconsciousness. Then silence. Then the slow, rhythmic sound of stitching.

Teyra and Ash sat in the clinic's waiting room, a cramped space with two chairs and a table covered in medical journals that were at least a decade out of date. They didn't speak. They didn't have the energy.

Teyra's ankle throbbed where the construct had torn it, her head ached from the magic drain, and her entire body felt hollow, scraped out, empty. The cold had settled so deeply into her bones that warmth felt like a thing she'd read about once and half-forgotten.

But they had the book.

She pulled it from her bag, the leather-bound volume that had cost them so much. It looked ordinary enough to shelve in the back of The Final Steep and never think about again.

"What happens now?" Ash asked.

Teyra looked at him. He was slumped in the chair beside her, his form barely visible, more absence than presence. The wards had done terrible damage. She didn't know if he could recover. She didn't know if any of them could recover.

"Now?" She touched the book's cover, felt the weight of two generations of lies pressing against her palm. "Now we rest, heal, and then burn Greythorn's world to the ground."

Ash's lips curved, something that would have been a smile if he'd had the strength.

"Together?"

She reached out and took his hand. Her fingers passed through at first, he was too weak to hold his shape, but then he concentrated, focused, and for a moment his hand was real. Cold, but real. There.

"Together," she said.

Outside, the sun was finally rising over Athergard. The clouds were breaking apart, letting through shafts of golden light that caught the rain-wet streets and made them glow. It was going to be a beautiful day.

They had three days left.

It would have to be enough.

Chapter Ten

THE WEIGHT OF CROWNS

DAY SIX: TWO DAYS REMAIN

TEYRA REACHED FOR THE cold and found nothing.

She was awake before she knew it, gasping and clawing upward out of a dream where the bone constructs were still moving and the vault was collapsing and the Command Word was tearing through her like a scream made of razor wire. Her hands flew to her chest, fingers splayed, clawing for the Grave-Chill in a blind, suffocating panic.

Nothing. The familiar frost at the center of her being was gone, and in its place sat a hollow, ringing emptiness full of air and nothing else.

Beneath the magical silence lay a deeper absence. She reached for the fragments the way she reached for the cold, instinctively, the way you reach for a tooth after the dentist has pulled it. The smell of bread was gone, along with the pull toward quiet mornings and the chill on winter nights. The ache between her third and fourth rib, gone.

All of them. She knew they had faded, had felt them thin after the Moonflower healing. This was absent. The spaces where they'd lived were scorched hollows, like rooms after a fire, the shape of the furniture still visible in the soot, but the furniture itself ash. She'd carried those fragments for six days. Some of them, the little girl's, she'd carried for fourteen years. They had been the background noise of her existence, the permanent low hum of other people's pain that she'd learned to sleep through, work through, live through.

The quiet was absolute, sharp and deadened as a severed nerve.

For the first time since she was twelve years old, Teyra Tepes was alone inside her own body.

She tried to sit up. Her body came apart in pieces of pain, ribs grinding, ankle shrieking, every muscle she owned staging a coordinated revolt.

"Don't."

Hands pushed her back down. A grey-haired woman leaned over her, pressing a cup of something thick and green into her shaking fingers. Dr. Croft. The harbour clinic, antiseptic and old blood.

"Drink," the doctor said.

Teyra drank. It tasted like rotting vegetables steeped in lamp oil. She barely noticed.

"My magic," she said through a scraped-raw voice. "I can't feel my magic."

Dr. Croft's expression didn't change. That was worse than sympathy. "Your necromantic channels have been burned. From the inside. I've never seen anything like it." She took the cup back, set it down with the careful precision of someone delivering very bad news. "You've been out for two days. Three cracked ribs, torn ankle ligament, severe magical depletion. But the channels are the part that concerns me."

"The Command Word," Teyra whispered. "I used it without anchoring."

"I don't know what that means. What I know is the fever alone should have stopped your heart."

Teyra looked down at her hands. Pale, trembling, the veins standing out dark against her skin. She reached again for the cold, frantic now, digging for it as you'd dig through rubble for someone buried alive.

Nothing.

The absence was worse than pain. Pain meant something was still there to hurt. This was erasure.

"Ash," she said. "Where is Ash?"

"The ghost?" Concern flickered across Dr. Croft's expression, quickly suppressed. "In the back room. He's stable. If that word applies to the dead."

"And Seraphine?"

"Still alive, barely." Flatness entered the doctor's voice. "I've done what I can, but she lost too much blood. The necrotic healing your friend attempted kept her alive, but it also damaged the tissue. Her body is fighting itself now. Without a proper healing mage, someone who can work with life energy and not death..."

She didn't finish the sentence. She didn't need to.

"How long does she have?"

"Days. Maybe less." Dr. Croft stood, brushing off her apron. "I'll check on you in an hour. Try to rest. Your body needs time to recover, even if your mind doesn't want to give it."

She left. The door closed behind her with a soft click, too loud in the silence.

Teyra lay back on the thin pillow and stared at the ceiling. It was made of rough-hewn planks, the kind you'd find in a building that had been standing for a century or more. Water stains spread across the wood in patterns that looked almost like maps, coastlines, rivers, and mountains, charted by decades of leaking pipes.

Two days. They had two days before Ash's anchor failed and he became a poltergeist.

Seraphine had days, maybe less.

And Teyra couldn't feel her magic at all.

They were running out of time. All of them.

She found Ash in the back room.

Barely more than a closet, a narrow space with a single window that looked out on the brick wall of the adjacent building. The glass was grimy, letting in only the faintest suggestion of daylight. A chair sat in the corner, ancient wood worn smooth by generations of anxious waiting.

Ash was sitting in the chair, or rather occupying the space where the chair was, sometimes present enough to rest against the wood, sometimes so thin she could see the wall through his chest.

He looked terrible.

The cracks the blood wards had burned into his spectral flesh hadn't healed. If anything, they had spread, thin lines of darkness running across his face, down his neck, disappearing beneath the collar of his coat. His silver glow had dimmed to almost nothing, leaving him looking washed out, faded, like a photograph left too long in the sun.

He looked up when she entered. His eyes, grey again, thank the gods, found hers.

"You're awake," he said. His voice was rough, tired, but there. Present.

"So are you." Teyra limped to the window, leaning against the frame to take the weight off her injured ankle. "The doctor says I nearly died."

"You did die." His voice cracked. "For almost a minute. I felt it, felt your heart stop, felt the life energy leave your body. I was ready to follow you. Into whatever comes next."

"Ash..."

"Don't." He stood, pulling himself together with what looked like enormous effort. "Don't tell me I shouldn't have thought that. Don't tell me it would have been foolish or wasteful or wrong. You were dying, Teyra. You were dying because you went back for me. Because you used magic you knew would destroy you to save my existence." He moved closer. His cold reached her before he did.

"If you had died in that bone chamber, I would have followed you. That's the truth. All of it."

She could have argued that his existence mattered more than hers, that he was a king with a kingdom to save and she was a failed necromancer with a mountain of debt. But the words wouldn't come, because she understood.

If their positions had been reversed, she would have done the same thing.

"We're a mess," she said instead.

"A complete disaster," he agreed.

"Seraphine is dying."

"I know."

"My magic is burned out. I can't feel it at all. It's like reaching for something that used to be there and finding empty air."

"I know."

"And we have two days before your anchor fails."

"I know." He reached out, his hand hovering an inch from her cheek. The Touch Barrier, still there, still enforced by magic neither of them fully understood. "But we also have the book. The truth. The weapon we came for."

"Can we even use it?" Teyra turned to look at him fully. The movement sent pain shooting through her ribs, but she ignored it. "Greythorn controls the city. He has the Hessians, the Guard, probably the courts. We can't just walk into the Palace and show everyone the prophecy. We'd be arrested before we got through the door."

"Then we don't walk through the door."

The voice came from the doorway. They both turned.

The Moth stood in the entrance, his grey velvet suit somehow immaculate despite the grimy surroundings, his silver mask gleaming in the dim light. His dead dead eyes moved from Teyra to Ash and back again, assessing, calculating.

"You're awake," he observed. "Good. We have the book. We have two days. And I have a plan."

Teyra looked at the Moth, at Aldric Vane, the scribe who had lost everything and rebuilt himself into a man who unsettled her, and felt the weight of his twenty-five years pressing against her own exhaustion.

"You sold Seraphine our location," she said. No question in it.

"You needed a tactician," the Moth said. "She needed a reason to defect. I provided the introduction."

"Sit down," she said. "Before I fall down."

He sat. Ash stood by the window, his unsteady light casting strange shadows on the walls. Lenore perched on a cabinet, watching the Moth with undisguised suspicion. She'd arrived while Teyra was unconscious—found her own way out, as she always did. The injured wing was healed. She offered no explanation and Teyra knew better than to ask for one.

Teyra found herself studying his gloves. She'd registered them in the Night Market, pale kidskin, she'd thought, clerk's gloves, but here in steadier light she could see the silver thread worked into the seams. Fine as hair. Precise as wards. Ward-threaded leather, and that was how he'd caught Ash's wrist. The gloves were stitched with containment sigils, the kind that could grip spectral matter the way iron gripped heat. Cathedral work, she realized. The kind of thing a scribe who'd spent years in the archives might have learned to make. Twenty-five years of preparation included preparing for ghosts.

But before the Moth could speak, Teyra felt them.

Wider than a fragment, quieter than the sharp press of a single spirit against her damaged channels. Like standing at the edge of a crowd and hearing a thousand people breathing in one room, their voices fused into a single murmur.

She closed her eyes. Reached through the cracks in her Resonance, through the scorched, barely functional damage. The places where the scarring had left gaps, where the walls between her and the dead had thinned to nothing.

They were in the walls.

These were the Unsettled, the ones her grandmother had named: the dissolved dead of Hollow Stair, turned to rain and residue and the grey film on every window. They had seeped into the clinic's foundations as they seeped into everything in the lower city, quietly, over decades, until they were part of the infrastructure. Nobody had ever listened to them. Nobody had ever tried. They were atmosphere, background, the spiritual equivalent of damp.

But they knew her.

She felt it like a current shifting direction, a thousand dim presences turning toward her at once, the way sunflowers turn toward light. They recognized the shape of her channels, the signature of a woman who had been absorbing their weight for years without ever being asked. Every ghost who had sat in her shop, every fragment she had carried, every cup of anchoring tea her grandmother had brewed before her. The Unsettled had been drinking from the Tepes women for three generations, and they remembered.

We know you.

It came without words or language, a feeling, warm and vast and very old, like touching a wall and feeling the house breathe. The Unsettled of Hollow Stair, of the Tanners' Quarter, of the Dockside and the Meat District and every low place where the drainage wards had never reached, they were aware of her. They had always been aware of her. And now, through the cracks the Command Word had burned into her channels, they were reaching back.

The recognition carried a low, collective dread, old as the foundations under Hollow Stair. The Unsettled were unsettled. They could feel something underneath the city, something deep, something patient, something that had been growing for a long time. The void. The darkness that Teyra had glimpsed in the bone chamber, in the jar on the Moth's shelf, in the patches of absence on the child-construct's frame. The dead of Hollow Stair had been living above it for centuries, feeling it press upward through the foundations the way you feel cold seep through a thin floor.

They had been trying to warn someone. For longer than Teyra had been alive, maybe longer than anyone remembered. Dissolving into the rain, pressing against the windows, leaving their residue on every surface. Beyond hauntings, beyond unfinished business.

Distress signals.

Teyra opened her eyes. The clinic room was exactly as it had been, dim, chemical-smelling, ordinary. The Moth was watching her with those dead eyes, head tilted, waiting. Ash had gone still by the window.

"What just happened?" Ash asked.

She didn't know how to explain it. The feeling was already fading, retreating back into the walls like a tide going out, leaving only the impression of vast, patient, unsettled company.

"I think the dead already know what's coming," she said quietly. "And I think they've been trying to tell us for a very long time."

Interest moved behind the Moth's eyes, the closest thing to surprise she had ever seen break through that carefully maintained emptiness.

"Interesting," he said. Then, with the air of a man filing something away for later, "Very interesting."

"The book," Teyra said.

"The book." The Moth nodded. "The original prophecy. The proof that everything the Greythorns have built, their power, their wealth, their position, is founded on murder and lies. Show that to the right people, and their entire stolen dynasty collapses."

"The right people," Teyra repeated. "Who, exactly?"

The Moth smiled behind his mask.

"The Coronation Anniversary is tomorrow night. A grand celebration at the Palace, attended by every noble house, every foreign dignitary, every person of importance in the kingdom. Lord Greythorn will be giving a speech, a tribute to the 'tragic' Thornwick dynasty and the 'noble sacrifice' that ended the curse. It's a tradition. He does it every year."

"You want us to crash the party," Teyra said.

"I want you to understand what you're walking into." The Moth's voice shifted, clinical now, precise. "The current Lord Greythorn inherited the conspiracy from his grandfather, who began falsifying the prophecy nearly fifty years ago, then used it to justify the fire that killed the Thornwick heirs twenty-five years later. The same fire that killed a Cathedral scribe's family, on the grandfather's orders, because the scribe had noticed the forgery. He also built the estate vault as a sealed repository for the original prophecy and his research into what lay beneath the Palace—everything too dangerous to destroy and too incriminating to keep above ground. Only later, once Elias was under Greythorn control, could the family access it regularly"

"The grandfather died in his bed a year later, peacefully, as tyrants sometimes do. His son, Aldous's father, expanded what Casimir built. Married into the military families, secured the Hessian contracts, put Greythorn money into every institution that mattered. He was cleverer than Casimir and crueller, and he died in a hunting accident that three people witnessed, and nobody believes was accidental."

The Moth's eyes flickered. "The current Lord had grown up inside it, raised on the conspiracy as though it were family tradition. By the time he was old enough to question it, he was already complicit. Why would he expose it? The lie has served his family well. He had also arranged for Elias to marry his niece, his late brother's daughter, the last direct Greythorn by blood, a Thornwick heartbeat with a Greythorn name beside it on the throne. Clean, if it had worked."

"But Elias," Teyra said. "Why keep him alive?"

"Because you cannot kill a Blood-Key, Miss Tepes. The ancient wards of Athergard, the seals that keep the dead in their graves and the darkness in its pit, are tied to the heartbeat of a Thornwick. If Elias dies, the walls fall." The Moth spread his hands. "Greythorn put the tether on him the week he was adopted. He was four years old. Told it was a family heirloom. He has worn it every day for twenty-five years, and he has never once been told what it costs him."

His voice didn't change, but something behind those dead eyes went flat in a different way. "One brother murdered to prevent the End of Days. One brother caged to keep the city standing. A perfect balance, if you're the kind of man who can live with it."

"Greythorn will have Elias at the coronation," Ash said. His light flared once, hard and bright, then steadied. "A Thornwick heartbeat to anchor the wards while every noble in the kingdom watches him give a speech about the tragic fall of my family."

"And if you can get to him before Greythorn realizes what's happening," the Moth said, "the wards will have two Thornwick anchors instead of one. A living one and a spectral one. The Greythorns built their security around a single heartbeat. They never planned for the prince to come back."

"I want you to tell the truth. In front of everyone who matters. With the evidence to prove it." The Moth stood, his movements fluid and unsettling. "I can get you inside. I can ensure you have an audience. But the rest, the confrontation, the revelation, the consequences, that's your burden to bear."

He walked toward the door, then paused.

"One more thing. The prophecy, the real one, with the clause that was removed. It explains what the Thornwick 'curse' actually is, along with how to prevent it."

"Which is?"

The Moth looked at Ash, and for an instant the emptiness in his eyes thinned enough to show something almost like understanding beneath.

"A gift. The Thornwicks were blessed to save the kingdom, never meant to destroy it. The 'End of Days' the prophecy describes? It's real. It's coming. And the only ones who can stop it are the ones with Thornwick blood."

He moved toward the door.

"Is it enough?" Ash said. "A ghost's blood. A dead man's anchor. The prophecy was written for a king who could hold a sword and give orders and actually rule. After what the blood wards took from me, I can feel the Moonflower guttering, I'm losing coherence faster every hour." He paused. "Is that enough to stop whatever's coming?"

The Moth stopped with his hand on the door frame without turning around.

"I don't know," he said.

The absence of performance in those three words was more unsettling than anything else he had said all evening.

"Twenty-five years," Ash said. "And you don't know."

"Twenty-five years of preparing for the moment a Thornwick came back." The Moth's voice was flat. "The prophecy doesn't specify living or dead. It says blood of Thornwick. Your blood opened the vault. Your blood is still potent enough to affect ward-magic. Whether it's potent enough for what's coming..." He paused. "That, my lord, is what tomorrow night is for. We expose Greythorn. We restore the Thornwick name. We give you back the crown, or what passes for one. And then we find out."

"Find out," Teyra repeated.

"Whether a dead king is better than no king at all." The Moth glanced back, once, and for the first time his eyes carried something that might have been the ghost of an apology. "It has been my working assumption for twenty-five years. I would prefer not to be wrong." He paused at the door. His gaze moved to Ash—not the assessing look he'd used at the Night Market, not the predatory attention of a man cataloguing assets. This was an unguarded look, quickly buried. The look of a man staring at a ghost who was roughly the age his son would have been.

He walked out, leaving them in stunned silence.

Lenore dropped from the cabinet. She didn't fly, she dropped, a graceless flutter that ended on the cot beside Teyra's knee. The raven sat there for a moment, utterly still, her feathers pressed flat against her body.

"Your grandmother's channels scarred," Lenore said.

Teyra looked at her. Ash looked at her. Neither spoke.

"The last year. She didn't tell you, you were at the Academy, and she didn't want you worrying through your exams. But the channels were closing. Slowly. The way scar tissue closes over a wound." Lenore's voice was stripped of performance. No timing, no wit. Just a raven who had lived in a woman's shop for decades and watched her fade. "She couldn't feel the dead anymore, at the end. She brewed from memory. Muscle and habit. The teas still worked because the recipes were good, and the magic had nothing to do with it." A pause. "She said it was like going deaf. The shape of where sound used to be was still there. She just couldn't hear it."

The clinic was still.

"She was fine," Lenore said. "She was fine with it. She said the dead had given her enough, and she could give them back their privacy."

The raven's beak opened and closed once, a dry click. "I wasn't fine with it. I sat on the back of that chair for eleven months and watched her pretend the world wasn't going quiet, and I have been bound to your bloodline for longer than this city has had plumbing, Teyra, and I am telling you—"

She stopped. The sentence just stopped, like a mechanism that had run out of spring.

"Telling me what?" Teyra whispered.

Lenore turned both eyes on her. The full gaze. The one she never used, the one that meant she'd put down every weapon in her arsenal and was standing in the open. Both eyes, unblinking, the way she'd looked at Maren in the chair that last morning.

"That I can't do it twice," Lenore said.

Then her feathers ruffled, a full-body shake, violent and deliberate, the way a dog shakes off water. She hopped to the edge of the cot.

"Well," she said, and her voice had its edges back, mostly, almost. "That was revolting. Let's never speak of it again. You have a book to read and a dynasty to topple and I have a reputation for emotional unavailability that I'd like to maintain."

She flew back to the cabinet and began grooming her wing feathers with furious attention.

They read the book together.

Teyra sat on the cot, the ancient leather-bound volume open on her lap. Ash sat beside her, present enough to maintain the position, though the effort showed in every flicker. The pages were yellowed, the ink faded, but the words were still legible.

The prophecy was written in the formal style of the old seers, ornate and circuitous, full of metaphor and allusion. But stripped of the flowery language, the meaning was clear.

"When darkness rises from the deep places of the earth, when the dead walk and the living flee, when the sun is swallowed and the stars go blind, then shall the blood of Thornwick be the last light. The crowned head shall become the saving hand. The sacrifice of one shall preserve the many.

"But if the line is broken, if the blood is spilled before its time, if the gift is rejected, then shall the darkness consume all, and no power in heaven or earth shall turn it back."

Below this, in a different hand, the hand of whoever had made the altered copy, was a note.

"The clause regarding the 'gift' and the 'saving hand' has been removed per Lord Greythorn's instructions. The altered version emphasizes only the 'darkness' and the 'consuming.' This should be sufficient to justify the necessary actions."

Teyra read the words three times, her hands trembling slightly.

"It was never a curse," she said. "The Thornwicks were supposed to save the kingdom. Greythorn twisted the prophecy to make them look like a threat, when they were actually the only protection against whatever this darkness is."

"And now the line is broken," Ash said, the words hollowed out. "My family is dead. I'm dead. There's no one left to fulfill the prophecy."

"You're still here."

"I'm a ghost, Teyra. A spirit bound to borrowed time. In two days, my anchor fails. In two days, I become a monster or I fade into nothing." He laughed, and the sound was dry and empty. "Some savior."

"The prophecy says 'the blood of Thornwick.' It doesn't say 'a living Thornwick.'" Teyra looked at him. "Your blood opened the vault. Your blood is still potent enough to activate blood-locked wards. Maybe that's enough."

"Enough for what? To stop a darkness that the greatest seers in history could only describe in metaphors?" Ash shook his head. "I don't even know what we're fighting. 'When the dead walk and the living flee,' what does that even mean?"

"I don't know," Teyra admitted. "But I know this. Greythorn murdered your family because he was afraid of what you might become. He altered a prophecy to turn a blessing into a curse. He built his entire dynasty on the corpses of people who were supposed to save the world." She closed the book, set it aside. "Whatever comes next, whatever this darkness is, whatever the prophecy actually means, we start by tearing down the lie. We expose Greythorn. We tell the truth. And then we figure out the rest."

Ash was quiet for a long moment.

"Two days," he said finally. "The Coronation Anniversary."

"Tomorrow."

"And then we walk into the heart of Greythorn's power and call him a murderer in front of everyone who matters."

"That's the plan."

His grey eyes searched her face.

"You're insane," he said.

"So I've been told."

"I love you."

The words hung in the air between them, heavy and fragile and impossibly real, and Teyra's breath caught.

"Ash..."

"I know." He lifted a hand, still not quite there, the lamplight showing through his palm. "The timing is terrible. We might not survive tomorrow night. Even if we do, I have two days before my anchor fails, and then I either pass on or become something that needs to be destroyed. I know all of that."

He moved closer, close enough for the cold to reach her skin. "But I also know that I spent five years in darkness with no memory, no identity, and no understanding of anything. And then I walked into your shop, and you saved me. You gave me a name. You gave me a purpose. You showed me that there was still something worth fighting for in this world."

His hand came up, hovering an inch from her cheek. The Touch Barrier, that invisible wall of magic that kept them apart.

"If I'm going to fade into nothing," he said, "I want to do it knowing that I told you the truth. That I didn't let timing or the impossibility of our situation stop me from saying what matters."

"What matters?"

"You matter. You, Teyra Tepes. The woman who weeps for ghosts. The necromancer who feels too much. The only person who ever looked at a dead prince and saw a man worth saving."

His hand touched her cheek.

The cold was immediate, spreading through her skin with the clean shock of winter water. She felt the magic of his anchor strain, felt the Touch Barrier push back against the contact. For a moment, she thought he would flicker, fade, lose his grip on solidity.

He didn't.

His palm pressed against her cheek, cold and real and present. His fingers curled into her hair. His eyes, those grey eyes that had seen death and betrayal and five years of darkness, held nothing but warmth.

"I love you," he said again. "Whatever happens. Whatever we become. I love you."

Teyra reached up and covered his hand with hers.

"I love you too," she whispered.

And then, for the first time, she leaned forward and kissed a ghost.

The kiss was impossible.

His lips were ice, colder than anything she'd ever felt, cold enough that it should have burned, should have sent her recoiling. Beneath the cold ran warmth. The echo of the man he'd been before death, before darkness, before a dynasty of lies stole everything from him.

He kissed her like she was the only real thing in a world of shadows. Gentle at first, hesitant, as if afraid she might break or he might fade. Then deeper, more urgent, his hands in her hair, her arms around his neck, the cold and the warmth tangling together until she couldn't tell where one ended and the other began.

The Touch Barrier fought them. She could feel it, that magical resistance, that push against intimacy, the rules that forbade touch, holding, any kind of love between the dead and the living. It pressed against them like a current, trying to tear them apart.

They didn't let it.

Ash pulled her closer, growing more real with every moment of contact. The cracks in his spectral skin were still there, still dark and spreading, but his presence was stronger than it had been since the bone chamber. Her touch was anchoring him, she realized. Life energy flowing into death, giving him something to hold onto. The violent feelings had always shattered him. But this, whatever this was, was making him more real than he'd been in days.

Then something tore.

She felt it through the contact, a snap, deep inside his anchor, like a thread pulled taut until it broke. Ash flinched. His body stayed pressed against hers, warm and cold and real, but something behind his eyes stuttered. A flicker. The briefest expression of loss, there and gone before she could name it.

"What was that?" she whispered.

"Nothing." He kissed her again, harder, as if he could outrun whatever had just happened. "Nothing. I'm here."

But later, after the desperate closeness, after the whispered promises, after the world outside had shrunk to the size of a cot and a window and two people holding each other, he sat very still. She watched him from the pillow, half-asleep, and saw him press his fingers against his temple the way he had in the Archive. The old gesture. The reaching-for-something gesture.

"Ash?"

"The roses," he said quietly. "The garden. The memory I had, the one from the Archive, the red roses, the feeling of being very young and very safe." He lowered his hand. His eyes were distant. "It's gone."

The word fell between them with the clean chill of steeped metal.

"Gone?"

"I can feel where it was. Like a gap in a sentence. I know something was there, but I can't…" He trailed off, flexed his fingers. "The touch. The Barrier. It took something when it let us through."

Chest tight, Teyra understood the anchoring magic, her life energy flowing into his death, hadn't been free. The Barrier had extracted its toll from him, spending the only currency a ghost possessed.

His memories.

"We stop," she said immediately. "No more contact. Until I can figure out…"

"No." His voice was quiet but absolute. "Don't."

"Ash, if every time we touch you lose…"

"Then I lose it." He turned to look at her, and his grey eyes held something she hadn't seen before. Certainty, clean and deliberate and total. "I spent five years in the dark with no memories at all. I know what that emptiness feels like. And I know what this feels like." He reached out, let his fingers hover a breath from her cheek. "If the price of touching you is forgetting a garden, I'll pay it. I'll pay it every time."

"You can't mean that."

"I mean it more than anything I've ever said."

His memories were all he had, the proof he'd been alive, the last evidence of the man before the ghost. Losing them was losing himself. But she looked at his face, at the calm, deliberate peace of a man who had weighed his entire existence against a moment of warmth and chosen the warmth, and the argument died in her throat.

"This is probably a terrible idea," she murmured against his lips.

"Probably," he agreed.

"If we're caught..."

"We won't be."

"If someone walks in..."

"They won't."

"Ash..."

"Teyra." He pulled back just far enough to look at her, his forehead resting against hers. "We have one night before we walk into a trap. We have two days before my anchor fails. We have a lifetime of loss behind us and possibly nothing ahead. For once in your life, stop planning, stop worrying, stop being responsible." His lips curved into what was almost a smile. "Just be here. With me. For whatever time we have."

The reflex to argue kicked in, the way it always did. But he was right. They had one night. Maybe less.

And she was so tired of being alone.

"Here," she said. "With you."

She kissed him again.

They stayed that way for a long time, longer than was wise, longer than was safe. The sun moved across the grimy window, painting bars of light across the floor. The sounds of the harbour drifted in, ships' bells, gulls crying, the distant shout of dock workers. The world kept turning outside their small room, indifferent to the two broken people holding each other against the dark.

Eventually, as it had to, the moment ended.

Ash's edges blurred, just once, just a breath of instability, and they both felt it. The anchor straining. The magic reaching its limits.

He pulled back slowly, his hands sliding from her hair to her shoulders to her hands. The cold lingered on her skin, but it wasn't unpleasant anymore. It was familiar. His.

She watched him carefully. He was staring at his own hands, turning them over the way he had that first night in the shop, examining them like they belonged to someone else. His brow creased. She saw him reach for another memory, testing. Probing the edges of the gap.

She didn't ask. She was afraid of the answer.

"We should rest," he said. Steady, but he wouldn't look at her. "Both of us. You're still recovering, and I'm…"

"Dying," she finished for him.

"I was going to say 'conserving energy,' but yes. That too."

She laughed, a small, broken sound, but real. "You're terrible at being comforting."

"I'm dead. We're not known for our bedside manner."

"I've noticed."

He helped her lie back on the cot, his movements careful, gentle. The room felt different now, smaller, warmer, less like a temporary refuge and more like a place that mattered, a night worth remembering.

She thought about telling him not to kiss her forehead. Thought about forbidding contact until she'd studied the mechanism, found a way around the cost. But when he leaned down, she didn't stop him.

Neither did he.

"Two days," she said, looking up at him.

"Two days," he agreed.

"And then we tear down a dynasty."

"And then we tear down a dynasty." He leaned down, pressed a kiss to her forehead. The cold of his lips left a mark she could feel long after he pulled away. "Sleep, Teyra. I'll watch over you."

"You always do."

"I always will."

She closed her eyes.

For the first time in six days, she slept without nightmares.

When she woke, the room was dark.

Night had fallen while she slept. The window showed nothing but blackness, and then it showed more than blackness. The grey film was worse. She could see it from here, pressed against the outside of the glass like fog with weight, like breath that wouldn't dissipate. And beyond it, through the grimy pane, the harbour glowed. The Unsettled luminescence she'd first seen the night of the Greythorn raid, the phosphorescent residue that lit the gutters and pooled in the low places, had risen. It had climbed to window-height. A slow, grey tide creeping up the walls of the Dockside District, soft and terrible and silent. From here she could see it lapping at the foundations of the rope-maker's next door, pooling against the clinic's front step, filling the street below in a luminous haze that turned the gas lamps into smudged halos.

The drainage wards were failing. Everywhere, by the look of it. The bronze discs she'd seen gleaming in the Garden District gutters must be overwhelmed, or cracked, or outpaced by a city producing more spiritual residue than three centuries of infrastructure could filter. The dead were rising as atmosphere, a grey tide without bodies. Athergard was drowning in its own unprocessed dead.

The sounds of the harbour had faded to distant murmurs, the city settling into a stillness that wasn't quite sleep.

Ash was sitting in the chair by the window, watching her. His form was more stable now, the rest had done him good, or maybe the kiss had. The cracks were still there, but they seemed less prominent, less threatening.

"How long?" she asked, sitting up.

"Another four hours. Dr. Croft checked on you twice. Said you were healing faster than expected."

"The magic?"

He was quiet for a moment. Then, "She said there's damage. Scarring in your necromantic channels. You might not recover full function. You might never be able to use a Command Word again."

The emptiness where her power should be, she'd been circling it since she woke, prodding the hollow where the cold had lived. Hearing it said aloud made it real.

What she didn't tell him was the other thing. The thing that had started while she slept.

The fragments were coming back.

The old ones were Ash, Thomas, the widow, the little girl, all consumed by the Command Word and gone for good. But new ones were arriving. Faint, uninvited, seeping in through the scorched channels the way water seeps through cracks in a broken pipe. She'd felt the first one settle while she was still half-asleep, a dockworker's last seconds, sharp and specific, the lurch of a deck beneath his feet, the black water closing over his head, lungs burning. He must have died in the harbour. His residue must have drifted through the clinic wall with the rising Unsettled tide, found her damaged channels, and slipped inside.

She hadn't opened the channel or invited it. But the channels were scarred now, scorched wide by the Command Word, with the careful walls around her Resonance pathways burned to nothing. Before, the fragments had come one at a time, each one requiring contact, proximity, a deliberate or semi-deliberate opening. Now they were arriving. The dead were in the air. The dead were in the walls. And her channels had no doors left.

Two more had settled while she'd lain there, a woman's sharp sorrow, the metallic taste of a locket held too long in a closed fist, and an old man's bewilderment, the feeling of waking in a room you don't recognize, reaching for a name that used to be yours. Three new fragments, absorbed in her sleep, without consent, without contact.

The collection was rebuilding. She had burned her entire life's burden in the bone chamber, and already the city was filling the empty rooms.

"I'll live," she said at last. "I've been a mediocre necromancer my whole life. I can learn to be a mediocre something else."

"You were never mediocre."

"Tell that to the Academy."

"The Academy was full of fools who couldn't see what was right in front of them." Ash stood, moved to sit beside her on the cot. "You're the most powerful necromancer I've ever known. The magic you can do matters less than the compassion you bring to it. The Academy taught control. You taught kindness. That's rarer. That's better."

But compassion hadn't saved Seraphine from being gutted. Compassion hadn't stopped the bone constructs. Compassion had gotten her failed out of the Academy and nearly gotten them all killed in the vault when she'd frozen, drowning in the entombed workers' three-hundred-year-old fury. And now compassion, or whatever the scarred, involuntary version of it was, had left her channels wide open to a city that was drowning in its own dead. By tomorrow, she'd be carrying a dozen fragments. By the Coronation, maybe more. The question she'd asked in the café, *how much feeling is too much*, had acquired a terrifying new dimension. What happened when you couldn't stop feeling, even if you wanted to?

But a thread in Ash's words tugged at a memory she couldn't place. *The strongest Commands don't run through the Chill at all. They run through connection.* An old theory. Pre-Academy. Dismissed in the footnotes.

She let it go. She was too tired to chase it. But the three new fragments pulsed quietly in her chest, the dockworker's drowning, the woman's locket-sorrow, the old man's lost name, and she thought, *If the city keeps pouring in, by tomorrow I'll be carrying more than Meridia ever did.*

What that made her, she didn't know yet.

She leaned against him, let his cold seep into her warmth. It was getting easier, the contact, the intimacy. The Touch Barrier still pushed back, still took its toll. But they'd learned to accept the price.

"One day left," she said.

"One day."

"We should probably come up with an actual plan. Something more detailed than 'crash the party and tell the truth.'"

"Probably." He put his arm around her, pulled her closer. "But that can wait until morning. For now, just stay. Like this."

She stayed.

Outside, the city slept. Somewhere in the Palace, Lord Greythorn was preparing for his annual triumph. Somewhere in the Night Market, the Moth was pulling strings only he could see.

Teyra had looked in on Seraphine before coming upstairs. The woman was asleep, if you could call it sleep. Her skin had gone the color of old tallow, and the veins around the wound had darkened to a bruised violet that spread a little further each time Teyra checked. The necrotic seal was gone, stitched shut now by Dr. Croft's steady hands, but the death magic Teyra had poured into her was still there, still working its way through the tissue, still eating what it had been meant to save. Seraphine's body was cold on the left side and warm on the right, the temperature divide running exactly along the line of the original wound. She was fighting the healing as much as the injury. Her body couldn't tell the difference anymore.

And in a small room above a harbour clinic, a necromancer and a ghost held each other in the dark, counting down the hours until everything changed.

One day.

It would have to be enough.

Chapter Eleven

THE CORONATION

SERAPHINE HAD WOKEN AT dawn. Barely, but enough to look at Teyra with eyes that knew they were running out of time and say three words. "Burn it down." The Moth's people had the uniforms ready by noon, the servant passes forged by three.

They spent the hours between planning over the Moth's sketches—servant routes, blind corridors, the single balcony moment when the book could reach the room before Greythorn shut them down.

Lenore had made her feelings about this plan very clear.

"A Palace full of Hessians calibrated to detect the undead," she'd said, from her perch on the clinic windowsill, "and you're bringing the ghost prince. Inspired." She'd clicked her beak. "I'll stay with Seraphine. Someone should be here when she wakes up, and I'm the only one not rushing headlong into a death trap."

Teyra hadn't argued. When the sun touched the Palace spires, she walked through its doors with a tray of champagne glasses and a dead prince at her shoulder. Her ribs complained with every breath, a dull grind she'd learned to work around by keeping her inhales shallow; Dr. Croft had wrapped her ankle so tightly it felt more like a wooden peg than a joint, though it held her weight if she didn't think about stairs.

The Royal Palace was a monument to excess. The pigeons that normally roosted in its eaves were gone, every ledge bare, every cornice empty, as if the birds had sensed before anyone else that something was wrong tonight.

Crystal chandeliers descended from ceilings painted with scenes of triumph, ancient Greythorns slaying dragons, conquering enemies, accepting the adoration of grateful subjects. The walls were covered in silk the color of wine. The floors were marble veined with gold, polished to such a shine that you could see your reflection staring back at you with every step. And everywhere, there was light. Candles by the thousands, magical luminescence that had no visible source. The Palace was built to dazzle, impress, humble.

But the Palace was working harder than it should have been.

The drainage wards embedded in the foundations hummed at a frequency she'd never heard before, a high, strained whine that lived just below conscious hearing. The wards in the Garden District had been bronze discs in gutter grates, modest and functional. These were vast sigil-arrays carved into the bedrock, the most powerful spiritual filtration system in Athergard, and they were running at capacity. The network's architecture lay open to her now, the Estate wards, the Palace wards, the drainage system beneath the streets, all threaded through the same bedrock, drawing from the same anchor-point, Elias's blood. It showed itself in the luminescence flickering at the edges of the room, brightening and dimming in cycles that matched the ward-pulse. Beneath her feet the marble floor vibrated with the shallow buzz of overloaded infrastructure, a surface hum above the deep tremor from below. The Palace wards were holding back the same grey tide that had risen to window height in the Dockside District. The difference was that here, the wards were strong enough to hold.

For now.

Outside these walls, the city was drowning. In here, the champagne stayed cold, the light stayed bright, and the dead were someone else's problem. The final, most extravagant expression of the class divide she'd been walking through since Weaver Street. The rich lived better than the poor, and even their dying was an improved thing. And even the machinery of better death was starting to crack.

Teyra was not impressed.

She was thinking about the bone chamber beneath the Greythorn Estate. About the skulls arranged in patterns on the walls. About the constructs made from stolen corpses, the blood wards designed to kill, the vault that held secrets worth murdering children over. She was thinking about the rot beneath the gilding, the darkness beneath the light, the lies that held this entire glittering edifice together.

"This way," Ash murmured beside her.

They were dressed as servants, simple black uniforms provided by one of the Moth's contacts, anonymous and invisible in the sea of staff preparing for the evening's celebration. Teyra carried a tray of empty champagne glasses, a prop to justify her presence.

Ash carried nothing, because his hands kept passing through things when his concentration slipped.

He was deteriorating.

The cracks in his spectral skin had continued to spread throughout the day. Now they covered half his face, dark lines that pulsed faintly when the light caught them wrong. His form was less stable than it had been even that morning, sometimes solid, sometimes transparent, sometimes barely there at all. The effort of maintaining visibility was clearly costing him, draining whatever reserves he had left.

Hours remained before his anchor failed completely.

If they survived tonight.

At the turning where the service corridor branched, Ash stopped. One hand against the wall. That reaching gesture, fingers pressed to his temple, grasping for something that wasn't there anymore. She knew it before he spoke.

"The waltz," he said quietly. "The coronation ball. The music, the dancing, I could hear it this morning. The melody Seraphine and I..." He stopped. "It's gone."

Without looking at her, he kept walking.

Teyra followed without saying what she was thinking. That made two: the garden, now the waltz. The Touch Barrier was stripping his life from the back end first, taking the good memories before the cold ones. She wondered, with a dread she couldn't voice, what would be left of him if it took everything that wasn't suffering.

They moved through the service corridors, narrow passages hidden behind the Palace's grand facades, designed for servants to move unseen while the nobility conducted their glittering affairs.

The Moth's network had done its work well: doors that should have been locked stood slightly ajar, and guards who should have been watching stared in the wrong direction. A footman passing in the opposite direction gave them a subtle nod and continued on without a word. In the basement below, one of his people, a former Hessian engineer who'd been dismissed for asking too many questions about the command ciphers, was already in position beside the machine relay, waiting for the signal to cut the frequency. He'd been working on the override codes for months, the Moth had said. The goal was to redirect the machines, keeping them active under new command. When Greythorn's command authority fell, the engineer would be ready to catch it.

What unsettled her was how smoothly it was going. Teyra kept waiting for the alarm, or for the palace wards to react to Ash's presence. But unlike the Greythorn Estate, the ancient protections here parted around the rightful heir like grave-mist around a headstone. The Hessians stationed in the corridor alcoves stood with their optical sensors dim, unresponsive, the engineer having already given his signal.

What the wards didn't part around was Teyra.

Every step deeper into the Palace added to the weight she was carrying. The servants' corridors were saturated with ambient residue, decades of it, centuries of it, the accumulated emotional leavings of every person who had ever worked in these passages and been exhausted, or homesick, or humiliated. The drainage wards filtered the Grand Hall beautifully. The servants' quarters were left to themselves. And Teyra's scorched channels, wide open, doorless, still raw from the Command Word, drank it in the way old paper drinks spilled ink.

By the time they reached the first staircase, her inventory had doubled. The three fragments from the clinic, the dockworker, the locket-woman, the bewildered old man, had been joined by a scullery maid's bone-deep tiredness, a footman's shame at being invisible, a cook's smothered fury at a lord who'd struck her across the mouth for serving cold soup. Small burdens. Ordinary burdens. The sort that never reached songs, prophecies, or history books. They settled into Teyra's damaged channels like sediment settling into a riverbed, just present. Layer upon layer upon layer.

She didn't tell Ash. He had enough to carry.

She stopped and pressed her palm flat against the corridor wall.

The stone was vibrating. A vibration deeper than the hum of the wards, rising from beneath the foundations. A tremor so faint she might have imagined it, except that the water in a servant's pitcher on the windowsill was rippling in tiny concentric circles, and the candle flames along the corridor were all leaning the same direction. Toward the center of the Palace, toward something below.

"Do you feel that?" she whispered.

Ash's expression tightened. "I've felt it since we entered. Something under the floor. Under the city." He paused. "It knows I'm here."

It was the same pull he'd felt on the bridge that first night, only stronger now. Closer. The thing beneath the city had moved beyond hunger. It knew he was here.

And beneath the wrongness, beneath the void's hunger, Teyra felt a second pressure, faint and almost inaudible. The same murmuring pressure she'd felt in the Greythorn vault, multiplied a thousandfold. The dead of Athergard, layered beneath three centuries of stone, waiting in the dark. A city's worth of ghosts, pressed against the underside of the world like breath against a chapel window.

We are here. We have been here.

She didn't know why the thought made her feel less afraid. But it did. Maybe because she was carrying so many of them now, their small burdens humming in her chest with the low, gathering sound of a choir before the first note, that the boundary between Teyra and Athergard's dead was blurring. She was becoming a vessel, whether she wanted to be or not.

This is what happened to Meridia, she thought again. But the thought had a different quality now. Less dread. More understanding. Meridia had drowned because the flood came and she had no way to use it. Teyra was drowning too, but she was drowning on the way to the one place where a flood might actually be useful.

They kept moving. Behind them, the candle flames straightened as if nothing had happened.

"How deep does his network go?" she whispered.

"Deep enough," Ash replied. "Twenty-five years of collecting secrets. Twenty-five years of cultivating contacts in every household, every institution, every corner of the kingdom. The Moth doesn't control Athergard, but he knows everyone who does."

"And he's using all of that for us."

"He's using all of that for revenge." Ash gave it to her without softening it. "We happen to be the weapon he chose. Don't mistake that for friendship."

They climbed a narrow staircase, the servants' route to the upper levels. The sounds of the celebration grew louder as they ascended, music and laughter and the clink of glasses, the murmur of hundreds of voices engaged in the peculiar theater of aristocratic conversation. The Coronation Anniversary was the social event of the year. Every noble house attended, along with every foreign dignitary and every person of importance in the kingdom, gathered in one place to celebrate the lie that had kept the Greythorns in power for two generations.

And in the middle of it all, Lord Greythorn himself, preparing to give the speech he gave every year. The tribute to the "tragic" Thornwick dynasty. The solemn acknowledgment of the "sacrifice" that had saved the kingdom from the curse.

Tonight, they were going to interrupt him.

Tonight, they were going to tell the truth.

The gallery overlooked the Grand Hall like a theater box overlooking a stage.

The gallery had been designed for servants, a narrow balcony hidden behind velvet curtains, where staff could observe the proceedings below and respond to the needs of the guests without being seen. The perfect vantage point for what they had planned.

Teyra parted the curtains just enough to peer through.

The Grand Hall was magnificent. A cathedral of marble and crystal, its domed ceiling painted with a mural of the heavens, stars, moons, and suns, all arranged in patterns that were supposed to represent the divine order of things. Columns of white marble lined the walls, interspersed with statues of previous Greythorn lords, each one posed heroically, each one gazing down at the assembly with carved expressions of benevolent authority.

The floor below was packed with people.

Teyra had never seen so many nobles in one place. They drifted through the hall in a riot of color, wine-red and sapphire, emerald and gold, fabrics that cost more than she would earn in a lifetime. Jewels glittered at throats and wrists. Medals and ribbons adorned military dress uniforms. The air was thick with perfume and the particular scent of wealth: expensive soap, fine leather, and bodies that had never known a day of physical labor.

They were laughing. Drinking champagne. Exchanging the kind of polished pleasantries that passed for conversation in these circles. None of them knew the foundation of their world was about to crack.

At the far end of the hall, on a raised dais draped in Greythorn colors, stood the man himself.

Lord Aldous Greythorn was older than Teyra had expected, sixty at least, with silver hair swept back from a high forehead and a face that had been handsome once, before age and power had carved it harder. He wore a coat of deep grey velvet, embroidered with the Greythorn serpent in silver thread. A chain of office hung around his neck, heavy with the seals of various honors and positions. He stood with the easy confidence of a man who had spent a lifetime unchallenged, unquestioned, and obeyed.

He was smiling. The smile of a grandfather at a family gathering. The smile of a man who believed, truly believed, that he was beloved.

And beside him, seated in a carved chair at the edge of the dais, Elias.

Ash went rigid.

His brother was dressed in Greythorn grey, the iron band on his wrist catching the chandelier light with every pulse of ward-energy it siphoned from his blood. He looked healthy, composed. The dutiful adopted son, displayed like a trophy at his patron's right hand. He had no idea what the bracelet was doing. He had no idea what any of this was.

And beside Elias, a young woman in Greythorn grey, her hand resting near the arm of his chair, close without touching. Her face was composed, but her eyes kept drifting to the exits with the quiet watchfulness of someone who had learned young which doors in her uncle's house locked from the outside. Greythorn's niece. The arranged bride. She looked like a woman enduring a role she had been made to perform.

Teyra felt Ash's cold spike, sharp enough to frost the curtain fabric beneath her fingers.

"I see him," Ash said. Barely audible. "I see him."

"We stick to the plan," Teyra whispered. "Expose Greythorn first. Reach Elias after."

His jaw locked. His eyes never left his brother's face.

"He looks so normal," Teyra murmured.

"He is normal," Ash said beside her. His voice was flat and hard. "That's what makes men like him dangerous. They don't look like monsters. They look like fathers, neighbors, pillars of the community. They do terrible things, and then they sleep well at night, because they've convinced themselves they had no choice."

"Did he have a choice?"

"Everyone has a choice." Ash's voice went cold. "His grandfather chose to murder my family for power. His father chose to maintain the lie. And he's chosen to keep building on a foundation of bones, because the alternative would mean admitting that everything he has, everything he is, was bought with innocent blood."

Below them, the musicians stopped playing. The murmur of conversation faded. A seneschal in formal livery stepped forward, struck his staff against the marble floor three times.

"Lords and ladies, honored guests, citizens of the realm, please welcome Lord Aldous Greythorn, Lord Protector of Athergard, Keeper of the Crown, Defender of the Faith."

Applause. Genuine, enthusiastic applause. The sound of hundreds of people celebrating a murderer.

Greythorn stepped forward to the edge of the dais. He raised his hands, and the applause gradually faded.

"Thank you," he said. His voice was warm, resonant, the voice of a practiced orator. "Thank you all for being here tonight. Your presence honors me, as it honors the memory we gather to preserve."

He paused, let the silence stretch.

"Three hundred years ago, a prophecy was sealed in the vaults of the Cathedral. Confirmed by twelve seers, verified by every test known to magical science, a warning of a doom that would consume us all. 'When a Thornwick sits upon the throne,' the prophecy said, 'the city shall burn and the kingdom shall fall.'"

His voice dropped, became heavy with performed sorrow.

"The Thornwicks were good people. Noble people. They had ruled this kingdom for generations with wisdom and grace. But a curse ran in their blood, a curse older than memory, older than history. A darkness that would awaken when one of their line claimed the crown."

He shook his head.

"What do you do, when the family you love carries a doom in their veins? What do you do, when the choice is between one house and an entire kingdom?"

His eyes swept the crowd.

"You do what must be done. You make the sacrifice that no one wants to make. You destroy the thing you love most, because the alternative is losing everything."

The hall was silent. Utterly silent. Every eye fixed on Greythorn, every ear hanging on his words.

"My family did not want this burden. My grandfather did not want to watch the Thornwick line end. But when the fire came, that terrible, accidental fire that claimed the king, queen, and their heirs, he saw an opportunity. An opportunity to take the weight of the crown onto shoulders strong enough to bear it. An opportunity to protect this kingdom from a curse that could never be allowed to return."

He straightened, his expression shifting from sorrow to resolution.

"Since my grandfather's time, we have kept that vigil. For two generations, we have borne that weight. And in that time, this kingdom has prospered. We have known peace. We have known what it means to live without the darkness that once threatened to consume us."

His voice rose.

"Tonight, as we do every year, we remember. We remember the Thornwicks, as victims of a curse they did not choose. We remember their sacrifice. We remember the price that was paid so that we might stand here, in this hall, in this light, alive and free."

He raised his glass.

"To the Thornwicks. May their memory be a blessing, and may the curse they carried never rise again."

"To the Thornwicks," the crowd echoed. Hundreds of voices, speaking in unison. Hundreds of glasses raised to toast the lie.

The chandeliers swayed.

The movement had nothing to do with wind, because there was no wind in the sealed hall. A single, synchronized shudder, crystal pendants chiming against each other in a discordant note that cut through the applause. Teyra saw a crack in the marble floor near the dais, hairline thin, new, running in a straight line toward the center of the room. A servant hurrying past with a champagne tray stumbled, looked down, frowned, and kept walking.

No one else noticed. The music resumed. The laughter continued.

But Teyra's necromancer senses, burnt and failing, were screaming. The wrongness she'd felt in the corridor was stronger here. Concentrated, as if the lie Greythorn had just spoken aloud had agitated a presence that had been listening for longer than anyone alive.

Teyra's stomach was clenched, her skin crawling, and the certainty she felt went beyond logic. They were running out of time in more ways than one.

She turned to Ash. He was staring at the scene below, his face locked down tight. The cracks in his skin were glowing now, a deep, burning blue. The poltergeist stirring beneath the surface.

"Ready?" she asked.

"No."

"Me neither."

She took his hand, knowing what it cost him. His fingers were cold, but they squeezed hers with desperate strength.

He looked at her. She looked back.

Neither of them said it. They didn't need to anymore.

They stepped through the curtain.

The balcony was twenty feet above the Grand Hall floor.

Teyra stood at the railing, looking down at the sea of upturned faces. No one had noticed them yet, the gallery was in shadow, hidden from the main lights of the hall. But that would change in moments.

She reached into her bag and pulled out the book.

Beside her, Ash stepped forward to the edge of the balcony. He closed his eyes. Drew in a breath he didn't need.

And then he blazed.

The light that poured from his form was pure, brilliant white, the color of stars, of moonlight, of things that had never known darkness. It exploded outward from his body, illuminating the entire hall and casting shadows that stretched to the walls and beyond.

Gasps broke first, then screams, then the clatter of dropped glasses and the scrape of chairs shoved back in alarm.

The crowd was staring. Every eye in the hall fixed on the figure on the balcony, the glowing figure, the figure that looked like something from a legend or a nightmare.

Greythorn's face went white.

"Guards!" His voice cracked, the composure shattering. "Guards! Seize that... that thing!"

But the guards didn't move.

They were staring too. Staring at the face of the ghost on the balcony, the face that looked exactly like the portraits that hung in the Hall of Kings. The face that every citizen of Athergard knew from coins, statues, and history books.

The face of the last Thornwick prince.

"My name," Ash said, and his voice was different now. The voice of a king, deep and resonant, echoing off the marble walls, filling every corner of the hall with an authority that couldn't be questioned. "My name is Ashen Thornwick. I was the heir to the throne of Athergard. I was murdered on the night of my coronation by a woman I loved, at the order of the man who stands before you now."

The hall erupted.

The crowd surged unevenly, bodies pressing forward while others scrambled backward and some stood frozen in shock. Voices clamored, questions shouted, accusations flung. The carefully orchestrated celebration had become chaos in seconds.

"Lies!" Greythorn's voice cut through the noise. He had recovered his composure, or at least the appearance of it. His face was flushed, his hands trembling slightly, but his voice was steady. "This is a trick! A necromancer's illusion! A ghost summoned by enemies of the crown to sow discord!"

He pointed at Teyra.

"That woman is a criminal! A failed necromancer, disgraced by the Academy, wanted for illegal practices and conspiracy against the state! She has conjured this apparition to undermine everything we have built!"

Some of the crowd was nodding. The military uniforms first, predictably, the old guard who owed their commissions to Greythorn patronage. Then the merchants, the shipping families, the men whose fortunes depended on Greythorn contracts. And scattered among them, quieter, the judges, the Academy deans, the ward administrators, the institutional class that had been appointed by and answered to the Greythorn machine for two generations. The lie was woven so deeply into the fabric of their reality that even seeing Ash with their own eyes wasn't enough to shake it.

Teyra stepped forward to the railing.

"I am a necromancer," she said. Her voice was smaller than Ash's, human, ordinary, but it carried in the sudden silence. "I work with the dead. I help spirits find peace. And I can tell you, with absolute certainty, that the man standing beside me is no illusion."

She held up the book.

"This is the original prophecy. The one that was sealed in the Cathedral vaults three hundred years ago and hidden in the

Greythorn vault after the coup. The one that Lord Greythorn's grandfather altered to justify the murder of an innocent family."

She opened it to the page they had marked.

"The version you've been told, 'When a Thornwick sits upon the throne, the city shall burn and the kingdom shall fall,' is a lie. A deliberate falsification designed to make the Thornwicks seem like a threat, when they were actually our only protection."

Her voice rang out across the hall.

"The real prophecy says this. 'When darkness rises from the deep places of the earth, when the dead walk and the living flee, then shall the blood of Thornwick be the last light. The crowned head shall become the saving hand. The sacrifice of one shall preserve the many.'"

She lowered the book.

"The Thornwicks were blessed to save this kingdom. And Lord Greythorn's family murdered them to steal a throne they had no right to claim."

No one breathed. The Grand Hall held itself still, a thousand lungs suspended, waiting for someone to tell them what to believe.

Then Greythorn laughed.

A good laugh, rich and warm, the laugh of a man confronted with something absurd. He shook his head, spread his hands in a gesture of disbelief.

"A book," he said. "You expect these people to believe you based on a book? A book you claim came from my vault, with no witnesses, no verification, no proof that it wasn't created yesterday by a skilled forger?"

He stepped forward, his voice hardening.

"I could produce a hundred books that say the opposite. I could produce a thousand. The prophecy has been verified by every reputable seer in the kingdom. It's been confirmed by blood divination and bone-casting. Are we supposed to throw away three hundred years of scholarship because a failed necromancer waves a piece of leather and claims it's authentic?"

He turned to the crowd.

"This is what our enemies do. They create confusion. They sow doubt. They undermine the foundations of our society with tricks and lies, hoping to tear down what generations have built." His voice rose. "I will not let them succeed. I will not let the sacrifice of the Thornwicks be perverted by charlatans seeking to destabilize our kingdom!"

His arms spread wide, his voice cracking with the desperate edge of a man losing control of his own script.

"You have no idea what my family has been holding back. No idea what sleeps beneath this city, what would pour through if the walls we built ever fell. You think this is about a throne? About power?" His laugh was wild, uncontrolled, the laugh of a man who had just said more than he meant to. "This is about survival. This has always been about survival."

A murmur rippled through the crowd. What walls? What sleeps beneath the city? Greythorn's eyes widened slightly, as if hearing his own words for the first time. He straightened, smoothed his coat, reassembled his composure.

But the damage was done. Teyra had seen it. Ash had seen it. And somewhere beneath the marble floor, the hairline crack she'd noticed during the toast had grown three inches longer.

The crowd was murmuring, uncertain. Greythorn's earlier words had been landing, the comfortable weight of three centuries of accepted truth. But his outburst had shaken something loose. The lie was developing cracks of its own.

Ash stepped to the edge of the balcony.

"You speak of sacrifice," he said. The King's Voice again, that deep, resonant tone that vibrated in the bones. "You speak of burden. You speak of doing what must be done."

He raised his hand. On his finger, the Thornwick signet ring gleamed in the light of his own radiance, the burning rose, the family crest that had glinted on his hand the night they met.

"This ring was on my finger when your assassin drove a blade into my heart. This ring was buried with me in an unmarked grave, because your family was too afraid to give me even the dignity of a proper funeral."

He descended.

His feet left the balcony, and he floated downward, slowly, majestically, like a king making an entrance to his own court. His light cast sharp, unnatural shadows of the nobles against the wine-red silk walls, every figure stretched and distorted, as if the room itself were bowing. The chandeliers dimmed by comparison. The gold veins in the marble floor caught his radiance and threw it back, turning the ground beneath him into a mirror of cold fire.

The crowd parted before him, nobles scrambling backward, guards raising weapons they didn't dare use, servants pressing themselves against the walls.

He landed on the dais, ten feet from Greythorn.

The two men faced each other, the living lord and the dead prince, the usurper and the rightful heir. The air between them crackled with tension, with magic, with two generations of lies finally coming to a head.

"I remember almost everything," Ash said. His voice was normal now, something more intimate than the King's Voice. More human. "I remember being seven years old, watching my home burn. I remember being carried away while my mother screamed my name. I remember growing up believing that my family was cursed, that I carried a doom in my blood, that I would destroy everyone I loved if I ever took the throne."

He paused. A flicker crossed his face, a reaching, a grasping for a thing that wasn't there anymore.

"There are gaps. Places where a memory should be and isn't. Your family didn't just kill me, Greythorn. You stole the person I was before the blade. And you are still stealing from me."

His eyes burned into Greythorn's.

"I remember Seraphine. The woman your family manipulated into believing she was saving the kingdom by killing me. I remember the look on her face when she drove that blade home, the tears, the whispered apologies, the utter devastation of a woman destroying the thing she loved most."

He took a step closer.

"I remember dying. Five years of darkness, of emptiness, of never knowing who I was or why I was suffering. And I remember the truth, the truth your family has been hiding since before I was born."

He was inches from Greythorn now. The lord had gone pale, truly pale, the color of a man watching his entire world crumble.

"The Thornwicks were never the threat," Ash said. "We were the solution. The only thing standing between this kingdom and whatever darkness the prophecy was warning about. And your family murdered us to steal a throne."

Greythorn's composure finally broke.

"Guards!" he screamed. "Kill him! Kill them both!"

The guards surged forward, a dozen men in Greythorn livery, swords drawn, charging toward the dais. Teyra noticed others held back. The Moth's influence only went so far.

Ash raised his hand.

"Stop."

The word was power. Pure, undiluted authority, the voice of a king speaking to his subjects. It rolled through the hall like thunder rolling through stone.

The guards stopped.

They had no choice. The King's Voice had frozen them in place, held them motionless by sheer force of will.

Ash was shaking. The light pouring from his form was dimming, the cracks spreading faster, his grip on reality visibly slipping. The effort was destroying him, burning through whatever reserves he had left.

But his voice was steady.

"I am Ashen Thornwick," he said. "Last of my line. Heir to a throne that was stolen. Voice of the dead who cannot speak for themselves."

He turned to face the crowd, the stunned, uncertain crowd.

Her eyes moved, involuntarily, to Elias. He hadn't moved. He sat perfectly still in his chair at the edge of the dais, his hands folded in his lap, his face the color of the marble beneath his feet. A man receiving news too large to hold yet. His lips moved—barely, almost soundlessly—but Teyra was close enough to read them.

"Brother?"

The word struck Ash with the clean violence of a blade. His form flickered once, hard, and for a moment Teyra thought he would shatter. His light guttered. His edges went transparent. Then something in him—the king, the duty, the five years of darkness that had forged him—pulled him back together.

"And I am telling you. Everything you have been taught is a lie."

The hall was silent. So silent that Teyra could hear her own heartbeat, could hear Ash's ragged breathing, could hear the soft click of a mechanism engaging somewhere in the walls.

And she could see the floor.

The crack she'd noticed during the toast, the hairline fracture near the dais, had spread. It ran the entire length of the hall now, branching and forking like a river delta, the marble on either side turning from white to grey, as if the stone itself were dying. The gold veins in the floor had gone dark. The reflections that had been so perfect when they arrived were gone, the polished surface now dull, opaque, as if the stone itself were drinking the light.

The crack had been growing throughout the entire confrontation. While Greythorn spoke his lies. While Ash spoke his truth. While the crowd listened and the guards charged and the King's Voice shook the walls. The void had been patient. It had been waiting.

a presence that had been listening for longer than anyone alive.

The chandeliers swayed. The columns groaned. Cracks appeared in the marble floor, spreading outward from some central point, glowing with a light that was older than silver or gold. Darker.

And the Palace wards screamed.

The high, strained whine Teyra had felt since entering the building rose to a shriek, a sound that bypassed ears and went straight into the teeth, the bones, the base of the skull. The vast sigil-arrays in the foundations, three centuries of the most powerful spiritual filtration in Athergard, overloaded and blew. She felt them go, a chain reaction, ward after ward detonating in sequence, the spiritual equivalent of fuses blowing down a power line. The luminescence in the Grand Hall died. The candles guttered. For one terrible, eternal second, the only light in the room was Ash's failing silver glow and the dark radiance pouring from the cracks in the floor.

The wards hadn't broken because of Ash. Unlike the Greythorn estate's blood-wards, which had been built to reject him, the Palace wards were older—Thornwick-keyed, foundation-deep. They'd welcomed him, parted for his blood the way they had in the corridors. But they'd been straining all night against the rising tide, and the void pressing up from below didn't care about bloodlines or rightful heirs.

Then the grey tide hit.

Three centuries of filtered spiritual residue released in a single catastrophic wave, fragments, Unsettled deaths, and every loss the Palace wards had processed, stored, and held at bay. The grey film that had been pressing against the Palace walls all night crashed through the shattered wards like water through a broken dam. It flooded the Grand Hall in a luminous tide, knee-high in seconds, waist-high in moments, filling the room with the phosphorescent glow of Athergard's unprocessed dead.

And Teyra's channels, scorched, doorless, wide open, caught all of it.

The fragments hit her like a wall. They came crashing, not settling. Hundreds, thousands. Every burden the Palace had filtered for three hundred years, every death the drainage wards had processed, every Unsettled spirit that had dissolved in the grey rain and been caught by the gutters and stored in the infrastructure that was now rubble, all of it pouring into the one person in the room whose channels were broken enough to receive it.

She lost breath, sight, and any separation between herself and the flood. She was a woman in a harbour clinic with empty arms where a child should have been. She was a soldier bleeding out on cobblestones during a riot that history forgot. She was a grand-mother watching the door, waiting for a son who'd sailed away and never come back. She was a hundred people, a thousand, their small and ordinary and devastating losses stacking inside her like books in a library that had run out of shelves. She lost herself. For a moment—a second, an hour, she couldn't tell—she was no one. Just a vessel. Just a channel with no walls and no name and no self to hold onto. Then Teyra Tepes came back. Because she had to. Because there was still something left to do.

This is what happened to Meridia.

But Meridia hadn't known what was coming. Meridia hadn't walked into the flood on purpose. Meridia hadn't spent six days learning that borrowed hurt was fuel.

"No," Greythorn whispered. His face had gone from white to grey. "No, no, no, it's too early, it can't be…" His head snapped toward the dais. "Elias! The ward-anchor, hold the ward-anchor…"

But Elias was on his knees, the iron band on his wrist blazing red, his face contorted with something he couldn't understand. The young woman in grey had seized his arm, steadying him, her composed mask finally cracked.

The ward system was drawing on him, draining everything the Blood-Key could give, and it still wasn't enough. The cracks widened. The shaking intensified. From somewhere deep below, from the foundations of the Palace, from the bedrock beneath the city, a sound rose. A rumbling. A roar.

The sound of a thing waking up.

"The darkness," Teyra breathed. Her voice came from somewhere far away. She was drowning in other people's lives and the words barely made it through. "The prophecy, 'when darkness rises from the deep places of the earth'…"

"It's happening," Ash said. His voice was hollow. "It's happening now."

The floor split open.

And something climbed out.

Chapter Twelve

THE LAST LIGHT

THE THING THAT CLIMBED from the breach was an absence.

A living shape cut out of the world, a void that moved and writhed and reached upward with limbs made of pure nothing. Where it touched the marble floor, the stone didn't break. It ceased to exist, simply vanished, leaving behind emptiness that hurt to look at. And the sound was a low, steady hum, a note being subtracted from music, a frequency that made Teyra's teeth ache and her eyes water.

The air around it stopped being air, became a thickness that choked and burned and tasted like the end of everything.

Teyra's necromancer senses, burned out, barely functional, still screamed at her. This was death, but a kind she'd never encountered. The peaceful transition her grandmother had taught her to shepherd had nothing to do with this. This was death as erasure, the ultimate nothing that waited at the end of all things.

The void-creature rose to its full height, if height was even a concept that applied to something made of absence. Ten feet, fifteen, twenty. It kept growing, kept expanding, kept becoming more of what it was. A wound in reality given form, the darkness between stars given hunger.

And it was alone only for a moment.

More shapes rose from the crack in the floor, dozens, hundreds, darkness pouring upward in a tide from a broken dam. They had no faces, no features, no substance, just the suggestion of forms, the memory of things that had once been alive and were now something worse. They moved in silence, but Teyra could hear them anyway. Could hear the screaming. Thousands of voices, layered on top of each other, the accumulated agony of centuries of death compressed into a sound that bypassed her ears and went straight into her soul.

The guests were running.

The Grand Hall had become a stampede, nobles trampling each other in their desperation to reach the exits, guards abandoning their posts, servants screaming as the darkness swept toward them. A duchess in emerald silk went down beneath the crowd and didn't rise. A general in full military regalia was grabbed by a void-tendril and simply stopped existing, his medals clattering to the floor as the body that had worn them vanished.

The chandeliers were swaying violently, crystal pendants shattering and raining down like deadly hail. One broke free entirely, crashing into the crowd below, the screams swallowed by the larger roar. The columns cracked, those beautiful marble columns carved with the serpent-and-crown motif, splitting from base to capital as the floor continued to buckle. The painted ceiling, those magnificent murals of Greythorn triumph, split and crumbled, angels, dragons, and victorious lords dropping in chunks of plaster into the chaos below.

The void-creatures carried no scent at all, an absence where smell should have been, somehow worse than any stench, because stench at least meant something still existed to rot. The absence of sense, the absence of everything that made the world real.

And in the middle of it all, Lord Greythorn stood frozen on the dais, staring at the apocalypse he had unleashed.

"No," he whispered. The sound shouldn't have carried over the roar of the void, but it did, a thin, brittle thread. "No, this is wrong. The prophecy said the darkness would come if a Thornwick took the throne. The Thornwicks are dead. There are no Thornwicks. The curse was broken..."

"The curse was never real."

Ash's voice cut through the chaos like a blade. He was still blazing with white light, still holding the frozen guards in place, but his form was dimming now, the effort of maintaining the King's Voice draining him faster than Teyra had ever seen.

"Your family invented the curse to justify murder," Ash continued. "The real prophecy was a warning, a warning about a darkness that was coming, a darkness that could only be stopped by Thornwick blood. And you killed every Thornwick who could have prevented it."

"That's impossible." Greythorn shook his head, his composure crumbling. "The seers confirmed, the divinations proved..."

"The seers were paid to lie. The divinations were manipulated. Your grandfather spent thirty years constructing a false reality, and you've been living in it your entire life." Ash took a step toward him, his light pushing back the darkness that was creeping across the dais. "Congratulations, Lord Greythorn. Your family's half-century of conspiracy has finally achieved its ultimate goal. You've doomed us all."

Greythorn's face contorted, the desperate spasm of a man whose entire world was crumbling around him.

"I am the Lord Protector!" he screamed. "I am the Keeper of the Crown! This kingdom is mine to command!"

He turned toward the breach, toward the tide of darkness still pouring upward, and did what Teyra least expected.

He dropped to his knees.

His hands pressed flat against the cracked marble, his fingers finding the Greythorn sigils carved into the dais, the blood wards, the family magic, the ancient protections his ancestors had woven into the very foundations of the Palace. His lips moved, forming words in the old tongue, the activation phrases that had been passed from father to son for three hundred years.

The sigils flickered. Red light pulsed beneath his palms, faint, uncertain, struggling to respond.

"Answer me," Greythorn whispered. His voice had changed. The bombast was gone, the practiced authority, the orator's resonance. This was the voice of a man talking to his gods. "This is Greythorn blood. This is Greythorn stone. I am the keeper. I am the protector. Answer me."

The sigils pulsed once more and went dark.

The red light died. The wards fell silent. Three hundred years of Greythorn magic, built on stolen foundations, powered by a conspiracy that had murdered the very bloodline meant to fuel them, extinguished. The wards had been designed to respond to the blood of kings. Greythorn blood had only ever been close enough to fool the surface enchantments, and now, with the void pouring through, the ancient magic could tell the difference.

The Palace itself had rejected him.

Greythorn stared at his hands, then at the dark sigils beneath them. At the nothing where power should have been.

"No," he breathed. But the word was hollow now. Emptied of conviction. The word of a man who had just heard the universe confirm what some buried part of him had always suspected.

He looked up at Ash.

What remained was smaller. Human. An old man kneeling on cracked marble, watching the darkness pour out of the earth, finally understanding that he had never been the wall between the kingdom and destruction.

He had been the door.

"Did you know?" Ash asked. His voice was quiet. Almost gentle. The voice of a man who had spent six days wanting to destroy this person and was finding, in this final moment, that destruction wasn't big enough. "Somewhere inside. Did you always know it was a lie?"

Greythorn's jaw worked. His eyes, those cold, calculating eyes that had looked out on a kingdom he believed was his by right, were wet.

"My grandfather told me on his deathbed," he said. The words came out thin and cracked, barely audible over the roar of the void. "He said the prophecy had been adjusted. He said the Thornwicks were never the threat. He said we'd done a terrible thing, one that could never be undone, and that the only way forward was to keep building. Keep the lie alive. Because if we stopped, if we admitted what we'd done..."

His voice broke.

"Everything would fall apart."

He laughed. A single, brittle sound, like a teacup hairlining under boiling water.

"He was right about that, at least."

The darkness shifted behind him. The void-creatures were closer now, drawn by the sound of his voice, by the heat of his body, by the simple fact of his existence. They moved without hurry. They had all the time in the world.

"Was there ever another way?" Greythorn asked. He was looking at the breach now, at the wound his family had spent three centuries ensuring no one could close.

"There was," Ash said. "Your family destroyed it."

Greythorn closed his eyes.

"Then let it end with me."

He opened his eyes. Not at Ash. Not at the breach. At the hall behind them, where a serving girl, fifteen, maybe sixteen, her uniform torn, her face blank, had tripped over a fallen chair and was crawling toward the east doors on bleeding hands. A void-creature was drifting toward her, unhurried, patient, that terrible hum preceding it like a herald.

Greythorn stood.

His legs shook. His hands were empty. He had no magic, no wards, no authority left to wield. He was just an old man in an expensive coat, walking toward a darkness that had already marked him for consumption.

He put himself between the girl and the void-creature.

"Run," he said. His voice cracked on the word. She stared at him, uncomprehending. "Run, you stupid child."

She ran.

He didn't scream when the darkness took him.

The void-creature nearest to him flowed forward, closing the distance in the space between heartbeats. Its limbs, if you could call them limbs, wrapped around him, embraced him, pulled him close. And Lord Aldous Greythorn, last of his name, keeper of a lie that had outlived its architect, did not fight.

Teyra watched, couldn't look away, couldn't close her eyes, as the darkness consumed him.

First his hands. The fingers turning grey, then black, then transparent, then nothing at all. The expensive rings he wore, the sigils of his authority, fell through space where fingers should have been and clattered to the floor.

Then his arms. The grey velvet of his coat dissolving, the flesh beneath following, the bones beneath that becoming visible for one horrifying moment before they too vanished into the void.

His face was last. His eyes were still closed. Whatever he saw behind those lids, whatever final truth or oblivion waited for a man who had spent his life building on bones, he kept it to himself.

And then there was nothing.

The darkness consumed Lord Aldous Greythorn in less than ten seconds.

When it was done, there was nothing left. No body, bones, or ash. Just empty space where a man had knelt, and two rings gleaming on cold marble, and the void-creatures already turning to find their next meal.

The screaming in the hall intensified. The stampede became a rout. People were dying now, trampled underfoot, caught by the spreading darkness, simply giving up and collapsing as the weight overwhelmed them.

Ash didn't hesitate.

"Guards!" His voice cracked through the chaos, raw, human, stripped of spectral power. Just a man's voice pitched to carry over a battlefield. The surviving members of Greythorn's personal guard, four men, swords drawn, frozen with indecision, turned toward him. "The east doors. Get them open. Evacuate the civilians through the kitchens, the void is spreading from the west. Move the injured first. Anyone who can walk helps someone who can't."

The guards stared at him. A ghost giving orders. A dead prince commanding living men.

"Now!"

They moved. Whether it was the authority in his voice or the simple human relief of someone telling them what to do, they moved. Swords sheathed, shoulders turned, four men becoming a rescue operation instead of a stampede.

For one breath, Teyra heard the echo of Greythorn's voice in his, the same authority, the same unquestioned expectation of obedience. Greythorn had pointed at enemies; Ash was pointing at exits.

Ash turned to the Hessians, three still standing, their command frequency severed when Greythorn died, their brass faces cycling through error patterns. "You. Perimeter. Nothing gets past the east corridor. Protect the exit."

The machines processed, recalibrated, and obeyed.

Then Ash turned to Teyra.

"The breach," he said. His voice was strained, cracking. "I have to close the breach."

"You can barely stand!"

"I know." He looked at the crack in the floor, wider now, ten feet across, still spewing darkness into the world. "But if I don't, everyone dies. Those things won't stop at the Palace. They won't stop at the city. They'll consume everything."

He met her eyes.

"I need you to anchor me."

Teyra didn't hesitate.

She vaulted the gallery railing and dropped, hitting the marble hard enough to jar her teeth, her injured ankle screaming as she rolled and came up running. She slid across the debris-strewn floor, nearly falling as a chunk of ceiling crashed down inches from her head. The darkness was spreading faster now, tendrils of void reaching out to touch everything they could find. Where they touched living flesh, people simply stopped, froze in place, their eyes going empty, their bodies collapsing like husks with the spirit gone out of them.

She grabbed Ash's hand.

The cold was immediate and overwhelming, the full force of his spectral nature, unfiltered, undiluted. It burned into her palm, raced up her arm, spread through her chest like ice water being poured directly into her heart.

"Whatever happens," Ash said, "don't let go."

"I won't."

He turned toward the breach.

And he blazed.

The light that erupted from his form was blinding, gold, pure gold, the color of crowns and sunlight and everything the darkness could never be. It poured from every crack in his spectral skin, every wound the blood wards had burned into him, every piece of his being that was still fighting to exist.

The transformation was agonizing to watch. Ash's human features, the face she had come to love, the eyes that had looked at her with such warmth, were dissolving into pure radiance. He was becoming something else. Something greater, something that might save them all if it didn't destroy him first.

He walked toward the breach.

Each step left a footprint of golden light on the ruined marble. The void-creatures recoiled, actually recoiled, pulling back from the advancing light like animals flinching from fire. For the first time since they'd emerged, they showed something that looked like retreat.

The ground shook with every step he took. Windows blew out along the walls of the Grand Hall, stained glass depicting Greythorn victories exploding outward in sprays of colored fragments. The remaining chandeliers swung wildly, several more crashing down into the emptying hall.

"The blood of Thornwick," Ash spoke, and his voice was the King's Voice again, amplified beyond human limits, resonant with a stolen legacy three hundred years deep, finally being reclaimed. The words carried power, each syllable pushing back the darkness, each breath a weapon against the void. "The last light. The saving hand."

He reached the edge of the breach. Below him, Teyra could see it now, a wound in reality itself, deeper than any crack in the floor. A hole that went down forever, into darkness so absolute it made the void-creatures look pale by comparison. The screaming was coming from down there. The screaming of the dead, the lost, and all those consumed by the nothing that waited at the bottom of everything.

Ash stepped into the breach.

He didn't fall. His light held him suspended over the abyss, a beacon in the dark, a star burning in the void. The golden radiance spread outward from his body, denying the darkness outright, and where his light touched the void, reality reasserted itself, existence anchoring against the nothing that sought to unmake it. The sphere of light grew and grew and grew.

But Teyra could feel it, feel what it was costing him. The cold in her hand was intensifying, spreading beyond pain into a sensation she had no name for.

Her blood crystallized in her veins. Her heart pumped jagged shards of ice instead of warmth. Her vision was going white at the edges, then grey, then white again.

Warmth trickled from her nose, blood, she knew, though she couldn't spare the attention to wipe it away. Then from her ears.

Then from the corners of her eyes, red tears tracking down her cheeks.

She was his anchor. The only thing keeping him tethered to the world while he poured himself into the light. And the tether was burning her from the inside out.

Her knees buckled. She caught herself, forced herself to stay upright, forced her fingers to maintain their grip even as the cold ate deeper and deeper. The marble beneath her feet was frosting over, ice spreading outward from where she stood, her body becoming a conduit for the deathly cold that was the price of his power.

"Hold on," she gasped, tasting copper. "Ash, hold on..."

"I'm trying." His voice was distant, distorted, coming from somewhere very far away. "There's so much of it. So much darkness. It's been building for three hundred years, waiting for this moment. Waiting for the last Thornwick to fail."

"You're not failing!"

"I'm fading." She could hear the truth in his words, could feel it through their connection. The light was draining him, draining everything he was, everything he had been, everything he might have become. "I can hold it back, Teyra. I can keep it contained. But I can't close it. The anchor won't let me."

"What do you mean?"

"The breach needs to be sealed from the inside. Someone has to go into the dark and pull it shut behind them." His voice cracked. "Someone has to become the door."

"No." Teyra's grip tightened on his hand, the cold burning deeper, the ice spreading to her shoulder now. "No, there has to be another way..."

"There isn't." He turned his head, just slightly, just enough to look at her. His face was barely visible through the blaze of golden light, but she could see his eyes. Grey eyes, human eyes, the eyes of the man she loved. "I've known since I read the prophecy. 'The sacrifice of one shall preserve the many.' I'm the sacrifice, Teyra. I've always been the sacrifice."

"I won't let you..."

A scream cut through her words—human, ragged, and close behind her.

A human scream, coming from somewhere behind her. She turned, keeping her grip on Ash's hand, and saw Seraphine.

The Commander of the Queen's Guard should not have been standing. Should not have been here. Should not have been alive. She had crawled out of a clinic bed, Teyra could see the clinic's threadbare shift beneath the coat one of the Moth's people must have thrown over her shoulders, could see the saline feed she'd ripped from her arm still dangling from her wrist, the needle trailing a thin thread of blood. Lenore must have gone for help when Seraphine woke, must have found whoever the Moth had stationed nearby and gotten her here, because no human body in that condition could have crossed the city alone. She had come here on will alone, because whatever physical reserves she'd had were gone, consumed by the necrotic damage eating through her torso, by the blood she no longer had enough of, by the simple biological reality that a body cannot sustain this level of damage and continue to operate.

But she was operating. Barely upright, one hand braced against a fallen column, the other pressed against the wound in her side that had reopened and was bleeding freely. Her face was the color of old wax, the specific yellow-white of a person whose organs were beginning to shut down. Her legs were shaking. Her breathing was audible from twenty feet away, short, wet, labored, the sound of lungs that were filling with what they shouldn't be filling with.

She had no weapon. She had no strength. She was dying on her feet, and she had dragged herself here to die in the right place.

But she was standing between the fleeing civilians and a void-creature that had broken through Ash's light.

"Run!" Seraphine screamed at the people behind her, a cluster of servants and lesser nobles who had been too slow to escape, who had gotten trapped in the corner of the hall. "Run, you fools!"

The void-creature flowed toward her, and as it moved, it changed.

The shifting darkness coalesced into a man-shaped thing. It wore a coronation suit made of shadow, a face Seraphine knew better than her own, the boy she had murdered five years ago, his chest a ruin of hollow darkness where her blade had gone in.

Seraphine didn't run. Her legs wouldn't have carried her three steps, the wound in her side wept through the coat, cold numbness spreading up through her torso where the necrotic healing had eaten away at her from the inside out. Her knees wanted to buckle. Her vision was narrowing to a tunnel.

She planted her feet on the blood-slicked marble because planting them was all she had left.

Her breath hitched, a sob she refused to release.

"I know you," she whispered to the nightmare. "I see you."

The shadow-Ash raised a hand, accusing, silent. It was her guilt made manifest, the End of Days wearing the face of her greatest wound.

"Come on, then," she snarled, tears cutting through the grime on her face. "Come and take me. I've been waiting for you since the night I drove that blade home."

The memory lunged.

And Seraphine caught it.

She caught it with a force that had nothing to do with hands or strength or magic, none of which she had left. She caught it with the same thing that had kept her alive since the night she'd dragged herself to their doorstep on wounds that should have killed her twice over. The flat, immovable refusal of a woman who had decided what she was for, and would not stop until she'd done it.

She caught the darkness with her soul. And it was already such a damaged thing, scarred by years of carrying what she'd done, eaten by necrotic magic, held together by discipline instead of hope, that the void found fewer clean surfaces to grip than it expected. The death magic Teyra had poured into her wound was still there, threaded through her tissue, and it recognized the void the way a scar recognizes the blade that made it. Her body had been learning to contain death since the safe house. The void was just more of what she was already holding.

Teyra saw it happen, saw the void-creature's essence wrap around Seraphine, saw the woman's body convulse as the darkness tried to consume her. But Seraphine didn't crumple. Didn't fade. Didn't cease to be like Greythorn had.

She held on.

Her scream became a weapon. Pure, undiluted refusal to be erased. The void-creature writhed, trapped, unable to consume her but unable to break free.

"GO!" Seraphine screamed at the trapped civilians. "GO NOW!"

They went. Scrambling past her, pouring toward the exits, escaping while she held the monster at bay.

For one moment, across the ruined hall, Seraphine's eyes found Teyra's. The void was eating through her, shadow rippling beneath her skin, but her gaze was clear and steady as a woman delivering a final briefing.

"I told you," she said. Her voice held the quiet devastation of a woman who had been right about the wrong thing and was now holding the consequences inside her own body. "I told you what was waiting beneath the city."

"You were lied to, Sera," Teyra said. "The prophecy was forged..."

"The door still opened." A spasm wracked her. She held. "Right and wrong don't matter anymore. Only what I can hold."

Teyra watched, helpless, as Seraphine's body glowed, with the darkness itself rather than with light, the void-creature's essence seeping into her, becoming part of her.

"She's absorbing it," Teyra breathed.

"She's becoming a vessel," Ash said. His voice was hushed. "She's taking the darkness into herself. Containing it. Choosing to be the prison."

The void-creature disappeared, absorbed rather than destroyed. Seraphine fell to her knees, her skin shifting between flesh and shadow, her eyes going dark and then bright and then dark again.

"That won't hold forever," she gasped, looking up at them. Her voice was layered now, human and other, the darkness speaking through her as much as she was speaking through it. "I can feel it fighting. Trying to break free. You need to close the breach now, before I lose control."

"I can't close it." The words were almost nothing. "I've given everything. My light is dying."

Seraphine's body convulsed. The void-creature inside her was winning. Her skin rippled, her eyes going dark and then bright and then dark again, the intervals between human and void growing shorter.

"Hold the line, Sera." Ash's voice cracked on the name. "Just hold."

"I'm trying." The words came out layered, human and void, Seraphine and the thing wearing her. "Minutes. Maybe less."

The world went quiet.

The breach still screamed, the void-creatures still howled, the Palace was still collapsing around them. But for Teyra, in that moment, all of it receded. The way sound goes underwater. The way the world goes soft at the edges when your body has nothing left to give.

She was sitting on the floor. She didn't remember sitting down. Her back was against a fallen column, her hands in her lap, blood from her nose dripping onto her fingers. Ash was beside her, what was left of him. More light than man now, more memory than flesh. But he was there.

"Hey," she said.

"Hey."

"Remember the first night? In the shop? You were dripping on my floor and Lenore asked if you were dead or just rude."

A sound that might have been a laugh. "I remember."

"I was going to drink Velvet Dusk and sit in my armchair and feel sorry for myself. That was my entire plan for the evening."

"Sounds like a good plan."

"It was a terrible plan. I'm glad you ruined it."

His hand found hers. Cold light against warm skin. She could see the floor through his palm.

"Teyra. When this is done, if there's anything left of me, I'd very much like to sit in that armchair and drink terrible tea with you."

"It's not terrible tea. It's excellent tea. You have no palate."

"I'm dead. We're not known for our palates."

"You keep using that excuse."

"It keeps being true."

She closed her eyes. Opened them. The breach was still there. Seraphine was still holding. The world was still ending. But for five heartbeats, she had sat on the floor with the man she loved and talked about tea, and that was enough. That was the whole point. That was what she was fighting for, the possibility of quiet mornings and bad jokes and someone to share a cup with, rather than kingdoms or prophecies or the grand machinery of fate.

She stood up.

Ash turned to her. His form was dissolving, more suggestion than substance, more memory than man. The golden radiance that had sustained him was guttering, the last embers of a fire that had burned too hot.

"Teyra. You need to run."

"No."

"The breach is still open. Seraphine can't hold it. I can't close it. If you stay here…"

"I said no."

She wasn't looking at him. She was looking at the breach.

At the wound in reality. At the place where the world ended and the void began. It was vast and hungry and screaming with the voices of the consumed, and it was the most terrible thing she had ever seen.

And somewhere beneath the exhaustion and the burned-out magic and the blood running from her nose, Teyra Tepes recognized it.

The breach was a door that had been forced open. Ash's light could push against it, had been pushing against it, but light alone couldn't close a door. It just illuminated the darkness on the other side. And Seraphine's sacrifice, her willingness to become the seal, that was a lock rather than a door. She could hold the darkness back, but she couldn't stitch reality together. The wound needed to be closed from this side. Healed. With the specific force that operated at the boundary between the living and the dead.

Necromancy.

The Academy's cold-channel necromancy was useless here. The Grave-Chill was gone. She could feel the scorched channels, the scarring where she'd pushed too hard, too many times, over the past seven days.

But there was another channel. The one the Academy had buried in footnotes. The one they'd warned against in three separate lectures. The one that had gotten her failed because she couldn't stop feeling what the dead felt.

Resonance.

The deeper the bond between necromancer and spirit, the more powerful the Word.

It's like replacing a faucet with a river. The power comes, but it comes all at once, and it burns out everything in its path.

The professors had tested Resonance with one spirit. One connection. One bond. And even that had overwhelmed her, the soldier boy, his homesickness, his love for his mother, the arrow wound she'd felt in her own chest.

They had never considered what would happen if a necromancer opened that channel to every spirit in a city.

At the Academy, she'd been empty, a girl reaching into a stranger's pain with nothing to anchor her. Now she was carrying a city's worth of borrowed weight. The fragments had become her foundation.

"Teyra." Ash's hand found hers. His fingers were barely solid, cold light, fading fast. "Whatever you're thinking..."

"I'm thinking about the soldier." She sounded far away, a woman doing arithmetic in a burning building. "Thomas. The Academy exam. I broke the circle because I felt everything he felt. One spirit, and it drowned me."

"Teyra, you can't..."

"One spirit drowned me." She looked at him, and her eyes were clear. Terrifyingly clear. "What happens when I open the channel to all of them?"

"You'll die."

"Maybe."

"Certainly. The Resonance from one spirit nearly destroyed you. A hundred will... a thousand will..."

"Will close the breach." She squeezed his hand. The Barrier didn't push back. She waited for the familiar resistance, the magical current trying to separate them, but it was gone, absent in the way a lock stops working when there's nothing left inside worth protecting. Whatever memories the Barrier had been feeding on, it had already taken them all. "Ash. I've spent my entire life being told I feel too much. That I'm too connected to the dead. That my compassion is a weakness, a flaw, a failure of professional discipline." She pulled him closer, pressed her forehead against his, solid meeting spectral, the living and the dying, one last point of contact. "What if they were wrong? What if the thing that made them turn me away is the thing that saves the world?"

He was silent. The breach roared behind them, hungry and patient.

"The dead of this city know me," she said quietly. "I brewed tea for their grieving families. I held their hands while they faded. I told them they were seen, and known, and not alone. For years, Ash. For years I did that, one spirit at a time, in a shop on Weaver Street that nobody cared about." Her voice broke, then steadied. "I'm going to ask them to help me. Ask rather than command."

"And if they say no?"

"Then we die." She almost smiled. "But the dead have never said no to me."

Seraphine screamed.

The sound was inhuman, the void-creature inside her surging, her skin rippling between flesh and shadow, her body arching backward as the darkness tried to tear free. She fell to her knees, hands braced against the cracked marble, holding herself together through will alone.

"Now," she gasped. "Whatever you're doing. NOW."

Teyra let go of Ash's hand.

She turned to the breach. She knelt on the cracked marble floor of the Grand Hall, in the wreckage of a coronation, in the ruins of a kingdom built on lies, and she closed her eyes.

Before she reached, she took inventory.

Her clinical magic was scorched, barely functional, the channels ruined by the Command Word. But the other thing was intact. The thing she'd been accumulating since a rainy morning in a tea shop on Weaver Street, one fragment at a time, day by day.

They were all there. The thousands from the ward collapse, the mother with empty arms, the bleeding soldier, the grandmother at the door. The servants' corridor burdens, the scullery maid's tiredness, the footman's shame, the cook's smothered fury. The clinic fragments, the drowned dockworker, the locket-woman, the bewildered old man. And underneath them, faded but present, the ghosts of the original collection. Thomas's homesickness, burned by the Command Word but echoing still in the shape of the scar it left. The widow's yearning. The little girl's winter-cold. The phantom blade. All consumed, all spent, but the channels remembered their shapes the way a riverbed remembers water.

She was carrying a city's worth of borrowed weight. The thing the Academy called a disorder, her grandmother a gift, the thing that had gotten her failed and nearly killed and dragged through seven days of hell.

And beneath them all, so familiar she'd nearly overlooked it, her own. The grandmother who'd died and left her a shop and a gift she didn't know how to use. Four years of empty chairs and unanswered bells. A lifetime of being told she was too much, by everyone except the dead.

She'd never included it in the inventory before. It had never occurred to her that her own counted.

It counted.

How much feeling is too much?

The question she'd asked in the café, a lifetime ago. The question that had followed her through every day, every fragment, every involuntary accumulation. The question the Academy answered with *any feeling is too much* and Meridia had answered by drowning.

Teyra answered it now.

There is no too much. There is only whether you're willing to carry it.

She reached.

She bypassed the clinical cold, the regulated channel the Academy had spent four years trying to teach her. She reached for the other thing. The connection. The bond. The river. And she opened the Resonance channel and the collected weight together, every fragment, every borrowed hurt, every piece of other people's suffering she'd been carrying, and offered it as fuel. Given freely, offered by choice, where the Command Word had burned them from her against her will. Given the way the spirits had given their feelings to her in the first place. In trust. In hope. In the belief that someone who felt this much might know what to do with it.

The first spirit answered before she'd finished asking.

Mrs. Pemberton's husband. The bitter ghost who'd ranted about the butcher's affair. His presence surfaced in her awareness like a hand breaking water, surprised, confused, but there. She felt his irritation, his stubbornness, his grudging affection for the necromancer who'd listened to him complain for forty minutes without judgment.

Help me, she thought. *Please.*

He didn't speak. But he stayed. And his bitterness, the fragment she'd carried since the first morning, flared in recognition. The fragment and the spirit, reunited, the borrowed feeling going home.

The second was the widow from last month, the woman who'd died in her sleep and couldn't understand why her cat kept walking through her. Her yearning, for mornings, for ordinary life, for the cat who couldn't feel her hand anymore, pulsed in Teyra's chest and then flowed outward, back to the woman who'd first felt it. The third was a dockworker who'd drowned in the harbour, a man whose ghost Teyra had spent two hours coaxing out of the water because he was afraid of heights and the afterlife seemed to involve going up.

They came. And their burdens came with them, as bonds rather than weapons or fuel to be burned. Each fragment Teyra had ever carried was a thread connecting her to the spirit who'd left it behind. The collection was a web. A network of bonds spanning an entire city, built one cup of tea at a time.

The channel opened.

And the river poured in.

Hundreds answered. Every ghost she had ever helped, and every ghost they knew, and every spirit still tethered to the old stones of Athergard by love or unfinished business. They rose through the cracks in the marble floor, through the foundations of the Palace, through the bedrock of a city that had been burying its dead for three hundred years.

The dead of Athergard answered their necromancer.

Every connection was a thread, and every thread carried weight, memory, emotion, identity, the full unbearable complexity of a human life. One spirit had nearly destroyed her at the Academy. Now she held hundreds. The Resonance tore through her necromantic channels like a flood through a drainage ditch, widening them, scarring them, burning everything it touched.

Blood poured from her nose. From her ears. From the corners of her eyes.

She held.

"Teyra!" Ash's voice, somewhere far away, urgent. "Your eyes are bleeding…"

She couldn't hear him. She could hear everything else. The dead were speaking, all of them, a chorus of voices that should have been cacophony but wasn't, because they were choosing. Every one of them, individually, freely, choosing to answer the woman who had treated them like people instead of problems.

She stood. Her legs shouldn't have held her. They held.

She walked toward the breach.

The void screamed at her approach, the hungry nothing that existed beneath reality, the absence that wanted to become everything. It pushed against her, a pressure wave of non-existence, trying to erase her the way it had erased Greythorn, the way it had consumed the guards and everything it touched.

The dead of Athergard pushed back.

They poured through her in a light that was neither gold nor silver. A warm amber glow of a thousand remembered lives, a thousand stories, a thousand cups of tea brewed in a shop on Weaver Street for people who needed to say goodbye. The light tasted of chamomile and the particular sweetness of letting go.

And each spirit brought its weight home.

The entombed workers came, the builders from the Greythorn vault, three centuries of fury finally given voice, pouring through Teyra's channels with a force that should have torn her apart. But it didn't tear. It built. Their fury became mortar. Their stolen labor became the seal's foundation. The class divide that had exploited them in life and death was, in this final moment, reversed. The forgotten dead became the structure that saved the living.

The scribe came, the old man who'd wept while forging a lie. His burden, which Teyra had carried since the bone chamber, flowed back to him and transformed. His tears became evidence. His trembling hand became steady.

And Thomas came.

She felt him before she saw him, the homesickness, the bread, the tin roofs, the mother's kitchen. The fragment the Command Word had burned to silence in the bone chamber. She'd thought it was gone forever. But the scar-shape was still there, the hollow in her channels where his homesickness had lived for four years, worn smooth as a riverbed, and it had called to him the way an empty room calls to the person who used to sleep there. Thomas had been waiting, the way spirits wait, patient, uncertain, hoping someone would call. And when Teyra opened the channel, when she offered the web as a bridge, he crossed back along the path his own fragment had carved, into the space that had always been his, with the force of a son coming home.

I'm here, the feeling said. *You carried me. I'm here.*

The full, unfiltered weight of a boy who'd died afraid and far from home hit her. It was the heaviest thing she'd ever felt. And the most precious. Because it meant the fragments hadn't been destroyed. They'd been returned, sent ahead, like seeds, to be planted in the ground the spirits would need to grow back.

Teyra raised her hands. She was weeping. She had always been weeping. This was who she was.

A necromancer commands the dead, Miss Tepes. She does not weep for them.

"I do, though," she whispered. "I always have."

She pushed.

The breach resisted. Reality buckled and groaned, the edges of the wound grinding against each other like broken bone. The void fought back, tendrils of darkness lashing out, trying to drag her in, trying to consume the spirits that surrounded her. A void-creature lunged from the breach, and three spirits intercepted it, wrapping around the darkness and pulling it apart with the quiet, implacable strength of people who had already died and had nothing left to lose.

Behind her, Seraphine was failing. Teyra could feel it, the void-creature inside the Commander tearing free, Seraphine's will crumbling, her human body collapsing under the strain of containing a thing that was never meant to be contained.

"Sera." Ash's voice, raw. "Sera, hold on."

"Can't." The word was barely human. "Ash, I'm sorry. For everything. For the blade. For the five years I stole from you…"

"I know." His voice cracked. "I forgive you. I forgave you the moment you turned left in that tunnel."

A sound from Seraphine that might have been a sob, might have been the void finally winning.

"Close it," she whispered. "Teyra. Close it now. I can give you ten seconds. That's all I have left."

Ten seconds.

Teyra poured everything into the breach. Every spirit, every connection, every thread of Resonance burning through her ravaged channels. The dead of Athergard surged forward, a tide of amber light, a city's worth of love and loss and stubborn refusal to be forgotten, channeled through one woman who had never learned to stop caring.

The edges of the breach knitted.

Five seconds. Seraphine's scream cut off. The silence where her voice had been was worse than any sound.

The breach narrowed. Three feet, two, one.

The dead pressed inward. Teyra felt them pouring through her like water through a shattered pipe, felt her necromantic channels tearing, felt the cost of the river she'd unleashed. It was destroying her. Every pathway, every conduit, every connection between her living body and the world of the dead was burning to ash.

She didn't stop.

The breach sealed.

The impact threw her backward. A concussive wave of displaced reality rippled outward from the point where the wound had closed, cracking the marble floor in radiating lines, shattering what remained of the windows, extinguishing every light in the Grand Hall. For a single held breath, there was absolute darkness.

Then light.

Amber, warm and deep, the color of tea held up to candlelight, the color of autumn, the color of things that had survived the worst and come out the other side. It pulsed beneath the floor where the breach had been, gentle and steady, a heartbeat of gathered spirits, a seal woven from the bonds between a necromancer and every soul she had ever loved.

And in that amber glow, embedded like a fossil in ancient stone, Teyra could see the faintest trace of silver, a woman's shape, arms spread wide, holding the last of the darkness in an embrace that would endure until the end of time.

And on her wrist, glowing faintly where the amber and silver met, the outline of a serpent eating its own tail. The cycle complete. The last thing she'd carried in life, the first thing she'd carried into whatever came after.

Seraphine. The cage that held while the door closed.

The void-creatures were gone, the screaming had stopped. The End of Days was over.

Teyra had sealed the breach.

And the cost was everything she had.

She couldn't feel her hands.

Her limbs were dead iron, impossibly heavy, numb at the extremities, responding to her will with a delay that felt like screaming into a canyon and waiting for the echo. The Resonance channel had burned through her like acid through copper wire, necromantic pathways scorched, connections severed, the last threads linking her to the world of the dead reduced to ash. The spirits had departed, returning to whatever rest they'd earned, and in their absence Teyra was left with an absence that should have been silence.

Instead, the fragments remained.

The fragments hadn't gone with them.

She'd expected them to, expected the borrowed burdens to return to their owners by their own nature, back to the source, leaving her clean and empty and alone. But the channels that had filtered them, the pathways that had kept the fragments borrowed, temporary, returnable, those channels were destroyed. Burned to ash by the Gathering. And the fragments that had survived the river, the ones that had been inside her when the channels died, had nowhere to go. They were fused now, permanent memories that belonged to other people but lived inside her, and would live inside her for the rest of her life.

Thomas's homesickness. Still there. The echo rather than the full, devastating weight that had hit her during the Gathering, because that had flowed back to Thomas with the rest. But the scar-shape of it. The bread, the tin roofs, the mother's kitchen. She would carry it the way she carried her own memories, as something she'd lived through, something that had happened to her body, even though it had happened to someone else's life.

The widow's yearning for mornings. The phantom blade between her ribs, Ash's death, fused into her like a splinter too deep to remove. The little girl's winter-cold, faint but present, a chill in her bones on nights when the wind sounded a certain way.

She hadn't lost them all. She'd lost the ability to return them. The collection was permanent now, a record of every spirit she'd touched, every life she'd been trusted to hold. The cost of the Gathering was permanence: the borrowed burdens were no longer borrowed. They were hers. Forever.

The silence of a house with every door closed. The silence of a well gone dry.

Her magic was gone. She could feel the absence as surely as a fingertip finds the chip in a favorite teacup, the hollow space where something vital used to be. But the house was crowded instead. The rooms were full of other people's furniture, their love, their small and ordinary and devastating lives.

And she would live among those rooms for the rest of hers. Carrying the weight of everyone she'd ever helped, because that was the price of being the kind of necromancer who felt too much.

It was, she realized, a price she would pay again.

But there was one more thing she needed to do.

Ash was fading. She could see him, barely, a ghost's ghost, a sketch of a man drawn in dying light, his form dissolving into the air. The golden radiance was spent. The anchor was gone. He had given everything to push back the darkness, and now there was nothing left to hold him to this world.

Nothing except her.

She crawled to him. Her arms wouldn't support her weight properly, so she crawled, dragging herself across the cracked marble, through the debris and the dust and the amber light that pulsed beneath the floor. Blood dripped from her face, nose, ears, eyes, leaving a trail behind her, bright as butcher's runoff.

She reached him. She took his hand.

Her fingers passed through him.

"No." The word came out as a croak. "No, no, no. Ash, stay with me. Stay with me."

"Can't." His voice was a whisper from the other side of the world. "Nothing left. The anchor's failing. I can feel myself slipping..."

"Then I'll pull you back."

"You can't. Your magic is..."

"I don't need magic." She grabbed for him again, and this time, this time, her fingers caught something. A thread. A wisp. The barest trace of what he had been, still clinging to existence by will alone. "I don't need magic, Ash. I need you."

She pulled.

She bypassed the burned-out channels and the spent Resonance, the river run dry. She pulled through the only thing she had left. The bond itself. The raw, unmediated connection between two people who had chosen each other across the divide between life and death. No magic. No technique. No academy-approved methodology.

Just a woman who refused to let go.

He screamed.

The sound tore through the ruined hall. It was the sound of something being dragged back from the edge of oblivion, of existence being forced to continue when it wanted desperately to end.

She didn't stop.

"I am telling you, Ashen Thornwick, that you do not have my permission to leave."

She pulled one final time.

Reality buckled. A blinding ripple of displaced energy erupted from the space between them, scorching the marble with the smell of ozone and burning air. Teyra was thrown forward, colliding with something that wasn't air, or light, or ghost.

And Ash snapped back into existence.

His form took hold, dense and real in a way it had never been before. The cracks from the blood wards sealed over, becoming silver scars that traced patterns across his skin like lightning frozen in flesh. His color deepened, alive and present and substantial in a way that made her breath catch.

He gasped, actually gasped, his chest heaving with a breath that was necessity rather than habit.

"What..." His voice was deeper, richer, more present. "What did you do?"

"Closed the breach." She was shaking, her body trembling, her vision going black at the edges. "Saved the city. Pulled you back from the dead. The usual."

He looked at his hands. At the silver scars. At skin that was no longer translucent.

"I can feel my heartbeat," he whispered. "Teyra, what am I?"

"Alive." She touched his face. Solid flesh beneath her fingers, with no barrier of cold between them. "You're alive."

She knew how. Somewhere beneath the exhaustion, she understood. The last pull hadn't been Resonance. It hadn't been the clinical cold. It had been a Command Word powered by nothing but the bond between them, raw and unmediated, the final spark of a necromancer who had burned out every channel she possessed. A Command Word fueled by the clinical cold could move a spirit. A Command Word fueled by the specific, stubborn, furious love of a woman who had been told her whole life that she felt too much could remake one.

The cost was everything she had.

Her grandmother would have understood. *Death is just a door, Teyra. And love is the only key that opens it from both sides.*

He caught her as she collapsed.

She woke to sunlight streaming through the shattered windows of the Grand Hall, painting the destruction in shades of gold and amber.

The morning sun, she realized: dawn. They had survived the night.

She was lying on something soft, a cloak, maybe, or a pile of curtains someone had gathered from the wreckage. Her head was in someone's lap. Cold fingers were stroking her hair.

Cold, but here. Present and real.

"You're awake."

She looked up. Ash was looking down at her, his face lit by the morning sun. He looked different in the daylight, the silver scars more visible, tracing delicate patterns across his cheekbones and jaw. His eyes were still grey, but there was warmth in them now that she'd never seen before.

Life. There was life in his eyes.

"How long?" she croaked.

"A few hours. The sun just came up." His fingers continued their gentle motion through her hair. "The Moth found us. He's been organizing the survivors, taking charge of the chaos." Ash paused. "Teyra. What you did, the spirits, the breach, people saw. The survivors in the hall, the guards who came in after. They saw you kneeling on the floor with a city's worth of ghosts pouring through you." His voice was quiet. "They're calling it the Gathering. The night the dead of Athergard answered a necromancer's call."

"I didn't call them. I asked."

"I know. That's what makes it unsettling to everyone who wasn't there." His lips quirked, but the humor didn't reach his eyes. "The Moth has been managing the fallout. When you eliminate the Lord Protector, close a breach in reality, and demonstrate that one woman can summon every ghost in the city, someone needs to step in and keep people from losing their minds."

"The Moth is in charge of the kingdom?"

"Temporarily. He says he has no interest in ruling, only in seeing the right people get the chance to." Ash's expression darkened. "He also says he knows where every skeleton is buried. Literally and figuratively. It gives him leverage."

Teyra laughed, a crowded sound, edged with the footman's startled relief at being seen, one of the fragments coloring her voice before she could catch it.

"What about the guests? The survivors?"

"Most of them made it out. The void-creatures focused on Greythorn first, then the breach itself. When Greythorn died, his command authority over the Hessians collapsed, and the Moth's engineer, the one who'd been waiting in the basement since before the Coronation began, caught the command frequency before anyone else could. The machines answer to him now. And where the Hessians go, the City Watch follows. His people had the exits clear before the worst of it." He paused. "There were casualties. Not as many as there could have been, but some."

She nodded. Even in victory, there was loss. There was always loss.

"Elias?" she asked first.

"Alive." The word came out like an exhale he'd been holding for hours. "The Moth's people pulled him out before the Grand Hall collapsed. The iron bracelet shattered when the wards went down, twenty-five years of siphoning, and the moment Greythorn died, the tether just broke. The new seal doesn't need his blood, whatever you wove down there holds on its own. He's in the east wing. Confused. Mourning for a man he thought was his father." Ash's jaw worked. "He doesn't know me yet. He knows the story, everyone will, soon enough, but he doesn't know his brother."

"You'll tell him."

"Today. After I can stand without leaning on things." His hand tightened on hers. "I've been watching him sleep. Through the doorway. The way I did at the estate." A pause. "He still looks four years old to me."

"And Seraphine?"

His expression shifted. An emotion moved behind his eyes, tangled and complicated, that she couldn't untangle from the outside.

"Gone," he said quietly. "She held the line while you closed the breach. The void-creature she absorbed, it consumed her from the inside. But she held." His voice caught. "The silver light in the floor, you can see it, if you look, that's what's left of her. The cage that held while the door closed. She's part of the seal now. Part of whatever you built."

"She bought me the time."

"She bought everyone the time." He was quiet for a moment. "I don't know how to feel about that. She killed me. She destroyed my family. She spent twenty years serving the people who orchestrated everything. And then she held the darkness inside her own body so that you could save the world."

"That's redemption," Teyra said softly. "The choice to do better, even when it costs you everything."

"Is that enough?"

"I don't know. Maybe that's not for us to decide." She reached up, touched his face. Solid. Warm, even. And real. "But she's the reason you're still here. That has to count for something."

He leaned into her touch, his eyes closing.

"I can feel that," he whispered. "Your hand on my face. No barrier. No cold burning. Just touch. Just you."

"What are you now, Ash? What did I turn you into?"

"I don't know." He opened his eyes, and there was wonder in them. "I can feel my heart beating. I'm still made of something that isn't quite flesh. Something in between, maybe. Something new."

"Are you okay with that?"

He smiled. A real smile, unguarded and warm, the smile of a man who had been dead for five years and was finally, impossibly, getting a second chance.

"I'm here," he said. "I'm with you. My life, my death, the darkness, the light, it's all still here. Loving you. Being loved." His thumb traced her cheekbone. "There are pieces missing. A garden. A waltz I can almost hear. But you, you're the clearest thing I have. If I could only have saved one memory, it would have been you." He leaned down, pressed his forehead against hers. "I don't know what I am. But I know who I am. And I know who I want to be."

"Who's that?"

"Yours."

She pulled him down and kissed him.

It was different now. There was no cold, no barrier, no magical resistance pushing them apart. Just his lips on hers, his hands in her hair, his body solid and real and present in a way it had never been before.

They were both crying. Neither of them cared.

"Ahem."

They broke apart, reluctantly, to find Lenore perched on a chunk of fallen column, watching them with one beady black eye.

"Not to interrupt the romantic moment," the raven said dryly, "but there's a mob of terrified nobles outside demanding answers, a kingdom without a ruler, a two-generation conspiracy that needs to be publicly unraveled, and approximately seventeen very confused Hessians who keep asking where their orders are supposed to come from now."

Teyra groaned. "Can't it wait?"

"Emphatically no." Lenore ruffled her feathers. "Though I will say, as disgusting displays of affection go, that one was almost bearable. Now get up. You've got work to do."

Ash helped Teyra to her feet. She swayed, exhaustion bone-deep, the kind that would take weeks to recover from, but his arm around her waist held her steady.

"Ready?" he asked.

She looked at him. At the silver scars that marked him as something the world hadn't seen before. At the grey eyes that held love and life and the memory of everything they'd survived.

"No," she said honestly. "Not even close."

"Me neither."

"But we're going to do it anyway."

"Together."

She smiled. "Together."

They walked out of the ruins of the Grand Hall, into the golden light of a new morning, into a world that had been broken and was waiting to be remade.

Behind them, beneath the cracked marble floor, two lights pulsed gently, amber and silver, intertwined. The gathered will of a city's dead, and the last remnant of a woman who had spent twenty years seeking redemption and had finally, at the end, found it.

The End of Days was over.

The Long Morning had begun.

THE LONG MORNING

THREE DAYS LATER

THE FIELD HOSPITAL SMELLED of carbolic soap and old sweat.

They'd set it up in the Palace's east wing, the only section still structurally sound after the breach. Rows of cots stretched across what had been a state dining room, the long mahogany table shoved against the wall to make space. Crystal chandeliers still hung overhead, absurdly elegant above the bandages, blood, and quiet suffering.

Teyra had been in cot fourteen for three days (she knew because the nurses had pinned the number to her blanket, and because she'd spent a lot of time staring at ceilings lately).

Her magic was gone.

The place inside her where the Grave-Chill had lived for as long as she could remember lay silent, an empty room in a house she'd always thought of as home. Dr. Croft had examined her twice, her expression carefully neutral in the way that meant the news was bad. The necromantic channels were scarred. The Command Word had torn through them like acid through fine wire. There was a chance they would heal. There was also a chance they wouldn't.

"Time," the doctor had said, as though that were an answer. "Give it time."

Time was the one thing she had too much of now.

Ash came every morning. He'd sit on the edge of her cot, his new clothes slightly too formal for a sickbed visit, and tell her about the world outside. The Council was forming. The Moth was managing the transition with an efficiency that unsettled anyone who understood what efficiency in a man like that really meant. The nobles who'd been at the Coronation were choosing sides, some rallying to the new king, others retreating to their estates to wait and see. The city was holding its breath.

On the second morning, he told her about the announcement.

The Moth had arranged it, of course he had. A public reading of the original prophecy, delivered from the Palace steps by the city's three remaining High Seers, with the book itself displayed under glass for anyone who wanted to verify the text. The crowd had filled the square and spilled into four adjacent streets. Some people wept. Some raged.

A group from the Thornwick memorial society, Teyra hadn't even known such a thing existed, laid dozens of candles on the steps, one for each year of the lie.

"There was a woman," Ash said. "Old. She pushed through the crowd to the front and just stood there, looking at me. She said her grandmother had been a Thornwick lady-in-waiting. That her family had been disgraced after the fire, stripped of their titles, driven into poverty. A lifetime of shame for a crime that never happened."

He stared at their joined hands.

"She didn't ask for anything. She just wanted me to know. And then she left."

He was quiet. Then: "She told me other things. That there were families who'd kept the old oaths. That the Welden name was gone—the farmstead burned six months after my coronation, Greythorn's Hessians—but their neighbors remembered. The household guard who carried me from the fire, his granddaughter runs a bakery in the Tanners' Quarter. Puts a silver rose in the window every year on the anniversary." His hand tightened on hers. "She said they never stopped waiting."

Another silence stretched between them. "I don't remember Margit. I don't remember the barn or the training yard or the boy who was my first friend. The Barrier took them." He looked at Teyra, and the loss in his eyes belonged to neither the void nor the coronation nor any grief she'd seen him carry before. This was the quiet kind. The kind that arrives after the crisis, when you realize the fire took things you didn't know you owned. "But someone should remember them. Someone should write their names down."

Teyra squeezed his fingers. There was nothing to say. The lie had been so large and so old that its damage couldn't be measured in a single conversation or repaired by a single king. It would take years, perhaps decades. And some of it could never be undone at all.

"The Moth says public sentiment is 'cautiously favorable,'" Ash added, with the faint irony of a man quoting someone else's euphemism.

"Meaning they haven't stormed the Palace yet."

"Yet." They shared a look, the kind that contained an entire argument and its resolution.

She tried, as she had been trying for two days, to feel him.

His hand was warm, present, unmistakably real in the way that still startled her, no cold, no barrier, no spectral resistance. That part worked perfectly. That part was a miracle she hadn't yet stopped being grateful for.

But when she reached for the feeling underneath the touch, the specific, private feeling that was hers alone, the one that had kept her holding on through the bone chamber and the void and the breach, she found it filtered. Thomas's homesickness sitting in front of it. The widow's yearning for ordinary mornings. The dockworker's superstitious unease about heights surfacing at inconvenient moments, which made no sense, she wasn't afraid of heights, except apparently part of her now was.

She could feel that she loved him. The information was there, the way you know a room is warm without being able to feel the warmth specifically on your skin. She could locate the love the way you locate a sound in the dark, approximately, by direction, without being able to put your hand on it.

She had not told him. She didn't know how to explain that the clearest expression of how she felt about him was still borrowed weight, Ash's own death wound fused between her third and fourth rib, the closest thing to direct knowledge she had of what he'd meant to her before she became what she was now. She loved him through the record of his murder. Through someone else's catastrophe. It was, she thought with a private exhaustion she would not be putting in the newspaper, a very Teyra Tepes way to experience joy.

She squeezed his hand. He looked at her with warmth in his eyes.

She smiled back, because she was, underneath all of it, genuinely glad he was here, genuinely grateful, genuinely something she would call happy if happiness weren't currently sitting three rooms away from her own chest, visible through other people's windows.

On the third morning, an aide appeared in the doorway, young, nervous, clutching a sheaf of papers, and said, "Your Majesty, the delegation from the Northern Provinces…"

Ash didn't look up. He didn't let go of her hand. "Five minutes."

"Sir, they've been waiting since…"

"Five. Minutes."

The aide retreated. (Wisely.)

Ash turned back to her, and it was already there, the pull. The crown settling onto him like a weight, invisible but constant. Every hour, something else needed him. Every decision waited on his voice. He was becoming the king, and the king belonged to the kingdom.

"Go," she said. "The Northern Provinces aren't going to negotiate with themselves."

"I don't want to leave you here."

"I know. But there are about four hundred people out there who need a king more than I need a bedside visitor." She squeezed his hand. "Go be what they need. I'll be here when you get back."

He leaned down. Pressed his lips to her forehead. Warm and real.

"Every morning," he said. "No matter what."

"Every morning."

She watched him walk away, straight-backed, purposeful, already shifting into the posture of a ruler before he reached the door. The aide fell into step beside him, talking fast, and then they were gone.

The cot felt very empty when a familiar weight landed on the footboard. Black feathers. One beady eye.

"You could go with him, you know," Lenore said. "The Palace has better beds. Better food. An entire wing of healers who'd fight each other for the honor of treating the woman who saved the Spectral King."

"I'm going back to the shop."

Lenore tilted her head. "Your magic might be gone, Teyra."

"I know."

"You can't run a necromancer's tea shop without necromancy."

"I know that too."

"Then why…"

"Because it's mine." The words came out harder than she'd intended. She softened. "The shop is mine, Lenore. My grandmother's blends. My counter. My bell above the door. I didn't save the world so I could live in someone else's palace. I saved it so I could go home."

Lenore was quiet for a long time. The raven stared at her with both eyes, the full gaze, the one she almost never showed.

"Your grandmother," Lenore said finally, "would be so proud of you that she'd be completely insufferable about it."

The little girl's winter-cold flared behind her eyes, abruptly and fiercely, eclipsed a heartbeat later by a heat that was entirely her own.

"Don't you dare make me cry in a field hospital."

"Wouldn't dream of it." Lenore hopped closer and settled against Teyra's ankle, the closest thing to physical affection the raven had ever offered. "Now get some sleep. You look like death, and I say that as someone who has worked alongside death professionally for several human lifetimes."

Teyra closed her eyes. The chandelier light played red through her eyelids. Somewhere beyond the hospital walls, the sounds of a city rebuilding, hammers, voices, the grind of stone on stone. Through it all ran the faint, steady hum of something that might have been hope.

She would go home. She would sweep the floor, stock the shelves, and put the kettle on. She would wait for her magic to come back, or learn to live without it. She would be there, every evening, when a king in borrowed time walked past her window.

She would begin again.

EPILOGUE

Two Weeks Later

IT WAS RAINING IN Athergard.

This was standard. It was always raining in Athergard, the city existed in a perpetual state of dampness, the cobblestones always slick, the gutters always running, the sky always that indecisive shade of grey that couldn't decide if it wanted to clear or storm. The locals had long ago stopped bothering with umbrellas. The rain was part of life, like taxes and the smell of the harbour and the way the gas lamps flickered at midnight.

But today, somehow, the rain felt different.

It was clean.

Teyra stood behind the counter of The Final Steep, watching the water run down the windows in silver rivulets, stripped clean of the grey-filmed runoff she'd grown up with, and tried to remember the last time she had felt this settled. The grey film was gone. The Unsettled residue that had coated every window and pooled in every gutter and risen to a phosphorescent tide on the night the world nearly ended had been cleared by the Gathering. The dead who had dissolved without passage, who had thinned into atmosphere and slipped free of memory, who had been filtered and stored and ignored for three centuries, the Gathering had given them what the drainage wards never could. Acknowledgment where filtration had failed. They had been heard. They had been felt. And having been felt, they had let go.

The rain running down the windows of The Final Steep was the cleanest rain Teyra had ever seen. In Hollow Stair, where the drainage wards had never reached, where the grey film had been thickest and the poor had lived among the spiritual residue of their unprocessed dead for generations, the gutters ran clear.

Happiness was too simple a word for the complicated tangle she'd been carrying since the night the world almost ended. But settled. At ease. Like she was exactly where she was supposed to be, doing exactly what she was supposed to be doing.

A Ward Inspectorate notice had been waiting under the door when she returned, weeks old, rendered irrelevant by the fact that the woman they'd meant to inspect had since summoned every ghost in the city. She'd used it to light the fire. Peace sat in her chest, strange and heavier than she'd expected.

"You're brooding again," Lenore observed from her perch on the spice rack. The raven was grooming her feathers—both wings whole now, the left one healed without explanation or apology, because Lenore did not explain herself—with the air of someone who had better things to do but was willing to put them aside to criticize. "I can always tell. Your forehead gets that little crinkle."

"I'm not brooding. I'm contemplating."

"Brooding."

"Reflecting."

"Brooding with a fancy name." Lenore abandoned her grooming to fix Teyra with one beady black eye. "You know, most people who save the world from an apocalyptic incursion of void-creatures take at least a month off to recover. They go to the seaside. They take up painting. They do not immediately reopen their tea shops and start serving customers like nothing happened."

"The rent doesn't pay itself."

"The rent situation has been restructured." Lenore chose the word with care. "The Moth didn't pay it. He acquired it."

Teyra's hands went still on the counter. "What does that mean?"

"It means the building now belongs to a holding company registered in the Merchant District. The holding company is managed by a trust. The trust answers to a man who doesn't exist on paper but wears grey velvet and keeps a jar of nothing on his shelf." Lenore clicked her beak. "Your rent is lower. Your lease is indefinite. And somewhere in the contract there's a clause about 'services to be rendered at the discretion of the managing party.'"

The words settled into Teyra's stomach like cold tea.

"He owns my shop."

"He owns your building. There's a difference. Technically."

Teyra stared at the counter she'd wiped down ten thousand times, at the shelves her grandmother had built, at the bell above the door that chimed when the wind changed direction. She thought of the Moth's dead eyes, how he'd put the Moonflower on the desk where they could see it. The way he gave you exactly what you needed and made sure you could never forget the cost.

"He's not done with me," she said.

"Men like the Moth are never done." Lenore's tone was unusually gentle. "His people say the void sample is still in the Night Market. The jar. Still eating its glass, still growing, even with the breach sealed." She paused. "He kept his piece of the darkness, Teyra."

"Of course he did."

"But you're alive. The shop is open. And the rent is manageable. For now, that might have to be enough."

It wasn't enough. But it was what she had. And Teyra Tepes had built a life out of what she had before.

"I like working," she said. "It keeps my hands busy."

"It keeps your mind occupied so you don't have to think about what you went through."

"That too."

Lenore made a sound that was probably meant to be sympathetic but came out more like a cough. "How's the magic?"

Teyra flexed her fingers, reaching for the cold at the center of her being.

It was there. That much hadn't changed. But it had become something different from the clean, clinical Grave-Chill the Academy had spent four years trying to teach her to regulate. That cold was still scarred, still healing, still the faint fragile thing Dr. Croft had called 'significant channel damage with uncertain prognosis.' That cold was recovering.

A second current had settled under it.

She didn't have a name for it yet. Calling it warm would be wrong, imprecise, the kind of category error that got necromancers killed. But it had nothing in common with the cold of regulated distance and professional detachment either. It lived at the boundary between the two. The place where a necromancer stood when she held a spirit's hand and felt what the spirit felt. The place the Academy had called a disorder and her grandmother had called a gift and Meridia Ashworth had called the only honest way to do the work, right up until it destroyed her.

Except Meridia had never survived what came after. The mass event had worked, six months of celebration, the harbour clean, the breach sealed, and then the bonds had woken up and broken her before she could find out what came next.

Teyra had burned, and healed, and burned again, and whatever had grown back through the scarred channels was running on something different now. Something she'd have to learn from scratch, because there was no textbook for it, no Academy module, no cautionary tale that had made it to the other side to report back.

What she did know, what she hadn't told Dr. Croft or anyone else, because there was no framework yet for telling it, was that the permanent fragments were still there, living in her now strictly as memory.

The fragments had settled into her body the way old injuries settle, present but quiet. She flinched at wet earth. She reached for a second cup on mornings when she was alone. She pressed her fingers to the space between her third and fourth rib sometimes, feeling for a wound that had never been hers. And on nights when the wind sounded a certain way, she still felt cold in places the weather couldn't explain.

She wore them as Seraphine had worn her bracelet. Evidence of what she'd chosen. What it had cost. She thought, sometimes, of the dark violet flower in its clay pot in the conservatory—the one plant that didn't belong among the exotics. She'd never asked Seraphine about it. Now she never would.

The borrowed weight didn't hurt the way it used to. It had settled, integrated, become part of the architecture. She could feel the dead without drowning. She had learned, was still learning, to carry it.

The Academy would still call it a disorder. Her grandmother would still call it a gift. Teyra didn't have a word for it yet. She was starting to think that was the point, that whatever she was becoming hadn't been named because nobody had become it before.

The harder truth, the one she was still learning to live inside, was what the permanent fragments did to the present tense. She loved Ash. She knew this the way she knew anything about herself, with certainty, without recourse to proof. But when he sat across from her, when she looked at his face in the morning light and tried to feel it directly, she kept finding the borrowed catalog first. The widow's longing arrived before her own, with Thomas's homesickness coloring the warmth. His own death wound between her ribs, which was the most intimate thing she knew about him and had happened before she'd met him. She was learning to navigate to herself through the crowd. It was slow work. Some mornings she found the way easily. Others she sat with his hand in hers and felt three other people's feelings about him before she found her own, like sorting through a drawer for a thread she knew was there.

She had not mentioned this to Lenore. Lenore would either understand immediately, which would be worse, or not understand at all, which would require explaining, and explaining would require saying out loud that the woman who had called every ghost in the city by name could no longer reliably find her own love without help. She was working on it. She had time. She thought she had time.

"Better," she said. "I managed to light a candle yesterday without passing out."

"Progress."

"Something like that."

"One more thing," Lenore said.

"The Moth's people found Whitmore. In the Night Market, still in the cage. Alive, if that word applies. They're transferring him to Dr. Croft's clinic." She paused.

"He asked for you by name."

The rag in Teyra's grip tightened. Whitmore. In a cage for three years, and he'd remembered her name. She didn't look up.

The bell above the door chimed as a customer entered, a young woman with red hair and a nervous expression, clutching a handkerchief that was clearly meant to serve as a focusing object. Teyra straightened her apron, put on her professional smile, and went to work.

This was what she did now. It was what she had always done: helping people say goodbye. Helping spirits find peace. The work hadn't changed, even if everything else had.

The morning passed in a blur of tea and tears and tentative closure.

The red-haired woman wanted to speak with her grandmother, a straightforward anchoring, the kind of gentle communion that had been Teyra's specialty before the Academy had decided proper necromancers required more cold than she possessed. The grandmother had things to say about the woman's fiancé (disapproval), her career choices (grudging approval), and the recipe for her famous apple cake (which she dictated in its entirety, including the secret ingredient that turned out to be a splash of cheap brandy).

After her came a middle-aged man seeking his late business partner, a widow looking for her husband's blessing to remarry, and a teenage boy who just wanted to know if his dog had made it to whatever afterlife awaited good boys who chased squirrels and always came when called.

The dog had. The boy cried. Teyra gave him a biscuit (and didn't charge for the session).

By midday, the shop was busy in a way it hadn't been in months. Word had spread, about the necromancer who had stood beside the Spectral King on coronation night. People came curious and grateful, wanting to believe that someone who had faced the void and survived might help them face their own smaller darknesses.

Teyra didn't know how to feel about that. She felt no kinship with heroes, only with a woman who had done what needed to be done and gotten very, very lucky.

But she took their coins and brewed their tea and helped them say goodbye, because that was what she did. That was who she was. The woman who felt too much. The necromancer who actually cared.

Maybe that wasn't such a bad thing after all.

"You're thinking about him," Lenore said during a lull between customers. The raven had relocated to the counter, where she was methodically destroying a biscuit that Teyra had foolishly left unattended. "You get this particular look on your face. Soft. Nauseating."

"I do not."

"You absolutely do. It's like watching someone get hit in the head with a romance novel."

"I'm going to stop buying you the expensive biscuits."

"You'll do no such thing. I'm the only friend you have."

"That's not true. I have..." Teyra paused, thinking. "There's the landlord. Mrs. Pemberton from the herbalist's guild. That nice guard who stopped trying to arrest me after the third time."

"None of whom would die for you."

"Would you die for me?"

"Absolutely not. I'm an immortal familiar bound to your bloodline for seventeen more generations. Dying isn't really in my wheelhouse." Lenore finished the biscuit and began cleaning crumbs from her beak with dignified precision. "But I would be mildly inconvenienced for you. Possibly even annoyed. That's practically the same thing."

Teyra laughed. It still felt strange, laughing, like a bell above a shut shop door rung after months of silence, but it was getting easier.

"Any news from the Palace?" she asked.

"The Academy sent a letter." Lenore delivered it with the precise casualness of someone presenting a grenade wrapped in tissue paper (gift-wrapped, naturally). "Formal stationery. Gold seal. They want you to come in for a 'reassessment of your certification status in light of recent events.'" She clicked her beak. "I believe the subtext is that they'd like to pretend they didn't fail the woman who just saved the city."

Teyra didn't look up from the counter she was wiping. "File it with the Ward Inspectorate notice."

"Ash already told them you're under crown protection. Apparently the Moth drafted the language himself—'extraordinary services rendered to the kingdom under conditions of existential necessity.' Very legal. Very permanent. The Academy can reassess all they want. They can't touch you."

"The Council met again this morning. Third time this week. The Moth is running them ragged, apparently he's got a list of reforms as long as my wingspan, and he's not letting anyone leave until they've voted on at least half of them."

Lenore tilted her head. "The corruption purges are going well. Turns out when you know where all the bodies are buried, literally and figuratively, people become remarkably cooperative."

She paused. "The Greythorn cousins are less cooperative. Three of them have barricaded themselves in the family's country estate up north and are refusing to acknowledge the new king. Two more have fled to the provinces with enough gold to raise a small army. And the nephew who married into the foundry contracts has gone very quiet in a way that makes people who understand quiet men very nervous."

"That doesn't worry you?" Teyra said.

Lenore's gaze sharpened. "What part?"

"The part where a man who blackmailed us with Moonflower while Ash was dying is now running the kingdom's reforms. The part where someone who collects secrets for leverage is now deciding which secrets get exposed." She rubbed her thumb along the handle of her teacup. "Greythorn built his power on knowing things about people. The Moth does the same thing. He just does it with a better tailor."

Lenore was quiet for a moment. "He helped us."

"He helped himself. We happened to be useful." Teyra set down her cup. "I'm not saying he's evil. I'm saying a man who uses dying people as leverage doesn't suddenly become trustworthy because we won. He becomes more dangerous. Because now he has the leverage of being the man who saved the kingdom."

Lenore digested this. "You should tell the King."

"I intend to." She paused. The Moth had said something to her at the clinic, in the quiet after his plan was laid out and before the world ended. She'd almost missed it. "He told me once that forced bargains are worthless. That there's no power in an agreement made under duress." She looked at Lenore. "He believes it. That's what makes him dangerous. He'll never force anyone. He'll just make sure every door except his leads somewhere worse."

"And the King?"

Lenore's expression turned knowing. "The King has been very busy. Meetings, ceremonies, public appearances. The people want to see him, the Ghost Prince, they're calling him, or the Returned, or the Last Light. He's become something of a folk hero."

"He hates that."

"He absolutely hates that. But he does it anyway, because it's what the kingdom needs." Lenore paused. "He also makes time to walk the city. Every evening, just before sunset. Through the Merchant District, past the Academy, down to the harbour and back. The guards want to accompany him, but he refuses. Says he needs to see the city as it really is, without armed men reshaping what he sees." Lenore paused. "The memorial society told him the old Thornwick kings did the same thing. An evening walk through every district, unguarded, so the Crown could see what the people saw. He didn't remember the tradition. But his feet found the route anyway."

Teyra's pulse skipped a beat, a sharp, physical flutter that had nothing to do with magic and everything to do with the fact that she already knew the answer to the question she was about to ask.

"Does he walk past here?"

"Every single day." Lenore's beak curved into what was almost a smile. "Usually right about... now."

But today was different. Lenore tilted her head. "He's late. Took a detour through the Tanners' Quarter yesterday too, after the memorial woman told him about the bakery. He stood outside for twenty minutes. The granddaughter came out and gave him a loaf, and he held it like it was made of glass." Lenore clicked her beak. "He told me the smell made him dizzy. Said it reminded him of a place he couldn't name. Safe, he said. The bread smelled safe."

Teyra's chest tightened. Thomas's bread-fragment stirred between her ribs, recognizing a kitchen it had never been to.

"And then she touched his face." Lenore's voice went quieter. "The scar above his eyebrow. She traced it with her thumb and said, 'Margit always stitched too tight.' He didn't know what she meant. She didn't explain."

The bell above the door chimed.

A stranger stepped through the doorway, shaking rain from a coat of deep blue velvet. Silver embroidery traced patterns along his cuffs, and his boots were polished leather that probably cost more than her entire wardrobe. It took her a second to find the man beneath the finery.

Then his eyes found hers, and everything changed.

The formality melted away. The stiff posture softened. The careful, composed expression cracked into a warmth she'd never seen on him before, the face of a man who had spent two weeks doing his duty and had finally, finally found his way back to the only place he wanted to be.

"Hi," he said.

"Hi," she said.

They stood there for a moment, just looking at each other. The rain drummed against the windows. The fire crackled in the hearth. Somewhere in the back room, water dripped from a pipe that Teyra kept meaning to fix.

He was different now. It showed in the way he stood, the way he moved, the way he occupied space. The silver scars that traced patterns across his cheekbones caught the light, marking him as something other than human, a ghost no longer, but something in between that hadn't existed before. Something new.

But his eyes were the same. Grey and warm and looking at her like she was the only real thing in a world of shadows.

"You look ridiculous," she said.

"I know." He glanced down at his formal attire with visible discomfort. "They keep trying to put me in things. Coats with too many buttons. Boots that don't bend properly. This morning someone tried to make me wear a crown. An actual crown. I told them if they brought it near me again, I would abdicate on the spot."

"Would you?"

"Probably not. But the threat seemed to work." He moved further into the shop, and she noticed the way his eyes swept the room, cataloging the familiar shelves, the worn counter, the raven watching him with undisguised amusement from her perch. "I've missed this place."

"You've been here for two weeks."

"I've been in the Palace for two weeks. That's a different thing entirely." He stopped at the counter, close enough to touch. "The Palace is full of people who want things from me. Decisions, declarations, appearances. Everyone has an agenda. Everyone is performing."

"And here?"

"Here, there's just you." His voice softened. "And you've never performed a day in your life."

"That's untrue. I performed extensively at the Academy. Usually in the 'disappointing the examiners' category."

"You know what I mean."

She did. That was the problem.

"How are you?" she asked. "Really. The answer you don't give the Council or the newspapers."

He was silent for a moment. The rain continued its steady rhythm against the windows. The fire popped and settled.

"I don't sleep," he said finally. "I can, whatever I am now, I'm capable of sleep. But when I close my eyes, I see the void. I see the breach. I see Seraphine holding the darkness inside her body." He paused. "I see you, bleeding from your eyes, calling every ghost in the city by name."

"Ash…"

"I'm not complaining." He met her eyes, and there was something fierce in his gaze. "Every nightmare reminds me that I'm still here. That you kept me here. That I have a chance to do something with this existence I didn't ask for but have somehow been given."

"That's a very optimistic way to look at trauma."

"I've had practice. Five years of darkness, remember? I've gotten very good at finding silver linings in terrible situations." His lips quirked. "Speaking of which, how are you? Really?"

She considered lying. Considered giving him the same cheerful deflection she'd been giving everyone else, I'm fine, I'm recovering, I'm happy to be alive. But this was Ash. He had seen her at her worst. He had watched her burn out her magic to save his existence. He would know if she was lying.

"I'm scared," she admitted. "All the time. I wake up shivering, reaching for a cold that isn't there, expecting you to be a fading ghost, that the void is still out there, that everything we did was for nothing."

"And when you realize it's real?"

"Then I'm scared of something else. That I've changed too much. That I can't go back to being the woman I was before." She looked down at her hands, the hands that had held his while the world fell apart, the hands that had refused to let go even when it cost her everything. "I used to be so angry. At the Academy, at my magic, at myself for caring too much about spirits who couldn't care back. Now I just feel tired. And grateful. And confused about how all of that fits in one body."

"They coexist because you're human." He reached out, and took her hand. His skin was cool, the pleasant coolness of someone who had just come in from the rain, far from the burning frost of a ghost. "You went through something no one should have to survive. You're allowed to feel whatever you feel."

"That's very philosophical."

"I've been taking lessons. The Council has a philosopher on staff. Apparently, it's traditional for kings to have someone around to make them feel inadequate about their intellectual achievements."

Teyra laughed, a real laugh, surprised out of her. "You're joking."

"I am absolutely not joking. His name is Abernathy, and he has opinions about metaphysics that could bore a corpse back to life."

"That's my job."

"You do it better." He squeezed her hand, and warmth bloomed in her chest. "I have to go back. The Council is expecting me for another round of arguing about trade tariffs or succession law or whatever fresh hell the Moth has dreamed up. The Valcoran ambassador has been waiting three days for an audience, and the Iron Coast lords are threatening a blockade if we don't renegotiate harbour fees." He paused, and a complicated look moved behind his eyes. "And after the Council, Elias. Dinner tonight. Just the two of us."

Teyra's hand found his. "How is he?"

"Still mourning. Still looking at me like I'm a ghost from a storybook, which, fair." A muscle worked in his jaw. "The first few times were all formality. The Moth's people in the room, councilors hovering, everyone watching the Returned King and the Blood-Key Brother perform a reunion for the history books. Tonight's the first time it's just us, no audience, and I have to figure out how to be his brother again when he doesn't remember having one." He exhaled, a real exhale, the kind that came with a body. "He still flinches when anyone touches his wrist. Where the bracelet was." He paused. "Last time, he asked me what our mother's voice sounded like. I couldn't answer. He said, 'Then we'll have to find out together.' He's braver than I was at his age."

His jaw worked. "The Greythorn girl is still at the estate. Refuses to leave. She says the arrangement was a cage, but Elias was the only real thing in it, and she's not abandoning him because the cage broke."

"Do you want me there?"

He looked at her. The way he had that night in the estate, standing at his brother's door, choosing to walk away.

"Yes," he said. "I always want you there."

But he'd come to see her first. He always wanted to see her first.

"Then stay." The words came out before she could stop them. "Not forever. Just for a cup of tea. You can tell the Council that you were delayed by matters of necromantic importance."

"Matters of necromantic importance?"

"It sounds very official. They won't question it."

He looked at her the way he had that first night when he'd stumbled into her shop, lost and desperate and searching for something he couldn't name.

"Tea," he said, "I would like that very much."

She brewed him something new.

She bypassed the anchoring tea she'd made that first night, because that was for binding, for holding on, for keeping spirits tethered to the world of the living. This was different. A blend she had been working on for the past two weeks, in the quiet hours when the shop was empty and the rain was falling and she had nothing to do but think about what came next.

She called it Sunrise.

The blend was her own creation, chamomile for calm, lemon balm for clarity, a touch of lavender for peace. But the secret was the roses. Red petals, dried and preserved, sourced from a garden that had once belonged to the Thornwick estate before the fire. The same roses that Ash had loved as a boy, the same roses that had been planted by his grandmother, the same roses that had stubbornly survived a quarter-century of neglect to bloom again in the ruins of his childhood home.

He wouldn't remember why they mattered. That memory was gone, the garden, the feeling of being very young and very safe, the red roses and the morning dew. Lost to the Touch Barrier on a rooftop above a harbour clinic when he'd chosen warmth over history.

But Teyra remembered for both of them. That was what necromancers did. They carried the dead's stories when the dead could not. And Teyra carried more than most. The permanent fragments,

Thomas's bread, the widow's mornings, the little girl's winter-cold, the phantom blade, hummed quietly in her chest as she worked, the way a house hums with the memory of the people who've lived there. They didn't interfere with the brewing. They *informed* it. Every tea she made now carried a trace of what she'd been through, a warmth that had nothing to do with temperature and everything to do with the fact that the woman making it had held a city's worth of borrowed weight inside her body and survived.

She had paid a small fortune for the petals. She would pay it again in a heartbeat.

The water was almost boiling. She measured the leaves with practiced hands, added them to the pot, watched the steam rise in curling wisps. The ritual was familiar, comforting, the same motions she had performed thousands of times, but somehow different now. Charged with meaning. Weighted with everything they had survived. Her channels were scarred, and the thing running through them now differed from what had run through them before. Quieter in some registers. Stranger in others. Twice this week she'd reached for a standard anchoring cantrip and felt something answer that wasn't the Grave-Chill, a force that moved through the fused fragments like a current finding the path of least resistance, warm where the Chill had always been cold, specific where the Chill had always been general. She didn't know what to call it. She didn't know yet if it was better or worse or simply different in ways that didn't map onto better and worse. What she knew was that it was hers, and it was new, and she was going to have to figure it out without a teacher, because no one who had ever had it had lived long enough to write it down.

The compassion that powered it was unchanged. It had always been the same.

The Academy had been right about one thing. Feeling this much was dangerous. They'd just been wrong about what it endangered. The comfortable lie that the living could ignore their dead and call it civilization.

She brewed the way she always had, with Resonance, with feeling, with the full weight of what she carried. And what she carried, she had learned, was a gift she'd given herself permission to keep.

Ash sat at the small table by the window, watching her work. He had shed his formal coat, rolled up his sleeves, loosened the collar of his shirt. The silver scars caught the firelight, tracing patterns across his forearms, his hands, the hollow of his throat. He looked like himself again. Like the man who had sat at this same table two weeks ago and learned to play cards.

Like the man she loved.

"What are you making?" he asked.

"Something new." She brought the pot to the table, along with two cups, the good ones, the ones her grandmother had left her, hand-painted with roses that matched the petals in the blend. On the shelf behind the counter, a blue willow cup sat alone, cracked down the middle and glued back together with a seam she hadn't tried to hide. "I've been experimenting. Trying to create something that isn't about death or binding or holding on."

"What's it about, then?"

She poured the tea, watching the amber liquid fill the cups. The smell was beautiful, floral and warm and somehow hopeful, like the first clear breath after fever, like pale light breaking through Athergard rain.

"Beginnings," she said.

She set his cup in front of him and sat down across the table. The rain was still falling outside, painting the windows in silver streaks, but inside the shop was warm and golden and quiet. Just the two of them, and the tea, and the fire.

Ash picked up his cup.

Their fingers brushed.

There was no cold, no barrier, no magic fighting to keep them apart. Just the warmth of his skin against hers, the simple human touch that they had fought so hard to be allowed.

He felt it too. It was in his eyes—the wonder, the fierce and fragile thing she didn't dare look at directly.

"Beginnings," he repeated softly.

"Beginnings."

He raised the cup to his lips and drank.

The tea was perfect. She knew it before he said anything—his expression shifting, his shoulders relaxing, his free hand reaching across the table to find hers again. Reaching out because he wanted to, because he could, because they had earned this moment and all the moments that would come after.

"It's good," he said.

"Of course it's good. I'm an excellent necromancer."

"You're an excellent everything." He set down the cup, laced his fingers through hers. "I love you, Teyra Tepes. I loved you while I was dying, I loved you in death, and I love you now, whatever I am."

Her eyes were stinging. She blinked rapidly, refusing to cry, failing completely.

"That's very dramatic," she managed.

"I've been practicing. The philosopher says I need to work on my rhetoric."

"Tell the philosopher he's done an excellent job."

"I'll do that." He lifted her hand to his lips, pressed a kiss to her knuckles. His skin was warm now, she noticed. Warmer than it had been when he walked in. As if the tea, or the touch, or simply being here with her had changed the fundamental nature of his existence.

Or maybe he had always been warm, and she just hadn't been able to feel it until now.

"Stay," she said. "Just for a while. Drink your tea. Let the world outside take care of itself for an hour."

"An hour?"

"Maybe two. I'm making dinner later. You could help."

"I don't know how to cook."

"You'll learn. I'm an excellent teacher."

He smiled, that warm, unguarded smile that transformed his face, that made him look at once like the boy who had loved too much, the man who had died for it, and the king who had come back to set things right.

"Alright," he said. "I'll stay."

They sat together in the quiet shop, drinking tea that tasted like beginnings, while the rain fell outside and the fire crackled and the world slowly, carefully, began to heal.

Hard days still lay ahead, the kingdom to rebuild, the conspiracy to fully unravel, the complicated work of becoming something new in a world that didn't quite know what to make of them. Teyra would struggle with her damaged magic. Ash would wrestle with a crown he'd never asked for. They would fight and doubt and wonder if they'd made the right choices.

But they would do it together.

And that, she thought, was enough. That was more than enough. That was everything.

The bell above the door swayed gently in a draft that shouldn't have existed, and for a moment, a silver light flashed in the rain outside, a woman's shape, standing vigil, then gone.

There was only the shop, and the tea, and the man she loved sitting across from her with warmth in his eyes and her hand in his.

"What are you thinking about?" Ash asked.

Teyra looked at him, at the silver scars and the grey eyes and the smile that felt like lamplight in a window after dark.

"I'm thinking," she said, "that this is a very good beginning."

He reached across the table. His hand rose to her cheek, and this time there was no distance. No inch of cold air. No barrier between them, no trembling, no dream-slow hesitation. Just his palm against her skin, warm and real, and the simple impossible fact of being touched by someone who loved her. She leaned into it. Closed her eyes.

He raised his cup.

She raised hers.

Their fingers brushed across the table, warm, real, easy, and for one clear moment she felt it without translation. The widow's version nowhere in sight. Thomas's echo silent. Hers. Just hers. A small, fierce, uncomplicated joy in a room with the man she loved.

It lasted three seconds. Then the phantom blade shifted between her ribs, and Thomas's bread-smell surfaced, and the feeling became a chorus again.

But she'd had it. Three seconds of her own. Yesterday it had been two.

Outside, for the first time anyone could remember, the rain stopped. The clouds parted, and pale sunlight broke through, touching the wet cobblestones of Athergard with living gold.

THE END

BONUS PREVIEW

MALANTHIA

The Story of Seraphine

Coming soon

SHE WAS FIFTEEN WHEN they sent her north.

The girl who would become the woman in the red dress carried one thing that wasn't in her orders: a violet flower pressed between the pages of a book, from her mother's window box, the week before she left.

She never told anyone she kept it.

Acknowledgement

To my daughter, who read this manuscript more times than either of us can count, gave wonderful feedback. Thank you, your feedback definitely helped make it better. To my other daughter and cover designer, whose creativity and patience through draft after draft, iteration after iteration, gave this book a face worthy of the story inside. You understood the vision before I could explain it. To my friend, who listened to me talk about the book across more car rides, flights, and late nights than any reasonable person should endure. Your encouragement kept me writing when the work felt impossible. To Steep House Press, for handling everything I couldn't and making the rest look easy. And to every reader holding this book, you're the reason it exists. this is only the beginning. You've seen one city, one crisis, one corner of a world that runs much deeper and much wider than these pages. The story is far from over. Stay close.

www.ingramcontent.com/pod-product-compliance
Lightning Source LLC
Chambersburg PA
CBHW020309160726
47992CB00004B/1455